11/23

The Quiet Way

REMEMBER REMEMBER

ROBIN MELHUISH

ISBN 1514851903
ISBN 13 is 9781514851906

ACKNOWLEDGMENTS

Grateful thanks to those who put up with me during the birth of this book, especially Mary-Frances Reilly who's perseverance got me this far and Yasmin Pade, who ruthlessly kept the story on track, and Neil Stewart for his encouragement, the Bush family and Osama bin Laden, without all of whom, none of this would have been possible.

Allahu a`lam. God knows best.

Remember, remember! The ninth of November,
The heinous treason and plot;
I know of no reason
Why the heinous treason
Should ever be forgot
(Paraphrased children's' verse circa 1870)

Ring-a-ring o' roses,
A pocket full of posies,
A-tishoo! A-tishoo!
We all fall down
(children's verse 1881, possibly older)

1

Sunday, another fine example of Britain's late autumn weather. Hanks stared out across the racecourse at the river Dee, half hidden by the rain. A brisk westerly was bringing in a steady drizzle off the Irish Sea, making the view bleak and unappetising. Hanks would have felt almost pleased to be in the office, had it not been for a headache coming on. He rubbed his eyes, sore from hours of poring over pages of tax data.

The door opened and his partner slipped into the room. Welks draped his soaking raincoat over the back of his chair, heedless of the runoff dripping onto the fine leather, pooling on the linoleum floor.

'DI Welks,' Hanks said, his tone laden with irritation, 'good of you to join.'

'Spare me the schoolmaster bit Alan, some of us have families.' Welks plonked himself down in the chair. 'What gives? What's so vital that we all get called in on Sunday?'

'Are the other two here yet?'

'Saw Whittaker outside in the other office, not seen Carlton yet. Whittaker didn't look too chuffed at being here; he was fiddling with his radio, muttering something about a cricket match.'

Hanks chuckled. 'Who the hell plays cricket in October for God's sake?' Welks shrugged and leaned forward to get away from the wet coat. Hanks flung his arm out and waved his hand.

'Hang it up, that's what that thing in the corner is for.'

'So, what's the deal?' Welks stood to hang his coat.

'Whittaker!' Hanks shouted, 'get your bloody earplug out and your arse in here.' Seconds later DC Stan Whittaker stood there, filling the doorframe with his intimidating bulk.

'Maan, you know iss raynin'.' His Barbadian lilt exaggerated for Hanks's benefit.

'Everybody can see it's bloody raining. I don't need the weather forecast for that.'

'The match is off, because of the rain maan,' Whittaker was exasperated, 'Australia against India, the last one day international,' he explained.

'Oh that's dandy then, isn't it,' Hanks said, 'so Stan the man can do some police work then? You have time?' Hanks smiled, taking the bite out of the barb.

'Sure, boss. I was only joking,' Whittaker's smile lit up the room. 'I was…' He was interrupted by the arrival of the fourth member of the team, DC Ian Carlton, a native Chester man with in-depth local knowledge and in Hanks's opinion little else.

'Oh good, we're all here now,' Hanks said. 'I know it is Sunday and if it wasn't important, I wouldn't have called you in. Get sat down, the pair of you,' Hanks nodded at the newcomers, 'I'll explain.' Whittaker sat on the only free chair in the room leaving Carlton no choice, but to get one from the other office.

'It's buggered my evening,' he griped putting the chair down and sitting opposite Welks. 'May I ask why Sunday night is going down the pan? So far, after weeks, we have zilch. What we need is another brainwave, like the 'Laundry scam' in Northern Ireland,' Carlton whinged.

'Laundry?' Welks said with a knowing smile.

'Yes, getting the dirty washing was the key. Dirty laundry, sheer genius,' Carlton continued, 'the security services tested the washing for traces of gun smoke and explosives.' Carlton leant back in his chair, certain he'd scored a point.

'Guess what Carlton,' Welks intervened. 'The man behind that is sitting right there,' he said gesturing at Hanks, 'The houses where the washing tested positive were raided the same day. It was the most effective tool for taking out terrorists ever devised. The terror suspects never twigged how they got found out. They were blaming and punishing their own people for informing.' Carlton coloured up, embarrassed,

'I didn't know that.'

'You couldn't have,' Welks snapped, 'it was a state secret. You don't think that things like that get advertised?'

Hanks was beyond tired of the conversation. 'Gentlemen, can we get on? Might I suggest a little scotch to lighten the atmosphere?' He opened the drawer of his desk, and pulled out a bottle. 'Glasses?' Hanks placed the scotch bottle on the desktop. Whittaker stood to get them from the kitchen, but was blocked by the presence of the immaculate uniform of Chief Superintendent Michaels standing in the door opening.

'Nice to see the team hard at work.' The Chief Superintendent said, rocking on his feet.

'Good evening sir, to what do we owe this honour?' Hanks attempted to keep the sarcasm out of his voice.

'Mayoral thingy at the town Hall, a Crime Prevention junket.' Hanks eyed the whiskey bottle on his desk at the same time Michaels saw it. 'DCI Hanks!' the words stopped hearts beating for a second, 'I will not tolerate alcohol on the premises.' Michaels stalked over to Hanks's desk and grabbed the bottle. 'You can collect this from my office when you leave tonight. I was going to ask how things were progressing, but it seems you are just partying.' He said as he turned on his heel and left. His departure was as much as a surprise as his arrival.

'Where the …? Like bloody school,' Hanks said to the closed door, 'what the hell is he doing here on a Sunday anyway?'

'Once a plonker, always a plonker, remember police training in Hendon,' Welks commiserated.

'Can I forget?' Hanks said resignedly, 'Okay, let's get on, we can always slip off the pub afterwards.' His hopeful words were met with little enthusiasm. 'Right, for your info, I have been going through the PAYE records of workers in Chester, which have been established since our chum Jemail went missing from Southall.' Whittaker was picking his fingernails and Carlton sat stone-faced, still angry at the way Welks had had a go at him. 'Do you need reminding gentlemen?' Hanks stood up his athletic form belying his age. 'A terrorist, part of a cell we cracked in London, got away. Our informants said Chester, and we have to assume that the man is undercover here playing the sleeper. We have finished checking with the DHSS (Department of Health and Social Security) and can conclude that he is not claiming benefits, which leads us to assume that he's working somewhere. Today, finally, we have two probable breakthroughs. I got a phone call intercept that the Yard rang me with an hour ago. It's a call from a coffee shop landline in Southall Broadway, from one of the 'Fellowship' suspects, someone called Kahn.'

'Significant?' Welks asked.

'Yes, Kahn, a slippery maggot that one, he owns the coffee shop in the Broadway.' Hanks explained. 'The message was short and in Urdu to a mobile prepaid number. Just said, 'BM delivery will be collected in Chester at the end of the month.'

Welks checked the calendar on the wall, '24th. So, we have a week to find this bugger and stop him delivering whatever he's supposed to deliver.'

'Exactly, Carlton, you mentioned that we needed a Laundry thing, well; I've got one for you, the PAYE (Pay as you earn) records.' Hanks announced. 'See, Chester, compared to other UK cities, is a City with a remarkably small immigrant population. I filtered out any non-British sounding names for anyone who changed jobs including new employees PAYE accounts set up since March, when we lost the man in Southall. Gentlemen, we have just 82 names.'

'And, is boyo on the list?' Welks asked.

'No, but he would have changed his name and that is what we need to do tonight. I want each one of these names checked and I want addresses for all of them by the morning, so that we can go visiting straight away. Time is of the essence here. Questions?' There were none, Carlton and Whittaker took the list, leaving the two senior detectives alone in their office.

Welks smiled, opening his desk drawer, withdrawing a bottle of scotch. 'Always good to have a plan B. What do you need me for?' Hanks wheeled his chair over, the castors screeching hideously. Welks poured the scotch into their coffee cups.

'Good man; Northern Ireland taught you a lot. I need you to organise the raiding teams for the morning. I want all those addresses visited and the people eyeballed. See what manpower we have available and blitz it. We need results fast.' Hanks took a sip of the whiskey, 'Anyway, how's the domestics now?' Hanks said, changing the subject as he savoured the drink.

'She's seeing the bloke nearly every night now, the girls are going loopy, ... cheers,' he said sombrely as he clinked his cup against Hanks's. 'And you seem to be stuck with this case?'

'Looks like until I retire. I hope the consultancy work is all it is cracked up to be and I will be able to do more working for them for six months than in the last ten years working here. We are tied down with regulations and paperwork,' Hanks said. 'But I am not leaving, I'll be back, it's just that the old contract enables me to double dip, a better pension, but that's a secondary consideration.' Hanks motioned Welks's cup with his for a refill. 'What're you up to tonight?'

'If she's in, another family row if I am unlucky, and if I'm lucky, a deaf and dumb dinner,' Welks replied filling the cups again. 'You?'

'I'll head over the road to The Boot, I fancy a drink tonight, and there are a couple of men who go there regularly that rent out cheap bedsits. Maybe they'll remember renting a room to some 'alien' in the near past. Bet seeing the missus tarted up and off with someone else is a bummer?'

'So, so, got used to it now. It's the girls that have trouble, they just don't understand. It's about time you let go as well. How many years has it been now?'

'Ten. Maybe you're right, it's bloody hard though,' Hanks nodded sagely, 'end in sight for you yet? Divorce, I mean?'

'Just the beginning,' Welks managed round a mouth full of scotch. 'This is probably my Sunday roast,' he quipped, laughing.

'It'll get better,' Hanks put his hand on his colleague's shoulder. 'It'll get better.'

2

From where they stood, the two women could see the gatehouse, which was one of only three buildings showing lights in the research facility complex. Teresa was waiting impatiently for the others to arrive with Jemma, nervous by her side, her blond hair, whipping in the wind. Jemma was on edge, Teresa simply infuriated that the rest of their team was still on their way down from the pub.

The research facility was silhouetted by the scudding clouds. The high razor-wire topped double fence was singing as the wind cut through it. It had just turned 11:30pm and as planned, the van was there, spotlighted the floodlights on the facility's gates. They could see Gavin and Clive leaning against it waiting, the white plumes of their breath being whisked away into the night.

'Where are the rest?' Teresa said, checking her watch. 'They know we have a narrow time window.'

Chester's industrial estate was deserted, which suited them well. The majority of the complex behind the fence was in utter darkness, as Jemma had told them to expect, everything was quiet.

Jemma peered anxiously down the road. Trembling with nerves, she was not so convinced now that she wanted to be part of the actual raid on her workplace. Her bladder signalled her nervousness, she grasped at her crotch for comfort.

'I think I can see them.' She stood on tiptoes straining to see down the infinite length of Sealand Road, which gleamed like it had been freshly oiled after the rain. 'Yes it's them! They're coming,' excitement in her voice now, adrenalin rushing.

In ones and twos, the rest of the group arrived, nervous, subdued and tense.

'Took your time,' Teresa scolded. 'You all know what to do now.' she said.

'Are we sure that the animals won't spread any diseases? What about the NAVS, they said it could be bloody dangerous.' Thomas, the tall lanky bespectacled student asked.

'Jemma said it's a lab bug, you berk, it doesn't affect people.' Clive replied looking at Teresa for approval. 'She bloody works there, so she should know.' Thomas looked unconvinced.

'We don't care what those pussyfooting mainstream anti-vivisectionists worry about. We are here to set the animals free.' Teresa shouted, angry at the question, 'We've been over all this time and time again.' Satisfied at the nods and grunts of agreement from the others, Teresa said, 'Let's go then.' They donned their balaclavas and approached the red and white barrier pole at the gate. A uniformed guard emerged from the gatehouse and made for the barrier ahead of them, in order to head them off. Before he could utter a word, Gavin, a bearded hulk of a man, vaulted the barrier and downed the guard with a tap on the head using the crowbar he was carrying. The guard went down like a dropped sack.

Jemma dashed into the gatehouse and pushed the gate release code, whilst retrieving the CCTV disc from the recorder on the desk. Too big for her pocket she tucked it down the front of her trousers. The huge metal gates seemed to take an age before the reassuring hum of the motor cut in and they began to open.

The group rushed through, Teresa sucked her breath in, listening. No alarms, a good sign, she thought. If there was an alarm, they'd have a maximum of approximately five minutes to do the business. She checked her watch. All police Fast Response Units were famously quick, although she couldn't possibly know where the nearest one was, only that the main police station was just over a mile away. Teresa led the group at a run across the almost empty car park, just two cars glistening wet in the floodlights. They ran to the first building on the right, which Jemma had told them housed the animals. The labs were one of the buildings that were lit up. Jemma punched in the key-code for the security lock and the door opened. Teresa split the party into two, motioning Jemma, Clive and Gavin to remain in the foyer, taking the main group down the corridor into the animal units. They rushed through the doors, ripping the plastic curtains of the sterile airlock down to be met by the pungent smell of mice, ferrets, rabbits and the chattering of monkeys. The row upon row of metal cages under the bright fluorescent lighting was what they had come for. They nervously checked around for cameras or staff, but there was no sign of either; empty apart from the test animals frantically scuttling around in their neatly stacked cages, frightened at the noisy intrusion. The only other object in the room was a large desk with a computer and a chair.

The team began releasing the frantic animals by using wire cutters to open as many of the cages as possible.

'Free as many as you can, as quickly as you can. Come on! Speed it up. Fast, faster!' Teresa shouted, urging them on whilst checking her watch again.

She then raced back to the group in the foyer, saying, 'Come on you three, with me. Quick, over this way!'

Teresa looked at Jemma for confirmation that she was heading in the right direction. Jemma nodded back nervously, her mouth too dry to speak. Gavin and Clive, with Jemma in reluctant tow, followed Teresa back across the wet yard towards the admin building. Inside on the ground floor, there was light in the staff canteen as they went in. Jemma hopped up on to the table to reach the DVD recorder and ejected the disc, the task made more difficult by her latex gloves, before tucking it down next to the other one in her trousers. The others burst into the empty canteen, to be confronted by a small portable TV on the table running, next to the half-eaten remains of a Chinese takeaway.

'Jemma!' Teresa shouted at the top of her voice. 'Where the fuck is he? You said he'd be here.' Jemma rushed in perplexed, having fully expected Khalid to be in the canteen on his break. She shrugged feebly, and picked up the takeaway bag as if it held the answer.

'He could be in the lab building.' she offered meekly.

'Okay, follow me.' Teresa beckoned urgently, making them rush back across the yard to the lab again. The activists there were busily cutting open cages and releasing animals. 'Where?' Teresa demanded. Jemma shrugged. Gavin saw a door to another room and kicked it hard to open it, realising too late, that the lock had already been forced and the door flew violently inwards. The sudden crashing of the door opening behind him surprised the duty technician who was squatting in front of the open door of a refrigerated safe. He hadn't seen or heard the intruders until now, until it was too late. Clive kicked the door of the safe shut causing Khalid to scream and curse in some unknown language. Gavin jumped on him and pinned him to the floor. It took a second for them to notice, first the blood, then the two fingers lying on the floor next to the safe door, which was ajar. Jemma, still holding the takeaway bag, followed them into the room, dropping the bag when she saw the blood on the floor. She rushed out, desperately needing the toilet now. Throwing the door of the staff toilets open, she dropped her trousers in the rush to relieve herself, ignoring the security discs falling and rolling on the floor under the divide into the next cubicle. She quivered fearfully in her toilet stall, hearing the noises through the thin walls, the sounds of Khalid's screams were terrifying. Afraid, Jemma stood on the seat and peered through the small fanlight to see what was going on.

'Fuck! Jesus! Shit!' Gavin shouted, 'You chopped off two of the bugger's fingers.'

'What? I just kicked that door shut, I didn't know.' Clive protested, seeing the fingers that the safe door had removed. 'Oh fuck, now what?'

'Serves him right for making the poor animals suffer,' Teresa snorted. The man's right hand was a mess, the index and middle finger missing. 'Bastard deserves it.' She added coldly. Her face lit up as an idea hit her.

'Jesus!' Clive interjected shaking his head in shock. Teresa looked at her watch again, as Jemma came into the canteen, putting her hands up over her mouth at the sight of fingers on the floor.

'Oh my God!' Jemma screamed before Teresa slapped her

face stopping her hysteria. Jemma held back a second scream and fled. Enough was enough; she just wanted to get out. She rushed past a running Thomas before she stopped outside in the car park, as the image of the severed fingers truly hit home. She never dreamed it would come to this, never imagined violence on this scale. She wanted nothing more to do with it. Feeling the bile rise in her throat she ran blindly through the gate, passing the prostrate guard as she pulled her balaclava off, just in time to reach the last Crossville bus into town. Gratefully she slumped sobbing into a seat.

Teresa stared at the door as it slammed behind Jemma, to see it burst open again, revealing Thomas's breathless form.

'There's an alarm been triggered, there's a flashing light on one of the security panels.' He gushed, catching his breath as he took in the scene in front of him. 'What the hell is going on? What have you done?' he demanded, staring aghast at the fingers on the floor, then at the blood, 'What in fuck's name are you doing? This wasn't what we were after!' He screamed at them. 'We were supposed to be making a statement about animal torturing and not about maiming humans. That isn't our message. It's against all we stand for.'

'Pompous idiot,' Teresa scoffed back at Thomas, 'it was an accident, but now that he has lost the fingers, we will put them in with the letter, it will make for much more impact.' She was worried now by the news of the alarm, 'You have a problem with that, then fuck off.' She screamed, spittle flying from her lips.

Thomas stood there, thunderstruck, unmoving. 'You, you….you.' he stammered.

'Oh just fuck off,' Teresa said dismissively, picking up the fingers and pushing past him and calling to the others over her shoulder on her way to the animal facility, 'Get going. Get him out to the van and get the hell out of here, we'll follow. Now go! Run! Both of you,' Teresa snapped. 'Get him out to Manning's Barn now. Move it!' she shouted.

Deflated, Thomas looked beggingly at Clive and Gavin who just turned away busying themselves with the hostage.

'You are going wrong,' Thomas half cried at them in frustration. 'Fools, all of you, get him to a doctor now. I'm out of here.' With that, he ripped his balaclava off and ran out after Teresa. Clive shrugged as he watched Thomas depart and grabbed the takeaway bag from the floor to wrap the technician's bleeding hand in.

'Twat!' he said to Gavin who was still trussing the technician with tape.

'Fucking students.' Gavin managed to say whilst biting a length of tape off with his teeth.

Teresa raced back to the animal lab as the two began dragging their hapless victim out behind her, heading towards the van. Panting with exertion, she checked the time. Four and a bit minutes gone by, Thomas's news made it more urgent now. She crashed through the door into the animal facility, startling everyone as she began screaming at the team releasing the animals,

'Come on, come on! Quick! Quick! We've got to be out of here fast. Go, go! Make sure all the outside doors are open,' she said as she kicked open the fire door to the yard. She checked the time again, five minutes. 'Let's go! Get out of here, now!' They all looked at her, in disbelief, as the work was unfinished; there were still dozens of cages they hadn't touched. The disbelief turned quickly to understanding, convincing them of the danger as they took off at speed out of the lab, splitting up as they ran out past the unconscious guard in the drive, ducking under the barrier and disappearing into the night.

The two men dragging their awkward bundle were the last out in spite of their head start. Teresa eyed them without emotion, as she deposited her letter with its gruesome contents on the gatehouse desk, adding a quickly scrawled addendum to the pre-printed message. She took a quick look at her watch and saw the time had jumped to 11:38; nearly 8 minutes. Her heart was racing. One last look round. She pushed the gate closure button before she slammed the gatehouse door behind her and took off after the rest of them.

Clive and Gavin had dumped their bundle unceremoniously in the back of the van that they had 'borrowed' from the local off-license. Gavin ran cursing to the driver's side and dragged off his balaclava as he got behind the wheel, Clive was already in the passenger seat. He looked at Gavin and said as the adrenalin drained, 'Wow, that was fierce. Let's get out of here.'

3

Detective Chief Inspector Alan Hanks was a detective of the old school and proud of it. He was close to early retirement and counting the days, having been accepted as a Security Consultant in an anti-terror security company. In spite of his successful career, he was actually looking forward to the chance of making a difference. Hanks had been recommended by a colleague who had done the same thing and re-joined the force six months later with a completely new perspective.

The initial euphoria of the chase for the suspect lost from 'Operation Fellowship' had faded into the drudgery of sifting records for someone who might be one of the biggest threats to the UK. The head of the Metropolitan Police had insisted that he, as their most senior AT (Anti-Terror) officer, go to Chester to continue the search for the missing suspect, as the last leads they had all pointed to the North West.

Now he was here in Chester on anti-terror duty trying to track a vanished sleeper, who Hanks was convinced was a part of a plot by al Qaida to destabilise Britain, but he was hampered by complacency, bureaucracy and was frustrated to the nth degree. His reputation as the top man for arresting terrorists after his successes in Northern Ireland and the 7/7 bombings. This had led initially to some friction inside the unit, but he soon turned the local detectives round, earning their respect with his razor sharp intuition, analytical talent and his impressive drinking capacity.

However, the only positive benefit of the move, as far as he could see, was meeting up with his old sidekick Welks, who he hadn't seen since their AT tour in Northern Ireland.

His new accommodation in Northgate Street wasn't a palace, but suited him for the ease of access to the town centre, and if all else failed, he could even walk to work at The Cheshire Constabulary Head Quarters.

It was the dream that had woken him, or maybe the stack of CDs falling to the floor, but he knew it was the dream, it always was. No amount of alcohol would stop it. The sickening sound of the explosion, the dreadful certainty, that it was his car, his wife, his beloved Kate. That was years ago, Kate had borrowed his car, because he'd parked behind her in the drive. It was his fault she'd died. If he'd have left the car in the road like he usually did; if only. In spite of years of personal investigating, the incident had never been cleared up. No culprits found, no claims from any terror organisation. He couldn't help harbouring the suspicion that it may have even been an inside job, one of his own. Lord knows, he'd made enough enemies in the Serious Crimes Unit.

His head was still scrambled, however he was able to see daylight through the curtains, so it must be Monday morning, he thought despairingly. He tried to focus on the wall clock to see the time, but there were still two of them, neither in focus. He gave up. His living room looked like a bomb had hit it, CDs and cases all over the place. What had happened last night?

He tried to put the events in sequence. He'd come off duty at six. He could remember the Bear and Billet at the bottom of Bridge Street. The landlord, Pete, had given him a bootleg recording of a Led Zeppelin concert, a new recording for his collection. He'd had a couple of drinks there, and then gone over the road to the Boot for another. He justified it as 'ground research', but really, he just didn't want to go back to the lonely flat. He'd gleaned nothing new in the Boot. Arriving home, he played the concert CD, then pulled out more of his music and had his own sad little party. He'd poured himself a few brandies, enjoying the soulful Page solos and Plant's high-pitched voice. He remembered vaguely finally listening to The Who 'live at Leeds' playing 'My generation'. He was still enthralled after all these years by Townsend's duet with his own echo off the back wall of the auditorium. Genius, he'd thought happily, as he then ffff---ffaded away. He smiled ruefully at the memory, head thumping as more consciousness returned.

He mulled over his future, unhappy at the prognosis he came up with. Relationships since Kate's death had been non-starters, his children gone; blaming him, like he did himself, for what had happened. An endless feeling of guilt, if only he'd parked differently, then he'd be dead and she'd be alive. Seeing his half-filled glass, he grimaced slightly and downed the dregs.

'Bollocks!' he exploded, as he poured another brandy into the greasy tumbler on the table in front of him. The neck of the bottle clattered against the rim. He'd had steadier mornings, he chided himself, and if Kate had been there, she'd have reprimanded him. He cursed as he lifted the glass and read through the bottom of it, as he tipped the fiery liquid down his throat, 'Unbreakable - Made in Turkey', stamped in the base. The thought occurred, that, if it was so bloody unbreakable, how come there were so many chips in the rim? He smiled at the profundity of this insight and returned to the thoughts of his career. He'd been in and out of favour almost as often as he'd changed his clothes.

There was that IRA stuff back in the eighties, clearing up the Victoria Street bombings. He'd been promoted for that and assigned to MI5, D Section in the 'Six Counties'. That's where he'd met Welks, a keen young detective who'd volunteered for the duty in Northern Ireland. The frustrations of being tied to the rule book had more than once pushed him over the line of legality, an attitude that had made him few friends in high places, but won him a lot of respect on the front line. 'Overzealousness in the pursuit of justice,' his then superior had called it. Damn! He was doing what the public expected of the police, taking the baddies off the streets. His colleagues in MI5 hadn't exactly played by the rules either, no one had. Many a 'suspect' had had an 'accident' or had been liquidated in 'own goals' as the euphemism had it. Back in London, he'd been a successful part of the Serious Organised Crime Team, before they transformed it into the National Crime Authority. He was behind many of the busts of syndicate crime, developing a special talent in surveillance technology and network structures. He had a nose for it.

The increasing restrictions on his freedom of action irked him more every day. He was suffocating in this strait-jacket that was being forced upon him. More to the point, the bastards were getting away with it. He desperately wanted to stop the rot. How? Paperwork? He thought about it day and night these days. End of a career, no burst of glory. No-one would remember him. Was the need for a memorial driving him? He studied the greasy tumbler in front of him, as if it contained the solution.

Almost on the point of refilling it again, his phone rang. He'd been tempted to use it a while ago, just to call in to see how the mission was getting on. His attempts at the two landlords having proved fruitless, maybe his team were luckier. In the end, he'd resisted. He picked the phone up. Before he could speak, a loud voice bellowed, 'You're late!' Hanks winced, the volume causing his head to spin. He was unable to counter with any witticism to his partner Colin Welks. But Welks was alright. He too had a good track record; they had a long and sometimes happy history together.

'Jesus, do you have to be that loud? What the hell's up?' Hanks winced.

'Suffering are we? Remy Martin then?' Welks knew him well, too well.

'Did you just phone to mock my hangover? Can't it wait until I am in?'

'Panic stations.'

'Shit, really? What happened?' Hanks asked alarmed now. 'What's going on?'

Welks paused for a moment, then, more seriously said, 'You'd better get in here fast. The Super's just given you two fingers.'

'You what?'

'Seriously, he's stuck you two fingers.'

'Bastard! All for putting a bottle of scotch on the table,' he put the glass down unfilled. 'I'm on my way,' he said heatedly disconnecting before Welks could say anymore.

Welks had left it at that and hung up. He knew Hanks would take the bait. Hanks headed for the shower; nursing a strong feeling he might need a clear head today.

The shower didn't quite hack it. Two Alka Seltzer, a couple of aspirin and a handful of indigestion tablets helped to get his guts back on track, and his head halfway functioning again. He hoped the toothpaste would cover the smell of the brandy lingering on his breath. He just about managed to shave himself without committing suicide, although his face didn't look too healthy after the attempt. He splashed a bit of aftershave on, immediately regretting it, the little cuts stinging savagely.

The drive into town down Sealand Road was easy, traffic was better than usual. He toyed with the thought that he should maybe make a habit of going in this late every day.

As he drove by, there was a bit of activity on the new industrial site. Some police officers were standing around in a yard, a SoC (SoC) van parked there as well. He didn't pay too much attention to it; too many other things were in the forefront of his mind. What the hell was the Super giving him two fingers for? Hanks got stuck at the lights going into Nun's Road. His mobile buzzed loudly, he saw Welks's number on the display and answered.

'Yeah.'

'Where are you?'

'Nun's Road lights. Why?'

'The manure is beginning to hit several fans simultaneously,' Welks said. 'The Super is up to his eyeballs in some regulations crap and an Army bloke is on the phone from the Brecon Germ Warfare Group. Can't see the wood for the trees yet; how long you gonna be?'

'Two, maybe three minutes.' Hanks choked back the questions.

'See you in the garage.'

'The garage? Why...?' Hanks began, but Welks this time had broken the connection, leaving him even more puzzled.

The lights turned green and a short time later, he swung into the police underground car park. Being a Detective Chief Inspector had its benefits, even if it was just a reserved space in the garage. Welks was already standing by the lift.

'What the hell is going on Welks? Why are we meeting here?' Hanks said impatiently.

'It's quiet and we need to talk uninterrupted.' Welks defended. 'There's been a break-in at Brinkley's. The Security guard is in intensive, a bang on the head.'

'I just came past there. I saw the action outside. Wondered what it was all about. So what's been at issue; I'm assuming straight B&E?'

'No, not a simple breaking and entering. AMIP is in a total spin.'

'AMIP? They've called Area Major Incident Pool for a break-in?' he shook his head in disbelief.

'Brinkley's as in virus research company, this is big, hence all the activity. The talk is that animal rights people did this, we've got a kidnapping, and loads of infected laboratory animals have been released into the wild. One of the night staff at Brinkley's has been snatched.' Hanks's thoughts stopped dead.

'Why the hell didn't you call me earlier?' Welks had no excuse, lamely he continued,

'I just wanted to get you up to speed, so when the Superintendent hauls you up, you don't look a complete twat when you go in.'

'When I need career advice ...' he left the words hanging with Welks looking at him in askance, '…I'll make you my sexual advisor.' He saw the puzzlement on Welks's face, 'When I want your fucking advice I'll ask for it.' Hanks snapped impatiently, as he made for the lift. 'Virus research facility and animals on the loose sounds like a real flap. We need to know if the freed animals carried any diseases.'

'What do you think we're doing?' Welks stopped and looked at his partner, unsure if all this was registering. 'Christ Alan, this is causing ructions, his nibs is doing a typical by the book, do nothing until something happens thing, and you come in looking like some dosser with a lobotomy.'

'Got it. Let's see what the picture is. Let's go up. You've got the witnesses and statements from Brinkley's? What about the animals then, any info on that? Dangerous, not dangerous?'

'DC Gunner is sorting that front, she's duty case officer at the moment. 'How did you get on last night, apart from the booze, you know the landlords bit? You picked a bad night to go on a bender. Was it Kate again?'

Hanks nodded miserably, as he appraised his image in the grubby stainless steel lift door. 'I don't look that bad! The enquiries you mean? Nothing useful, dead end.'

'You should stop blaming yourself for Kate, you know. She's dead, it wasn't your fault. Sure, it could have been you that night, but it wasn't. Alan, it's time to move on. It's doing you no good, 'bout time you got into a relationship again. By the way, all the teams are out knocking on doors this morning; let's see if your tax idea thing takes us anywhere.'

The doors opened spilling them into a big open plan office. Hanks had never seen the place so full; the noise level was breath-taking. There were people milling everywhere. DC Harris saw him and waved him over.

'Sir, the Super wants you as soon as you arrive. 'Urgent' he said.' Harris gestured with his thumb towards the operations room.

'Hmm, no rest for the wicked,' muttered Hanks, patting him on the shoulder on the way. 'Well Welks, looks like it's into the lion's den.'

He followed Welks towards the Ops room, remembering the first time he'd met Michaels, who was now Superintendent, at the police training school in Hendon. They'd been plain buttons in those days, but Michaels had stood out even then. He'd been the goody-goody who had got up everyone's noses, except perhaps those of some of the instructors, although he had won no-one's respect. Nicknamed Mr Perfect, the nauseous man, was everything but, and had told tales on everyone and was proud of it. Hanks would never forget the incident of the syndicate exercises, where Michaels had neglected to pass on the full information to his team mates in order to shine. Michaels had done that three times in succession, getting Hanks and his colleagues' lower grades as a result. They'd all been livid when they found out afterwards. Michaels, of course, was only too pleased to point out that all was fair in love and war. Hanks had punched him; it had been his first disciplinary procedure. Over the years, Hanks and Michaels' paths had crossed surprisingly often. Hanks had never forgiven him for the training college thing, and had had no reason to reassess his negative judgement of the man even now. This posting to Chester, on the trail of a missing al Qaida suspect had been a matter of dread for him, facing the thought of working closely with Michaels again, even though he wasn't directly under him.

As head of the Scotland Yard ATU (Anti-Terror-Unit) team, Hanks had managed by and large, to avoid the Super since he'd been in Chester. The man's reputation seemed to be legendary, even amongst his own troops he was the source of many cruel canteen jokes.

Doing this difficult and complex job under the direct control of Mr Perfect, who would, at the first opportunity drop anybody in the proverbial to make himself look good, wasn't an appealing thought. He took a deep breath and opened the door.

4

Hassan Washiri was back in Northern Pakistan and glad to be part of the active fight again. He had travelled from London on a devious route designed to throw off any tail that might have been assigned to him. Hassan, who was Watford born of immigrant parents, was visiting Osama bin Laden's deputy to plan the fight against the West, against Britain, the very place he knew as home, but had learned to hate. Yet, this corner of North West Pakistan wasn't Hassan's favourite place either, nothing to hate, but it was arid and bare. Why the leader had chosen this Godforsaken hole was beyond him. A primitive village with a few basic mud brick houses, non-existent plumbing and hardly any electricity. There was nothing inviting about this barren area, which matched a harsh landscape with an even crueller climate.

Washiri had trekked up from Islamabad to meet Osama's senior strategist. Qamar al Surira remained active in his retreat in Achar, a remote little hamlet in the mountains high up in the Swat Valley. The allied security forces had driven Osama bin Laden underground, which had considerably weakened the operational side of al-Qaida. A couple of internet videos a year wasn't exactly the role Osama had envisaged for himself either, Hassan thought, as he sat chilled and uncomfortable in Qamar's primitive house. He was drinking a glass of hot tea whilst taking in the mud walls of the room and the grubby mats on the packed earth floor. The only glimpse of modernity in the chaos of floor cushions and mats was a sleek laptop, the screen full of figures, which they had been studying. The data came from a USB stick that he had delivered to Qamar from England.

'The information is good. I told you he was an achiever.' Qamar enthused. Hassan hadn't a clue, what the man was talking about and just nodded.

'Do you know Masoud?' Hassan shook his head.

'You will meet him.' Qamar went back to his laptop engrossed in the information thereon. Abruptly, he sat up, looked Hassan in the eye and said, 'Masoud has started a plan which will do major damage to the British economy. Osama himself thought it up.' The name Osama caught Hassan's interest even more.

'Yes?' Fully alert now, he listened.

'We have managed to get a man into a highly sensitive facility. With what we will get from there, we will be able to achieve a great blow for the cause. They won't know what hit them.'

'What's the plan?'

'You don't need to know at the moment. I'll see you do when the time comes.'

'Uh huh.' Hassan nodded, none the wiser for the discourse. He had been there two days now at this supposed planning meeting, although they had very little they could plan. Qamar had said, something 'spectacular' had to happen to turn the balance, as retribution for the humiliation of the great Osama being forced under cover. Hassan needed little convincing of that. However, what could they or should they do? The West needed to be taught a lesson.

The problem was that their options were getting daily ever more limited. The West was getting better at spying, both electronically and physically, infiltrating their networks and, not the least of their worries, tracking their sources of money.

Blowing up market places full of people was easy in Afghanistan or Pakistan, but the impact on the outside world was pretty near non-existent. Nobody cared anymore. It didn't matter to the Mr John Smiths of Manchester, if another fifty or seventy Afghanis were massacred. They were just more abstract statistics, another newsreel clip, a bit of footage with expert commentary; something else to endure before the sports news came on. There was no connection to the real world, no relevance to Mr Average. The only purpose it served 'back home' was to frighten the dumber members of their population into the al-Qaida ranks; people who'd rather be the suicide bombers going to paradise than victims with uncertain afterlives.

'Masoud's thing is going well, but we need another 9/11!' Qamar said, slamming his fist into his palm. Hassan just nodded blankly and sipped his tea; he'd seen this too often to react and since he had no idea of Masoud's plan, he refrained from comment.

'The 7/7 London attacks gave the world just a little jolt. It's a shame that the tracing of the chemicals by the infidels reduced the impact, and the police arrests afterwards soured our glory.' Glancing out at what served the hamlet as a mosque, Qamar turned back to Hassan. 'We need Allah's help,' he shook his head despondently.

He'd seemed odd since Hassan had delivered the package containing the USB stick. The wrapping, an old British newspaper, lay discarded on the cushions at their feet, next to a bundle of pre-paid SIM cards, which Hassan had collected from Karachi on this way up. Hassan was surprised at Qamar's lack of reaction to the news of money being skimmed from the UK drugs operation. In ordinary times, he would have gone mad about it. He seemed, however, to be lost in another world. 'Masoud, our friend in England, has people on the ground ready and waiting. He has one good man placed in the north west, but we need to do more with the resources we have!'

The money skimming seemed not to have impinged on Qamar, although the UK operation was an important source of funds. Masoud had sent the details of the monies from the heroin trade in the UK, and had warned that the takings were being fiddled; the figures had been manipulated. Someone was taking a cut; cheating his brothers and the cause. Identifying the person, Hassan felt, would be difficult, with so many individuals involved, too many in fact.

'Allahu a'lam.' Hassan muttered as he looked out at the cold night through what passed for a window. He pulled the bit of sacking back over it to keep at least some of the warmth in the room.

'Yes, Allahu a'lam, indeed.' Qamar murmured, obviously deep in thought.

Qamar, born in Saudi, had been brought up in a privileged household, the eldest of four brothers. An educated man, he had studied in Caltech and Berkley in the States. In contrast, Hassan had come up the hard way, attending a technical college in Watford and then travelling the world working in the mining industry. He had left his last post as a ventilation engineer in the Iranian coal fields and had come back to Swat to take up 'the cause' full time. Yet, they both shared one thing in common, a deep hatred for the Western world, and America and its lapdog Britain in particular. Osama's father, Salem bin Laden, had been a close friend of Qamar's, before the tragedy of his sudden death. Qamar hated the Americans, because of their complicity in Salem's death. It was known to all, that Salem was betrayed and killed by the Bush family, after he had invested 33 million dollars from Saudi in the '80's with them. Salem had died in a Bush plane that had crashed 'mysteriously', and the money had disappeared.

Qamar had been in this black mood for days now, brooding, malevolent, and unapproachable. Hassan was sure that the virtual incarceration of their leader Osama had something to do with it. He would often rage, eyes dark as coal in a face burned like old leather by the sun, pacing the earthen floor like an angry demon. Qamar the fighter, no, Qamar the avenger fitted better. With Osama laid low, effectively out of action, Qamar had the reins, but the load was a heavy one and it was clearly telling on him.

'We need to tackle the skimming on the heroin trade in the UK.' Qamar grunted. 'We should take Baitullah's warning seriously. It's hard to believe that one of the faithful is stealing from the cause. It all points to the Preacher himself from the data we have.'

Hassan just nodded sagely. 'Baitullah?' he queried.

'Baitullah, yes why?'

'I thought his name was Masoud?' This was greeted by a rare rasp of laughter from Qamar. 'Oh, my friend, sometimes I wish I had more of you. Baitullah is his surname.'

'Whose?' Hassan said suspecting the answer.

'Masoud's.' Qamar confirmed.

'Oh well, yes,' Hassan said as if that had been obvious all along. 'Certainly, it seems that the preacher himself is skimming.'

'If it is the Luton Preacher, he must be punished. A thief is never good news, a bad example for others,' said Qamar, shoving a pile of books aside to make more space for himself on the cushions. He clapped his hands, summoning a servant to bring fresh tea.

'The new conduits for opium and heroin are working well. It's just the skimming that's the problem.' He turned from the laptop's screen to Hassan. 'The money laundering is going well, with all those holiday property scams,' He stretched yawning and added, 'we have companies based in Cyprus which do nothing but resell sold houses. The money is banked as property commissions. We pay the 3% tax on each transaction, which keeps the government happy. The money is then clean, so we're happy. The banking system there is so corrupt you can get them to agree to absolutely anything.'

'No wonder they need a bailout then. So what sort of funding do we have on hand?' Hassan asked.

Qamar shrugged, 'It's not just the Republic of Cyprus, we have accounts in the North as well. There is probably around half a billion dollars swimming in the Cypriot banking system. Apart from the skimming job, everything is how it should be.' Qamar looked at him directly, a scowl on his face as he sipped his tea. 'Finding out who is skimming is police work, not work for men of Allah,' he complained.

'Nearly ten per cent down on the previous month,' Hassan commented. 'Not good.'

'What is money to us? We are men of the true faith. It is only a tool against Allah's enemies.' Qamar waved imperiously, dismissing his friend's words as if he were clearing smoke. 'Nevertheless it's good to know that we have plenty of it. I'm sure Osama will be pleased. We'll need the funding when the time comes.'

Qamar idly picked up the pages of the newspaper the SIM cards and the USB stick had arrived in. It was a section of the London Times. Distractedly, he began reading the headlines. The paper was four days old, but in this part of the world, that was fresh news.

Only 30% for Tony Blair
'Tony Blair was only thought to be a possible candidate for European President by 30% of the voters.'
'That arrogant Bush lapdog,' he muttered. Hassan just looked at him questioningly. The next headline brought Qamar up with a jolt.

Huge Chemical disaster at Jaipur'
The Jaipur fuel storage and distribution terminal in India has been badly damaged when it exploded. It is owned by the Indian Oil Company (IOC) India's largest oil Company in the Sitapura Industrial Area on the outskirts of Jaipur, Rajasthan.' A series of major explosions occurred in the early morning. The Jaipur Meteorological Department recorded an earth-tremor measuring 2.3 on the Richter scale around the time the first explosion at 7:36 am, which caused the shattering of glass windows nearly eight kilometres from the epicentre. The disaster occurred when petrol was being transferred from the Indian Oil Corporation's oil depot to a pipeline. Forty Indian Oil Corporation employees were at the terminal when it caught fire, who are now presumed dead. The initial collateral casualty figures are some 509 dead, 214 missing and 4323 injured, most with severe burns..... Jaipur'

Qamar's heart missed a beat; he dropped the newspaper to the floor. This sort of thing would be much more effective in Britain, he thought. This kind of 'accident' would be an encouraging job for the front line; it would make Allah proud of them. Hassan saw Qamar's mood changing visibly as the initial excitement grabbed him.

'What's up?' Hassan asked concerned. 'What's happened?' Qamar, now full of excitement, pointed at the newspaper and explained what he had read.

'I think I have an idea for our next big attack, but I need to do some more research.' Qamar said as Hassan read the article, 'The infidels may be able to follow the movements of explosive chemicals, but they can't stop people moving petrol about, I mean, they can't follow every load can they? Tomorrow we must go to Dir and look some stuff up. I think it's far enough from here to be safe to use the internet.'

For some time, they discussed the accident and the details they could surmise from the article, considering location, material and detonation methods. Hassan recalled the explosions they'd had in the mines in Iran. The build-up of gas in the shafts was always a big problem and in the confined spaces of the tunnels, the effects were often devastating. They drifted into anecdotal stories and successes of the cause and eventually, still full of excitement, they turned in for the night.

At dawn, the sun did its weak best to stagger over the rim of the distant mountains as the pair, together with their local guide, made ready for the ride into Dir. The journey on their horses, would take the best part of six hours. The very cold, combined with the bitter wind and the scarves wrapped tightly round their faces, stopped conversation during the ride. In one of the rest stops they again discussed the problem of the 'skimmer', agreeing that when his identity was confirmed, they should make an example of him.

'Behead the whore's son and film it. It will be a good subject for a video.' Hassan said as they remounted. Qamar nodded his approval. The terrain they were negotiating was rough and desolate and without a guide, they would not have found their way to Dir. There were no roads as such, only a few goat tracks. Saddle-sore and weary, they travelled on through endless rocky outcrops, plodding on in an uphill, down dale monotony, both lost in their own thoughts, as the steady jogging of the horses and the penetrating cold slowly numbed them. Eventually, the road to Dir appeared. The high electricity masts dotted along it, were visible from miles away and stood like skeletal aliens against a bizarre background of jagged rocks and low scrub. They arrived in the small town, tethering the horses next to the petrol station. It was a picture of incongruity, the scrawny horses beside the petrol pumps. The internet café was full of youths smoking, most were trying to access sites the government had censored or banned and they were either complaining about it, or making lewd jokes and laughing loudly. Hassan and Qamar found a corner away from the crowd and started their online search for accidents.

Qamar soon found out that there had been some amazingly destructive accidents, and he was becoming increasingly excited at the idea of engineering the next big one.

'Here, look!' Qamar said quietly, leaning towards Hassan who was sitting next to him. 'Don't talk, just read. Who knows who might be listening?'

Hassan turned and rolled across on his chair, checking that they hadn't attracted any attention from the youths at the other end.

'1998 Pipeline at Jesse Frankria exploded', he read, 'instantly killing more than 500 people and severely burning hundreds more. Up to 2000 people had been lining up with buckets and bottles to scoop up oil. The fire spread and engulfed the nearby villages of Moosqar and Oghara, killing farmers and villagers asleep in their homes…'

'Or this one might be better still,' he enthused, as he scrolled down further. Hassan read on,

'1946 On April 16, the SS Grandcamp, carrying ammonium nitrate fertilizer, exploded in the Texas City harbour, followed the next morning by the explosion of the SS High Flyer. The disaster killed 576 and injured several thousand. The explosion was felt 75 miles away in Port Arthur, and created a 15-foot tidal wave destroying a large number of boats and coastal installations.'

'No good! They track all that stuff now,' Hassan whispered deflated, 'because of the IRA.'

Qamar nodded and went back to his search. 'Here,' he prodded Hassan again.

'1948: A thirty-ton tanker filled with diethyl ether caused a deadly explosion at German chemical conglomerate IG Farben, which is now Bayer Chemical's Ludwigshafen plant on the river Rhine killing more than 200 and injuring more than 3,800. Houses within a radius of 20 km from the site were damaged by the blast and the industrial complex was out of operation for two years thereafter.'

Hassan whispered to him, 'I wonder if they follow movements of ether?'

'Ether! I think that is it! Ether is far more explosive than petrol. We have found something beautiful here and have to do some thinking now.'

Qamar downloaded the details onto his stick as the sun disappeared. He turned to Hassan and whispered 'I think we will call it the operation 'Bayer'. That has a nice easy ring to it. We could camouflage it even more by making it 'Buyer',' he sniggered, 'I think we've found a 'Buyer', Hassan.' he chortled loudly, enjoying his play on words in English. Hassan smiled tolerantly. Qamar pulled at Hassan's sleeve and turned back to the keyboard, 'Come! Let's announce 'Buyer'.' He typed a short email to Masoud in England and then turned away from the computer looking very pleased with himself. He deleted the browser history whilst saying loudly to Hassan, 'It's great being able to contact my son so quickly like this, it takes so long for mail to get back and forth to Karachi.' More quietly he whispered, 'Let's leave here fast, we probably have already attracted the attention from..., you know.' he said, nodding upwards with his head.

'Allah?' Hassan whispered incredulously.

'No! The NATO devils! They spy everywhere,' Qamar hissed angrily, and led the way out of the cafe.

The horses had been fed and watered and the guide bowed obsequiously as they approached.

'This 'accident' will be the end of Gordon Brown and his cronies', Qamar crowed happily as he mounted his scrawny mare; ready to start back up the mountain. Hassan turned his horse to follow the others along the track.

The trek back up into the hills was arduous, the darkness making the journey colder and even more challenging than their descent. In Achar, the welcoming smoke of the kitchen fires was already decorating the dawn tinged sky as the weary pair arrived back.

'Let's get inside and sit by the fire,' Hassan said, hugging himself for warmth.

'No! Come, we can walk on up the hill a bit. You, I trust.' Qamar said. 'The others, the women, I don't. Walls have ears! I want you to go back to England and inform Masoud about everything we have discussed. We will get you back into the UK from France. You should work with Masoud closely. I'll see to it that he's warned you are coming, highly recommended by me, and he must set you up with an invisible cover. Have you got that?'

'Yes of course,' Hassan was secretly pleased to be leaving this terrible place; even England never got this cold. 'I have been thinking; if we detonate the ether on the surface we'll get something like we read on the news. What if we contain it, I mean, put it in a building or maybe a road tunnel? The effect would be multiplied enormously.'

'I like that,' Qamar said after some thought. 'Yes, that would strike a good blow for the faith. It would be just like your Iran stories from last night.' He paused to get his breath on the steep incline. 'It was our brothers who were killed in those mines. This time it will be our enemies who die.'

Hassan nodded, 'So, I will become invisible in England and our only contact will be through 'one off' phone cards sequence. You still want to use the satellite number sequences as we used in the past?'

'Of course, the +881 numbers, same system, a progression every day,' Qamar confirmed. 'Set up the system as soon as you get there and courier me the sequences for each of you when it's done.'

'We phone you when we must on the incremental daily number change.'

'Yes, it is always a risk using the internet for communication. I like your idea of maybe using a tunnel. It's good, so talk to Masoud about it. He is bound to know someone who can help and he will organise the logistics. He's clever, even if he is crazy sometimes.' Qamar cast his mind back to the stories about Masoud's private life. If only half of the tales were true, then he was a truly evil man, he thought, but he's Allah's tool nonetheless.

'What do you mean crazy? Dangerous?' Hassan asked, worried.

'No, not for you, how shall I say it? Masoud has a penchant for women.' He answered, padding Hassan on the shoulder. 'Do you still have contact with that chemist in Islamabad? What was his name?'

'You mean Shadeed?' Hassan asked, 'The organic chemist who our brethren in the north use for the purification of the harvest?'

'The very one, have you had contact recently?'

'No, not for some time.'

'You should visit him on your way to Europe. I'll text him now via satellite and tell him you are coming, ask him to give you information about ether, collect the data and take the information to Masoud. Be very cautious, we cannot be too careful with so many drones and satellite watching and listening. I just hope our little session in the internet café didn't get noticed.' Qamar looked concerned.

'You think it's a problem?'

Qamar shook his head slowly, 'I don't know. I really don't know.'

'You have to get this information safely to Baitullah, my friend. If the information falls into the wrong hands, we will lose a great chance to further the cause of our Jihad. You saw what happened two weeks ago when the American dogs fired missiles from their drones and attacked our people in Waziristan. Over 60 of our people were killed. Naturally, for publicity purposes we are claiming they were all innocent civilians, but we lost many good fighters that day, and the day before they killed 16 of our fighters the same way, when the drones targeted Aabid Baitullah, who only escaped by good luck. These attacks on the tribal regions increase daily and are depressingly more accurate. Above all, they mostly go unchallenged.' Qamar stared intently into Hassan's eyes, looking glum at the thought. 'How do they know where they are? Do we have spies? Do we have traitors?'

'My brother, I assure you, our men are all loyal, all of them,' Hassan tried to cheer him up. 'When we succeed in our new venture, all will be avenged.' he boasted.

Qamar put his arm around Hassan's shoulders and turned him to face back down to the village. 'If only it were so simple,' he mused, 'if only it were so simple. In Islamabad, I don't want any traces. You mustn't leave a trail. You follow me? Come,' Qamar said, 'I'm freezing. Let's get back into the warmth.' Hassan pulled his robe more tightly around himself and grunted agreement.

'Do you know Aabid?' Qamar asked conversationally on the way back.

'I never met him.'

'Aabid, our friend, is considered by the regime in Islamabad to be one of the state's most dangerous enemies. He has been coordinating attacks across the border on US and NATO forces in Afghanistan for the past two years. The Americans somehow know this and hunt him like a dog. They justify the drone strikes on our tribal regions for this reason. Aabid is a believer, a carrier of the faith and an inspirer of men. He can fight like a tiger and plan like the master Osama himself. He is a good man. A man you can trust.'

'There is a point to this?' Hassan asked as they approached the huts on the outskirts of the village again, the goats nervously bleating at their approach.

'Yes of course. You must know that Aabid has a brother, almost his equal and he is in England. He is Masoud.' Hassan looked stunned at the news.

'Brothers?'

'Brothers, indeed! I think you will be a good team together, with your experience in the mines and his organisation talents and contacts. Don't let his 'hobbies' with women put you off. He has some strange, sometimes-violent ways. Just ignore them, go to him in England and work with him.

5

Nick Kitson, the lab manager at Brinkley's checked his e-mails to find one from Sally, one of the members of the scientific media research unit, a bunch of students who trawled the web on Brinkley's behalf to flag up any developments about virology that might be of interest to the company. It was a cost-effective method of getting up-to-the-minute information.

He started to read, thinking it was probably boring rubbish, another load of verbiage from some conference, but maybe it was something, as Sally had flagged it. He braced himself for the chore of reading it, and sat back stunned afterwards and read it a second time before picking the phone up to talk to his boss.

'Hi, Nick.' Voss answered.

'I just got an e-mail with some stuff that could be of interest to us. A Dr Strout has done a presentation in South Carolina on the reasons for the differing severity of infection in the same host species. Sorry, I forgot to mention, he's talking about influenza viruses.'

'What have we got?'

'The most interesting points are that the intensity of infection appears to be genetic, and immunity to infection is a combination of environment and genetics. He's quoting work on the Spanish Flu pandemic, which left certain racial groups untouched.'

'Uh huh! Worth looking into, get hold of the paper for me,

will you?'

Andy Voss was Research and Development Director and founder of Brinkley Medical Services. The small company had prided itself in its pioneering work on the H1N1a flu and its derivatives. They had also made a fortune in the manufacture of anti-flu vaccines. He was sitting on massive stocks of vaccines at the behest of the World Health Organisation and the UK government. Currently, they were working on the new H5N6a virus that was predicted to become the cause of the next pandemic. The Disease Control Centre in Atlanta had issued a 'significant threat warning' about it six months ago, although all indications were that this strain would not transmit from human to human. The only success they'd had in the transmission chain was between small mammals, mice and ferrets. Airborne tests had indicated that the new genotype was not viable. Voss had a nose for innovation and that was what made him a highly respected as well as a highly paid member of the team, a lateral thinker and an astute manager as well.

He phoned down to the lab. 'Hi Mary. Do you have anything new on the latest transmission tests?'

'Yes Mr Voss, I was just about to call you. Some of the ferrets seem to be getting resistance to the bug,' Mary answered.

'How is it showing up?' he asked, his interest piqued.

'First I thought it was a statistical blip when a couple of ferrets I'd expected to die of the disease didn't. I bred some of the survivors and the new generations are showing signs that the virus affects less.'

The minute hand on the clock clicked over loudly in the quietness of the room, Mary looked up at the clock. It was showing Friday 22nd October 9:27. She rubbed her temple with her free hand, hoping she wasn't going to get a migraine. 'They are not dying, that's what is significant.' She added.

Andy reflected on this as well as the news from Nick. Was there a tie-in may be? He felt a mild adrenalin surge.

'Can you bring the test reports up to my office? Oh, and get Jemma to do some DNA analyses on the ferrets that died as well as the survivors. I want to see the differences. Get her to check the mice tests with Khalid as well; I'd be interested to know what is going on on that front.'

'Sure. I'll be up in about five minutes.' She sighed, her heart missing a beat as she hung up, frowning yet pleased. Any time she was alone with Voss, she hoped that he might notice her as more than just Nick's assistant. She smoothed her hair and straightened the neck of her blouse under her lab coat and quickly checked her reflection in the window. Satisfied, she returned to the task in hand. The extra work was beginning to worry her, stretching and went over to where the clipboards with all the current data were hanging on the wall. Jemma looked up and smiled sympathetically.

'Are you not feeling well, Mary?'

Mary sighed briefly, running her hands through her hair and throwing it backwards over her shoulders. 'I think I'm getting a migraine. Voss wants you to do DNAs on the ferrets, the dead ones and the survivors. He says he wants to see the differences. Oh, and he wants the mice tested as well. Can you get started on that?' She hesitated, not sure if the new girl would be up to it. 'He wants all the latest on the ferrets as soon as possible, ask Khalid for help.'

Jemma shrugged, 'Might get blood out of a stone first,' she said crossly, 'He's on nights again. He thinks at night we won't notice that he does naff all,' she commented wryly, punching holes in the latest lab sheets before filing them.

'Fat lot of help he'll be then.' Mary collected the last of the test sheets she needed, and for safety, put them through a UV light bath to sterilise them. 'Will you be ok with the DNAs alone?' she asked, waiting only for Jemma's affirmative nod, before she herself took a UV shower in the airlock between the 'Clean zone' and the offices. Jemma visibly relaxed as the door closed behind Mary, as she was getting nervous about what she and her friends were planning to do at the weekend.

Mary took the stairs two at a time, knocked on Voss's door and went in without being asked. Voss was on the phone and he motioned her to take a seat. She tried not to stare at him as she waited for the call to end.

'Yes, but we need more information on the types of viral binding sites. I need to get access to the electron microscope at the Poly Tech. No, no! There's no danger of contamination. We're talking DNA samples here, not viral samples.' Voss paused, listening intently to the other end of the conversation. Mary only heard a faint incoherent babble. 'Just send the damn authorisation to bookkeeping, will you? I need at least an hour, no make it two, booked for every day next week.' There was more mumbling from the other end. 'Of course it comes out of the H5N6a budget, Goddammit! We're only talking about a couple of grand.' Andy listened again. 'Just do it, understand? Or do I buy our own electron microscope?' He hung up without waiting for an answer, startling Mary who had been observing him.

'Bureaucrats, don't you just love them.' he said to no-one in particular. 'The place could be on fire and they'd want to know who was going to pay for the water to put it out.' He sighed in frustration, 'So Mary, show me what you've got for me.'

She stood and placed the reports on the desk, pointing out the graphs of the animals' temperatures marked as Test group I and Test group II.

'Test group one is the high mortality group.' she clarified.

'So group two are obviously the survivors?'

She nodded in affirmation. The graphs' curves mirrored each other practically identically hour for hour in the first ten hours of infection. Then the second group started to drop, whilst the first continued to climb. Until, that is, the animals died.

'We're doing twenty-four times a day routine temperature checks on the survivors now. All are perfectly normal. The H5N6a didn't harm them at all as far as we can tell. They seem to breed, but there might be a fertility issue. The males have abnormally swollen testicles. We're still checking.'

'Good work. I've been looking at the peer-to-peer transmission aspect. The virus seems pretty stable as it is, so I don't imagine we have a mutation here. It must be something in the host. Get Nick to check the binding sites in the DNA of both groups, and while he's at it, ask him to do the DNA in the inoculated specimens as well. I want common factors.' He stopped to see if she had understood him. She nodded again.

'I don't want to be rude, but you seem stressed,' he stated. 'Is everything okay?'

'Yes, well…,' she paused, glad for the chance to get things off her chest, 'the work load, it's getting very heavy now. Khalid is on nights and Jemma, although she's trying hard, still comes up short on skills and experience. It makes life hard having to do most of it alone.

'Let's assess staffing levels with Nick next week.'

'Thanks Mr Voss,' she said, turning to leave.

Voss watched her go out, thinking; she was a good worker, intelligent and bright. She was, his 'eyes in the lab'. Maybe she couldn't make all the connections, but she certainly picked up fast on discrepancies and anomalies. It was just time before lunch to talk with London on this; Randell needed to be brought in on it all, he thought, reaching for the phone.

Barry Randell had made millions by picking the right company or the right product at the right time. He came across as a canny bargainer and a cold businessman. Brinkley Medical was one of many profitable companies belonging to his investment holding company. He was sitting at his desk, working on a batch of potential contracts when his phone rang.

'Hello Andy,' Randall said, recognising the number. 'What's up?'

'Hi Barry, we need to talk about investment.'

'Oh!' Randell said interestedly. 'What?'

'The old chestnut I'm afraid. I had a conversation with accounts just now and am getting cheesed of trying to buy time on the polytechnic's electron microscope. I think it is high time we got our own.'

'It's a big chunk of money Andy,' Randell replied, 'I know your arguments and about labour saving, and more efficiency, but those beasts cost a lot of money, not simply capital investment, but upkeep and maintenance.'

'Leasing,' Voss was prepared for the argument. 'I've got a couple of firms I can call for quotes.'

'I'm not promising anything and not trying to put you off, but I've got an appointment in five and must rush. Get numbers and we'll talk.'

6

Masoud Baitullah waited at the entrance to a little side road between the Bank of Burundi and what used to be Woolworth's in Southall Broadway. He was cold. The temperature difference between here and Yemen, where he had just flown from, was too much for his body to acclimatise to rapidly. The temperature in March in England wasn't his idea of warm. His instructions to place volunteers in strategic places were clear, hiding people in plain sight. Putting them where they might become useful was more challenging. He had personally built up a comprehensive network of believers, which he had at his disposal. Masoud was watching the door to a coffee shop opposite.

His contact in Yemen had given him the address and a photo of the man he was due to meet. His name was Ahmed M'Beki. The man was a devout Muslim originally from Mogadishu, highly recommended by the local al-Shabaab commander. He had been kitted out with Yemeni papers by the organisation's experts and had flown into Britain two months ago, ostensibly visiting family already in Britain. They had used this ploy often and successfully in the past. He wanted to make sure the place wasn't under observation by the security forces. Masoud was a careful man; he had to be, the enemy was everywhere and getting more sophisticated every day. He'd seen many fellow fighters taken out because of the smallest lapses. He vowed that there would be no such failures by him; he could not afford one.

Southall Broadway was busy, traffic heavy, pedestrian flow steady, it was somewhere he would remain unnoticed. He had arrived early at the arranged meeting point and had been sitting on the pavement with his back to the wall of the bank for over an hour now. He hadn't spotted any activity that he'd call suspicious. He paid particular attention to the customers entering and leaving the coffee shop, looking for any signs of something out of place.

His pitch as a street beggar didn't raise any eyebrows. Indeed, he was one of about half a dozen along this part of the street; he'd even managed to collect a couple of pounds in donations. At exactly two o'clock, the man he was expecting appeared from the direction of the bus stop, having just got off a bus. Masoud didn't have to check the photo in his pocket, he had the man's face embedded in his memory. The man, dark-skinned with a little goatee beard, who was slim to the point of being skinny, turned into the coffee shop doorway, entering without looking back or around, appearing perfectly natural, behaving like a regular visitor. He was sure it was Ahmed M'Beki. He's good, Masoud thought. M'Beki must have been doing this for the last three weeks at least, if he had been following his instructions.

Masoud moved his pitch to be nearer the bus stop, but still in sight of the coffee shop door. He suffered the griping of one of the other beggars bemoaning the trespasser on his territory with indifference. Masoud ignored him and waited. The previously agreed sixty-five minutes seemed endless before M'Beki came out of the coffee shop again. He dodged the traffic crossing the road. Masoud immediately stood up. To the beggar's utter amazement, he dropped the money he had collected into his grumpy neighbour's cup and then took his place in the queue for the bus, arriving before Ahmed, who joined it behind him. As the bus pulled up, Masoud allowed M'Beki to board, and then followed and sat down next to him. His target glanced round, surprised at the company.

'I bring you greetings from your father.' Masoud whispered softly to Ahmed, using the coded introduction phrase he would be expecting. His contact's expression changed to a broad smile and he offered his hand. Masoud didn't accept it, but waited stonily for the reply. 'Well?' he snapped.

'Oh! My aunt will be pleased to have news from him.' M'Beki recited mechanically. This was the reply Masoud needed to hear.

In a low voice he instructed, 'tomorrow at two o'clock in the Bentall's Shopping Centre in Kingston. Meet me in Starbucks.' With that, he stood to leave, and got off at the next stop.

Ahmed M'Beki was elated, he had made contact. His only problem now was the immigration authorities. His paperwork had been screwed up. A careless mistake and he'd been forced to claim asylum in order to prolong his stay, but the appeals had brought no change. Unless he could manage to pull some trick out of the bag, he'd be deported. That would put an end to his destiny and to his moment of glory! He fervently hoped there was something he could do about it.

The following afternoon, Masoud again staked out the site for an hour before the meeting was due to take place. M'Beki was on time at Starbucks and was as nervous as a teenager on a first date. Masoud, satisfied that no-one had followed Ahmed into the place, went to join him at a small table at the back of the cafe, exclaiming, 'You are on the way to paradise, my friend!' Ahmed did not respond, but seemed concerned. This doesn't feel right, Masoud thought. The others had been overjoyed to hear that particular sentence. The indoctrination usually never failed on that front, yet here was this frowning volunteer. Masoud was anxious as well as irritated.

'What's the matter brother? Do you doubt the cause?'

'No brother.' M'Beki said, 'I have a problem that's all.'

Masoud's hackles rose. 'What sort of problem?' he demanded.

'Police and Immigration, Border Control.' M'Beki replied. 'You know how thorough these officers are. I pray it does not affect my role in Allah's work.' he whined.

'What sort of problem?' Masoud persisted, yet dreading the answer. 'You were told to keep clean, out of trouble and to integrate!' What have you done?'

'Nothing! I do as I was told. It's just that, well, my papers were wrong. Immigration checked with Yemen and found the birth certificate was for someone who died four years ago. The Border Control people tell me I cannot stay here. My lawyer has been a waste of time. If nothing changes, I must be out of the country within three months or they will deport me.'

Masoud considered whether something could be rescued from the situation, although he didn't know what or how.

'Listen. I don't want you changing your lifestyle or doing anything different. You have any friends here?'

'Yes.'

'You mustn't let them know anything, behave as you always have, act normal, do your normal everyday things. Back home you drove tankers, is the information correct?'

M'Beki nodded affirmatively. 'Yes, I have a dangerous goods licence.'

'That license won't be valid here, now listen, you go to the Job Centre in Kingston on Monday and ask for Mr Kasam al Bari, he's a good friend of ours. He will be expecting you. He'll send you on a sponsored training course; you'll get a Heavy Goods License and training, plus a job seekers allowance. Come back here next Monday, after you've seen Kasam al Bari, sit at this table and wait for me. You must be patient and wait for Allah's call. It may be quite a wait.'

'Yes, of course.'

Masoud got up and left. 'Don't follow me.' he called over his shoulder.

As M'Beki saw the brown-suited figure merge into the crowds and disappear, he reflected on events. He was thrilled. This was nothing like Mogadishu, where the fighters patrolled the streets and did whatever they thought necessary to bring errant people into line. Here, the unbelievers dressed abominably. The harlots showing flesh and hair, something he would not have tolerated back home, but he had been told not to show his feelings and to be 'tolerant'. He was finding it hard. The meeting with his contact had given him strength, knowing now that he was a part of the real Jihad.

Masoud went into the next shop, cut through the back way and back into Starbucks from the other direction. He could see M'Beki still sitting there drinking the last of his coffee. Masoud observed unseen from the crowd. Eventually, Ahmed stood and walked slowly towards the exit. Masoud checked carefully for any signs of watchers, but couldn't see any. He trailed M'Beki to the bus stop and saw him board the number 71 as the last passenger. Satisfied he wasn't being followed; Masoud walked back to the car park and picked up his old Vauxhall. He was excited, as he always was when he was organising action against the enemy, and a familiar urge overtook him; he felt the craving for a woman and knew Allah would forgive his desires. His mind drifted to things he could do with these faithless women. He felt the stirring in his loins. The adrenalin and the sexual arousal at the thought of the destruction the new recruit would cause raised his yearning for a woman to fever pitch. His hands gripped the wheel more tightly as he remembered the way his hands had closed on the throat of the last one, feeling her expire as his seed filled her mouth. He was highly aroused now, sweating slightly and smiling at the memory. Happy he had killed for the cause, happy that he'd destroyed another adulteress who had needed to die. Allah would be pleased that he had removed so many of them.

He pulled over to the side of the road and flipped his mobile open. Al Bari at the Kingston Job Centre answered almost immediately.

'He's coming to you on Monday.'

'Fine. Anything else?'

'Yes, you mentioned you had, you know, female accompaniment available.'

'Yes,' Al Bari replied cautiously. 'What do you want?' Masoud thought about it for a moment, lustful visions filling his mind. He was brought back to reality by a hooting car behind him; he was double-parked.

'Blonde.' Masoud blurted, torn from his reverie. 'Tall, thin, blonde.'

'Okay, ring this number.' Al Bari recited a number and Masoud noted it down.

'Thanks.' He hung up and drove off in the direction of Surbiton. He passed the university buildings in Penrhyn Road and pulled into a parking slot. He brought out his phone; dialling the number he'd been given.

'Hello. You've dialled Claire's. How can we help you today?' A sweet feminine voice husked in his ear.

'I want a woman.' Masoud blurted. 'Now, quickly!'

'I see;' the voice chirped unperturbed on the other end, 'anything in particular? We cater for all tastes.'

Masoud was getting more excited as she talked. 'Oral, anal, hard,' he managed to stammer.

'And now, immediately?' the soft voice crooned on.

'Yes, where do I go?'

'One moment, I need your credit card details first. You do have one?'

'No;' he grunted, 'I will pay cash, I always pay cash.

'Okay,' the voice responded, 'give the girl £250 for the service. You have an hour, but the fee doesn't include tips.' The voice was more business like now. 'Where are you now?' He told her. 'Right! We will send a lady who will fulfil all your dreams. She'll be waiting for you at three pm on the corner of St Mary's Road in Surbiton by the bus stop. All you have to do is say Primrose sent you. She'll be wearing a red skirt.' She went on to give him directions.

Masoud checked the dashboard clock, he had half an hour to the appointment. He thought about checking his mails, then decided against it and just sat watching students crossing the car park. There were some pretty ones too. Maybe he could save the money, he thought, as he leered at the young women walking by.

M'Beki and the Border Control issue would become a real problem if he couldn't find a way of keeping him here. He pulled his phone out and dialled another number. The ring tone seemed to go on endlessly before the call was answered.

'You know who this is?' he stated brusquely, waiting briefly for confirmation. 'Good! Then listen. The papers for M'Beki were wrong. The identity you used was of someone who had been dead for years. I won't accept that kind of work,' he growled, letting his anger show. 'You owe me!' He disconnected. The thought of the man panicking made him even more excited. The clock said it was time to move.

He was driving by the park towards Surbiton when, as described, he saw the woman on the corner under the railway bridge; a blonde in a short red leather skirt with long legs and high heels. It was obvious what she was, as she stood there at the roadside. Those legs, he groaned, feeling his groin respond as he swung over towards the kerb and slowed down. He felt his hardness with one hand as he stopped alongside her and wound the window down. Closer up, she was cheap and common, with the aura of detachment that went with the trade. Her blonde hair was straggly and spiky atop her over made up face; her tight outfit showed her ample cleavage. 'Primrose sent me,' he said as the window hit the bottom stop.

'My name's Hollie. Claire told me what you want. Park over there.' she said, nodding with her head at the little lay-by near the newsagent's shop. 'My pad is up here.' She pointed to the dark blue door between the two shops. 'I'll wait.'

Masoud swung the car over to the opposite side of the road and parked. Locking it, he walked back to her, taking in the details of her body as he crossed the road. He thought about what he would do, and how he would hurt her. Smiling, he put his arm around her, his hand clutching her breast clumsily as she unlocked the door. Masoud followed her up the stairs unzipping his trousers and watching the woman's buttocks move provocatively, as she ascended before him. The landing was small; four doors, which he assumed to be four flats, confronted them at the top of the stairway. Masoud reached out and pulled her skirt up roughly as she fumbled for the key to one of the doors. He was in no mood for waiting; he pinned her to the wall and rammed his erection brutally into her from behind. She managed to get out one short scream before he clamped his hand over her mouth. He pounded into her, not heeding the woman's pain or terror. He exploded inside her and pulled out, then, immediately grabbing a handful of her hair, he twisted her around and pushed her on her knees in front of him. He could see the fear in her eyes now, as he thrust his dying erection towards her mouth.

'Suck!' he ordered brutally, tearing at the woman's hair. She tried to resist, refusing to open her mouth. Masoud angrily ordered her again 'Suck!'

'No,' the woman sobbed through clenched teeth, 'Not like this!'

Masoud pulled his knife from his pocket and made sure that she saw it and then placed the tip under her chin pricking her skin.

'I said suck, you filthy slut.' Reluctantly she opened her

mouth, gagging and sobbing as he shoved into her. 'Suck, you cow,' he said again, pressing the knife to her throat.

He felt a draught as a door behind him opened.

'I think that's quite enough.' It was the voice from the phone, soft and erotic. He pulled the knife away turning to confront the voice, leaving the terrorised girl sobbing on her knees.

Masoud managed to get out the words 'Who the hell ....' before his mouth froze open as he saw the beauty of the woman behind the voice. He punched the sobbing Hollie hard on the side of her head, sending her sprawling on her face. 'Stupid bitch!' he spat, as he shoved his penis back in his trousers, all the while taking in this exquisite new arrival. She was a stunning five foot nine, elfin like, with long blond hair and penetrating blue eyes.

'You've had your fun, now go.' The soft voice had an edge of hardness in it now. 'Nobody does that to my girls.' Masoud stood spellbound by the voice alone, for once unsure of what to do. He still had the knife in his hand and he was still aroused, not sexually, but violently.

'I do what I want. I've paid for her. She's mine!' came out in a staccato growl. Hollie tried to scramble to her feet, clutching her skirt to her, tears and make-up streaming down her face. The blood from the nick on her throat was trickling onto the neckline of her top. Masoud lashed out savagely at her again, his foot catching her in her midriff, Hollie flew backwards onto the floor, hitting her head against the wall. In an instant response, Claire launched herself at him, ignoring the knife and kneeing him in the groin. The knife flashed and as she leapt back, she heard the fabric of her blouse tearing. She waited, expecting the pain, which never came. Unbelievably, the blade had only sliced through her blouse. Claire whipped round and lashed out again, her foot connecting with Masoud's wrist and the knife clattered down the stairs. The grateful thought flashed through her mind of how her recent self-defence course was coming in so handy right then.

She carefully appraised the man crouching opposite her, gripping himself in pain.

'You finished, or do I call the police, you bastard,' she hissed at him.

Masoud's adrenalin surge was rapidly abating, due to the dual pain in his wrist and his groin.

'You will regret that,' he snarled. Claire pulled her mobile from her pocket.

'I'm calling the police now,' she said, bending to help the stricken Hollie and at the same time trying to register characteristics of the man, so she could describe him to the police if need be. She was scrutinising him carefully now, asking herself what she could tell the police. He was forty, maybe fifty years old, overweight and going a bit bald on top. He had one of those glass eye thingies hanging from a pendant and showing in his open shirt. It was like the one she'd bought as a key ring when she was in Antalya on holiday. What was it again? Oh, yes the 'eye of Allah'! It saved you from evil. The man was wearing a brown suit and sandals. His shirt looked like it hadn't seen a wash since it was bought and that was a while ago by the state of it. She was torn from her inspection by his shouted, 'Don't! We can sort this.' The panic in his voice was obvious.

'So?' Claire said imperiously, 'how do you propose to do that? This poor woman needs hospitalising after what you've done to her. You're a monster!' She opened her phone, but Masoud stepped forward and snapped it shut.

'I said we could sort this.' He reached into the back pocket of his suit trousers and pulled out a wad of fifty-pound notes. He peeled off a dozen or so and shoved them at her. 'Here for the girl.'

She bent back down and helped Hollie to her feet, not taking her eyes off the dark stranger in his dirty brown suit. She pitied Hollie what she had had to suffer, and not just for the beating. Claire's stomach churned at the thought.

'You okay?' she asked, as Hollie clung shaking to her arm.

'Yes I think so.'

'Go inside and lie down. I'll be with you in a minute. I'll deal with this guy first.' It was then she realised the guy was staring fixedly at her torso; her shredded blouse revealed her near-naked trim figure covered only by her tiny, pink, lacy bra.

'You'll need to pay more.' She held the notes in an intimidating fist under his nose. 'My blouse cost more than this.'

Masoud, unused to such aggressive behaviour from a mere woman stepped back, and put his hands up defensively.

'I said that was for the girl. Here, this is for you.' He peeled another five notes off the wad. 'Next time I come, I want you.' he leered.

'There won't be a next time.' Claire took the money and began to wrap the remains of her blouse around herself.

'Stop!' he commanded. Confused by the demand Claire stopped for a moment. Masoud reached out and touched the top of her breast.

She smacked the hand away and shouted, 'You need another kick in the groin?'

Masoud backed off. 'Nice!' he said. Next time I come, I'll pay you to watch.' He was on the top stair now, and Claire could have pushed him easily, but she held back.

7

In the long run, things had changed. Claire thought back on the previous year, wishing fervently that she hadn't married that sullen dipstick after all. It had been more trouble than it was worth. All that rubbish about going to paradise and getting his 72 virgins was just so much nonsense; the idiot wouldn't know what to do with one virgin, let alone 72. Now, seven months on, she was stuck here, having to put up with his mumbo-jumbo religion in this tiny flat, and play-act the happy wife in case of a spot check by Immigration. After a shower, dressed only in her bra and jeans, with a towel wrapped round her wet hair, she sat in the tiny kitchen, fuming at the restrictions this mock marriage placed on her. A visceral fear swamped her every time she remembered Masoud's deep set eyes and emotionless expression when he'd set up the deal. Claire reflected on the past, thinking about the time since the regular payments had begun.

The money had given Claire new impetus in life, and had expanded her horizons business-wise, but she became increasingly frightened as she sat week after week in her office, while the vicious animal abused her girls. He even had the gall to offer her even more money, if she would agree to service him too. She shuddered as she recalled the man's cold disdain for women and the utter contempt he showed for the ones he regularly mistreated. He was paying five hundred pounds every week for an hour with Hollie and three hundred pounds to Claire, as security for Hollies' safety. Her role was to sit next door listening to ensure that Masoud didn't kill her. He also had brought some new business; a skinny man with a goatee beard who seemed quite shy and unassuming. Claire had given him a girl whom Masoud had paid for. While Claire was checking what Masoud was doing with Hollie, Chantelle was more than happy to deal with 'goatee beard'. For her it was easy money, three hundred pounds to watch a punter masturbate. All Chantelle had to do was to sit there in skimpy underwear and play spectator.

The initial incident with Hollie was now history; this was business. The little wall safe in her office was regularly stuffed with wads of fifty pound notes, which Masoud brought every Tuesday. Never a visit went by that he didn't proposition her, offering more money each time. He bought her gifts, presenting gold trinkets, a ring encrusted with diamonds, bouquets of flowers; he claimed he was in love with her. His attention left her cold as well as uneasy. The marriage of convenience was a total farce.

Her assessment of Ahmed, as the goatee turned out to be called, hadn't changed from the first time she'd met him. He was a moron with an IQ between that of a cabbage and a caterpillar, he came across as a brainwashed religious nut with nothing in his head but chunks of religious texts, learned verbatim and recited at every opportunity. He maintained to be a practicing Muslim, he had never touched her. The way he looked at her was something she'd identify as disgust. She knew very little about Islam and had never been consciously close to a Muslim before.

Staying under the same roof for three years was the deal, just so he could get his permanent residence authorised. Then she'd be free. Even a hundred thousand pounds, she thought in retrospect, was too little for having to live with a nutter like Ahmed.

Shortly before leaving her office that evening, she'd emptied the safe in St Mary's Road on impulse and taken the contents home. Her handbag was bulging with banknotes.

The slamming front door broke her train of thought. She stiffened, ready for the usual confrontation; he would be at the kitchen door in a few seconds, ranting on about the cause again, no doubt. For the first time, instead of her uneasy fear of him, she felt an overpowering rage that she had to put up with his mindless ravings. As he finally walked into the kitchen, she turned her back on him deliberately, not wanting to confront or talk to him.

'What you wearing nothing for in Allah's house? Showing off at the window and all that?' He shouted, pointing in her direction. 'What you get undressed for? No decent wife looks like you. Why you don't wear a veil or cover your hair?'

'My hair is my business and as you can see you idiot, it is covered you piss-head.' She snarled, retreating to the corner of the kitchen, as she knew he could get violent. She grabbed a sweatshirt from the loaded drying rack, hurriedly put it on and picked up her denim jacket.

'You watch your mouth,' he shouted, 'you trash slag. You make Allah cry, you so bad.'

'You and your half-arsed God. I don't give a pig's fart what he thinks.' She was sidling towards the back door slowly but surely. 'You and your God wouldn't know 'good' if it got up and bit you. Get a life, you loser!' She spat at him.

He lunged at her over the table, sending sundry, crockery and bottles flying. Claire threw open the back door, remembering just in time to grab her handbag, and then she was off. Something flew out of the door after her. She neither saw nor cared what it was as she ran down the garden path to the back gate. Claire made an instant and exhilarating decision never to go back, wondering why she had stayed in such a hell for so long. At last, voting with her feet, she rushed breathless into the road, casting a nervous glance back to see if Ahmed was following. Claire continued down the road, drying her hair as she went and tossed the towel into a bin. The outside world had never seemed sweeter nor the air fresher. As she walked, her mind cast back to how it had all started when Masoud had made the offer.

Three weeks after the first brutal attack on Hollie, Masoud, accompanied by a skinny man with a goatee beard, turned up at her office. Masoud had growled, nodding towards the African,

'I want a girl for him'. Then he added, 'And I want you to listen to me as well.'

Claire buzzed Chantelle, who accepted the trade and disappeared with the man into the apartment next to the office. Hollie was waiting apprehensively; the bruises on her cheeks from the previous week's session with Masoud still showing, but faded to a pale brownish blue. She had tried to cover them rather unsuccessfully with make-up. Hollie continued to accept the weekly abuse because she was being paid very well plus generous tips for servicing the animal.

As Chantelle and Hollie left to go to their apartments, Claire turned back to Masoud, 'Listen to what?' she asked, eying him suspiciously.

'I have a proposition for you.'

'Okay.' Claire nodded, offering him a seat opposite her desk. Masoud sat staring at her, his eyes fixed on her breasts. The bulge in his trousers highlighted the ridiculousness of the situation, making her want to laugh. 'Let's hear it.' She stared him down managing to hide her smile.

Masoud felt uncomfortable and angry being stared at in the face, especially by a woman. At home he would have beaten her, taught her respect, but here in Britain it was different, and so was this bold woman. He wanted to conquer her, dominate her and then maybe kill her. The woman would be good; he felt that as strongly as he felt the erection building in his trousers. He grunted in frustration, focusing on the task in hand now.

'He is my son,' obviously talking about the guy who had just joined Chantelle across the landing. 'He's trying for asylum here in the UK, but it isn't going good for him. The Immigration Office wants to expel him, deport him, you know. My dearest son,' he had whined in a tone that suggested he was seeking some kind of sympathy. 'They think he is, maybe some kind of bad type, but he is a good boy, never been in any trouble.'

'So what,' she thought.

'I give you a hundred thousand pounds if you marry him. He's a nice boy. He is a good religious man.' Claire didn't actually register much of the rest. The bit about him getting residency status and all that. She only had the thought of a hundred grand going round in her head. That would solve all of her problems.

She'd married the 'son' two weeks later, a basic civil

ceremony in the registry office in Epsom and a Spartan lunch in the Spread Eagle pub over the road afterwards. If there were ten people attending, it was a lot. Three of them had worn long white Arab frocks instead of proper men's clothes, and they had been eerily quiet the whole time, not even speaking to each other. They'd given her the creeps. Claire wasn't bothered that this new husband was no more the punter Masoud's son, than her dad was prime minister. A hundred grand was a hundred grand.

They had rented a flat for the marital arrangement in Chessington, Masoud carried the tab for that as well. Claire chose the furniture for the apartment and they immediately moved in. Ahmed didn't care. She barely saw him. He went out early for work, and the rest of his free time he spent with friends in Southall. Claire didn't care about that either. The money had enabled her to settle the mortgage on her house and the property in St Mary Road was also in her name. The income was now all profit.

'Brown Suit' had been in the background ever since, never far away. He would call her on her mobile when he wanted servicing, always Tuesdays. It never occurred to her that it was always a different number. He continued as a regular customer, even after the marriage to his supposed son.

Well, that was behind her now. Knowing that this day would come sooner or later, she'd trained Chantelle how the business was run on the proviso that she kept it secret from Al Bari.

She toyed with the idea going up to London, deciding instead to go to her sister in Chester, where she could have a rest, a break and some privacy. Nobody there would remember anything about her other than as that cute little schoolgirl in her Catholic school uniform, if they remembered her at all. No-one knew about her life in Surbiton or Ahmed. A fresh start, at least her sister would put her up for a bit, until she sorted things out.

Claire increased her pace; feeling more positive and energised than she had in years heading for the railway station, hoping the wait wouldn't be a long one. As she walked, reflecting that it was good that she'd insisted on keeping her maiden name at the registry office. At least she wasn't lumbered with M'Beki's cruddy name, fleetingly wondering how he would get on without her. The marriage hadn't lasted even a year yet. If the authorities found out, he'd be on the next boat home, wherever that was. She grinned at the thought. Then, suddenly a frisson of terror passed through her, the likely violent consequences of breaking the deal with Masoud was causing icy gooseflesh on her whole body. In an attempt to ignore her fear, she carried resolutely on towards the station to buy a ticket to Chester.

It was late when the taxi dropped her off outside her sister's house. She was not surprised that the lights were out at this hour.

The doorbell sounded unnaturally loud in the stillness of the street of terraced Victorian houses. Bouverie Street hadn't changed much since her childhood, except that most of the houses were now converted into cheap bed-sits, or housing those who could barely afford to buy in at the bottom end of the market. The families she grew up with were gone, having long since moved up the housing ladder. Mary's house was their old family home, she had never left it. She'd stayed after their parents had died and after a few disastrous relationships had managed end up on her own with two beautiful daughters.

After an age, a light went on upstairs. Claire stood in the dark porch, increasingly nervous, not only about the reaction of her sister, but the thoughts of what that evil man in the brown suit might do when he found out she'd run out on the deal. She heard her sister's grumbles all the way from the landing to the front door. The chains and deadbolts rattled as the door was eventually opened.

'God! Do you have any idea what time it is?' her sister snapped recognising who it was standing there.

'I need your help,' she blurted out.

Mary stepped back at the directness allowing Claire entry.

'What's up?' an edge of concern creeping into the tone, but still suspicious, 'What's happened?'

'I've run out on him.' Claire managed not to sob but her eyes were moist. 'I might be in trouble.' Claire turned to face her and opened her handbag allowing some of the fifty-pound notes to spill out onto the floor. Mary scurried after her picking up the bank notes as she went.

'You've got a nerve,' she said attempting to count the cash as she followed her sister into the kitchen. 'You robbed a bank or what?'

'Side job,' Claire slumped, glancing around the kitchen, onto one of the straight-backed still familiar chairs of her childhood.

'Claire, where's all this money from?' Mary was agitated now. 'You arrive in the middle of the night, say you're in trouble and have a bag full of cash. What is it? Thousands and thousands of pounds and you say it's a side job?' Mary sat opposite her. 'What the hell is going on? I thought you and your husband, what's-his-name, Mehmet, were happily married?'

'It's Ahmed not Mehmet. Claire said tiredly. 'Any chance of a cuppa? I'm whacked.'

'Only if you tell all,' Mary said putting the kettle on.

'I need a place to crash until I can get sorted.'

'You want to leave him? It's not even been a year, so why'd you marry him? Can't have been your hormones, he's an ugly little git, judging by the photos. Or is he hung like a horse?' She laughed derisively, seeing her sister flinch at the barb.

'Long story, and as far as the horse goes, I've never seen it, no idea.' Claire looked at her sister to see if that would do as an answer. Mary stood staring at her, open-mouthed in amazement.

'Jeez, you were married, weren't you? And you never, you know ...?'

'No, we never, you know, did any of that. That wasn't the deal.

Mary poured the tea and sat down again. She reached out and took her sister's hand in hers.

'So, what's the deal? Come on tell.'

'I've screwed up,' Claire said bluntly. 'I went for the soft option again. Like Uni, like work, like everything I damn well do.'

'Yes, well Claire, your future could have been bright, but you chose the high life. What's happened this time?'

'The Job Centre. The guy there, he got me a job.'

'It's what they're there for. Getting people work.'

'Not this kind of work,' Claire sniffed, trying to find a tissue, but settling for the kitchen roll instead, 'I nearly had to sleep with the bastard.' Mary was stunned.

'You nearly what?'

'He ran a prostitute ring, a ring of unemployed housewives.

He wanted to make me one of them.' Claire explained.

'You should have reported him. My God, that's terrible!'

'I thought about reporting him, but if I had, I would have lost my house and everything I worked for.'

'And then what?'

'He slept with loads of women on benefits, and then forced them into prostitution, blackmailed them, go on the game or no benefits.' Claire sipped her tea, feeling more confident now. 'He recruited me too.'

'What, as a call girl?' Mary looked genuinely shocked.

'No, actually to run them, he set up a discrete little place in Surbiton, as my own business. He got a cut and sent favoured guests for servicing. But I didn't sell myself.'

Having feared the worst, Mary sighed with relief, she nodded encouraging her to continue.

'A man rang one day and said he needed a woman. We called him 'Brown Suit', made me an offer to marry his son Ahmed, it was just to keep him in the country.' Mary's eyes widened in disbelief, 'Don't stare at me like that.' Claire looked her sister in the eye, searching for her response. 'In any case, a hundred grand and there I was married to the berk.'

'A hundred grand!' Mary said, awestruck. 'But you ran out today?'

'Yes.'

'That's why the panic. What's going to happen?'

'I don't know, 'Brown Suit' is very violent. He beats up the girls. He'll be very angry that I've backed out on the deal. Reckon he'll kill me.'

'Jesus! You do dramatise, don't you? How's he going to know you're here? Its history repeating itself, isn't it? You're a bit like me in many respects, the thrill seeker. I just managed to keep the lid on. If you ignore the two kids, that is,' she smiled ruefully.

'Anyway how's it going with the girls?' Claire asked changing the subject.

'In a word, crap.' Mary answered.

'Why, what's up?' The concern in Claire's face, evident.

'Long story, but basically it is all about money and child support payments. I am at the end of my tether. Honest Claire, I don't know where to turn.'

'Which of the fathers isn't paying?' That got her a sharp look. 'Sorry! I forgot you don't know who Elaine's father is.' Claire slid her teacup across the table trying to hide her embarrassment. 'You taken the worm to court?'

'Yes, but Derek won't pay. It makes things so tight for me and the girls. But I have a great job, and a great boss,' Claire saw the brightening in her sister's attitude, 'He is so considerate.'

Claire tried to read more into the comment and waited for some sort of explanation. 'So?' She left the question-mark hanging.

'He's just really nice,' Mary said coyly.

'You fancy him then?

'Well,' Mary hid behind her mug, 'he's a bit dishy and super clever as well.'

'Is there anything going on between you?'

'I wish.' Mary put her mug down on the table. 'I don't think he even sees me. It's eating me up inside.'

'He's being sensible Mary,' Claire took her hand in hers, 'he is the boss and if he is as intelligent as you say, then he won't pee on his own doorstep.'

'God, you're so coarse at times,' Mary appeared both hurt and shocked. 'You never been in love with anyone?' Claire thought about it and decided not to respond. 'Seems like we both have problems, doesn't it?' Claire nodded.

'Yes, but we're not going to solve them tonight, are we?' Mary stifled a yawn and stretched. 'Let's get some sleep. The world will be different in the morning. You can have the sofa. I'll get bedding.' Mary went, leaving Claire staring at the stains in her teacup, unable to stop drawing the analogy of how her life was stained. It could have been so white. Trance like, realising she had only the clothes she stood in, she undressed slowly. As she folded her sweatshirt on the arm of the chair, a sudden feeling of exhaustion overwhelmed her. Nothing had changed from the living room of her childhood, it was comforting and somehow sad, and she'd have to talk to Mary about that as well. The kids shouldn't live in a museum. That was for another time though, she was too tired now.

Mary reappeared with a quilt and pillow and bedded Claire

down on the settee.

'You'll get woken at seven by the kids going to school, you know that?'

'Uh huh!' Claire murmured sleepily turning over and pulling the quilt around her. 'Lights,' was the last word she mumbled. Mary switched off the lights and went belatedly back to bed.

Claire Grigson had been a model pupil at The Chester Convent School. At fifteen winning the science prizes for Chemistry, Physics and Biology, and when the GCSE's came round, she flew through them effortlessly and was streamed in to the sciences in the sixth form. Claire was bright and enjoyed the experience of learning. Her head teacher had said that, if anything, she was too keen to experiment. Claire absorbed information presented to her like a sponge, rather than having to learn it. It had surprised no-one when she passed all three subjects with distinction. Her scholarship from the Cheshire Education Trust Foundation was an honour her family and the school and, in fact, a first for the school. The local papers had been full of the City's star pupil off on her way to London to study.

After her Scholarship award, at the tender age of 18, Claire had embraced Imperial College and the Genetics and Biochemistry course with gusto, excelling at everything, until the end of the second year that is. By then she had discovered the London scene and the clubs. A stunningly attractive girl, in great demand and as an 'experimenter', leaving few stones unturned. She developed into an exotic woman, a butterfly who was admired by all. Then she met Marcus. He simply bowled her over, causing her to fall madly in love with him and his jet-set life style. The flash cars, top clubs, the best Discos and parties, it was thrilling stuff. At first she was missing days at Imperial, then whole weeks. Marcus had a flat in Teddington, a modern, ultra-cool pad by the Thames. She had never questioned of the source of his income. It never occurred to her it might not have been legal. She experimented with hashish at some of the parties and was never impressed with it. One day she was introduced to LSD at a party in St John's Wood. The new experiences and the exhilaration were too thrilling to resist repeating. Something she did with abandon, causing her to miss more and more lectures and failing to hand in course work.

At Marcus's, life was a whirlwind of lust, ecstasy and parties. The party was brought to an abrupt end, when the university threatened to send her down. Her inner-self panicked, huge pangs of conscience plagued her. Changing her mind set, she pulled herself together and started feverishly to work again. That sobering episode had shocked and galvanised her into a to fore unseen level of self-discipline, working at her studies round the clock to catch up and complete her degree. Afterwards embracing the job of party girl full-time, and loving it. The inevitable clouds appeared at 4:30 one morning, two years after graduation. She was woken by incessant hammering on the front door accompanied by the shouted,

'Open up, police!' Claire struggled into something to wear as Marcus freaked, trying to dump all sorts of stuff down the toilet. The door burst in at the first flush and two burly officers pinned Marcus mercilessly to the wall before they handcuffed him and dragged him away. At the same time a female officer escorted Claire from the premises. That was the beginning of the end; her life had just gone pear-shaped.

The day spent at Kingston police station being interviewed and quizzed about her friend Marcus and her role in his life was a pain, doubly so, because of being unable to see him again afterwards. Claire was out on the street that evening, nowhere to go, depressed and tired. Possessing only the clothes she stood up in plus the contents of her handbag, but determined not to give in to the overwhelming feeling of helplessness that was consuming her, Claire phoned a fellow student from her course and at least she had managed to get a bed for the night.

The next day she went dejectedly to Kingston Job Centre and was allocated a counsellor, a dark-skinned man with an infectious smile. He'd managed to get her a job almost immediately at Grant's Forensics in Teddington. All that was needed was a place to live and she was absolutely resolute that nothing was going to stop her getting back on her feet again.

Mr Al Bari, the counsellor had called her every now and again, purely to see how she was getting on and if she needed anything. His calls were not frequent but unnerving. He was always civil, but Claire never succumbed to his repeated overt sexual innuendos. The job at Grant's Forensics wasn't brilliant and certainly not patch on the life of parties and excesses with Marcus. She'd visited him a few times in prison, but he had grown increasingly distant and after a few visits, she had ceased the trips to Wandsworth. Ten years on, promotions saw her salary more than double and she was, although not flush with cash, living a self-sufficient life.

Her world folded again in late 2008; when Grants went bankrupt and she was out of a job. The administrators brought in counselling staff from the Job Centre, but the financial crisis was in full swing and jobs in her speciality were rare as chicken's teeth. Six months of applications and rejections, her contribution based JSA (Job seeker's allowance) entitlement finally ran out. Her mortgage was deeply in arrears, the bank was threatening to repossess, her credit card was up to the limit, and the ATM had swallowed her bank card. She was at her wits' end. The 'Hardship Allowance', for the next phase of unemployment would mean losing the house and everything she had worked for. Even if she could live on that allowance, she wouldn't be able to keep the house. Claire was more than depressed as she faced the meeting in the job centre, she was desperate. As chance or fate would have it, Claire got to see Mr Al Bari again. He was very sympathetic and offered her an evening meeting to discuss her future. Claire couldn't refuse because of the veiled threats of a block on her benefits, which was enough persuasion for her. She'd met him at the Swan in Thames Ditton for a cosy meal; the restaurant was crowded, yet he had somehow been persuasive enough to get a table with a view of the river. If there was one thing about him, he was smooth.

'Claire,' he said, practically before she had time to sit. 'Nice of you to come.' She flinched at his stare, which was patently not focused on her face.

'Well, you didn't give me much choice, did you?' She folded her napkin in her lap for something to do. 'You made it clear I might have problems with my benefits if I failed to turn up. How did you put it? A kind of job interview?' Claire stared at him sceptically, trying to judge the reaction. He just smiled disarmingly and gestured to the menu.

'Choose,' he said, 'my shout.' He scanned around for the

waiter. 'To drink?' he raised his eyebrow. 'Champagne perhaps to celebrate?'

'Celebrate? Celebrate what?' She saw the lewdness in his eyes and was watching him uneasily.

'Let's order, then we can talk.' The waiter was now hovering over them. 'A bottle of Moet and a large mineral water.' No please, and no thank you, as if he was used to giving orders and totally unused to them not being carried out.

Claire studied the menu, full with things she hadn't been able to afford since her relationship with Marcus had ended. Her thoughts drifted back to that time, until Al Bari broke the reverie.

'Shall I order for you?' The tone intimated that she was probably too stupid to know what she was confronted with.

'No,' Claire said firmly, 'I'll have the escargots, and will follow that with the lobster salad. It'll go well with the Moet, although a Cliquot or a Mouton Cadet would have been better.'

The game of one-upmanship was not new to her; and it pleased her to see the surprise in his face as he realised he'd underestimated her.

'You choose well,' he smiled insincerely at her, 'I'll have the same. I hope all your decisions tonight are as good…,' He left the words hanging. They could have meant anything, but instinctively Claire knew there was something more than a job offer afoot here. The champagne was poured into ice-cold glasses, condensation forming on the outside as the bubbles rushed to the surface.

'To us,' he raised his glass in a toast. Unsure about what he meant, Claire responded with a tilt of her glass. 'You see, you're making the right decisions already,' he leered.

The meal was unspectacular; the snails were frozen supermarket things, baked to little chewy lumps and the lobster was watery and relatively tasteless. Al Bari ate with appetite, extolling the quality, Claire didn't bother to disillusion him. 'You know,' he said mopping the last of the salad dressing up with his bread, 'I can make life very comfortable for a beautiful woman like you.'

'I thought we were talking jobs.' Claire was on her guard. 'Or are we talking benefits?'

'Both,' he smiled ambiguously, staring, but again not at her face. 'You do understand that in order to qualify for benefits, you'll have to convince me that you deserve it. I am sure you can imagine how.' He said running his finger over her wrist never taking his eyes off her. Claire had half expected a pass, but this? No, she hadn't anticipated anything as blatant.

'That's a gross abuse of your position,' Claire managed to stammer at him. 'I've a good mind to report you!' She exclaimed and stood up abruptly to leave. Al Bari grabbed her hand and stopped her, his grip painful.

'Don't make a scene, sit down!' he commanded, 'that's better,' he said as she twisted her hand away and sat again. 'There's more to it than only benefits. My offer is an exciting job and money. You can earn what you like and still get benefits.' Claire, repulsed by the sliminess of the man, was desperate. She was broke, she nearly cried. 'Well?' he asked gruffly. 'What's it to be?'

Claire felt herself collapsing inside. 'What's the job then?' she asked in a harsh whisper.

'Come to my office on Friday we'll talk about it.' He leaned back in his chair arrogance radiating. 'Trust me.' She nodded, although trust was far from her mind.

He paid the bill and got up to leave escorting her to the door. Outside, the parking area was full of luxury cars. He pushed her against the side of a Jaguar and kissed her, his tongue forcing her mouth open, his hands on her breasts. She shoved him away gasping. 'Do that again and you'll feel pain,' she threatened panting.

'Get in,' he said, ignoring her and operating the remote control. The Jag was opulent, with top of the range leather seats and all the gismos and gadgets that one could ask for. He pulled his wallet out and peeled out ten twenty pound notes. 'Take it. We'll go to my place.'

She took the money and kneed him in the groin hard. Al Bari doubled up grunting in pain. 'That wasn't the deal.' She said as she pocketed the money. 'The deal was you tell me the job. If I don't like it, I'll hang you out to dry. You understand? Anyway, in your condition you won't be up for much tonight.'

She turned and left him bent in pain, trying to open the car door. The two hundred pounds in cash in her pocket would sort a few things she thought, not at least a taxi home. She wouldn't let him mess with her, but she couldn't take the risk of losing benefits before she had sorted out a new job.

There were all sorts of people milling around in the Job Centre on Friday morning. Some stood in queues, some in front of the job advert boards. Outside al Bari's office there was a string of women, all a little younger than Claire. She passed the women and knocked on the door, dreading what demands Al Bari would make. Al Bari opened the door personally.

'Come in.' He smiled nervously at her as he invited her in with a flourish of the arm. Claire slid past him, half expecting a grab for some part of her body that never came. Tensely she sat on the chair on the far side of his desk, safe from his wondering hands.

'Claire, you are a clever woman, I think you will like what I have to offer,' she shrugged as he continued, 'outside, there are some women. First I thought I will make you one of them. Maybe you saw them?' She nodded. 'I call them my women.' She stared at him questioningly. 'Yes, unlike you, they have all slept with me.' He smiled smugly as the message sank in on her.

'Make me one of them? You slime bag, you tried and failed!'

'Wait!' He held up his hand, 'That was my plan, until our little 'meeting' in the car park.'

'Yes, that didn't exactly go to your plan, did it?' Claire eyed him apprehensively as he stood up. 'What was your plan?' She said, dripping scorn.

'They work for me and I give them their benefits.'

'I was to be one of those?' Claire stood up and stepped towards him aggressively. 'You think I would fuck anyone for money, and give you some share of the cash as well?' She prodded him in the chest making him sit down abruptly in surprise.

'Yes, but they are stupid and you are not,' he stuttered. He bridged his hands in front of his face, smiling at her as he regained composure. 'I have a different deal for you, but you have to keep your end of the bargain as well; remember? In the restaurant?'

'You naive bastard,' she hissed at him, 'what planet are you from? Women in your part of the world can't be worth much if they take this kind of shit from people like you.' Al Bari bristled as she watched the effect of her words making his temper rise. Good, she thought, feeling more in charge of the situation now. 'What is this special deal then?'

'I want you to run them,' he said clapping his hands, 'manage them.'

'You've lost me.' She stammered. 'Run them?'

'They are all getting job seekers' allowance and housing benefits and are selling themselves at the same time. I see to it that they get no hassle from this end.'

'So what do you need me for if everything is set up so perfectly?'

'I initially started this as a small side-line, but you wouldn't believe how many girls are willing to sign with me. It's got to the stage where I cannot manage it without my superiors getting suspicious. My private mobile never stops ringing and I've had one near miss, where a client barged into a meeting in my office, and nearly blurted out what he wanted, just because I couldn't answer my phone at the time. So you understand, that I have to distance myself from the operational side of things, it's getting too risky,' he answered, ignoring her disapproving look. 'In order to keep the things running I need someone competent who can manage the girls for me. If there is an investigation here, I can cover the benefits payments as a computer glitch, but there cannot be any trace of my direct involvement in this project.'

'What do you want for this act of chivalry?' Claire asked her voice oozing contempt.

'I just want 30% of the take, and I will refer all my clients to you. Your share will be 20% plus your job seekers' allowance and housing benefits. The girls get the remaining 50%, plus tips. Easy, and everyone is happy. If you want in, I'll set you up with premises and you do the admin.'

Claire thought rapidly about it. It was the answer to her problems. The revulsion she felt was secondary, her situation made her accept the reality, but she was only going to do it on her terms. Claire perched herself on the corner of his desk, looming over him aggressively.

'You expect me to sleep with you for that?' She laughed derisively, putting on an act to hide her desperation. 'The premises must be in my name only and freehold,' she insisted, jumping way ahead of him.

'Yes, yes.' he stammered taken aback by the suddenness of her demand.

'30% for me plus all my state benefits.'

'Fine,' he responded, shaken by Claire's firm taking of the lead. 'We'll take it from the girls' share,' he added nervously.

She was doing sums in her head to figure out how long she would have to endure this distasteful business. 'I'll choose the premises and you sort the finances,' she said. 'And to make it quite clear, I am not going to bed with you and that is final. We'll meet the staff now, shall we?' She stood up proffering her hand to Al Bari who stood, open mouthed, shocked by the turn of events.

Ten months later she found herself at her sister's with a bag full of money on the run from this life.

8

The police had called Voss out in the middle of the night; they'd sent a car to his house an waited while he got dressed. It was just after 1am when he arrived at the lab, the first thought on seeing the damage in the animal lab was the virus safe. He was horrified to see the door open and the floor covered in blood. After conferring with the forensics officer in charge, he was allowed in to check the refrigerated safe and was relieved to see all the samples still in their racks.

He wondered who'd used the large screwdriver to prise open the fridge when he saw that the door to the storage room also had been forced open. The place was milling with police specialists in full chemical suits checking everything for potential traces of the criminals. Voss's office had been checked by the SoC (Scene of Crime) officers, apparently untouched by the intruders, he was escorted there by a woman detective called Gunner. She gave him a quick briefing on what had happened, and then asked him questions about where he was at the time, as if he was the perpetrator. Eventually she had left him to sort out his day.

He was stunned, feeling helpless after the events of the night; the unreality of it all, even now hours after he had arrived, hampering any constructive thought. The break-in deeply disturbed him; the fact that a member of staff had been abducted and harmed and another lay critically injured in hospital weighed heavily on him. His worry was also about the research work, a lot of which had been destroyed in the savage attack that had taken place. Years of painstaking work by him and his team had been destroyed in the night.

Voss waited until eight o'clock before phoning the company's owner in London. Randell was less than happy at the news. His major concern though was about any financial liability that the company might incur as a result of a virus getting out into the public domain. He promised he would get the company's legals on it straight away. What other viruses would it meet and what would happen when it did? The variables were too many and too complex to predict. He tried to imagine containment strategies, and even considered preparing vaccines, but the problem was, vaccines against what? He didn't know.

Later in the morning, when the police had left and he again had access to the whole building, he went along to the animal units. About half of the mice which had been found still running around inside the building, had been recaptured by the staff and were once again caged up, but the ferrets and rabbits were nowhere to be seen. Thankfully the monkeys hadn't been touched. He had checked if any research notes or computers had been taken, but as far as he could see, the only target had been the animals. The lab reports were all still in their folders, he estimated that around sixty per cent of the animals were gone. Frustrated, he kicked out at a cage that was lying on the floor and it skittered across the lab careening off the fridge. A wave of anger and despair flooded over him. It was the animals that were irreplaceable. Once released, they had all been contaminated by the world outside. So, as stringent lab conditions had not been maintained, the few still left and those that they had managed to recapture were worthless as test animals now and would have to be destroyed. In reality, the fanatics who had done this had not achieved their aim, freedom for the animals. Instead, they'd guaranteed the premature death of the poor, now worthless creatures. And these people considered themselves animal lovers? He shook his head in dismay.

The puzzle he couldn't understand was why the fridge had been broken into, but nothing taken. It didn't make sense. The second riddle he had was that the security camera discs had been taken. Who knew where they were and why had they bothered to take them and then leave them behind? When Mary had first arrived, she'd found the company's CCTV discs lying on the cubicle floor of the female staff toilet. They were now sitting on his desk awaiting the arrival of the chief investigating officer, who was due to collect them.

His biggest worry, however, was the thought about what would happen to the virus, which was now no longer under laboratory conditions. The unknowns were giving him stomach cramps. To take his mind momentarily off these seemingly unsolvable questions, he bent down and picked up one of the empty cages. The doors had been cut, damaged beyond repair by side cutters or tin snips; he dropped it despondently back on the floor. After the SoC people had left, Mary had begun clearing up; she was working on her own this morning, as Jemma's mother had phoned in first thing to say her daughter was sick.

'We'll have to scrap all these Mary,' Voss said to her. 'Can you get a count done on them and I'll get Nick to do an insurance report? Since Jemma's not in, I'll also get him and a couple of lads from packing to come and help you clean up here.'

'Thanks Mr Voss. I'd appreciate the help,' Mary responded gratefully, but worried about the mountain of work in front of her.

'Did you send the police the list detailing the missing animals?'

'Yes, first thing. I'm worried about those animals that got loose.'

'Me too Mary, I've been worried sick since I heard the news.' The tension was clear in his voice. 'I can't even begin to get my head around the dangers. I don't think that the mice would be a problem, they'll die out quickly. The attrition rate will be helped by cats and other predators, due to the fact that most of the mice were infected and will die of the flu shortly anyway. It's the ferrets that'll be the problem, if there's going to be one. They live longer and may pass infections on.' He trailed off deep in thought again.

'Well, we've seen that the transfer from peer to peer is very fast and effective, but cross transmission between species hasn't happened yet. We don't have a zootic virus, do we?' Mary asked.

'No Mary, we don't. We can be pretty sure that what was released outside this lab wasn't zootic, so it won't spread across species, but we don't know how it will react in contact with other flu types. It is flu season, and if we get the wrong kind of antigenic shift, it could spell disaster.'

Mary put a comforting hand on his arm. 'You know that the antigenic changes are nearly all negative. The chances of a viable and deadly strain being created are lower than the odds of winning the national lottery two weeks running.'

Voss smiled. 'Thanks for the words of comfort Mary. I think I've been overdoing the nightmare scenario. But there are an awful lot of viruses loose out there and that's billions of lottery tickets, to use your analogy. I'm not convinced we're out of the woods yet.' he said. 'Come on, let's have a break. A nice cup of tea and things will look better.' Voss opened the door and they went out to the foyer and then over to the canteen in the next building. 'They're not finished in here yet.' Voss commented, nodding at the tape. 'Will it disturb you?' Mary shook her head and moved across to the serving hatch. They sat down with two teas in front of them, Mary's expression softened a little and she relaxed. Voss noticed the rings under her eyes.

'Is everything alright?' He probed gently; glad to be distracted from the worries of the break-in for a moment.

'Well,' she smiled up at him ambiguously, 'the break-in and all that, plus, my sister turned up in the middle of the night, marriage problems. I didn't get much sleep. That's all.'

'Mary,' he said earnestly. 'I need you now more than ever, awake and fully alert.'

She watched him closely for any signals, flattered by his words and unsure how to react. 'Thanks Mr Voss, I'll be fine, it's just a lot of extra work now.' Mary was embarrassed as she caught her boss's eye and dropped her gaze quickly again.

'My sister promised to search for a job and find a place to live, but she seems worried and uptight about the Job Centre.' she said.

'What has she been doing up to now?' he asked.

'Let's say she is capable of a lot more than she has actually achieved. She got top grades in her 'A' levels and then went down 'South' to Uni on a scholarship to Imperial.'

'Imperial? Voss sounded interested, 'What did she read?'

'Genetics and Biochem like me. She settled in a job at a forensic lab firm for a few years, but that fizzled out when the place went bankrupt, since then she's been doing a bit of this and a bit of that, you know…' She checked to see if her boss was admiring her and not just following her story, but only saw genuine interest in the story on his face as he listened to her. Disappointed, she continued, 'but she doesn't have much in the way of work experience outside forensics.' Mary paused again, gauging his reaction.

'Lab experience isn't always a bad thing,' he chuckled and walked round to her, putting a hand protectively on her shoulder and leading her towards the canteen doorway.

'Maybe you should ask her to fill out an application form for here? I'd be glad to help if she fits the job.'

'You're very kind, Mr Voss.' She looked up at him pleadingly. 'Even if she didn't get the best degree, she was brilliant, and I could use some help,' she waved her arm around helplessly, 'with all that mess over there.' Then she sighed and sagged visibly, as if anticipating an immediate refusal.

'We'll see,' Voss said, 'you don't have to sell her to me. I can't promise you anything.' Voss reflected, 'You get her to fill in an application form and we'll see what we can do. I have to examine her details first.'

9

The Chief Superintendent, resplendent in his full uniform, seemed frazzled, as he stood closely surrounded by unfamiliar faces. Hanks surveyed the room. Not the usual bunch of 'yes sir, no sir, three bags full sir,' wallies this morning. The Superintendent seemingly overwhelmed by the magnitude of the events was having difficulty answering the questions from the surrounding officers. He appeared to be reciting the regulations by rote.

'The response to a terrorist incident in this country relies on a coordinated approach between those responding at a local level, including emergency services and local authorities, and the central government departments with a key role to play. Our approach, should this incident at Brinkley's be defined as a terrorist attack, would follow a meticulously planned outline. Naturally, once agreed by the Chief Constable that we need support from the government, the Home Office would notify all key departments and agencies. The Home Office would then liaise with the Cabinet Office and a decision would be taken as to whether or not to activate the central government's crisis management facilities, the Cabinet Office Briefing Rooms (COBRA). The Cabinet Office has responsibility for maintaining the alerting mechanism for the UK central government response.

However, ladies and gentlemen, we are still not decided as to whether this is a terrorist attack or solely a bunch of lunatics on the rampage. I'll be speaking to the Chief Constable shortly and will advise you later on the outcome on that front. Thank you.'

People started drifting out murmuring amongst themselves.

'Waffle, waffle, waffle. Where are all the sycophants?' Hanks asked out of the side of his mouth to Welks, but his partner was no longer there. The Super noticed him at last. He looked ostentatiously at his watch and in his best 'public address' voice said,

'Oh, DCI Hanks, I'm so glad you could fit us into your busy schedule,' his voice dripping sarcasm. Those officers still nearby turned in his direction.

'Good morning, Chief Superintendent,' He replied formally. He thought about needling him, but resisted the temptation. 'What's on?' he coughed.

'You know what's happened of course?'

'Let's say I know what I've been told.'

'Come with me, we need to see the forensics boys and the SoC stuff from Brinkley's.' Hanks trailed behind him, shaking his head at being treated like a school kid. They left the Ops room together and went across the corridor.

'Sir,' Hanks stopped the man in the corridor, 'a virus research establishment gets broken into and animals released, this could develop very quickly into a massive crisis. With due respect sir, I think it would be better to overreact here and be safe, rather than to soft peddle. This should go national now.'

'And if it is just lunatics at work? I'm not going to risk my reputation panicking because of a few nutters. You find me something concrete to take up to national level and what we are dealing with here. Then I can make some decisions. In the meantime; concentrate on your job of catching these people and leave policy to me.' Hanks remained silent as he followed, fuming, into the small windowless room; the bright neon lighting caused his head to start throbbing again. Two white-coated technicians were examining something in a glass dish.

The Super stopped. 'Stand back please!' he commanded. 'Take a look for yourself,' he gestured. Hanks stepped forward obediently and peered into the Petri dish on the worktop. He gasped at the unexpected sight confronting him, the severed index and middle fingers of someone's right hand. Ah, 'the two fingers', he smiled wryly to himself.

'The fingers,' he commented, 'a non-white then.' The Superintendent rolled his eyes skyward.

'Your political correctness leaves a lot to be desired, but yes Hanks, as you ought to classify, an IC4. They belong to the kidnapped staff member at Brinkley's. There was a letter with the fingers. DC Welks knows the details on that.'

Hanks bit his tongue to stop another snide remark erupting; instead, he posed the question that had been bugging him since he got into the lift.

'Why me sir?' trying to insert some modicum of deference into the words.

'Terrorists! Your neck of the woods!' Michaels said sharply, 'you haven't made much progress on the man you supposed to be chasing so maybe you'll be better at this.'

'Sir, I was relocated here to chase a subversive known to be part of a radical Islamist group. I have a feeling that we are close to getting him...'

Michaels puffed out his chest in a pompous gesture, 'The Incident Officer Sarah Gunner is waiting to talk to you downstairs and Welks has been digging around as well this morning. No holds barred on this one.'

Hanks was about to protest, but then seeing there was no point in another battle, gave in. 'Well then,' he said after some deliberation, 'I'll set up a major incident team. You will find the official request papers on your desk today. I trust you don't mind me going ahead immediately, before your formal approval.' The Superintendent nodded, turned and went back to the ops room, leaving Hanks dumbfounded at the paucity of the information, and the quality of the briefing he had just received. Hanks went over to the fingers again. The technicians stood by, a little more relaxed now, since the departure of the Super.

'Do me a favour, will you?' Hanks asked, 'get me a DNA and fingerprint analysis as fast as you can. I need to know who these belong to.'

'Well, that's easy sir, they belong to the bloke from Brinkley's, as the Super just said,' the taller of the two proffered. 'It's in the letter that was left. His name is Khalid Akar and according to the staff records at Brinkley, he's a 27 year old Moroccan who's been working for them for two months now.'

'I didn't ask you what you think,' Hanks glowered into the man's face. 'I asked you to do some tests to find out who they damn well belong to.' The man averted his eyes, in a mixture of annoyance and embarrassment. 'I can read the damn report myself. I need the facts and evidence to prove it, or we will have a problem. Do we want problems?'

The man backed away. 'No sir,' he replied meekly.

Hanks went back to his office, his head was thumping.

'Damn fine thing with the fingers, Colin. You had me going on that one,' he growled, chucking his jacket unsuccessfully onto the table under the window, and then watching it slide gracelessly to the floor. Welks picked it up, grinning at his partner as he hung it up.

'What've we got?'

'Fingers, two for the use of.' Welks answered, as Hanks settled back in his chair.

'Name rings a bell though. Khalid Akar?' Welks produced a facial twitch resembling a smile that turned immediately into a frown. 'I have a feeling he was on our list of PAYE miscreants.'

'He is,' Hanks said. 'I put the names alphabetically for the investigating teams. He's the only 'A' we had.'

'Well he's not at home,' Welks grinned, 'we can call the dogs off on that one.' He picked up the phone to call back the team from Akar's home until they got a search warrant, and then shouting through the door for Harris to get a warrant for Akar's place issued.

By now, the two of them were a practiced team. Welks had worked with Hanks before in Northern Ireland and each had impressed the other with his ability to annihilate vast quantities of booze and manage to be effective in trapping the baddies. They'd been separated after Hanks's wife was killed in the bombing. It had been a happy surprise to Hanks finding that Welks was to be his partner again in Chester.

'There's more,' Welks went over to his desk and got behind his PC, turning the screen, so Hanks could see it.

'We have an email sent at 02:20 this morning. Apparently, it's from the ARF, some 'Animal Rights Front' group. The IP

Address is a fake or at least an alias; they're using a VPN to cover their tracks. Our 'geeks' are trying to do a track-back exercise to see if they can find the source.'

'They're using a what? Colin, this is all Greek to me. What the hell are you talking about?'

'Simply put, an email sent this morning with copies to all the major Fleet Street newspapers. We cannot as yet locate the source computer as they have used some software to create a virtual private network, that's a VPN, behind which to hide. The 'geeks', our computer specialists, are seeing if they can track it back anyway. We'll know more soon. Oh, and DC Gunner, the incident officer, has been texting me about a possible epidemic due to viruses. We'll have to get some experts to examine that. We don't want to catch the plague while doing our job, do we?'

'The plague was a bacterial infection, not a virus! Don't they teach you lot anything in schools anymore? Oh God, do I need a coffee!' Hanks groaned holding his head more in real than mock anguish. After helping himself at the office dispenser, Hanks perched on the edge of the desk.

'What's in the text of the letter left on site with the fingers?' he asked, slurping his coffee loudly.

'Here, read it yourself. It's the usual self-important, self-righteous dross.' He held out a plastic wallet with a piece of paper sealed in it. Hanks read it,

'You motherfuckers sit up and take notice. Khalid Akar, your lackey in your vile capitalist, inhuman shit hole Brinkley Medical is our prisoner. We will keep him until you do a new law against animal testing. Stop killing animals.

The Animal Rights Front'

Just to make sure you understand how serious we are, here is two of the bastards fingers.

'That's the hard copy which was left behind at the scene at Brinkley's this morning, the one with the fingers. It wasn't printed off at Brinkley's, by the way. It's the same text as the email so I reckon it was prepared in advance. The last bit is hand written, the press didn't get that.'

Hanks said, 'It means that they knew before the event, who they were going to take hostage. That does suggest insiders. What puzzles me is the handwritten bit about the fingers, looks like it was not part of the plan.'

'Never thought about that,' Welks said, making a note.

'That's why I earn a fiver a week more than you,' Hanks joked. 'The A.R.F, what have we got on them?' Hanks paused, slurping his coffee again, a habit Welks couldn't stand.

'I've got DC Whittaker and DC Carlton up and running on that side of things. We should have something shortly.'

'I'm thinking,' Hanks said, 'we need to keep a lid on as much information as possible for operational reasons. Good, now tell me slowly and in detail what happened last night at Brinkley's.'

Welks read off the report from his computer, 'As far as we know the initial alarm was raised at 23:30 yesterday. The front gate silent security alarm went off at the alarm call centre here at headquarters,' he checked some notes on his desk, 'with only an automatic date stamp and no further details. The Alarm Centre put in a request for immediate assistance. A radio log was filed at 23:32. It was an all cars call. Alfa Oscar 420, being the nearest operational unit on call, responded. The unit arrived on scene at 23:40. The gate guard was found clubbed to the ground and an ambulance was called straightaway. The company's virus safe was broken into, according to the principle there was nothing taken.

'I find that strange, they break open a safe and take nothing?'

'Not a real safe, more like a lockable fridge.'

Hanks thought about the detail, aware that it might be vital later. 'Right then' he said, 'what's the latest on the condition of the guard? Can we talk to him?'

'Last I heard he was in intensive care, pretty serious. He's in a coma and it's touch and go. He took a mighty whack on the head, so we could well be dealing with a murder case here if he doesn't make it.'

'Any witnesses?' Hanks grunted expecting a negative. 'CCTV?'

'Nada!' Welks spun his chair towards him, 'CCTV discs are

missing. Someone took them.'

'Definitely seems like an insider then, doesn't it? The hostage name, and now the missing disks.' Hanks turned towards his own desk. 'Whatever, we need to keep the name of the hostage out of the press for as long as possible. Whittaker!' he shouted through the door, 'get onto the Press Council and stop them putting out Akar's name, tell them, until we've informed next of kin.'

'I'm on it boss.' Whittaker responded from the other room.

'Hey Welks, one more thing,' Hanks frowned, 'how did you know it was Remy Martin this morning?'

'I'm a detective,' Welks laughed, 'you always drink it when Kate starts bugging you. Sorry that the Northern Ireland thing came up yesterday. I knew it would affect you.' Hanks grinned ruefully back.

'I'm fine, just that it happens when you least expect it. Trust Carlton to open that particular wound. I still have the nightmares. Anyway, let's talk to Gunner.'

Welks picked up his phone to call Gunner and ask her to come up to the office. Hanks's phone rang. He walked back to his desk and picked up. 'DCI Hanks.'

'Mr Voss?' pause, 'Ah yes, Brinkley Medical. Bad thing that. What can we do for you?' He listened and then commented, 'That's good news! Are you sure they are the right ones? Yes? Good. Where were they found? What? Ladies toilet, right! We're on our way over. Please don't touch them more than you have already.' He put the phone down.

'Colin, get SoC over to Brinkley's again. I want the staff toilets given a real good going over. Then get your jacket on, because we're going to see a Mr Voss at Brinkley's. He's got something that will help us.'

Welks's interest was aroused. 'What's he got, Alan?' as he grabbed the papers that had come off the printer. Gunner walked in, as they were about to leave.

'Bad timing? I thought you wanted to talk to me?' Gunner asked, obviously put out that the pair were just leaving.

'Sorry, off to Brinkley's,' Welks said.

'Yes, I wanted to talk to you Sarah. Walk with us for a bit,' Hanks said. 'I need to know if anything else went off last night.'

'What?' She was caught off balance. 'No sir, nothing exceptional. There was a fight outside the Bear and Billet in Bridge Street and a Taking Without Consent (TWOC), a delivery van from a Threshers off-licence. Other than that, only the usual string of traffic offenders, as well as a domestic in Chichester Street in the small hours of the morning. Nowt out of the ordinary, really, oh, and the shout from Brinkley's.'

'Uh Huh,' Hanks thought for a second, 'Which officers dealt with the theft of the Threshers van? Has it been recovered?

'Williams and Peterson sir, they were on that one. And no sir, no sign of it yet.'

'Chase that up. How's the door-to-door going on? Get anything there?'

'Nothing. No-one noticed anything. Not many doors to knock on there. Sealand Road is one long industrial estate these days. Only thing of interest was an unusual crowd whooping it up in the Cricketers. Landlord reckons they were off to a sex orgy the way they were tanking up.'

'Find out who talked to him and tell them I want to talk to them when we get back.'

'Okay,' Gunner answered, 'I have to go to the Town Hall Public Health Department to brief them on risks tomorrow. Me, of all people! What do I know? Voss at Brinkley's is also in the dark as to what could happen with the released animals, so how am I supposed to tell the Health Department anything, when even the experts don't know?' She sighed wearily, 'I'll let you know when I get back. By that time I'll have found out whoever it was that interviewed the publican.'

Welks held the door open as Hanks stared into his plastic coffee cup, 'How come, even with a filter machine, we still get this crud in the bottom of our cups?'

'Rocket science! Way above your head Alan,' Welks ushered him outside, 'Are we ready now? I thought this was urgent.'

'You'll never get promoted. I'll personally see to that.'

'I hear there's a vacancy in security at Brinkley's,' Welks said blackly and Hanks laughed as they went out leaving a bemused Gunner staring after them.

10

Flight Sergeant Bullock was nearing the end of another shift in the 'Video Games Room' as it was jokingly called. Only this one was the real thing. What happened here on screen, actually happened outside. You couldn't reload by winning virtual medals or clicking on sidebars, you had what you had, and that was it. This was a war room.

The dimmed lighting was punctuated by the screens of computers on each side of the eerily quiet windowless room. The operators were all concentrating on their tasks: The left-hand side was 'Recon', where the screens all had a green LED on the top and the right-hand side was 'Action'. Bullock's current shift was in 'Action', as he'd already done a week of Recon. It was a pretty boring routine, like so many others. The positions of the six airborne Predator drones were projected on the huge display map on the end wall; little red dots moving on the map. The names of towns and villages on the other side of the world didn't mean a great deal to the recruit from Tennessee. They were printed next to the aerial pictures of clusters of buildings. His drone, Pred 4, an MQ 9 Reaper, was on autopilot cruising at 4000 ft., flying low over part of the northern Pakistan Afghanistan border area.

It was deepest night in Pakistan; Bullock's screen was showing night-enhanced pictures in real time from half a planet away. There was nothing spectacular going on. He was waiting for a call from 'Recon', a call to do something. Most shifts he never got such a call.

On the 'Recon' side, the operators were a little more involved in their work. They had not only visual images to digest, but also sound bites and Signal Intelligence (SIGINT) to cope with. Flight Lieutenant Janet Cody was sitting on Recon 4, the control panel for a UAV unmanned aerial vehicle. In this case, it was a QinetiQ Zephyr, a HALE class (high altitude long endurance) unit. She checked the flightlog on the display. The plane had been up for a fraction over seventy hours, so there was plenty of reserve before she'd bring it back to Bagram for refuelling and maintenance. The longest mission she had had to date was nearly three hundred hours; the new solar packs added a great deal of scope to a mission. The Zephyr was in night mode over the Swat valley. She had her brief. The CIA had forwarded a list of SIM card numbers from agents on the ground in Pakistan and satellite numbers from Intel. The Mobilink telephone numbers were in the active filter of the software module. She was hunting, waiting for one of these to be activated, for someone down there to make a phone call. Come on ET; phone home, she thought wryly.

The Zephyr was at 18,000 ft. and Cody knew the surveillance tools were insufficient at this height to do face recognition or number plate identification. She'd have to come in lower to do that, but this height was the best mix of coverage and sensitivity. Her UAV was covering a patch sixteen miles wide by fourteen miles deep, progressing over the ground at about thirty miles an hour. There wasn't anything going to happen down there, electronically or thermally, that she wouldn't know about.

She activated the open Wi-Fi sniffers, in case there was some smart bastard out there who'd use a laptop and the internet to access the phone system. A SIM card was all they needed, either that or a satellite connection. Up here in the hills of North West Pakistan the latter was the more likely. It was her job to find out who used the numbers and identify them. It was like playing a game she thought, as she watched the Zephyr crossing the Afghan border into Pakistani airspace. The threat-warning radar sensors were quiet. No-one had noticed the incursion. She was relaxed. It was an ordinary day, an ordinary mission.

A small light went on at the bottom left of her screen, a

notification of an email intercept. The message from Langley SIGINT was hours old, but none the less Intercepts of open traffic emails in the mountains of northern Pakistan were rarer than honest bankers. Janet Cody immediately straightened up, fully alert now. The clear text ran over the bottom of the screen. It made no sense to her, even though it was in English. 'Brother, we are pleased to inform you that we have started operation 'Buyer'. We wish you the best from your father.'

Cody noted that Pred 4 was quite close to her Zephyr. Casting a glance over to the Pred 4 control desk, Bullock was boredly chewing a pencil, checking the Pred's capabilities, in case they had a strike situation. The small list appeared at the base of her screen. The details of the drone, such as its location, speed and altitude were shown, plus its fuel reserve and weaponry. Pred 4 was loaded with most of the goodies the USAAF could get on it and it still had about 65% of its fuel left. Good to know. Any targets would regret being on the end of one of Pred 4's Hellfire missiles. They sure could mess your evening. She smiled and sent her Zephyr a bit nearer to Pred 4.The red and green dots practically overlapping on the map.

Bing! Bing! Bing! The alarm went. One of the SIGINT filters had picked up a known satellite phone. She checked the map to see where the nearest other Recon was. Recon 1 was a hundred miles away to the west.

She called over the headset, 'Recon 1, I have an alarm lock-in to signal on frequency 3,434 GHz try and get a fix for me.' She gave the geo coordinates.

'Roger Recon 4. Will come over your way; try to get a better signal,' came the dry response.

'Pred 4, I am over you and getting a signal, do you have signal recognition and tracking capability?'

'Sure do honey,' Bullock drawled. 'Wanna give me your number?' She was unimpressed with the innuendo.

'Got a sat number active on the ground, that's one you can have.'

'Ouch that hurt,' Bullock joked. 'Okay, let's see what this baby can find. Gigahertz band?'

'Yep'.

'Got it. Signal coming from some village called Achar

according to the map.'

'I'm going down; take your bird off on 30° east, so we don't interfere.'

'Roger, 30° east it is, confirmed.' He flicked the autopilot off and manipulated the Pred using the joy stick. The two blips on the map began to separate.

Cody took the Zephyr down to 3000 feet, with the night cameras on full sensitivity. She didn't care about motor noise; this wouldn't be a problem until she got much lower. All she wanted now was an ID, a photo. That would be a real lucky break, but even a house where the card was being used would be a great help to her colleagues. She edged the plane lower 2000 ft., then 1000 ft. from the ground. There were two red specs. Two dots moving slowly, obviously on foot going towards the village. The signal was emanating from one of them, she was sure of that. The enhanced zoom image showed two men, one with his arm around the shoulders of the other. She got complete full facials from both of them.

'Bingo!' she cried excitedly, causing heads to turn in the room. 'Sorry guys,' she whispered into the intercom. Then, as her orders specified, she beamed the pictures off to Langley's SIGINT.

'Okay guys, back on Auto pilot, the excitement is over for now'. Bullock switched back to Auto and logged the time. His relief was due in just under five minutes.' Shame, he'd have enjoyed the adrenaline flash that came with triggering a Hellfire. Never mind, another day, another dollar. His relief arrived.

Cody's full facials were being fed into one of Langley's highest powered Cray super computers. The facial recognition programme was amazingly accurate. The algorithms and search functions were as slick as they were thorough. It would take a man a lifetime or two to go through the database of millions of photos, but the machine could check some 9000 photos a minute against any given comparison.

The pair from the Swat valley were being well scrutinised; electronically speaking, they were under the microscope.

Cody got a flash message on her screen. Target identified. A picture of one of the two men appeared.

Qamar al Surira AKA Qamar Surira: Age: 56 Born: Jeddah.

Notes: Last seen Nairobi shortly before US Embassy bombing. Nationality: Saudi Arabian

Written next to the second picture was: Identification failed due to poor image quality. Lt. Cody mailed this data to her controller as well. The joint intelligence committee will be busy soon, if this pans out, she thought, going back to her mission board. Maybe we'll get lucky twice tonight. She focused back on her screen. In Langley, the alarm bells were ringing already. The duty SIGINT operator got Cody's messages and immediately red-flagged them. Qamar Surira's details were forwarded to MI in Britain along with the open text email. The Langley operator mailed the controller requesting more pictures. The Controller picked up the phone and buzzed Cody in the War Room.

'Sir?'

'They need a clear shot of the other guy.'

'Not a hope sir, they've gone into a hut in the village. We will never be able to tell if it's the same man, even if he shows up again we can't know if it's him.'

11

Shadeed was still asleep in his room when the visitor arrived. Although twenty-nine years old, he still lived with his family.

'I'm his sister, I'll wake him for you,' Nalini, offered. 'Please be seated. Can I offer you a drink or something to eat?'

Hassan appraised the sparsely furnished apartment, wondering how many of the family lived here. The small window overlooked a courtyard, where some children and dogs were sharing the water from a small pool in its centre. The sun wasn't up high yet and the temperature was still in the comfort zone. That would all change in about an hour. First the humidity would climb sky high and then the rain would come. Water masses that threatened to drown you where you stood. He hated the rainy season, but at least there were no serious floods here. He could hardly wait to get to the airport and out of this place.

He politely declined Shadeed's sister's offer, 'Just get him please. It's important.'

The petite Nalini disappeared behind a curtain. He could hear her quiet whispering on the other side. Hassan thought, if she were his daughter, he would insist on her covering herself up. She was half-naked in her hot pants and T-shirt, far too western. A harlot, he thought to himself as the curtain moved again and Nalini reappeared.

'He's coming. Please, won't you sit?'

Hassan sat on the sofa, a large red velvet object with deep

buttoning and little lace coverlets on the armrests. There were pictures on the walls in ornate golden frames.

'Have you come far?' Nalini interrupted his thoughts. He pondered his response.

'Yes,' he said. 'I have travelled a long way and have still a long way to go. Your brother is still working?' he asked.

'Yes, at the university. He's assistant to the Head of the Chemistry School,' she answered with pride in her voice.

'And you?' Hassan stared her down till she turned away embarrassed, 'What do you do?'

'I work in Mobilink telephone services. I sell mobile phones and phone contracts.' She self-consciously tucked her T-shirt into her shorts. 'I only work afternoons,' she added, almost apologetically.

The curtain moved again, a slightly bedraggled, tall, dark man came out; running his fingers through is coarse black hair.

'Ha…' he started only to be met with a cautionary raised finger from Hassan.

'No names please, my friend,' Hassan smiled at Nalini. 'It is enough I know yours. Nalini, I think maybe you should attend work earlier today to avoid the rains.' Nalini, unsure, asked Shadeed, who nodded tensely.

'Okay,' she said 'but don't you want drinks first?'

'I'll sort that out.' Shadeed said, 'You run along now.'

A little put out; she picked up her handbag and opened the front door. The fresh air and the light were welcome in the stuffy room. The two men waited until she was gone.

'Hassan, I got your text, but I was in Karachi, I got back very late last night. I didn't expect you so early.' Shadeed greeted his visitor with an embrace.

'We have the makings of a mission of Allah, a strike for the true faith. Qamar thinks you may be able to put some parts of the puzzle together for us.'

'You want drugs?' Shadeed asked astonished.

'No, we don't need drugs.'

'But that is my area of expertise. I know practically nothing else.'

'Don't underestimate your talent, young Shadeed. What is it you use to purify your raw opium and heroin?'

'Heh? Ether! I'm not sure what you mean?' Shadeed looked worried.

'Relax my friend, all is in perfect order. We need detailed information about ether, that's all.' Hassan put on his best smile and patted the sofa, indicating Shadeed should sit. Cautiously, Shadeed sat next to him. 'We need some information and details of safety procedures for handling ether, like flashpoints, boiling points, side reactions and all that sort of stuff.'

Shadeed nodded sagely. 'What do you want me to do?'

'I want you to write notes, put them on an SD card and give them to me. I will wait. The information will be put to very good use, I promise you. Please don't use the net for this, I want no traces.'

'We are talking about the diethyl ether, aren't we?' Shadeed held his chin in thought. 'I will do it now. Please sit. A drink while you wait?'

'Thank you. How long do you need?'

'Give me a few minutes.' Shadeed stood and retrieved his laptop from under the sofa switching it on before disappearing into his room to return with a text book.

'You should make your sister dress properly,' Hassan chided Shadeed as he worked.

'She is young and hot-headed,' he replied, 'and she goes her own way. I too am disappointed with her.' Applying himself to the task, rattling it off from memory, one thing he was good at was chemistry. He typed rapidly, adding everything he thought was relevant about ether. 'You need storage information data, Hassan?' his head came up from the text book. 'Do you need pumping information, like static electricity charges and max flow rates?'

'Everything my friend, everything is important, down to the smallest detail.'

'It's vital to know how you are using it, for safety. If it's only small quantities then it's not relevant but big loads…' He paused, 'big loads are more dangerous and you must observe very strict precautions. I'll tag all the details on. You'll also need to earth any tanks you may be pumping too or from.' He continued typing.

'How's it going?' Washiri asked after a while, getting

impatient and wanting to be off.

'Nearly done! Just have to save to the SD card and we're finished.'

'Okay, give me the card.'

'Sure.' Shadeed pulled the card from its socket and dropped it in his friend's hand. 'All there.' he announced as Hassan tucked the card into a pocket in the folds of his gown.

'You've been a great help.' he said, 'I will make sure Qamar knows of your part in all this. He holds you in high esteem,' He then embraced the man, before turning and picking up the laptop, which he threw violently on the floor, ignoring the protests of the chemist. Hassan stamped on the wreckage until he was able to rip the hard disc from inside. 'I have to be certain,' he said coldly, withdrawing a wad of dollars and thrusting them into the young man's hand. Without another word, he went to the window, alert for any signs of observation, checking for parked cars or delivery vans out of place. There was one vehicle parked on the corner of the road, a service van for air-conditioners. He watched it carefully for a while, checking particularly for any movement of the suspension, indicating that people were hiding inside the van.

Finally satisfied, he walked out into the bright sunshine searching for a taxi. The day was getting warmer, he thought, as he neared the van on the corner. A man in overalls came out of the apartment building with a toolbox in hand, nodding casually and heading for the parked van. Hassan relaxed, and raised his hand to summon a taxi.

Within minutes, he was heading through the dense traffic along the Expressway to the airport to catch his flight back to Paris. On the Kaak Pull Bridge over the river Soan, he ordered the driver to stop. Ignoring the ire of other motorists forced to slow up behind, he stepped out of the car and flung the chemist's hard disc in a spinning arc over the parapet into the swirling currents below. He smiled as he got back in the cab and patted the card in his pocket. He then concentrated on the plan. One of the main elements they needed was a tunnel, a tunnel full of people. Maybe Masoud would have an idea.

Benazir Bhutto Airport was busy as Hassan got out of the cab and paid the driver. He disappeared fast into the terminal building. He was now finally on his way to London. He read the scrap of paper Qamar had given him; one line of text in Urdu: Kahn's Coffee Shop, The Broadway, Southall and an email address, nothing else. That's where he'd meet Masoud. He just had to wait for him there.

Nalini got to the shop early. Her colleague was surprised when she arrived. The shop was empty. The coolness of the room was a relief after the humidity outside. She dropped her handbag behind the screen at the back of the shop.

'What are you doing Rashid?' she asked her colleague, seeing him scrolling the prepaid subscriber numbers on the screen.

'Oh, just checking something for head office. They want me to send a daily list of prepaid sales. I have to copy and paste the numbers into an email. No big deal.' He needed another minute, and noticing how hot she was, he offered, 'My mum gave me some lemonade, it's in the fridge. Can you bring me one as well, please?'

'Oh sure. Thanks, I will.' She smiled heading for the fridge. Pleased to have her out of the way, Rashid sent the mail to his American friend, happy at having earned another hundred Dollars for the information. She didn't have to know that his email wasn't going to head office.

12

Voss was surprised that the two plain-clothes detectives didn't resemble police officers. The older one was more like a slimmer, very fit, athletic version of Tom Jones. The younger man, in his early forties, had the air of a man doing kids' birthday parties as a magician or clown; he had a jolly face and a disconcertingly happy aura.

'Gentlemen, come in.' he ushered them into the office. 'Please take a seat', he offered, showing them to the two chairs in front of his desk.

The elder briefly showed something that may have been a warrant card and introduced his colleague and himself.

'Thanks for your time', Hanks said eying the DVDs on the desk. 'Are those the discs?'

'Yes,' Voss answered, 'Mary, I mean, Ms. Grigson, found them in the ladies toilet this morning.' Welks wrote something in his notebook. 'As far as I know she's the only one, apart from me, who has touched them.'

'Alright, I trust you have nothing against us taking your prints for comparison purposes, so we can identify them from any others that might be on the discs. It would be good if we could have the prints of all employees. It would make our job much easier,' Hanks said.

'Might be good if we could have DNA swabs as well,' Welks said. 'Belt and braces so to speak.'

'No problem.' Voss said 'We have DNA analyses for each member of staff in the personnel files. I can mail them to you.' Welks reached into his pocket and produced a visiting card with a contact email address on it.

'Today would be nice,' he smiled. 'If we can have it quicker, all the better.'

'Well, I can do better than that.' Voss got up and walked over to a filing Cabinet. He pulled a key ring out of his pocket and unlocked the top drawer. 'Of course, I'll need these back gentlemen.' He withdrew a bundle of thin files, which he placed in front of Hanks. 'The full staff files, all DNAs, fingerprints, addresses, everything. Can I expect them back by the weekend?'

'We'll see what we can do,' Hanks replied gruffly as he turned the files round towards him, pulling Akar's file open checking the address and pointing it out to Welks.

Welks jotted it down in his book noting it was the same as on the PAYE records. He glanced out of the window into the yard, watching the white-suited SoC officers arriving.

'So, where can we play them?' Hanks asked.

'Here,' Voss said, reaching out for one of the DVDs. 'I'll put them in my computer.' Hanks put a restraining hand on his arm.

'Please, allow me.' He pulled on a PVC glove and carefully picked up the first disc. 'Do you have any blanks, so we can make a copy?'

'Yes, of course:' Voss answered and pulled a drawer open revealing a box of DVD blanks.

'Do you mind?' Welks got up and took over Voss's computer, his practiced hands slipping the DVD into the drive and copying it to the hard disc. He then inserted a blank and made the copy and repeated the process with the next disc.

Hanks let Welks get on with copying the discs and asked Voss about the safe with the samples in. Voss told him that the storeroom was locked when he wasn't on the premises and the keys were in his office, pointing to the small intact key-safe on the wall, neither man could understand why nothing had been removed from the safe; a mystery.

Hanks's mobile rang; he stood up and walked towards the window, seeking a measure of privacy.

'Hanks here,' he said quietly. 'I see. All right! We're out

interviewing. Put the details on my desk. We'll be back by four o'clock at the latest.' He rang off as he peered down into the yard. 'The SoC team is here,' he said to Welks, 'you can give them the discs, when you're finished copying.'

'I've just finished, I'll catch the lads before they leave.' Welks lifted the bagged originals and left the office.

'Mr Voss,' Hanks said, 'I suggest we watch.' He gestured to Voss to take the chair beside him. 'I want you to observe closely and let me know if you see anything that might be of help, anything unusual, however trivial it may seem.' He clicked on the start button. A remarkably clear picture in colour appeared on the screen. He found the fast forward and advanced to 23:31. A group of seven people dressed in dark clothing and balaclavas were approaching the main gate. Hanks noted from the gait that one of them was more than likely a woman; his suspicion was confirmed when he saw the profile of the person in question as she looked up at the camera; a woman, no doubt about that. The group were stopped briefly by the guard. One of the larger members of the group hit him with a stick like object and the guard slumped to the ground. The rest of the footage showed the group crossing to the lab building, then nothing, the disc obviously having been removed.

'Mr Voss, that white van,' Hanks pointed at it on the screen, 'any idea who it belongs to? Is it one of yours?'

'No, definitely not,' Voss peered at it more closely, 'we only have a little Renault and that's a Ford. It's got something written on the side, though,' he said helpfully.

Hanks zoomed in and squinted at the picture. 'I can't make it out.' He took out his notebook and scribbled down the vehicle's model and colour. 'It puzzles me.....' Hanks began, thinking aloud. 'There were dangerous viruses locked in your safe, which was opened, but nothing was taken, what also is my question is who knew where the recorders were and how did they get the access codes?' He looked in askance at Voss as he was getting up to leave. Voss was perplexed.

'Well, thanks Mr Voss, you've been most helpful. If you can think of anything else or something else crops up, ring me.' Hanks put his card on the desk. 'Oh, and one of your employees, Jemma, has called in sick?'

'Yes, well her mum called for her.'

'We'll need to go round and talk to her. Thanks for your time and for these,' Hanks said, tapping the files. 'You know where we are.' He put on his best smile as he shook Voss's hand and turned to the door, bumping into Welks who was walking back in as he opened it. 'Time to go,' he said.

They crossed the car park in silence. Welks got in behind the wheel and Hanks slumped into the passenger seat.

'I want to get some detailed information on these animal rights wallies. Who is behind them? Where do they meet and who are their members? That would be a good start.' He ran his hand through his hair in frustration.

'Carlton sent us the information, I picked them up from the printer before we left, but I didn't have a chance to read them.' Welks stopped the car and pulled the handbrake on, then reached out for the papers on the back seat and handed them to Hanks.

'Aims and ambitions', Hanks started reading, 'a curt analysis stating that they were a fringe group, even the RSPCA distanced themselves from them, because of their excessive lust for spectacularism.

'They are all absolute bloody nutters.' Welks stated.

Hanks read on. 'Their founding member is Heather Craig, currently living in Eccleston, Cheshire. Welks, where's Eccleston?'

'South of here, just south of the North Wales expressway. Why?'

'How long to get there?'

'Blues and twos?'

'No.'

'Then ten minutes at the least,' he stated, sounding disappointed. 'Where about in Eccleston?'

'Rake Lane. Number 42.'

'Wow, that's the moneyed end. Posh there Alan, I tell you.'

'Spare me the tourist patter, get us there.' Hanks turned his attention back to the papers.

'Right.' Welks turned the car round at the next junction and headed back the way they'd come towards the expressway.

'Says here that there's a factional split within the organisation. What the hell does that mean?' Hanks ruminated.

'One faction wants to be kind to animals and the other wants to be even kinder?' He stifled a grunting laugh as he flung the papers onto the back seat. The roads were clear as they drove into Eccleston, a tranquil picture postcard village.

'Round here I think.' Welks took the corner a tad too fast causing Hanks to swear.

'Do that again and I'll play you the Hammersmith Odeon Rory Gallagher Concert.'

'Oh Christ! You still on that trip? Haven't you grown up yet?' Welks needled him whilst searching out of the window for house numbers. 'You know, sometimes I wish you were old enough to have seen all these groups live, in their heyday.'

'What?'

'Yeah, you'd have retired by now and I wouldn't have to put up with this.'

His partner thumped him playfully on the shoulder, 'Bastard.'

'Last week it was the unreleased recordings of the Allman Brothers fighting in the dressing room at Fillmore East. Now it's Gallagher. You want the radio on for some decent music?' he continued scathingly, happy to see Hanks needled.

'Philistine! It's a classic. Best version of 'Catfish' you'll ever hear,' Hanks growled back at him.

'Here!' Welks said, braking.

'This it then?' Hanks asked, peering out of the window at the high hedge. Welks swung the wheel, bringing the car into the well-tended gravel driveway of an impressive mock Tudor house. He brought the car to a scrunching stop in the forecourt of number 42.

'The Craig residence,' he announced with a flourish. A green Range Rover standing in the driveway confronted them. A prominent sticker in the window stated, 'I stop for animals'. Hanks eased himself out of the car and waited for Welks to join him. The porch had a tiled gable roof, its sides adorned with geraniums in troughs and hanging baskets in full bloom. Obviously, someone paid a lot of attention to them, for there wasn't a dead-head to be seen. Hanks pushed the door chime, sending a melodic 'ding dong' rolling through the house.

'Doesn't seem like a nutter's house does it?' Welks said, leaning back to see if there was movement at any of the upstairs windows.

'They never do,' Hanks replied laconically, opening the letterbox and bending to squint through it. 'Jesus!' he jumped back. 'How many cats can you keep in a house?'

'Dunno. Why? Don't think there's a law about it.'

'Take a look through there.' He stepped back to make room as Welks bent over to peer in.

'Bloody hell!' Welks almost shrieked, 'There're hundreds of the buggers. Can we do her for hoarding cats, or what?'

'Ahem!' a lady-like voice came from behind them. 'What are you doing here? I'll call the police. I have my mobile in my hand.'

'We are the police.' Welks turned to the woman behind them, flashing his warrant card. 'Are you by any chance Mrs Craig?'

'Why? What's it all about?' the woman said defensively, stepping back from the two men.

'Are you Mrs Craig?' Hanks followed, stepping right up to her and making her flinch.

'Er... no.' she stammered. 'I'm from next door. I saw the car and thought it might be burglars, so, I sort of, came round.'

'Brave, but a wee bit foolish, Mrs…? Sorry, I didn't catch the name.'

'Forbes, Marjorie Forbes,' she answered, flustered now.

'Next time, Mrs Forbes, when you see burglars, call the police first. We could have been dangerous.' Hanks said, getting even more into her space. 'Where is she then?'

'Who?' she asked, trying to draw back from him, but hindered by the car.

'Mrs Craig!' Hanks was menacing. Welks wasn't sure the woman deserved it, but said nothing.

'Oh,' Mrs Forbes tried to get away from him by sliding along the car, 'she... she went off with the… the big guy,' she stammered. 'I think he's the gardener… or houseman, or something of the sort. She asked me to feed the cats as they're gone for a few days.'

'The Range Rover is hers, I presume? Did they take another car?' Welks asked.

'Well, yes,' she confirmed, nodding. 'They went this morning about seven-thirty. His car is a Peugeot, a blue Peugeot and it's got a big Smiley on the bonnet.'

'Number?' Hanks asked.

'No idea,' the neighbour shrugged, bewildered.

'What did she say when she left?' Hanks kept on.

'Not a lot, she just gave me the keys and asked me to check on the cats for a few days. It happens quite a lot, nothing unusual.'

'Didn't say where they were off to then?' Hanks persisted.

'Can you please let us in Mrs Forbes? Just in case anything untoward has happened,' Welks came in on the act, trying to rescue her from Hanks' aggressive interview technique.

'Untoward. What do you mean?' She looked worried now. 'What do you want to talk to her for? This is very odd.' She was getting feisty now that she was out of Hanks' reach, having succeeded in putting the car between them.

'Mrs Forbes, simply open the door please. You're not helping us, you know.'

'Don't you need a search warrant or some such to go in there?'

'You've been watching too much TV, Mrs Forbes. It isn't like that at all. Are you going to check on the cats or do we have to break the door down?' Hanks snapped impatiently. Mrs Forbes pulled the key from her apron pocket and opened the door. The house stank of cats. There were a dozen or so rubbing themselves around the detectives legs as they went through the front door into the hall. Hanks held his nose ostentatiously whilst trying not to trip over any of the animals.

'All posh outside and stinks like the local tip inside. Glad I'm not rich, Welks.'

'Your place any better?' Welks grinned.

'Much,' he stared at him hard and then countered, grinning back, 'No cats.'

'Let's see what we can find.' The dining room door was open and there were papers strewn over the table. 'Holyhead to Ireland ferries brochures; maybe that's where they've gone?' Welks pointed out the brochure to Hanks.

'Maybe that's what they want you to think, Colin. It might be a red herring. Unless, of course, it's about cat food?'

'Cat food?' Welks was startled by the comment.

'Red herring, fish, cat food.' Hanks explained laboriously, with a pained expression on his face like he was talking to a backward kid.

'Your humour…,' Welks shook his head rolling his eyes. 'Don't give up your day job.'

'Phone in to base and get them to check the ferries just in case. Can't hurt to be thorough, can it?'

They wandered through to the kitchen, seeing a pile of animal rights brochures and some photos lying on the worktop. Hanks picked up one of them. There was a cage with what appeared to be dead mice in it. The logo on the cage was Brinkley Medical. He moved the others more cautiously. This could be serious evidence. There were more pictures of animals in the labs at Brinkley's. He pulled a bag out of his pocket and swept the photos into it.

'I think we'd better put out an 'all points' for them. They seem to be involved at any rate.'

'Involved in what?' Mrs Forbes asked, patent incredulity in her voice.

'Mrs Forbes.' Hanks addressed her patiently. 'Are you going anywhere today?'

'No, but what's that got to do with it?'

'I'm going to call SoC and forensics over here to check on a number of things. This time I promise you they'll have a search warrant. I'm asking you to let them in for us. Would you be so kind?'

'This is serious isn't it?' Mrs Forbes said, shaking her head in disbelief.

'Yes ma'am, I'm afraid it is. Deadly serious,' Welks confirmed.

13

It was gone nine in the evening when Hanks finally called it a day. A warmed up microwave dinner in his flat didn't appeal, so he drove down the road to the Crown Plaza. It was brash, modern and not what was increasingly getting on Hanks's nerves about Chester, cliché 'olde'. The doorman nodded a greeting as he walked through to the bar.

'Beer, please,' Hanks asked hoisting himself onto a barstool. The barman delivered his beer, as Hanks saw the newspaper behind the bar. 'Anything on the Brinkley's raid in there?' the barman looked puzzled and placed the paper in front of Hanks.

'No, not that I know of, but feel free.'

Hanks scanned the front page and confirmed that the news had been too late to catch the Monday morning edition. He turned to page two, to check if there was anything of interest, disappointed, he laid it down and picked up his glass. It was then he noticed the woman on the next barstool. She was half turned towards him, her blond hair hanging on her shoulders.

She slid the paper towards herself, before folding it neatly. 'My sister works there,' she stated, her speech a little slurred and her accent clearly not local. He regarded her closely over the edge of his glass, registering the elegant figure and pretty face. An attractive woman, not unlike Kate, he thought as a moment's discomfort caused him to shiver. Her perfume had a heavy and musky scent and she had the bluest eyes he'd ever seen.

Expressive pools of life in a face that was just short of stunning. He was spellbound for a moment, taken back in time. He experienced the giddy feeling of 'Deja vue' before he snapped back into the present.

'Where, at the newspaper?' Hanks asked politely.

'No, the place that got broken into, Brinkley's.' Hanks nodded, 'bird watching' no longer his prime interest now. 'She's right in the middle of it. She told me about the hostage, the guy who got his hand chopped off.'

'Do you always take newspapers from strangers?'

'Not yours, is it?' she picked up her wine glass, the slim fingers twirling the stem. 'It's the hotel's.' She smiled and took a sip of her wine.

'Very observant,' Hanks commented, smiling back.

'But why chop his hand off? Maybe they want a ransom or something?'

'Really?' Hanks, amazed she'd made the connection with the fingers and a possible ransom demand, there was nothing in the media about that yet.

'My sister says that animals with a virus infection have been liberated. This could become a problem. The virus can change,' she continued, 'it could even get to the point of an epidemic, killing people, like in those horror films. It kills the mice, so obviously, it can kill humans too.'

He got the impression she was deliberately keeping the language simple, probably assuming that he, like most people, wouldn't understand the technicalities of genetic mutation in viruses. Her apparent knowledge coupled with her sensitivity impressed him. Hanks thought about his short conversation with Sarah Gunner earlier and her appointment with the Health Department tomorrow. 'By the way the viruses changing thing, it's called an antigenic shift.' He replied, to see her reaction.

'How come you know that? Not many people know what an antigenic shift is.'

'Let's just say, I read a bit here and there, with my age comes experience.' He smiled at her, his beer forgotten.

'What is that supposed to mean?' She blushed a little, 'Antigenic shift is not local paper stuff,' she countered, changing subjects.

'What you told me now wasn't in the paper either.' Hanks stared her in the eyes.

Embarrassed she looked away. 'My sister; I don't think she should have told me.'

'And I don't think you should be telling people that either, there's probably a reason it isn't in the paper. Your sister got a name?' he probed.

'Mary; she's my older sister.' She paused and indicated that the barman fill her glass again. 'I'm visiting her at the moment. Just come up from London. Needed to get out of the house though, I'm not used to the quiet family life. You're from there as well, aren't you? I can tell by your accent. Where are you from?'

'Kingston actually,' he turned away from her, uncomfortable at answering questions, but never the less intrigued.

'Well I'll be ...! We were practically neighbours,' she bubbled.

'Neighbours?' Hanks replied, giving up playing cool now, he was interested.

'I was in Chessington and Surbiton.'

'So what brought you to Chester?' He asked trying not to sound too interested.

'Well,' she paused looking at him directly, 'if you want the truth, I walked out on my husband.'

'Uh-huh.' Hanks had a feeling of elation at the news.

'He is some kind of warped guy,' she continued, 'a nutter to boot! I shouldn't have ever married him.' She fidgeted nervously with her hemline, drawing his eyes to her smooth legs. 'Not sure why I told you that.' Her voice was shaky as she gripped her glass.

'Why marry him then?' He asked ignoring her discomfort.

She stopped, 'I don't know,' waving her hand, dismissing the thought. 'Are you married?' She asked, drawing the topic from herself.

'I was.' Hanks broke eye contact.

'Divorced?' She asked softly seeing the hurt in his eyes. 'Or what?'

'Or what.' Hanks used the euphemism.

'I told you my story, so you tell yours!'

'God, you are persistent.' Hanks said irritably, 'if you must know, she died, years ago.'

'Oh. I didn't realise, I mean, I didn't …' She trailed off. Hanks pulled himself more upright, hoping she wouldn't see his eyes.

'So, you had to get married then?' He focused on her again.

'Not like that!' she mocked offence, and then giggled at his reaction.

'So?' he smiled, softening the question.

'Hmm, complicated,' she paused looking for a way to tell the story. 'I was financially up against the ropes; I was made an offer I couldn't refuse.'

'You don't appear buyable.'

'I'm not, not in that way.' She replied thoughtfully at the comment.

'So why then?' Hanks persisted.

'You don't give up do you?'

'Character defect,' Hanks said, without smiling, 'same as you.' Which caused her to smile her cheeks dimpling alluringly as she did so.

'I was down, I mean really down, and this man, 'Brown Suit' told me that he had a son with an asylum problem,' she continued with a lower voice, almost whispering, 'and he offered me a hundred K for marrying him, but I couldn't stand it. He was horrible, uncouth and constantly babbled on about paradise and his 72 virgins. I shouldn't be talking like that, should I?'

'Was he a Muslim then?'

'Sure, so was 'Brown suit', they both were.'

'Brown suit'? Funny name, how did he get that name?' Hanks was intrigued and saddened, that he would have to report this at some stage.

'Never saw him in anything else, just the cheap, dirty brown suit.'

'What happened to him? The husband I mean.' Alarm bells rang in his head as he made a connection, right or wrong, between illegal Muslim immigrant and missing terrorist, even if it was the wrong end of the country.

She was puzzled at the question, 'No idea, we had a blazing row and I left him. God, I need to sober up, my sister will give me hell if I come home this drunk.'

'So you came back to Chester?' Hanks tapped on the bar, she nodded.

'Yes, I was brought up here. My parents' house is in Bouverie Street. My sister lives there now.

'The one that works at this Brinkley's?'

'Yes, I left after school and went down London to Uni.' the university bit did not surprise him. 'I'm staying at her place until I find something. I only hope that the bastard doesn't find me here. I bet he'll want his money back.'

'Mmmm,' Hanks scratched his chin, 'do you think he's followed you to Chester?'

'I only walked out yesterday. He hasn't a clue where I've gone. Anyway, it's not him, it's 'Brown Suit'. He's the evil one.' Hanks was at loss how to continue the conversation without it sounding like an interrogation. 'Anyhow, I left him, and came here' she repeated, unaware of his problem or that she'd already told him that. 'So here I am, looking for a new start. Don't suppose you know anyone hiring?'

Hanks was taken aback again. Flustered, he replied, 'No, I don't know of any jobs going at the moment, sorry. What was your husband's name?'

'Ahmed, with a stupid surname, M'Beki. How can anyone be called M'Beki? You're a good listener, by the way.' She stared at him ambiguously, before reaching for the newspaper, she borrowed a pen from the barman, turned the paper over and began to rapidly fill the difficult Sudoku puzzle on the back page. Hanks could only sit there quietly amazed by both her skill and her beauty. He was captivated by the signals this woman was sending him. He observed her more closely, wondering if she knew how attractive she was. He was fascinated by her sultry voice as well, so like Kate's. He tried to put an age on her and failed.

As she finished, she smiled at him again and said, 'I like these,' putting the paper down, and giving the pen back to the barman. 'I can't resist them. You know,' she reflected, 'I appreciate you lending me your ear. You are easy to talk to and I needed to talk. I am feeling much better now, thanks.'

'No problem, the pleasure is mine.' he answered, feeling

somewhat guilty not having warned her about his occupation. 'Well,' he said, 'I'll have to be off now. Nice meeting you...my name is Alan. ' he said holding out his hand.

'Claire.'

'Well, Claire, nice to meet you. Good luck with the job hunting. Maybe we'll meet again.' He put the money for his beer on the bar. 'Can I get you another drink before I go?'

'No, thanks, I think I've had more than enough.' She looked directly into his eyes and smiled again. Had she held onto his hand just that fraction longer than necessary, or was that wishful thinking on his part?

'No bother.' he said, as she finally let his hand go. There was something disarming and deeply attractive about the woman. He felt younger than he had in years and was disappointed that he had had to leave. I'm probably way past it, he sighed.

Outside he pulled out his mobile to phone in to get the man M'Beki checked out, but noting the low battery symbol was flashing yet again, he decided to leave it until morning.

14

Hassan's journey to London had been memorable only for the tediousness of it. His flights across the planet seemed to have lasted an eternity, finally getting him to Heathrow. Only on this last leg from France did he use his real passport. Immigration at Heathrow were masters at spotting fake passports and he couldn't risk being caught on something that silly. He had an address in Kensington, a small place with minimal comforts, but better than anything Achar had to offer. He arrived late morning, exhausted and at the same time elated to have got through all the airports unscathed. He unpacked what little luggage he had brought with him and set up the laptop on the bed in the small room. He checked his mails and then turned to check the way to the coffee shop for his journey the next day. Masoud was good; he'd have to wait for a contact from him, any day after 4 pm was the arrangement. He didn't know how long he'd have to wait.

Hassan had waited impatiently from half past three until the coffee shop closed for Masoud to show up. He was sick of reading the old editions of Pakistani newspapers that people had left in the café, a lot of minutiae about chickens, farming and irrigation, none of which was of use in central London.

Kahn's was empty when he arrived the following day, the proprietor, who was mindlessly polishing a glass behind a primitive counter showed no visible sign of recognition.

'You want?' the man asked him gruffly.

'Chai, sweet please,' Hassan saw the time on the clock over the counter, 3:15, he had a wait in front of him. He sat at a grubby table and listlessly studied a magazine as the tea was served.

'You are from far away?' the man, whom Hassan assumed to be Kahn himself, asked. This was the first bit of conversation he had proffered.

'You could say that, my friend. I bring greetings from father for a friend.'

'Ah, I see,' he said knowingly. 'You are welcome; I will bring you some sweets.'

Before Hassan could protest the man had gone, vanishing into the back of the shop. He checked the time again, nervous now because of the disappearance of the proprietor. The front door opened and a young boy of maybe ten or eleven came in. He was wearing a grubby kaftan and an ill-fitting Pashtu. Hassan dragged his attention away from the rear doorway and observed the boy, who sidled up to the counter with his back to the wall, never taking his eyes off Hassan.

'Mr Kahn!' the boy's voice strident in the quietness, 'Mr Kahn?'

'Yes Zia.' The proprietor's voice came from the back of the shop. 'What is it?' Kahn reappeared with a small bowl of sugared maize balls and dropped two of them into the boy's hands.

'Mr Kahn, I have this for you. The man said it was important,' as he held a scrap of newspaper up towards him.

'I see,' Kahn said, accepting the snippet.

'It's for the man from father,' the boy blurted out.

Kahn looked at his other visitor. Hassan was fully alert now. Kahn studied the piece of paper, turning it over and scratching his chin. He then cuffed the boy playfully round the ear.

'What! You still here?' The stunned boy froze and was about to say something, when Kahn's expression stopped him. 'Be off now, go on, get home.' Kahn patted him on the rump as he fled.

'This is for you I think.' Kahn approached Hassan's table slowly, laying the paper and the maize balls in front of Hassan and returned to polishing glasses behind the counter. Hassan stared at the paper ripped from the classifieds in the Evening Standard. An advert was roughly circled in red ink with the words 'public phone' in Urdu scribbled above. The text read: 'FAMILY REUNIONS AND PARTIES CATERED FOR. Ring for details,' and there was a telephone number below. Hassan sat back and sipped his scalding hot tea, savouring the taste on his tongue.

'How much?' he asked Kahn, who waved him away with a negative gesture.

'Is there a phone booth nearby?' Hassan asked.

'Outside, a hundred yards or so on the left.' Hassan stood and stuffed a maize ball in his mouth.

'Excellent.' he managed to say around his mouthful as he left.

The telephone booth was free, not surprisingly, as it stank of stale cigarette smoke, urine and vomit. Hassan shoved fifty pence in and dialled the number.

'Yes?' His call was answered immediately.

'A message from father,' he managed, taken aback at the speed with which the call had been picked up.

'Hold.' The voice ordered before line went dead, leaving Hassan fretting in the squalor of the telephone booth.

'Yes.' a new voice said.

'A message from father.' Hassan repeated.

'Yes!' the voice said. 'I can see you, stay where you are and wait!' With that, the line went dead. Hassan panicked looking around for signs that he was being watched. Seconds later, an old white Vauxhall pulled up beside him. The now familiar voice called out of the open window. 'You from father?' Hassan nodded. 'Get in!'

The door was hardly shut before the driver sped off into the traffic, ignoring the priority of other motorists, and throwing Hassan back roughly into his seat.

'So, what do you have, my friend?' The driver smiled a cruel, mirthless smile as Hassan settled himself and belted up.

'Masoud?' He studied the man, dressed in a brown suit and a shirt that needed a wash, his left hand sporting a big gold ring. Nice, Hassan thought eying it appreciatively, must have cost a bit.

'Yes,' the man nodded curtly.

'Qamar sent me,' Hassan added superfluously.

'I know.' The car screeched around a corner into a side street where Masoud stopped savagely, ripping up the hand brake and turning off the engine. Hassan saved himself from injury by bracing his hands against the dashboard.

'What have you got for me?' Masoud repeated his question. It was an hour later by the time Hassan had explained Qamar's idea and passed on all the ether information. 'We must work together on this. Qamar says you have people in place and that you know who to talk to,' Hassan finally added.

Masoud was deep in thought. 'A superb idea,' he mumbled, more to himself than Hassan. 'By all that is holy, it is genius.' He smacked his thigh emphatically with his palm. 'I like it!' he shouted, almost joyously. Hassan was nervous, apprehensive in the man's presence, having heard about the violent temperament and the outbursts of rage.

'I have sequence phone numbers for you, so we can communicate.' Hassan said passing him a bundle of SIM cards with the matrix he had prepared.

'Good. I will call you when I have something.' Masoud was deep in thought again. 'There is someone I must see, we will get what we want from him.' Masoud started the car. 'You go now. I will ring you.'

Hassan jumped out onto the pavement and closed the door. Shivering in the cold air, he stood looking after the car which drove off in a swirl of exhaust fumes.

15

The week had started off tough, his official request for the Super to take the issue to governmental level had still not been dealt with, and to cap it all, Michaels had stopped the PAYE operation under the guise of it not being 'cost effective.' Of the 82 addresses Hanks wanted visited only 16 had so far been done. If Monday had been bad, Tuesday had been worse; a series of irritations, bad judgement and technical glitches that had driven him to the verge of insanity. The highlight of the meeting on Monday evening with the blonde woman in the bar was now only a distant, but happy memory. Hanks sat behind his desk horrified at the amount of paperwork sitting in front of him.

His sidekick Welks was out at Brinkley's, still wrapping up the last of the staff interviews. The repercussions of the break-in were still causing Hanks to have visions of horror. He buzzed through to the outside office to ask if the Superintendent had responded to his request for a 'national call' on the issue, to be told there was nothing yet. Angrily he put the phone down, unable to fathom why Michaels was delaying. To get his mind off Michaels, he decided to concentrate on the kidnapped victim. He called Whittaker in to get the report on the house search of Akar, which was one of the 16 addresses visited.

The big Barbadian ducked under the door frame as he came in. 'Sir?'

'You did the Akar place yesterday?'

'Yes sir, Carlton and I went over it.'

'Anything of any note there?'

Whittaker sifted through the reports on Hank's desk, pulling out a single sheet. Hanks studied the list of the items found and traced the list down with his finger. 'Nothing significant here.'

'No, sir, other than a bunch of virus books there was not much there.'

Hanks's phone rang interrupting them, 'Okay Stan, thanks, I'll catch you later.' He said picking up. 'Yes sir, we are working on all possible leads.... No sir, I don't think a press conference or a press release would be helpful at this juncture. Of course, I'll keep you informed. Sir, did you get my memo? Are we going national on this now?' The line was dead leaving Hanks shaking his head in disbelief at the man. 'Idiot!' he muttered under his breath, 'he still thinks he's earning brownie points at some training course,' putting down the dead receiver, wondering what else it would take to make Michaels react. 'Idiot,' he muttered again to himself.

What to do next was the question. He entered his password on his PC to call up the case files when the screen locked as it tried to load the page. Frustrated he waited as the little egg timer spun.

'Anyone got a problem with the main databank,' he shouted through the door.

'Downtime,' a voice came back from the outer office, 'routine maintenance apparently.'

Hanks got up and walked to the door, leaning on the frame looking out. Carlton was furtively filling his overtime sheet trying to appear busy filing reports. The other desks apart from Harris's were empty, they were all out. 'Never heard the expression then,' Hanks said in frustration, 'if it ain't broke, don't fix it.' Carlton's head bobbed up, Harris shrugged his shoulders.

Despondently, Hanks walked to the coffee machine eying the reports Carlton was filing. 'Have we got anything back from the Holyhead Ferry or from forensics from Craig's house? Are there any clues there?'

'There's a report of a blue Peugeot on the ferry at 10:00 pm on Sunday. The licence checks out to a Mike Thompson. He's the gardener.

'They're probably in Ireland then, better get the Garda to keep a look-out for them, and forensics?'

'Not much, apart from cat's hairs, and a micro SD card with the originals of the pictures you picked up at the house. The pictures were taken on a mobile phone.'

'Been busy guys?' Welks's over happy voice jarred in the atmosphere in the room.

'You being sarcastic?' Hanks grunted, 'Anything of value?'

'Nah, nada, still have to see the missing lab girl,' he checked his notes, 'Phelps, the woman has not been in since Friday, tummy trouble according to Brinkley's.'

'Get her visited; I don't want a loose end. Did fingerprints get anything from the security discs?'

'No, only the security man, Ms Grigson and Voss.'

'I've been trying to get a background check, but our system is down, bloody great time for maintenance, another of Michaels' brainwaves.'

'You making any headway?' Welks asked ignoring the snipe at Michaels.

'Spent the whole day yesterday chasing shadows on the ARF front, still no sign of the hostage. Went to see the Brinkley's guard in Chester General. He's not going to be any use to us for any time in the near future.'

'He's bad then?'

'Seen fitter beef-burgers,' Hanks chuckled blackly, 'would be a damned miracle if he makes it. Apart from the Craig woman and the guy she's done a runner with, we don't have any other local ARF names. Checking the others, they are all miles away in other parts of the country; it is taking a hell of a time. I'm just getting negative feedback for all the visits that have been made so far. Listen, when you get the server available again, I have a name for you to have a go with, see what you can find out on an Ahmed M'Beki, write this down,' and he spelled it for him. 'Try border control, HMRC and Immigration for starters. He most probably is an illegal. If that doesn't switch on any lights try Surrey, as he was last known to be in Chessington.'

'Christ Alan, you think I have nothing to do?' Welks complained. 'Anything concrete?' Hanks smiled at the grumbles.

'No, a hunch, it's maybe nothing. Seen the Chronicle today?'

'An Ebola outbreak wouldn't have made as big a splash.'

'Sure, let's get back to work, any news from Gunner yet?'

Welks shook his head, 'No.'

With that the door opened and Sarah Gunner stood in the doorway. 'Talk of the devil.' Hanks smiled.

'Sir?' Her confusion showing, 'I know it's late, but here are the details of the van stolen from Threshers.'

'Taken from Christleton?' Hanks said as he studied the form she presented him with. The van was a Ford Tourneo, white.

Taken aback Gunner stammered, 'Yes, how did you know that?' Hanks didn't need to tell her it was the off licence he used coming into Chester from the motorway, and the only Thresher's branch within 40 miles of Brinkley's.

'Crystal ball,' Hanks joked grimly as the connection made click in his mind. 'This must be the one outside Brinkley's on Sunday night; remember I told you about the CCTV Colin?'

Welks nodded, 'We would have been a damn sight surer, if we'd had the licence plate.'

'Bloody obvious.' Hanks growled. 'Sarah, put everything we have out there on finding that van. Maybe put out a local radio call; let's get the public involved on this one.'

'Certainly sir,' as the phone started to ring in Hanks's office stopping the talk. Hanks rushed over and grabbed it. 'Hanks.' He managed breathlessly. Gunner backed out, unsure of what was happening in the minds of the two senior detectives.

'Sir, it's Thornton.'

'Yes,' he snapped, recognising him as one of the lab guys with the fingers on Monday.

'The DNA and fingerprints are back on the kidnapped employee. Did you have a sixth sense when you had a go at us?'

'Why, what's happened?'

'Well, you said you wanted to know who he was, and not who we thought he was.'

'No, that's my usual bullshit, just to get you wound up.'

'Well, it worked, jackpot so to speak. He isn't who everyone thought he was. He's not Khalid Akar, in any case.' There was a stunned silence at Hanks's end.

'Say again!' Hanks shouted now, 'He isn't Khalid Akar?'

Welks heard him, and let it sink in for a second, shocked.

'Hello sir? You still there?' Hanks grunted, 'Now you want the good bit, sir?'

'It gets better?'

'Our hostage is none other than Jemail Kasab,' he sounded well pleased with himself. 'I got the fingerprints checked on the national databank, 100% positive.'

'Damn!' Hanks said so loudly, that even things in the outer office stopped, there was silence.

'He's the brother of the sole surviving attacker at the Taj Mahal Hotel massacre in Mumbai. The one that's in the papers right now; due for hanging; a full blown terrorist! I googled that,' Thornton said proudly. 'Our system was down.'

Hanks almost dropped his phone. Unable to say, that he knew the man's history. This was the man 'Operation Fellowship' had lost. The very one he was supposed to find. He felt the hairs on his arms standing on end.

'Thornton, thanks, that's great work.' He put the phone down and turned to Welks, 'It's our man, we have found him. I have to get upstairs to the Super, now!' Hanks was perspiring, 'I'll be back soon.' He took off for the lift; the gazes of his officers followed his progress. Ten minutes later he was back, steaming mad and in vile temper.

'Good meeting then?' Welks jested, trying to lift his mood.

'Bastard wouldn't see me, too bloody busy, his secretary told me to send him a note.' Hanks was calming slowly, 'I'll go over his head. This is a major disaster now.' He sank into his chair and typed an email to the Superintendent with a copy to the Chief Constable. 'So, what do we make of a known terrorist working in a virus lab?' Hanks posed. 'Especially one with a false identity and seemingly with his hand in the till, so to speak? It ties in with the forensic evidence showing the imprint of the fridge door seal on the severed fingers.'

'Stinks in my book, especially with the phone intercept from the Yard about collecting in Chester at the month end.' Welks added 'Well, at least that's one delivery that won't happen.'

Hanks said, 'Now that we've identified him, we only have to find him.'

'So, do I get the easy job then?' Welks joked.

16

Rahmani was greeted by the smell of cooking as he dumped his briefcase in the hallway and called out to his wife that he was home.

'I'm in the kitchen.' She called back to him as his daughter rushed out and threw her arms around him.

'Daddy, daddy your home early!' She said excitedly.

'Yes sweetie, I finished early today. So what has my little one been up to?'

'I've been chosen for one of the lead roles in the school ballet!'

'That's fantastic news darling, I'm proud of you!'

'And daddy, I need to interview you. I have to write a report for school on what my parents do.'

'Sure, bring your pad and pencil and we'll talk in my office, while mum is getting the dinner ready.' She dashed off to get her stuff as he climbed the stairs; and arrived back as he opened his office door.

''Wow, that was quick,' he smiled patting her dark hair, so, what questions have you got for me?'

Dalila referred to her notes. 'Where do you work?'

'Hatfield University.'

'What's your responsibility?

'Head of civil engineering.' She paused while she earnestly wrote down the information.

'What do you like most about your job?'

'Well, the best thing for me is tunnels, at least the most interesting.'

'Tunnels? Why tunnels, daddy?' She asked surprised.

'It's kind of complicated. Not many people give much thought to tunnels, they are just there; that they function is taken completely for granted. I am a specialist in Computational Fluid Dynamics (CFD); people come to me for advice from all round the world.'

Dalila looked confused, 'What do they want to know, daddy?'

'For example, I am working on a project for the London Underground at the moment. They have a problem with the heat in the train tunnels; do you know how warm it gets there?' She nodded, remembering the times they had been in London on the tube, and how uncomfortably warm it had sometimes been. The call to dinner from downstairs interrupted them. 'Come on petal, we have to eat now or you'll be late for your piano lesson.' He half dragged his protesting daughter down to dinner.

After the meal, Rahmani went back into his office and heard the door shut behind his wife and daughter as they left for the piano lesson. He poured himself a glass of tea when the phone rang. Unfamiliar with the caller's number on the display, he answered cautiously. 'Yes?' He nearly spilled his tea in surprise when he recognised the voice. 'Masoud, brother!' he hastily deposited the cup on his desk, stood up and walked nervously to the window, checking outside. 'To what do I owe this honour?' he asked regaining a little composure, seeing nothing out of the ordinary outside. He hadn't seen Masoud since first coming to England, when Masoud had been the 'helping hand' enabling him to get the right papers and the right introductions; fully aware that he'd signed a deal with the devil in so doing. They'd met initially in the mosque in Luton, where he had come to stay with some acquaintances after fleeing Egypt, because of his political views, not to mention a loose involvement with the assassination of Anwar Sadat. All that had been carefully brushed under the carpet with the loss of his old identity. The name he was born with was gone forever.

Masoud ignored his question, 'Still of the faith Hamid, my

friend?' deliberately using the man's original name.

'Of course, Masoud. What can I do for you?' Rahmani felt an icy chill down his back.

'I will be with you in ten minutes. Tell no one.' The line went dead.

Almost to the minute he opened the door for Masoud and took him upstairs to his study.

Masoud picked up the worn copy of the Koran on Rahmani's desk, glanced at it before replacing it again.

'Would you like tea?' Rahmani asked nervously, 'please be seated.' He removed his daughter's notepad from the chair opposite his desk so his visitor could sit.

'Tea is good. Can we talk here undisturbed?'

'Yes, my wife and daughter are out visiting.'

'I know.' Masoud answered coldly.

'Oh!' Rahmani's heart missed a beat.

'I meant, are you expecting anyone?'

'No, I was planning to do some modelling work, but that can wait. You, my honoured guest, have priority over everything.' Rahmani was sweating now.

'Your daughter is very pretty,' Masoud said slowly, 'she goes to Hatton School, doesn't she?' Rahmani blanched, 'she came home at lunchtime today.' Rahmani attempted to protest. 'Don't interrupt me!' Masoud ordered. 'She had lunch with your wife and changed from her school uniform into her tracksuit and then went to her dancing class.' Rahmani was white with fear.

'And now,' Masoud checked his watch; 'your wife and daughter are at 113 Railton Road at Mrs Shah's for piano lessons.' Rahmani was speechless. 'Mrs Shah does not take just any student, your daughter must be quite talented.' Masoud's cruel eyes bored into him. 'Do you remember my assistance when you arrived here?'

'Most certainly, I most certainly will never forget your kindness.' Rahmani was close to panic, but brought a second cup of tea to the desk, his hand shaking as he placed it down.

'I need your help, precisely in the area of ventilation and cooling of tunnels.'

'You are remarkably informed,' Rahmani was surprised his guest knew what he was doing and more to the point the movements of his family.

'I want you to do some important work for me. It concerns the London Underground. You must not mention our conversation to anyone. We have never even met, do you understand?' Masoud said, menace oozing from him.

'I understand,' Rahmani said resignedly, as the horror of his situation hit him. 'What do you need?'

'Your computer modelling, I want to know more about it.'

'Of course, the programme I have developed is used for the study of air currents and thermal currents in complex tunnel systems. Computational fluid dynamics enables the analysis of fluids and gasses in a 3-D domain, including heat transfer, mass transfer and chemical reaction.'

Masoud nodded, pushing his empty teacup towards Rahmani for a refill.

'So, you can predict how a layer of cold air interacts with hot air or gas in a tunnel system. How it spreads and how it travels. Is that so?'

'It is an over-simplification, but yes, in a nutshell, that's it.'

'My friend was right, you are the right man. A question, if we replaced hot air with a hot gas, would your computer model do this too?' Masoud said, as his excitement mounted.

'I'd need to know the density of the gas and the temperature, but in essence, yes, of course. What gas are we talking about?'

'Ether. I want you to find me the busiest underground station with the most traffic and do a simulation on how much ether we'd have to put in to do the most damage.'

'Oh my God, that will kill hundreds at least.' Rahmani was sweating more profusely now. 'I can't do this, my conscience won't let me.'

'Do you think that your family is being followed for protection? How naive can you get?' Masoud sneered.

'You wouldn't...,' the lecturer stammered.

'I will not hesitate. The information I need from you will be accurate and correct to cause the maximum damage and casualties. I promise you, if you don't come up with the goods, you will watch your family die.' Masoud paused to let the threat had sink in, 'So, I have all the information about the ether on this SD card.' He reached into his pocket and slid it over the table, studying the lecturer closely.

Rahmani pushed the card in the reader slot of his laptop and studied the details Shadeed had provided.

'Well,' he paused, 'you want me to combine the airflow in the tunnels with the information on your SD card. This will take time; Masoud.'

'You make the time. I give you three days. You know what's at stake?' Masoud said aggressively. 'When you are done, save it on the SD card and send it to this address.' He laid an addressed envelope on the table.

'I will do my best.' Rahmani said trembling.

Masoud stood to leave. 'You would do well to perform the role Allah has sought for you,...' He didn't repeat the threat, seeing that Rahmani had understood the message.

'I will get the information to you in three days.' Terror made his voice waver.

'Good. I need to make a phone call. Do you mind?' It took a while for Rahmani to twig that he was being asked to leave the room.

'Yes, of course. I'll wait outside.' He closed the door behind him.

Deliberating between using the secure SIM card method or the phone on Rahmani's desk, he decided that Rahmani's phone was probably not on anybody's radar and would be safe. So, Masoud used the man's house phone, after a short interval, the call was answered. 'This is Masoud, the plan is in full progress, do you want to press on? ... Of course ... The date? Not critical. We'll think of something.' He disconnected and put the phone back. 'Hamid, you may join me again,' he called and Rahmani came back into his study, alert, and the fear evident on his face.

Masoud stood to leave. 'You provide me with the information as discussed.' With that he turned and left, leaving Rahmani gawping after him.

As the door shut on Masoud, Rahmani muttered 'Inshallah!' resignedly and went back to his computer, adrenalin coursing through his veins as he began his task. The envelope addressed to Mr John Smith C/O Kahn's Coffee Shop, The Broadway Southall, stared up at him from his desk.

17

'Sir, we have a report of a sighting of the lab animals from the Brinkley's break-in.' the telephone operator at the main police station on Nuns Road called over her shoulder to the duty sergeant whilst holding the mouthpiece closed.

'You sure?' he said putting his pen down and walking over to her. 'Who is it?'

'The head of the kindergarten in Blacon, a Mrs Willis.'

'Check. Make sure.'

'How can you be sure these are the lab animals Mrs Willis?' she asked. He stood next to her attentively, indicating she should put on the call speaker.

'...we've seen quite a few over the last few days and they all have these yellow ear tags with numbers, so I reckon they're the ones I read about in the Chronicle. We saw several inside when we opened up this morning. The kids are terrified. We managed to get four locked in a classroom; I don't think they can get out.'

The sergeant nodded. 'All right Mrs Willis, you've done very well. We'll get some handlers down to you as fast as we can.' she said, 'Keep the classroom doors and windows shut please, and don't touch the animals. Thank you for calling this in.'

The duty sergeant was agitated. 'We better take this upstairs immediately. Lab ferrets in a kindergarten could be a disaster.' He picked up the phone and dialled.

'DI Welks.' The call was answered right away.

'DCI Hanks, please.'

'I'll take it. He's not here yet.'

'Oh, right, Duty Sergeant Vickers here. We've just had a shout from a kindergarten in Blacon. They've locked some of the lab ferrets in a classroom.'

'Okay, we will take care of it from here. Thank you Sergeant.'

A haggard looking Hanks walked into the office as Welks ended the call.

'News?'

'Bad night?' Welks asked, 'they have trapped some of the escaped laboratory test animals from Brinkley's in a classroom at the Rainbow Kindergarten in Blacon, apparently, they've been seeing animals for the last couple of days there, but these are the first they've managed to trap.' Welks related what had happened.

'We'll have to make sure that the emergency crews don't make physical contact with anyone at the kindergarten until we know what we're dealing with.' Hanks thought aloud, with the worst case scenario of an epidemic in the back of his mind. 'Call Mr Voss at Brinkley's and let me know what he says we should do, and get it documented as well. We mustn't disappoint the paper pushers, must we? By the way, we had a shout that there was a blue Peugeot on the Holyhead ferry, which arrived on Monday morning in Cork. The driver/owner is a Mike Thompson. I need to get border control alerted, because they will have to come back some time.'

Welks just nodded in acknowledgement, 'Get me Brinkley's please,' he said to the telephonist. She dialled for him.

'Voss, Brinkley's Medical.' The voice was a little distorted.

'Welks here from Chester police, Mr. Voss. We've had a call from the Rainbow Kindergarten in Blacon. They appear to have trapped some of your ferrets in a classroom. Tell me what we have to do to contain the virus.' He listened for a bit, making notes as he did so. 'Can you get someone round there immediately and reclaim them?' Hanks gestured Welks to put him on speaker.

'Certainly we can. Will send my team out now. In order to be on the safe side we should quarantine the kids and staff. Get some strong UV lamps set up around the perimeter. That'll stop any transfer over the boundary. If the emergency services personnel wear facemasks and allow themselves to be bathed in UV light, they should be all right. It's important to avoid sneezes and coughs. The disease infects in the aerosol phase. Put a cordon round the whole place and put the staff and kiddies under observation; please arrange for me to talk to the Public Health Officer at the Town Hall, just to be extra safe.' Voss paused for a long moment.

Welks was concerned that the call had dropped because of the long silence, 'Mr Voss?'

'Yes, sorry, I was lost in thought. Mr. Welks, please also get the emergency services people to take a throat swab sample from everybody in the kindergarten.' He stopped for a few seconds and then continued, 'No, don't worry about it. I'll get one of my staff to do the necessary.'

Welks called the incident centre next. 'Get a fast response unit out to the Rainbow Kindergarten at Blacon, as well as the car, will you? Maybe six men and an incident van as well. We've got to put a lid on this fast.' That done, he wrote up his notes on the file, emailing Hanks as to what had been done. If paperwork was what Hanks wanted for the Superintendent, then he'd get it.

At Brinkley's

Voss rang down to the labs and told Mary and Nick to drop everything, go to the school to pick up the animals and do the sampling. 'Full Bio suits,' he reminded them, 'you cannot be too careful.' He was apprehensive about what the results would turn out to be. He needed to maintain an outward calm, even though he suspected the additional data they'd get as a result of this disaster would be pure gold.

The rest of the morning, he spent sifting the claim forms and trying to get hold of the hospital to get some update on the guard. The man's wife had been in earlier; she had been very distraught, no surprise there. It was such a shame. Jemma had phoned to say she wouldn't be back until the following week, increasing his worries that they wouldn't be able to cope with the new increased workload. He signed the final forms and put them in the envelope for the insurance company. His appointment with them was at three o'clock. He decided to go and see what was happening at the kindergarten until then. Grabbing his jacket, he drove over there, arriving just as Mary and Nick were packing up the samples.

'Anything out of the ordinary, Nick?' Nick, looking like a spaceman in his bulky suit, removed his mask.

'Not up to now, boss. We've got four ferrets in a cage in the back of the van.'

'They're group two,' Mary added excitedly, pulling off her suit. 'You remember? The survivors.'

Voss nodded. He hadn't expected anything else. The group one animals wouldn't have lasted that long.

'Wrap it up here. Let's get testing. Will be interesting to find out what kind of cocktail we will find in them. Nick, get going on a vaccine solution to anything you find in these beasts. We don't want to be surprised if this gets into the wild.' He patted the shoulder of Nick's 'spacesuit' and added, 'See you back at the lab.' Voss then went off to thank Mrs Willis for her help in recovering the animals and to give her a few reassuring words, even if he wasn't sure if he was right in what he was saying. His apologies for the quarantining were met with astonishment.

'No-one told us that,' she stammered as one of the police officers came over to break the news that they'd all have to stay in the kindergarten until further notice and that they would be under observation, just as a precaution. She was told that the parents could come in, but if they did, they mustn't leave.

'We'll need to see about beds and bedding then,' she said, beginning to recover from her shock. As she departed to plan what needed to be done, technicians were setting up big banks of floodlights.

Two hours later Mary brought the insurance agent to his office. Their meeting was pretty straightforward in spite of his doubts. The assessor explained that the company was going to have their lawyers check the epidemic aspects of any claim as well. Voss thought that it was funny how you could sometimes decide what a person's job was simply by the way they dressed.

This man was an insurance assessor down to his polished brown brogue shoes. His card lay on Voss's desk, his name,

Jason Salameh. Voss asked him about the name as he certainly didn't seem 'foreign'. Mr Salameh wasn't taken aback by the question, he'd obviously been asked it hundreds of times. The insurance man explained that his father was a Palestinian who had moved to the UK and married an English girl. That was all.

During the meeting they'd walked downstairs to inspect the damage on site. Mary and Nick took over the guided tour.

Salameh had promised to call back the next week to sort out any final details and see if any other insured damage had become apparent in the meantime.

'So, how's it going, team?' Voss said pushing the lab door open after Salameh had gone.

'Poor man,' Mary said, 'I think he was getting a terrible cold. Anyway, I told him that we've accounted for nearly seventy per cent of the released animals now, this is with those still in the lab when we got here after the break-in and those that we have found dead in the grounds.' She added.

'It seems odd that we haven't found any of the rabbits,' Nick said, as he took mucus samples from the four kindergarten ferrets.

'How are the patients doing?' Voss asked.

'Hungry,' Mary grinned, tossing some sprats into the cage, which were immediately devoured.

'Okay, what about the swabs? How many did you manage to get?'

'You are a sly one, Mr Voss.' Mary looked him directly in the eye. 'If I didn't know you better, I'd say you were interested in some free human testing here.' She winked at him playfully to show there was no malice.

Voss was initially taken off balance, thinking how she had made that connection. 'What, me Mary?' he answered, with an exaggerated wide-eyed expression. 'It could cost me my license.' he winked conspiratorially at her.

'Right, I understand.' Mary picked up the wooden box containing all the swab samples. 'It's going to take some time to test all these.'

'The work is getting over our heads.' Voss said, scratching his head. 'Mary, is your sister still interested in a job? I read through her CV and it seems that she has got enough laboratory experience and she studied genetics. Please ask her to come and see me.'

'Thanks, Mr Voss. I'll ask her. We could definitely use some help.'

Voss went back up to his office, playing through possible solutions of speedily creating a vaccine if this thing did get out. It was time to phone London he thought, as he slumped into his office chair and grabbed the phone.

'Barry! Good to get you so quickly, I wanted to update you on the break-in situation.'

'Let's have it, Andy.'

'We have recovered four ferrets from a kindergarten up the road from here. The animals are infected with the H5N6a virus. We've got them under observation back in the lab. No news about Mr Akar though, and the guard is still in a coma in Chester General.'

'The nutters haven't a clue what dangers they may have let out on the public. You still haven't got any better assessment of the possibilities we could be facing on that front?'

'No, the whole thing is a Pandora's Box. The situation is so unpredictable; it's all unfounded conjecture at the moment. The insurance people seem easy on the issue though. The assessor was here today and the material damage will be paid for, no problems there, though we still have to sort out the personal injury and loss of profits bit.'

'What is the situation with the kindergarten?'

'That's under control. On my advice, authorities are quarantining the kindergarten. We don't want to take chances.'

'Good idea, though I don't like all the publicity this is going to bring down on us. I don't want a bill for all this.' Randall always got agitated when it came to profits in jeopardy.

'It's good news though, that all the derivatives of H5N6a have proved unviable so far and won't transmit, so it could hopefully be a dead end as far as onward transmission goes.' Voss tried to add a high note.

'Let's pray. Anything else?'

'Just one thing, we took swab tests of all the kiddies and most of their parents in the kindergarten to do tests on, in case they were exposed to the ferrets.'

'What are you going to do with them?'

'We will test all the swabs for viral infections and see if there's been any transmission. More urgently, we need to check if there has been any significant change in the virus's physiognomy. We have to be very alert for any antigenic shift that may affect the virus's infectious capabilities.'

'That is phenomenal news, Andy. How long before we get any results?'

'Well, if we put everything into it we could be talking about a couple of days. Then we'll see a picture.' Voss said.

'Pull out all the stops.' Randell ordered. 'Check if any other work is being done anywhere as well. We don't want to walk into any patent fights, they can be expensive.'

'Sure, we are all hard at it.'

18

Voss arrived in his office early on Friday. The kindergarten issue yesterday and the uncertainty about the insurance cover were nagging him as he sat behind his desk, still too engrossed in his thoughts even to turn his computer on. The phone on his desk rang; from the tone it was obvious that it was an internal call. The security guard announced there was a Ms Grigson to see him. Glancing at the wall clock, he saw it wasn't even 7:30 yet. He asked to get someone from packing to guide her to his office. Minutes later, there was a discrete knock at the door. He stood up and went to answer it.

'Oh!' Voss stepped back, surprised by the woman before him. 'Hello, you must be Mary's sister. You look very much like her. Andy Voss,' he introduced himself. He appraised her again. She bore a striking resemblance to her sister, but was taller than Mary and slimmer. Her shoulder-length hair was longer in contrast to her sister's. 'Come in, come in.'

Claire walked into the office and glanced around nervously.

'Yes, I'm Claire. Mary said you wanted to talk to me about a job?' She observed the man opposite, remembering what her sister had said about him. The slim active man did have a certain something about him, she had to concede that. His office was neat, unfussy, nothing out of place. Definitely not a 'mad scientist', but a disciplined man, she thought. The only personal touch in the office was a small framed picture on the shelf behind the desk. Peer as she might, she couldn't quite make it out.

'Can I get you something?' Voss asked which gave her the opportunity to lean forward and see the picture as she accepted a glass of water from him. The picture was of a small hut, the foreground full of pigs.

'Hah, the picture.' Voss smiled. 'The pig-farm, that was here in the beginning. I took that the first day I came here, difficult to believe what we have here now, isn't it?'

Instead of the expected, insipid comment along the lines of 'oh that's nice,' Claire asked if she could take a closer look, he nodded assent.

'Interesting,' she commented, 'they're saddlebacks, aren't they? I didn't realise they were bred outside Schleswig Holstein.' Voss was amazed.

'You know pigs then?'

'Let's say I know this one, by chance mind you. It was a DNA thing back for when I worked in forensics. The murder of a pig farmer, I got to test the DNA of umpteen different pig breeds for comparison purposes to identify the killer of a German farmer at an agricultural show. The Saddleback was one of the pretty ones, that's why I remember.'

'Did they catch him?' Voss asked clearly impressed at what she'd said.

'They never told us.' Claire shrugged. 'We were just part of the investigation; it was rarely we found out about arrests or convictions.'

Voss nodded taking the information in, using the time to study her more closely; at first glance, she was young and attractive, and then he had to reappraise her. In her mid-thirties, a mature beauty had replaced the first flush of youth and little crows' feet enhanced her eyes giving them a mischievous air.

'I have been through your CV and what you have described is right up our line of work. Under normal circumstances the selection process would be a great deal more complicated, but we don't have normal circumstances, the break-in, the missing employees and the damage have left us with a huge problem and piles of work. People with your skills are rare.'

'My sister went to see Jemma, the sick girl, last night. She said she looked depressed as hell. She didn't want to talk or look her in the eye. Mary reckons that it seems more like a love lost than a dickey tummy.' She added.

'Well, that's an update at least; we haven't even had a sick note from her either.' He paused, 'Ok, Claire, you've impressed me to the extent that I'll take a risk. We'll have to get background checks done and all that, but in the meantime, welcome aboard. I think we'll get along just fine. When can you start?' Voss stretched his hand out; Claire, surprised and excited now, hesitantly got up and offered her hand in return.

'Thank you very much Mr Voss. I can start straight away.'

It was Voss's turn to be taken aback at her willingness to start immediately, which encouraged him in his decision to hire her so hurriedly. She had a way of inviting trust, even involuntarily. He was glad that he did not have to go through a long painstaking selection process, which would have cost time, a commodity he didn't have, and if she was just half as good as her sister, he would be satisfied.

'Right.' He explained, 'Nick starts work in about ten minutes. Let's get you a cup of tea and show you round and then he can do all the paperwork.'

'About that, I forgot to ask what the pay will be. A bit stupid, wasn't it?' They both laughed. 'We'll sort that,' Voss said, smiling as they went through the door, 'Well, I just offered you a job without checking you out, and so we're quits.' They both laughed.

Later That Day

It was late Friday afternoon, most of the day staff was packing up for the weekend, and Ashok Nayyar had just started his shift. He was tracking mobile phones and radio signals from half a planet away, which wasn't exactly his idea of fun. He glanced up at the elegant woman in her fifties walking towards him. He admired his section head, recognising that her expertise in the field of radio communications was second to none, she was the best in her field.

'Here is a pile of intercepts from Dir in the Swat valley. We downloaded this from Echelon. It's yesterday's news I'm afraid, but see if there's anything in it. The auto filters are flagging it red, so there maybe something interesting there for us.'

'Sure, I'll get right onto it,' he affirmed, accepting the printout from her. This work was preferable to tracking phones.

'Let me know if there's anything unusual.' He was already so absorbed in his task that he didn't reply.

The first intercept was an IP number that was already red flagged. It belonged to an internet café in Dir in the Swat Valley. He scanned the URLs that the IP had called up. It never ceased to amaze him how little security there was on the internet. The first one he read caused him goose bumps - 'Chemical disaster 2009 at Jaipur.blogspot.com'. He froze at the next one, 'Frankria pipeline blast kills at least 200, USATODAY.com'. The third one, 'www.buncefieldinvestigation.gov.uk' made him reach for the panic button.

He grabbed the phone and punched the red button. He was going direct to the top. Whoever was there, whatever they were doing, the red strobe on the phone would interrupt anything.

'Hi,' he said breathlessly. 'Who do I have?''

'Whitworth,' came the curt answer. 'This had better be good. I'm holding a call to the Secretary for Defence for this.'

'Sir, someone in the Swat Valley is doing serious internet research into major industrial disasters.' Nayyar was still going down the list of sites visited from the café and spotted another, 'Ludwigshafen Ether Explosion 1946'. Someone's been checking out some pretty bad industrial big bangs. Remember the Buncefield explosion?'

'Yes,' came the apprehensive reply. 'And?'

'Well, how does industrial accidents and diethyl ether strike you? Not just Molotov cocktail proportions, thirty tons to be precise.' Nayyar heard the sharp intake of breath. Followed by,

'Mr Browne, I'm sorry sir, I'll have to get back to you. A situation' is developing here which needs my attention.' Then the click as the other line was disconnected.

'Nayyar, make printouts of the sites and bring them to Task Room 2. I'll get some others together. Print four copies, that should do for now. See you in ten minutes.'

'Yes sir. I'll be there.' The line went dead. Nayyar had never sat in on one of these meetings before. He was excited as he started to call up the URLs, made screen shots to print them.

Task Room 2 was a totally secure screened room with a secure internet connection, an encrypted phone and definitely not the usual run of the mill meeting room. It had no windows and the furniture was all specially made with no hollow spaces and non-splintering materials in case of explosions. Apart from the secretary, he was the first there. He used the time to start collating the copies into ordered stacks. Whitworth came in without acknowledging either Nayyar or the secretary. He picked the phone up and dialled a number.

'Where is he now? Hereford? So he's airborne. Estimated arrival? Eight minutes? Right, got that.' He hung up. 'There'll be a bit of a delay. Mr Browne's on his way from Hereford by chopper, he'll be here in about ten minutes.'

'Who else is coming, sir?' Nayyar asked nervously, but Whitworth was gone again and he was talking to empty space. The secretary smiled at him sympathetically.

'First time, heh?'

'Yeah! Does it show that much?'

She smiled as she set up the overhead.

'Relax! It's probably just another false alarm. If you want a coffee, or some other drink, help yourself, over there.' she nodded in the direction of the coffee machine.

'Thanks.' He walked over, poured himself a cup, and picked out the best of the wafer biscuits from the pile on the plate.

The door opened and a man in army uniform came in. 'Hello, who are you?' he asked Nayyar .

'Nayyar, sir. Ashok Nayyar, staff researcher and general dogsbody,' He noticed the man's epaulettes and swallowed hard, 'No pun or offence intended, General.'

'None taken, Nayyar. It's Wheeler by the way, Military Intelligence, and it's Colonel, not General. What's the panic? Whitworth said something about industrial accidents?' at that moment, Whitworth reappeared.

'Colonel, good to get you here. I hope we didn't disturb anything important? The Defence Secretary will be here shortly, he's flying in any minute now. I've asked Chris Hall from the Think Tank to step in on this as well. He does have a knack of spotting things.'

Wheeler sat on the edge of the table and picked up a biscuit. 'Quite so, quite so,' he glanced over at Nayyar, 'high level stuff indeed. Who got the ball rolling on this, you Nayyar?' He munched on his biscuit.

'Well, yes sir,' Nayyar looked sheepish, 'I just got a list of the intercepts and filled out the details.'

Hall burst into the room, exclaiming, 'Sorry I'm late, been on the phone to Chester all morning, chaos up there, they have a kidnapped terrorist sleeper and a possible virus epidemic going off. The Chief Constable at the request of the chief investigating officer has asked for our assistance. What's so important here?'

He slumped into a chair and dangled a leg over the arm. Wheeler regarded the gangly man with overlong hair and a bald pate with disapproval, but Hall's weasel-like face showed no reaction to the Colonel's frown.

The door flew open and Defence Secretary Browne rushed into the room. Introductions were made and the participants all took their seats again. Whitworth took the floor first.

'Gentlemen, we have scenarios unfolding, which makes me uncomfortable to say the least. The first is the matter of the intercepts from Pakistan, which reached us through the Echelon satellite system via Troodos yesterday. Mr Nayyar analysed these and pushed the red button. He will show us what he has found. Mr Nayyar, if you please.' Nayyar stood up, coughing nervously.

'Well, it's all happened so fast, so I do not have much yet. It's mostly a gut feeling at the moment, but I think the events are highly alarming. The intercepts are from a wireless internet service operation, an internet café in Dir in the Swat Valley in Pakistan. We're using X-Keystroke software to run through texts, this software enables us to analyse billions of messages a day with a set of parameters we choose to set. By the way, we have a database of over ten thousand words in eighty-two languages to call on to help in this. Someone in Swat Valley; I think we all know what a hornet's nest that is these days,' he laughed nervously, 'has been researching industrial accidents. In Dir, in the middle of radical Muslim territory, someone is searching the net for things like exploding ships, blazing oil terminals and chemical disasters, all concerning high casualties and mega damage to property and industrial productivity.'

'What else do you have?' Wheeler asked, visibly agitated.

'An email sent from the same internet café.' The email intercepts were difficult to decipher as the various routing acronyms were mixed,' Nayyar pressed on; passing the prints he'd made around the table as well as the email intercepts.

'I haven't had time to trim off the fat on the emails to make them easier to read, there just wasn't enough time. This is the raw data.'

Chris Hall suddenly stood up, clutching the email list, scratched his chin vigorously and loped out of the room, leaving the other three participants opened-mouthed in surprise.

Whitworth stepped in. 'Make nothing of it,' he said, 'Mr Hall is renowned for his idiosyncratic approach.' He was met by smiles from the Colonel and the Defence Secretary who obviously knew Hall of old. 'Well, Nayyar, anything else?'

'Only a guess I'm afraid, sir,' he said.

'Well, out with it young man!' the Defence Secretary said.

'I'd like you to look at the printout of the 1948 disaster in Ludwigshafen, the IG Farben thing.' They all leafed through the printouts until they got the page in question.

'Well,' he continued, 'when I saw this amongst the others I wasn't particularly drawn to it, but if you now look at the email intercept number 1211/ad from 24.10.2010, we see the following in plain text: '*Brother we are pleased to inform you we have started operation 'Buyer', the envoy will be bringing greetings from father*'.'

'So, what's the connection?' Whitworth was checking his watch impatiently and the other two appeared bewildered.

'IG Farben later became the Bayer Chemicals Group, 'Bayer' equals 'Buyer', phonetically anyway. So, in my mind, it has to be the Ludwigshafen explosion.' He hesitated, intimidated by their apparent incomprehension. 'If it hadn't come from the same café as the searches, I'd not have picked up on it, but this is too much of a coincidence, don't you see? It's a play on words.'

The door burst open and Hall rushed back in again with yet more papers in his hand.

'See this!' he shouted agitatedly, 'See this!' He placed the papers on the desk in front of him, stabbing with his finger at the middle of a page of email intercepts, unconcerned that he might be interrupting something. The others looked on baffled. 'It's the same addressee, don't you see?'

They all stood and huddled round the notes. Sure enough, the sender was the same as the addressee in the mail Nayyar had. They had a link. The subject was different though.

'Our friend is now employed in BM Chester. Delivery at month end. Greetings from father.'

'I got the news a moment ago, that the kidnapped victim from Brinkley Medical in Chester is the brother of the surviving member of the Mumbai attacks last year, i.e. a known terrorist, the confirmation is the BM.'

'This puts a possible epidemic and the industrial accident off the Richter scale in my book,' Nayyar concluded.

'Hell, how long has Chester been sitting on this?' Colonel Wheeler nearly exploded. 'We should get COBRA involved immediately. Get me the Chief Investigating Officer in Chester on the line now,' Colonel Wheeler called over one of the secretaries, 'and you'd better get copies of all this over to Langley fast as well. They need to know what we have here. Maybe they'll have some input for us. Oh, and make sure Scotland Yard ATU are also informed.' The Defence Secretary was already on the phone to Whitehall.

19

Hanks logged on and called up the ever-growing case file, noting that the virus was, now officially, the subject of some concern regarding transmittal and the possible change into a different virus. He added the connection of Kasab and Brinkley's to it, yet another reason to get COBRA involved, he thought, annoyed and frustrated that still nothing had come down from upstairs. The wall clock showed 7pm.

'You fancy a beer Welks? I got a mouth like the Gobi Desert.'

'How about the Kings Arms?'

'Sounds good,' he grabbed his jacket. 'So much for 'POETS' day. He pointed to the clock.'

'I was hoping go to the footie at Old Trafford tomorrow for Man U – Everton, but I reckon that's not gonna happen, is it?'

'You got a ticket?' Hanks stared at him in astonishment. 'Jammy bastard.'

Welks held up his warrant card. 'Season ticket,' his grin widened. 'Always works. Tell 'em you're after someone in the middle block. Might not get a seat, but a good spot though.' They both laughed and headed for the door.

The Kings Arms had seen many makeovers during its history. Once a Tudor coaching house, it was now, well, just another pub. The latest revamp had tried to make it a twee character pub. The only thing the brewers had managed to do was destroy the atmosphere of the old place. The clientele was mixed this early in the evening and there were many, like them, on their way home from work. The place had a reputation, a bit like the Boathouse, as a pub for easy pick-ups. Hanks didn't care, the beer was excellent and he ordered two pints straight away. Welks found the one-armed bandit irresistible, that is, until it had swallowed up £5 of his coins. He gave up and came over to Hanks who had sat himself down at a small table overlooking the entrance.

'I have a bad feeling about this case.' Hanks said. 'There's simply too much we're not seeing. Same again?' he asked, draining his glass completely with a big slurp.

'Wish you'd stop brezzling like that. It's not polite you know.'

'Tastes better, gives you the full aroma as well,' Hanks wiped a trace of foam from his top lip. 'You're not gonna go maudlin' on me are you Colin?' he grinned.

'Gonna eat something, are we?' Welks asked, 'Or are we having all our calories in liquid form?'

'Answer my question. Same again?'

'Yes and a bag of crisps, salt and vinegar. I'm starving.'

Hanks headed for the bar, which was becoming busier by the minute. He jostled a couple of young people, apologizing as he passed. He got the beers and held the bag of crisps in his mouth as his hands were full. Turning around, he got a look at the couple he'd bumped into on the way past. The woman's face was familiar. He'd seen it before. He was sure it was in relation to the case. Who was it?

'Well, I didn't want you to eat the damn crisps,' Welks joked as Hanks spat the bag onto the table and put the beers down.

'Welks, who's the woman with the straggly blond hair over there, the skinny woman?' Welks screwed up his eyes and squinted across the bar.

'Oh that's, eh, what's her-name. Damn it, the… the Phelps woman from Brinkley's, that's it!'

'I thought so, registered her face from the Brinkley files. Who interviewed her in the end?'

'Carlton and some WPC went round to the house. The girl was genuinely sick. She'd been up talking to God on the big telephone all night. Her mum reckoned she was preggers, but the girl said it was some junk food her boyfriend had brought back after the pub.'

'Anything of use come out of the interview?'

'Nah. She hadn't heard of the break-in, at least, not until Carlton broke it to her. He was pretty certain of that. The boyfriend backed the story independently, so, no, nothing of use.'

Hanks thumped his empty glass on the table. 'It's your shout.'

Welks struggled to down the rest of his pint whilst getting up to head for the bar.

The atmosphere in the bar changed palpably. A sudden quiet came over the place, it was as if the temperature had dropped abruptly. Hanks's attention was drawn towards the door and he saw two uniformed officers standing there looking round. Their eyes met. One of the two came over towards him, followed by all eyes round the pub.

'DCI Hanks, sir?'

'Yes, that's me,' Hanks sighed wearily. 'Am I double parked or something? What is it?'

'Sorry to disturb you, but the Chief Super asked us to look out for you. Your mobile, it's switched off.'

Hanks took his battered mobile out of his pocket. The battery was empty again.

'So?'

'Well sir, he needs you back at the fort now.'

'What's going on?' Welks arrived with the pints.

'We are being summoned back to base.' Hanks said his annoyance clear.

Welks looked at Hanks and then turned to the officer. 'It's bloody Friday. Friday after a long and gory week's graft on the grubby coalface of humanity. We're tired, we're dirty and we're off duty. You understand?' He sat down next to Hanks, looking pleased with himself.

'Quite so,' the policeman said, obviously embarrassed, 'I'm sorry sir, but the Chief Super was adamant that we take you back. Something has come in about the case you are on sir.' His voice had dropped to a whisper on the last bit.

'Okay, we'll drink up and come quietly,' Hanks said resignedly.

'We'll drive you there sir,' the officer said after a few seconds of no reaction.

Hanks was shaken out of his reverie by the words. 'Yes, sure. You go out, I've got to get a couple of things,' he said, heading for the bar. 'I'll be there in a minute. Don't go without me,' he grinned.

Welks was sitting in the police car outside when Hanks appeared, his pockets bulging with bottles. Hanks nearly lost a bottle climbing into the back of the car. Only a bit of deft juggling saved the house red from an end far different from the one Hanks intended for it.

'Let's go team,' he said despondently as he slammed the door shut. 'Back to the coalface.'

The mood in the car was quiet, if not sombre on the short drive back to the station. The patrolmen, at loss as to how to deal with two senior detectives the wrong side of the breathalyser limit, just kept silent. The car turned into Nuns Road. Police headquarters was practically in darkness, the only lights showing were at reception and in the underground car park. Hanks regarded the wall of grey glass that some architect in the 60's had thought was the latest thing. Prince Charles's comment sprang to mind, *'a carbuncle on the face of...'* He couldn't remember the rest.

'Where's the Super then? I don't see any lights on up there.

'I don't know sir, my instructions were only to find you and bring you back here.'

Hanks turned to Welks, 'We should have eaten in the pub, I've got a feeling about tonight, and it looks like it's going to be a long one.'

They got out of the car and Welks helped Hanks who was having more trouble with his bottles. They took the lift up to the second floor, entered their office and switched on the light. Hanks deposited the bottles inside his desk drawer along with six packets of chilli peanuts and two bags of crisps. They were startled by a discrete cough behind them.

'Gentlemen, I'm glad you've made it back.' The Chief Superintendent stood in civvies in the doorway behind them. 'Sit down and listen! We have an awful lot on our plates as of now and DCI Hanks, thanks you for going over my head. I would have appreciated it, if you'd informed me about the developments in the case before I have to hear it from high above.' The Superintendent's anger was evident. 'I've had a call from a Colonel Wheeler at GCHQ, he wants you to call him back. His team thinks that there may have found a connection between Brinkley's and something much bigger. What it is exactly, I don't know, they want to talk to you and only you.' He paused a moment allowing for Hanks to get a word in.

'With all due respect, sir, I have informed you via memos and emails on several occasions. This should have gone to COBRA at the latest when we found out about the terrorist in the virus place.'

The Superintendent looked daggers, 'Hanks, you must realise how busy I am and how much responsibility I hold. I get hundreds of mails and memos a day. With something this important, you should have come to me immediately and personally.'

'What?' Welks interjected amazed. 'He did ...'

'Inspector! I'm talking to DCI Hanks, I'd advise you to keep out of this.' Welks coloured up and swallowed hard. 'Colonel Wheeler wants you on this, Hanks. I hope you don't let him down. He's is waiting for your call and then you need to talk to Langley. Here are the numbers.' He laid the piece of paper which he produced from his pocket on the desk in front of Welks, seemingly nervous of going too close to Hanks. 'Oh, and by the way, Detective Chief Inspector, I'd be grateful, if in future you'd leave policy matters to those who understand them.' He turned and left before a flabbergasted Hanks could respond, leaving them both staring at the cheap wood veneer of the office door.

Welks peeked over his PC screen at Hanks. 'Another top briefing Alan?' He laughed cynically. 'He still skirts round you; he must remember the punch you landed.'

'Good that he did, I nearly lost it again.' Hanks said fighting to get his brain around the events that had just happened. 'I don't believe I heard that.' Hanks shook his head.

'Just because that man is late getting things into gear we have to sacrifice the weekend,' Welks grumbled 'We've got a suspected sleeper taken hostage,' he scratched his head, 'at least most of him is kidnapped anyway, and a virus on the loose and he talks about policy.' He grinned at Hanks.

Hanks laughed raggedly. 'Oh well,' he sighed settling down at his desk, 'let's see what we have.' He dialled the number in Cheltenham. The phone rang for what seemed an age before it was answered.

'Wheeler.'

'DCI Hanks here, Cheshire Constabulary. The Chief Super said I should ring you. By the way, I've got this call on the speaker so my colleague DI Welks can sit in on it. Is that ok with you Colonel?'

'Certainly, certainly, Hanks. Thanks for getting back to me so quickly. Some fine work at your end about Kasab. Without you we'd still be in the dark.'

Hanks thanked him for the compliment. 'It was just a gut feel and we hit the jackpot with the false identity.'

'Hanks, due to your *piece de resistance* our men latched on to a connection between emails, which would appear to be connected with your terrorist and another operation. We have identified a major suspect in Pakistan who seems to be behind it all, Qamar Al Surira. He is a very high ranking al Qaida member wanted by the Americans for his part in the Nairobi bombing. You follow me?'

Welks shook his head and Hanks was confused.

'In a word sir, no. Haven't got a clue.'

'Do you have a secure fax line? I'll fax you some transcripts and then we'll talk again.'

'Yes, sir.' he read the number off to him. He had hardly broken off the call when the fax in the corner beeped into action. Funny with emails and all that, he never seemed to use the fax these days. What a boon it used to be, he thought, getting up to retrieve the fax message. Welks pulled his chair over to Hanks's desk. They read the pages in silence. After a pause, they re-read the messages, this time both of them made notes.

'Christ!' Welks said. 'I remember the big explosion at the Shell refinery in Ellesmere back in the early seventies. A pipeline with hydrogen sulphide blew up under the railway bridge on the South Side refinery. Miracle no-one was hurt, but we heard the bang here in Chester, twenty miles away. The damage looked like a war film. No, more like the aftermath of a giant earthquake. Only nine tons of the stuff exploded there. Even that threw railway trucks more than fifty yards through the air and lifted a bridge over ten feet off its foundations. A mega blast! Here, they're talking like thirty tons.'

'The connection...' Hanks interjected. 'You see the connection with the email address? There's one confirming the placement of a man in an establishment in Chester; too much of a coincidence for it to be none other than our hostage. Fits in with the message our people intercepted about the delivery at the month end in Chester. The other is announcing 'Operation 'Buyer' with the footnote by this Nayyar guy about IG Farben, and Bayer. He must be a WWII fanatic to have picked up on that so quickly.' Welks was furiously scribbling notes in the margins of the fax as he talked. 'You're not going to quote this in your memoirs are you?' Hanks jibed.

'No.' Welks looked at him disdainfully, 'got better things to do than that. Anyway, a book of some crackpot London DCI's memoirs isn't exactly going to be 'the' bestseller, is it?' Before Hanks could reply, the phone rang again, he picked it up.

'You got the fax,' a statement not a question, 'now; do you understand where I'm coming from? You realise how important it is to find this hostage so we can question him?'

'Most certainly, sir, with the greatest respect, we'd already reached that conclusion, albeit not in connection with the Pakistan side of things, but in connection with an intercept about Jemail Kasab making a delivery in Chester.' He paused for a moment, 'I have another telephone number in the States, a Langley number, any idea what they can add to this?'

'Ah yes, you'll talk to a Bob Dos Santos. He's the SIGINT officer for the UAVs in the Afghan mission. This guy is live on line with Edwards Air Force base watching suspects; he's watching this Qamar chap round the clock, real-time.'

'Is that so? I'll phone him now.' Hanks hung up and redialled. The pre-recorded mechanical voice informed him he was not authorised to make international calls from this extension. 'Sod it.' He dialled the front desk. 'Got a number for the Chief Super? Ring him, he should be at home by now and tell him we can't dial out to the States as the telephone in our office is blocked; tell him it's DCI Hanks. It's urgent! He may even understand what it's about.'

Welks was at his PC scouring the databanks for anything and everything he could find about Qamar Al Surira and Kasab, his notepad filling with scribbles and cross references. He scrupulously added each piece of information to the online case file. The phone rang, the display showing it was the front desk. 'The Super says that you can use the phone in his office. I'll get someone to nip up and unlock it for you.'

'Hey, do you have the Pizza Taxi menu down there?'

'Yeah sure, but the Greek takeaway is better. You get a bottle of red wine with all orders over a tenner and they deliver.'

'Great! What do you want Welks? It's Greek.' Hanks held his hand over the receiver.

'What about souvlaki and a shepherd's salad, oh, and some of that tsatsiki, the garlic stuff and some fresh rolls as well.'

'It'll stink like a wrestler's jockstrap in here by the time we've finished.' Hanks snorted and repeated the order to the desk sergeant and told him to make it two of each. He headed for the lift.

An officer was waiting with the key outside the Super's office.

'I've been told to let you in sir.' he said, unlocking the door and backing off. Hanks turned the lights on inside and sat putting his feet up on the pristine desk as he pulled the phone towards him and dialled the number in the States.

'SIGINT, Bob Dos Santos.' The phone was answered on the first ring.

'Detective Chief Inspector Hanks here from England, Cheshire Constabulary, Police,' he added in clarification. 'Colonel Wheeler at GCHQ asked me to ring you. Qamar al Surira and maybe some other snippets regarding an operation calling itself 'Buyer''.

'Right on,' the American drawled. 'I can't give anything out on the phone. No disrespect, but you could be anyone. If you have one of the CIA's listed secure numbers we'll call you back.'

Hanks was dumbfounded. CIA listed secure number. What the hell was one of those? He dialled Wheeler again relating his problem. Wheeler asked for the number he was dialling from and said he'd sort it. Hanks redirected incoming calls to his extension and went back down stairs to see Welks still feverishly tapping away at his keyboard.

'Any joy? It's nearly ten thirty. I'm starving.' He opened a wine bottle and filled two cups. Then he pulled out his jotter and started to put things in two columns, the 'knowns' and the 'maybes'.

The phone rang, making him jump. 'Hanks!'

'Hi. That Colonel of yours has sure got some clout. Gets things done pretty damn fast.' The American accent left no doubt who was calling. 'Alright, I'm cleared to give you all I have on the villages of Dir and Achar.' Hanks said nothing, he just wrote the names down on his pad. 'We have good reason to believe that al Surira is hiding in Achar, and we suspect he's behind the enquiries. You have the intercepts, I believe. We now suspect that he has been in telephone contact with someone in London on a prepaid card from the Orange Company. GCHQ put us onto it, but we haven't located the satellite phone yet. Seems that there's an operation being set up in London. It's all a bit cryptic, but the thing is called 'Operation 'Buyer'. That's all we have at the moment, but all our antennae are bristling.

We located the first call from a place near Heathrow, a T-Mobile number to a satellite phone in Pakistan. It was very short, too short in fact, so they didn't get enough time for an accurate fix. The second call from Afghanistan to an Orange number was longer and we were luckier there. The recipient was in Surbiton, Surrey, England when the call was received. I can give you a map references if you need.'

'Email to me,' Hanks said, reciting his email address, 'Please continue. Can you give me the dates and times of the calls?'

'Certainly sir, I'll give you those directly.'

'Any idea what they spoke about?'

'No sir, they were in some Urdu dialect we haven't translated yet. It's being worked on, unfortunately we didn't realise the significance at the time. Oh, there's one more call from a 'Three' number. This one is clear and very short and says 'Meet me under the bridge at three pm'. Male voice, no identifiable accent as far as we can tell. We're having it run through our voice recognition programme now. It'll be a while though, nowhere near as fast as facial recognition, both recipient and caller were in Surbiton.'

'Interesting,' Hanks mused. 'Can you give me the numbers?'

'Sure,' Dos Santos referred to some notes. Hanks could hear the rustle of paper even over the transatlantic line. 'Here goes.' Dos Santos recited the list of known numbers, which Hanks painstakingly noted down. Dos Santos then gave him the dates and times of the four traced calls. Hanks finished the call as the door opened, revealing a PC burdened with a carrier bag and two bottles of red wine.

'Where?'

Hanks pointed to the table under the window, thanked him and gave him the cash as Welks started dividing the spoils. As the smell of the food reached him, he realised how hungry he was. They ate in silence apart from Hanks slurping his wine.

'How're you doing?' Hanks asked wiping his mouth.

'Getting there, there's a whole file on the databank this Qamar guy, very interesting reading, but it's all history. It doesn't tell us what they're planning, but a must for background though; I'll plod on. Have to check with Special Branch next, see what they have. How about you?' He picked up his Styrofoam cup and drank some of the wine. 'Does this get better on the second bottle?' he grimaced.

'Right, it's number crunching time. Do we get cooperation from telephone companies this time of night? Who do the Yanks have as their 'on the ground spies' here in Britain? Really crazy world,' Hanks muttered more to himself than Welks.

'Might do, if you try going through Wheeler.'

Hanks rang Wheeler again and explained the problem. Wheeler promised someone from Orange and all the other networks would cooperate promptly. He'd call the Home Secretary immediately and get it sorted. There were specialists on 24-hour call for just these kind of incidents. He'd see to it that Orange got to him within the hour.

'I might need all the connection data for the numbers and the connection data for the SIM cards as well.' Hanks added.

'We'll see what can be done, Inspector.' The Colonel hung up.

'Well, a natural break, Welks.' He stood up stretching. 'Wonder how many people are getting shaken out of their Friday night reverie at the moment?' he smiled. 'They've buggered up our night out, so I don't feel sorry for them either,' he added with malice. Welks rubbed his eyes; stood up and stretched as well.

'You go cross-eyed staring at that screen for so long. My girls play computer games for hours on end; I don't know how they cope.'

'You know what intrigues me?' Hanks leaned back in his chair. 'Our missing terrorism suspect, the hostage, who didn't want to be missing the way he is... what's his connection with industrial accidents? Is that just a decoy?'

Welks stroked his chin and walked to the window. It had started to drizzle again outside and the watery light of the street lamps glistened off the wet road surface.

'I agree I'd hazard a guess and say it was piss poor timing. Our boy was just in the wrong place at the wrong time. It's doubtless that he was trying to get what he was supposed to deliver out of the fridge, but my gut tells me that the 'hug a rat' mob have no clue that they've kidnapped a wanted terrorist.'

Hanks stood, lost in thought for a long moment. 'If our premise is right and the break-in by the ARF is a totally separate incident and the hostage wasn't a target as such, then we are still completely in the dark about what they are planning. This is doing my head in.'

Hanks opened another bottle of house red, Château Gargoyle, and placed two fresh Styrofoam beakers on the table. Unlike good wines, where you checked the vintage, Hanks checked the best before date. 'Never trust a Greek bearing gifts.' He chuckled at his paraphrased quote, and once satisfied the wine wasn't out of date, he filled the cups.

'Cheers.' He lifted his beaker in a toast and sighed, 'I can't help but feel that we're just beating our heads. It's like trying to nail custard to the wall. You just get a messy wall and messy fingers.'

20

It was now four days since Hassan had first met Masoud in Southall. A slip of paper under his door had told him to be in Kahn's today. Hassan had complied. He was on his third tea of the day, pacing his intake to save himself from an acid stomach and emptying his bladder too often. He could miss something while in the toilet. An old man shuffled through the door and went up to the counter. 'You have my post?' the old man said in a whisper. The voice was clearly younger than the body, and Hassan was immediately more alert.

The owner smiled and reached under the counter. Two envelopes, one large and the other normal-sized changed hands. The old man sat down at the far side of the café as the owner's son brought a glass of water for him.

Hassan examined the man closely, but he still wasn't sure. He stood up and walked over carrying the newspaper he had been pretending to read. The Jang Urdu News was part of the symbolism for initiating the contact. He placed the paper in front of the old man and saw immediately that his face was covered in make-up. He was sure now.

'My father thought you would enjoy the news from home.' he said smiling, using the agreed contact phrase.

'Your father is most kind. Let me thank him for his trouble.'

'Let me read the paper my friend and we will talk about the news later.' He noticed Masoud prominently placing two fingers on the table. Two hours, he thought, but where. Masoud was ahead of him though.

'I think I will go to the local cinema today. I think it will be a good film.'

'I wish you a good read about our beloved homeland. May your day be blessed.' Hassan backed off to his own table, where he threw some coins down next to his tea cup, picked up his bag and left. Two hours to kill, he mused. Kill who? He smiled.

Anyone who knew the area, having overheard their conversation, would have known the cinema had been closed for a decade. The steps up to the main doors were strewn with rubbish, not cleaned for months, clear evidence of the council spending cuts. Hassan approached the place cautiously, checking to see if there were watchers. He saw two beggars nearby, and the odd pedestrian ambling past, but nothing that looked like 'observation' to him. The sun was out, its warmth spreading across his back as he walked. He wondered what part of the puzzle Masoud had. It was going to be an interesting day and he was itching to get started on 'Operation Buyer'.

Masoud had changed his appearance. He appeared now as an Indian shopkeeper with a brown suit and polished shoes. He even had a battered old briefcase. Hassan was impressed.

'Round here,' Masoud whispered, guiding Hassan into an alleyway down the side of the old cinema. An emergency exit was gaping open, the push bar long since torn off. They pushed through, to be met by the rank smells of urine, rotten food and other indefinables. Hassan almost ran into the back of Masoud when he stopped at the foot of a staircase.

'Up there.' Masoud nodded his head in the direction of the projection room. 'It's safe and we can see anyone who comes. The stairs are dark so be careful. Rubbish from these degenerate infidel dogs is everywhere.'

They negotiated their way up through the litter of old hypodermics, mouldering cartons and paper cups and reached the projection room door which Masoud unlocked. This room, in comparison to the rest of the cinema, was spotless. The space was lit from an overhead skylight, which at some time had also served as ventilation for the projectionist.

'You have made progress I assume?'

Masoud stepped over to a table by the wall and unpacked a laptop from the briefcase. He switched it on before responding to Hassan's comment. The computer had booted up as Masoud took a small envelope from his pocket and tipped an SD card out of it. Deftly he slid it into the docking slot on the laptop.

'Here, isn't it wonderful?' he exclaimed as the data appeared clearly on screen. 'Our engineer has done great work for us.' he said turning the screen round.

Hassan saw a sectional drawing of an underground station. Only on closer examination could he see that it was Bank Station in London. The caption was, *'This is what you are looking for*. Underneath the diagram was another snippet of text. *'Only the fourth biggest as far as passenger flow goes, but easily the most congested in the rush hour. More people here than in any other station on the network at 8:05 am every weekday.'* The engineer was good, very good. Even had his source listed as: Transport for London Station statistics.

There were many scenarios, many different calculations and many possible outcomes of the use of ether in the tunnels. Masoud, fascinated, studied them carefully. Hassan, with his coal mining experience, was also equally impressed with what he saw. There was an obvious balance between the amount of the chemical and the size of the bang.

'You understand the significance Hassan? The engineer is saying that we don't need the full thirty tons, less will create a greater bang.'

'The ether air mix just has to reach a concentration between 18-32%, and a temperature of over 25° C, then, any surface over 160° C or the smallest spark will ignite the mixture. It's the gas-air mix that does it, not the quantity of fuel.' Hassan said sagely, realising that the calculations of the chemical reactions with air were breath-taking. It was all down to timing and the right quantity; he knew that the maximum impact would be a finely tuned, delicately performed work of art. 'The first train will set things in motion, the collector shoe on the live rail will surely create enough sparks or failing that, there are so many electric motors in the system, escalators, train engines, light switches, or whatever to do the job.'

'Wonderful!' Masoud clapped his hands joyously. 'Look at

the diagram my friend, especially at the detail! See the telephone cable ducts from the surface to the tunnels on the Docklands Light Railway. Brilliant, simply brilliant!' Masoud settled back satisfied. 'This is from the tunnel expert, one of us, a believer.' Hassan just nodded as Masoud turned to him.

'We will need funds; I will talk to Qamar and organize the money side of things.' Masoud opened the larger of the two envelopes he had picked up. Inside was a print of the station drawing that had been on the chip. 'We'll need to check the details very carefully. Nothing can be left to chance. 'I would like you to go to London today and check out the details of the drawing we have here, especially the telephone cable bit. Can you do that?'

'Yes, of course. Do we have contacts in British Telecom?' Hassan asked seeing the ducts on the drawings.

'Unfortunately no, we lack skilled technicians on many fronts. Life is so hard fighting technology with peasant farmers and stones, but the fight is a just one and we will win, Inshallah.' His eyes took on a fierce glint as he said it. 'Do your best with the drawing and we will meet in the coffee shop tomorrow at 4pm. I have to go up north; I am worried about one of our brothers.'

'Sure! I will be there.' Hassan said folding the drawing and putting it in his pocket. 'I will check and mark any deviations I can find,' Hassan said, standing to leave.

'You must tell me if there are any restrictions for heavy goods vehicles in the vicinity. You understand? Access, tonnage, all that kind of stuff. I'll find you at Kahn's tomorrow.'

As Hassan went out down the stairs, he heard the key turn in the lock behind him. The station plan was safely tucked in his pocket. Now he had to get to the Bank of England. He hopped on the next bus to Hounslow which would take him to the tube station.

Hassan made good time to the City. He got off the Northern Line at Bank and wandered slowly through the tunnels up to the central ticket hall; just fast enough to avoid the suspicions of the CCTV camera operators and just slowly enough to make a mental note of the details. He made his way upstairs to street level registering the sudden change in air quality, a joyful transition from the stuffy, dusty, hot winds swirling through the tunnels to the relative freshness of the London streets. He breathed in deeply, enjoying the cooler air.

The imposing edifice of the Manor House was in front of him. He pondered a moment if the Lord Mayor would he be there when it happened? It would be a big bonus if he was. On the street, he allowed himself another quick glance at the plan. The telephone cable duct was in Poultry on the other side of the road. He waited for the lights to change and was carried along with the flow of pedestrians. He looked up at the road sign, Poultry EC1. This is it, he thought to himself. He scanned the pavement searching for the cover with GPO on it. Then cursing as he realised his disorientation from being underground had taken him to the wrong side of the road. Spotting the newsstand opposite, he waited for a relative break-in the traffic and sprinted back across, causing a taxi driver to swerve and hoot furiously. Worse than Afghanistan he thought; you could get killed here.

A newspaper stand, a tin box for copies of the latest newspaper stood on the manhole cover, half covering a concrete inspection cover. He leaned firmly against it and pushed it away freeing the whole of the inspection cover, took his phone out and photographed it. It was an old type, possibly from the sixties; a brass plate in the middle announced GPO Telephones and a service address that probably no longer existed. He noted that it was not lockable. That was good. If the plan he had was correct, then this route took all the cables from street level down to the Docklands Light Railway tunnel below. He scouted the traffic signs. Apart from the double yellow lines and absolute no parking signs, he could not see anything that restricted heavy goods vehicles. In fact, several were passing as he stood there; even a tanker went by. Excellent! He set off back to the underground station entrance and went down the stairs to the central booking hall. He counted the tunnels leading off, eight. Good! He tried to appear like a lost visitor checking the maps for stations and checking the time; in reality, he was looking for signs that the cable duct he'd discovered, did come down here. He was sure he had the right area, although being underground was disorienting. The neatly tiled walls appeared to give nothing away.

He walked slowly along, surreptitiously studying the walls. Suddenly, someone running past jostled him. He stumbled, just managing not to fall by supporting himself with his hand on the wall. The cold tiles felt smooth, although not very clean, and, drawing his hand away, he saw that there was a thin double brass strip in the grouting between two rows of tiles. Five tiles to the left, the same again, floor to ceiling. He was elated. This could only be a cover for services, water, telephone, electrics and so on. Chance had played into his hands. It was a good omen, the will of Allah. Yes, the duct came down here, this far anyway. He was overjoyed.

Hassan had the photos of his outing to the city of London on a SD card in his pocket as he returned to Southall the next day. He wandered past the old cinema where he'd met Masoud. Eventually, at four, he went into the coffee shop. Apart from a young boy buying sweets, he was the only customer. No Masoud.

The owner served the boy and sent him on his way. 'Your friend is waiting for you in the Burundi Bank.' He pointed across the road with a long crooked finger.

Hassan left hurriedly and was dismayed to see the bank was closed; he scanned around for where his friend could be waiting for him. Masoud suddenly appeared behind him.

'Come on,' he said, 'we go to a friend's house nearby.' Hassan followed Masoud into a side road, they walked between the front garden walls of once elegant semi-detached properties now all gone to seed, the gardens, either overgrown with weeds or turned into parking spaces. They made their way to the door of a house, manoeuvring round a grubby push-chair; Masoud produced a key and opened the door.

The smell of curry was overpowering, coriander, turmeric and cumin with the harsh bite of burnt chilli thick in the air, like some chemical weapon designed to repel the unwanted. Actually, a welcome aroma, as it covered the more unsavoury smells of the defunct sanitation and other lapses in hygiene in the house. They entered the long hallway, the carpet gleaming like linoleum in the centre. Hassan's thought was that even Achar was cleaner than this. Masoud pushed open a door to the right leading to an empty room.

'We are safe here. I will organise tea. Please sit.' He waved airily towards the three-piece in the room. The furniture had seen better days, with seats sagging badly, Hassan decided not to risk sitting down on one, but perched himself on the arm of the sofa instead.

Masoud returned placing the mugs on the table in front of them and whisked his laptop out from his case.

'I think we have a very brilliant plan.' Hassan said, 'The only problem is that we cannot say if the telephone cable ducts underground are the same as on the drawing. We have no way of checking, but the engineer has accurately drawn access to them on the plan,' he said, showing some photos he'd taken on his phone, glad at last to get his pieces of information into the planning mix.

'Good, very good!' Masoud said before outlining how he envisaged the plan in great detail. Hassan had to bite down on his tongue not to remind Masoud that he fully understood the engineer's information. It had been his job to stop tunnels blowing up after all. They touched on the fact that there was no guarantee that the cable ducts weren't sealed and the whole thing wouldn't literally backfire. Furthermore, they were fully aware that the site they had chosen would be under round-the-clock camera surveillance. The Bank of England and Mansion House, to mention only two of the significant buildings, which were in the mission zone. They spent the best part of three hours refining the plan and defining the methodology.

'Fine,' Masoud said at last, 'I will get all the information together on this card now. Qamar must be informed.'

'Yes, he is waiting to give the start signal.' Hassan replied.

Masoud was scarcely listening to him, so intent was he in his typing.

Hassan dozed off on the arm of the sofa, uncomfortable as it was. He was startled when Masoud disturbed him, holding an SD card in his hand.

'Here, my friend, this you will take to Hemel Hempstead, to our friend Shener. Go through the contents with him and make sure he understands. He will carry out the job. Impress on him the importance of sticking to the quantities. Not too much, not too little. Shener will be easy to find. Go to his place in

Buncefield; mention my name and he will be accommodating. I will see to it that funds are transferred from the IBKK bank in Cyprus to cover the expenses.' Hassan felt the digital data card almost burning into his palm as Masoud spoke.

'You must take charge,' he added after a pause. 'If I am caught or dead, you know that.'

'You think there is a problem, Masoud?'

'I don't know.' Masoud replied. Hassan didn't know what Masoud was referring to and couldn't understand the mood swing, but he could clearly see the worry reflected in the man's whole body. It made Hassan feel uneasy. Had Masoud been followed? Was he under observation? He felt goose bumps on his arms and legs.

Meanwhile Masoud's worry was at the other end of the country, Masoud was desperately concerned that he hadn't heard from his operative in Chester for a week now. That was not only unusual, but also disturbing. His letter to the safe house had gone unanswered. Then there were the reports in the papers about the break-in at the laboratory where Khalid worked. Animal Welfare idiots he thought, after reading the newspaper. If only these animal lovers had real problems, they'd behave differently. He must find out if Khalid had been compromised.

He had to go to Chester urgently, he had decisions to make. As if that wasn't enough, Masoud thought, there was Ahmed M'Beki, who had made the move to Hemel, but his wife had left him. If the border control people found out, or if the stupid bitch filed for divorce, then he could have another problem. The woman wasn't taking any of his calls either. He'd have to take out that loose end at some stage, of that there was in no doubt. She wouldn't be his first dead prostitute after all. Just thinking of that, he felt himself stiffening, remembering the thrill and sense of pure power he'd felt at that sublime moment of killing. Yes, he'd do it to her as well, but first things first; he needed to get to Chester. He packed a small overnight bag just in case and hid all the 'Buyer' stuff safely in the back garden of the house.

Masoud drove through the night, chewing gum and energy drinks kept him awake. He reached the 'Welcome to Chester' sign in the early hours. He drove passed Khalid's house, which was in darkness and the doorbell drew no response. Next he drove to the safe house, which on examination has been untouched since his last visit, his letter lying unopened on the floor inside the front door. As a last resort, he decided to try his work place, not giving up on the hope of finding him. The horizon wasn't yet showing the coming dawn, which was over two hours away as he parked up opposite Brinkley's main gate. Maybe he'd spot Khalid going in or coming out. Making sure his phone was switched on, he stuck another piece of gum in his mouth and settled down, preparing himself for a long wait.

Traffic was light and the only real activity of note was a security guard occasionally walking out of the guardhouse to have a smoke under the small tree next to it. The dampness, which fell just a tad short of light drizzle, stopped him from dallying outside for any longer than his cigarette lasted.

A church clock in the distance struck six. There was movement over the road. People started coming out of the place. Masoud was wide-awake now and he studied the workers leaving Brinkley's, on the lookout for Khalid. He froze rigid. Unbelievable, it couldn't be! It was her! Claire walking across the car park, saw him almost at the same time as he saw her. Masoud noted the shock on her face, not aware that his expression must be mirroring hers. Getting out of the car and walking briskly towards her, he ignored the traffic causing cars to brake and swerve. She searched for somewhere to hide, somewhere to avoid him. He called out to her but she ignored him, instead she whirled round and hurried back into the building. The security guard was suspicious now, coming out of his cabin as Claire did her turn, he came towards him. Masoud backed off; he didn't need this trouble, and returned to his car. She'll be back, he thought. She has to come out sometime. He started the car and moved to a position where he could continue to observe the entrance without being obvious. He could have kicked himself for being so careless.

21

The Cabinet briefing room was austere and functional, without the opulence of the 'Number 10' room; it was a crisp white-walled neon-lit room screened from the outside world by everything technology had to offer. The gathering consisted of the main Cabinet members and secretarial staff plus some military people and the head of the Metropolitan police. Jacqui Smith, the Home Secretary, was tense.

'Here we have at least a chronology of the events leading up to the incident,' she began, as she distributed a thin file to each of those present, 'I'll run through it briefly. First, we are confronted with an apparent kidnapping of an employee of a bio-medical company called Brinkley Medical Research in Chester. Brinkley is involved in the forefront of research into transmission of viral diseases. This is an A grade Biological Secure facility.

The group claiming responsibility for the break-in, the Animal Rights Front, freed hundreds of lab animals. Most of these were infected with a new strain of influenza.'

'Jacqui, are the infected animals a health hazard?' asked the Prime Minister.'

'Well, Prime Minister, as far as we are aware, the animals were infected with a flu strain that is non-viable. However, I've taken the liberty of bringing in Dr Rogers of Port of London Health Authority. He's our expert forensic anthropologist and has agreed to help us to understand the situation. Dr Rogers, please could you give us a short ‘walk through’ on what we can expect on that front.’

The thin sharp-featured figure with half glasses rose, walked slowly to the front of the room and placed his collection of papers on the lectern. He coughed nervously and shuffled his notes.

‘Ladies, Gentlemen, I thank you for the opportunity to address this meeting. I’ll try to keep this as simple as I can without omitting anything that I think may be of relevance. To begin with, we are talking about flu viruses, Influenza A type. These may be transmitted from animals to humans in two main ways: Number one is from virus-contaminated environments to people, like contaminated food or objects. Number two is through an intermediate host, such as another animal. All Influenza A strains have eight separate gene segments. The segmented genome allows influenza ‘A’ strains from different species to mix and create new influenza ‘A’ strains.’ He stopped seeing the blank expressions around the table. ‘Am I going too quickly for you?’

‘Can you dumb it down a bit for us? Tell us in layman’s terms what the risk is from these freed animals.’ The Prime Minister answered.

‘Right, well, there is no danger as yet. The only problem would be, if the infected animals got a new infection with a different ‘A’ strain. Let me put it like this. If two different viruses infect the same person or animal; for example, if a pig were infected with a human influenza ‘A’ and an avian influenza ‘A’ at the same time, the new replicating flu could mix, exchanging existing genetic information and producing a new breed. This new one would have the genes from the human flu, but also a hemagglutinin and/or neuraminidase from the bird flu. So, the resulting new hybrid might then be able to infect humans and spread from person to person or animal to animal. You see?’ he paused again. The silence round the table told its own story. ‘Quite simply, the question of whether the animals pose a threat is unanswerable. Theoretically, no, they don’t. The disease they carry is non-transmittable, except through close contact between members of the same species. In a closed lab, the bug is contained. But the freed animals may have become exposed to other viruses in the wild and we don't know what can or will develop from this lab strain. We just don't know enough,' with that Dr Rodgers sat down.

'So in other words we could be sitting on a bomb or a dud,' the Home Secretary summarised.

'Well, a time bomb anyway,' Dr Rogers answered, 'you see the life span of a ferret or a lab mouse is limited. Once they die the risk is gone, unless of course they infect something else.'

'When does it become dangerous then? I mean for the public, and what needs to be done to limit the damage both in human and economic terms?' Jack Straw the Secretary of State for Justice asked as he turned his lanky frame in his chair, trying to find a more comfortable position.

Dr Rogers explained from his chair, 'Well, this type of crossing of two 'A' strains may lead to a major change in the virus. This change is known as an antigenic shift. If this new virus causes illness in people and can be transmitted from person to person, an influenza pandemic can occur. A classic example was the Spanish flu pandemic in 1918, or on a smaller scale, the swine flu going around now. So, we will have to monitor any new cases of influenza in the Chester area and analyse them very carefully. My department will be more than pleased to help here.' The Health Secretary was now scribbling notes furiously.

'That's good, thanks Dr Rogers. Does anyone have any questions?' Jacqui Smith waited for a response from around the table.

'Dr Rogers, just one question. How do we stop the virus if the worst case scenario happens?' Jack Straw asked.

'Well, there are two ways to stop viruses spreading,' the Doctor said pushing his glasses up on his nose, 'either put a barrier between them and their host, like a screen, as they did in Chester with the UV lamps, or launch a massive inoculation programme like it was done with the avian flu.'

'Good grief, d'you know what that cost us?' the Prime Minister complained.

'You know what it would have cost if we hadn't had done it.' Straw cut in impatiently.

'Does that cover everything?' Jacqui Smith asked breaking

the tension between the two men.

'Yes, I think that's it.' Gordon Brown said.

'Thank you for joining us Dr Rogers and giving us your time.' The Home Secretary indicated he was no longer needed and stood up to show him the door.

The Prime Minister turned to Lieutenant General Sir David Richardson, Deputy Head of the British Army. 'Sir David, we need to plan. The army should be prepared to make use of our germ warfare capabilities if it comes to a major quarantine operation. Maybe you can get some preliminary scenarios worked out for containing any infectious diseases, in say, the Wirral peninsula or maybe North Wales and the Wirral.'

'Yes sir, but I think on the operational level we need to act on a need to know basis, otherwise, if word gets out, there's going to be panic everywhere. There'll be a mass exodus from the North West.'

'Good point. How about putting the think tank onto it?' Browne asked. Get a plan put together to isolate the Wirral and greater Manchester areas, including say North Wales and Cheshire.'

'It's big bit of country. I'll see to it.' He made a few notes.

'Get them on to it fast, who knows how much time we have.'

The Lieutenant General passed his note to a secretary and whispered something in his ear. The secretary nodded and left hurriedly.

'So, Jacqui, explain to me, why the panic? Why call in COBRA? Surely, this is a health thing and it's up to the Health Department to keep outbreaks of flu in check?'

Jacqui Smith had been waiting for this question. She pushed the Cheshire Constabulary file across to Gordon Brown.

'Here,' she said, 'is the reason for this meeting.'

He flipped it open to read the first page. The silence in the room was palpable as he slowly raised his head and put the page down.

'Good God!' was all he could muster in a half whisper. 'The virus may not be our only problem. Jacqui, would you like to tell it.'

The Home Secretary took the floor. 'Let's get to the meat of this issue,' she started, 'Cheshire Constabulary, or rather an ATU team headed by an expert from Scotland Yard have identified the hostage from Brinkley's in Chester as a known al Qaida terrorist. The man's name is Kasab, Jemail Kasab, he's a Pakistani national and a probable al Qaida sleeper. His trail goes back to training camps in Afghanistan and Border Control Services records show that he re-entered Britain at Heathrow on 23rd March this year and then dropped off the map. Now he turns up in a sensitive infectious disease research facility under a false name and is kidnapped by animal activists. The fingerprinting and DNA testing results leave no doubt that this man is the hostage. His false name was Khalid Akar. The papers he had were immaculate forgeries, so someone went to a lot of trouble getting him inside a secure facility. For those unfamiliar with the name, he is related to the last surviving Mumbai Terrorist. It would appear from the various intercepts that he was supposed to deliver something at the month end. He had his hand in the virus safe when the break in happened.'

'What do you mean?' Jack Straw asked.

'According to the Managing Director of Brinkley's, Kasab had no access rights to the locked store, where the bio hazard's safe was located. We assume that, when the activists broke in, the caught him in flagrante. It was maybe a blessing in disguise that the Animal rights Front kidnapped him, thus stopping him delivering.'

'There's a virus out there though, or we wouldn't be sitting here.'

'Of course Jack, just maybe not the one al Qaida wanted us to have, according to the report on what goodies were in the bio-safe at Brinkley's, there was everything from Anthrax to Ebola in there.'

'Jesus Christ!' the Health Secretary burst out. 'We need someone on the ball for this. Who is going to do it?'

'So this investigation is handled by Scotland Yard?' Gordon Brown asked, ignoring the outburst.

'Yes sir, DCI Alan Hanks is heading it up. He was instrumental in solving the 7/7 attacks and achieved high acclaim through his work in Northern Ireland, personally I think he is greatly underestimated. There's also the issue of the recent GCHQ stuff, they have been having some interesting intercepts of late,' she added, 'but I'll let the Secretary for Defence give you the gen on that,' she sat down relieved to have got her bit over with.

The Defence Secretary stood and took his place, 'There might be a tie up between the two issues here. One is the germ warfare thread and the other, a big industrial accident. There seems to be a connection as messages are emanating from the same source in Pakistan. We have a name of an operation, 'Operation 'Buyer', and some obscure reference to an envoy. One of the analysts ties Buyer in with Bayer, the chemicals giant, and a mail intercept about an industrial accident in 1946. Of course we have to treat it seriously, but we are not sure how much credibility to place in this information. At the moment, it's just an intercept out of context, albeit from a part of the world known for its extreme religious and political views.'

'Heaven help us if anyone gets the technology to launch germ warfare in the UK.' the Health Secretary added in an undertone caught by his neighbour.

'I think they already did,' his colleague whispered, nudging him. The Prime Minister shook his head.

'Put the country on maximum terror alert. I want the security services at all levels in all forces put together on this.' He said standing to indicate the meeting was at a close. 'I'll have no internecine squabbles queering the pitch on this one. Is that quite clear?' He fixed the Home Secretary with a beady glare. 'Get them all together on this one, Jacqui. One office, one head of investigation and a result before this thing becomes a real nasty. Put someone good at the head. You say Hanks is in Chester?'

'Yes. He was sent up to trace the man we now know to be the hostage.'

'I'd say we have the right man in the right place, wouldn't you?' His comment was met with nods of assent. Most Cabinet members had assumed the question to be rhetorical anyway.

'To be honest I think he's doubly right for it. Hanks has the input from GCHQ and the insight into 'Operation Fellowship' as well. He is fully up to the mark with the case. It'd be frankly stupid to put someone new on it. Put Hanks in charge.' He'd continued in justification, in spite of there being no detractors.

'Will do Prime Minister.' Jacqui Smith responded, as the

meeting broke up into smaller groups, animatedly discussing events.

'Oh, Lieutenant General,' the Prime Minister called over as he left. 'Get that quarantine plan on my desk tomorrow.'

'Yes sir,' he said moving across to the Home Secretary as the PM left, 'Jacquie, wasn't Hanks wife killed in a car bomb or something?' he asked her.

'Yes, bad thing that, he still blames himself for her death.' she replied, 'He's one of the quickest minds I know, but you wouldn't guess it from seeing him. He's very anti authority, has a real attitude problem, but in spite of appearances, he's a very dedicated man,' she ruminated, smiling as she said it. 'I'll get on to Cheshire and organise Hanks' transfer back to London. Maybe you should put in an appearance there. The Chief Super's a bit of a one for high profile visitors. He likes rubbing shoulders, if you get what I mean.'

'Ah, a climber rather than an achiever? Tell me about that sort! We have a regiment of them.'

'Get your quarantine things arranged; then we'll start pulling teams together. I'll have to get this terror alert thing coordinated now. 'Phone me when you're ready to go.'

'I suppose, the next ratchet up will be a state of emergency.' The Lieutenant General said grimly.

'I just hope we don't get that far.'

22

Whittaker stuck his head round the door. It was still only eight in the morning, but Hanks already felt like he'd been up all night at it. He glowered over his screen at Whittaker who was filling the doorway.

'Good morning sir, the Chief Constable is here and wants you and Welks in the Super's office in half an hour.'

'Chief Constable? Here at eight in the morning? It's Monday, you berk. You think I'm going to fall for that, you sad sod?' Hanks threw the morning paper at him, laughing. 'You'll have to get up earlier than this to catch me. No brass gets anywhere at eight on a Monday morning.'

'Seriously, he's here and wants you.' The big dark West Indian bent and retrieved the newspaper.

'If you're pulling my plonker, I'll nail your goolies to the front door. I'm not in the mood for wind ups.'

'No sir. Really, it's no joke. He's here. Big fuss apparently, a Lieutenant General Sir someone or other is with him as well. Rumour has it that there's been an emergency Cabinet meeting on the break-in at Brinkley's.' He sounded both impressed and excited at the prospect as he put the paper back on the desk.

'Hear that Welks? We're at Cabinet level now. Bet that'll scare the shite out of our Animal Front lot. Bet they're having kittens wherever they are.'

Welks grinned inanely at the thought of animal rights people having kittens. 'Got time to go home and change, have we? Can't go up in front of the brass seeming as if we've slept out all weekend.'

'In case you've forgotten, we have been out all weekend.' Hanks grunted. 'Okay, let's get a bit freshened up,' Hanks said nodding over at his colleague, 'Can't go in stinking like a bear's arse, can we.' Hanks grabbed his 'emergency' kit. Toothbrush, comb, razor, a deodorant stick, aftershave, some toothpaste and a spare shirt, which, from lying in the drawer for weeks, was more dishevelled than the one he was wearing. 'Oh hell!' he cursed quietly, on examining the shirt, before stuffing it back in the drawer, deciding the one he had on looked better. 'Coming?' he called over to Welks.

'Yeah, two ticks, just finishing this off. You go ahead; I'll be right behind you.' Hanks pushed through the doorway past the bulk of Whittaker, who moved back to let him pass.

Hanks was almost finished with his wash and brush up when Welks walked into the gents.

'Wanna bit of good news, Alan?'

'Daft question on a Monday morning. What've you got?'

'Missee Craig and Master Thompson late of 42 Rake Lane Eccleston. The Garda have picked them up in Cork in a little hotel.'

'Having a bit of hanky-panky, were we?' Hanks brightened at the news. 'Who pulled them?'

'I got the message from a Detective Sergeant O'Malley.'

'O'Malley.' Hanks paused as if bemused by the name. 'O'Malley, there's a coincidence now. Good old Paudrig. Paudrig O'Malley. Jeez, that's a name from the grave,'

'You know him?' Welks was amazed.

'Yeah, we were on joint cooperation teams in Ireland. Great bloke,' he reminisced, 'we met up again in Paris on some Interpol jaunt four or five years ago.' Hanks paused for thought, hand on head, 'that was it!' he said gleefully, the flash of happy memory coming back to him. 'The Five Nations Cup. Parc aux Prince, Wales-France game. The match was snowed off so we ended up getting steaming drunk and trying to take Paris apart. O'Malley drank the Head of the Paris Gendarmes under the table in a red wine drinking competition at the Interpol club. Legless doesn't describe it. They were both like rubber men afterwards, no joints, no coordination, totally gassed. We all thought they'd need dialysis,' he chuckled at the memory. 'Surprised either of them survived that night. Paudrig O'Malley, now there's a thing!' He turned to Welks, 'So?'

'We're waiting for extradition procedures to be started.'

'The hell we are! You got a phone number for O'Malley?'

'Yes, but the procedures say we have to…' but he couldn't finish, because Hanks was out past him shouting over his shoulder,

'Where's the phone number?' Welks rushed out behind him following him to his desk where he showed him the file entry. Hanks dialled the number, and then there was a brief delay as O'Malley was summoned to the phone before the pair engaged in a bit of reminiscing and verbal backslapping. Hanks then told his colleague what he wanted. Hanging up finally, he shouted for Whittaker to come in from the next room.

'Whittaker, tell the Holyhead boys that a blue Peugeot car will be on the next incoming from Eire. Collect the driver and his passenger and bring them here tout de suite. Hold 'em on anything, try the Prevention of Terrorism Act, slap a control order on them; you can hold them for a week at least on that. I don't want any mess ups.'

'How the hell does that work?' Welks exploded. 'They'll stuff us when this gets out.'

'Nah, O'Malley will let them go on the proviso that they go back on the next boat. He'll see to it that they're on it, believe me. It's totally fair and above board. A voluntary accommodation by two good citizens of the realm wanting to help the police with their enquiries, I wish we had more of that sort out there.'

'What, Craig and Thompson?'

'No, bloody O'Malleys, you berk!' Hanks said. 'I thought you were gonna get tidied up for this meeting? At least comb your hair and splash a bit of aftershave on. You pong like one of Brinkley's ferrets.'

'Thanks Alan, I appreciate the concern.' He ran a comb through his hair and wisely decided not to avail himself of Hanks's aftershave. There were afterall, he thought, only two things that smelled worse than ferrets and one of them, in his opinion, was Hanks's aftershave.

They went up in the lift trying vainly to smooth out the creases in their suits. The wall mirrors only emphasised how shabby they still looked, in spite of their efforts. Hanks knocked on the Super's door and after a brief uncomfortable wait outside, they were called in. The Chief Superintendent's office was almost devoid of any of the clutter normally associated with police offices. Hanks noted with inner satisfaction that his footmarks were still on the immaculate desktop.

The men were sitting around the small round table to the side of the main space and they all stood as the pair entered.

'Chief Constable, this is DCI Hanks and this is DI Welks,' the Chief Superintendent made the introductions and they shook hands. 'This is Lieutenant General Sir David Richardson, Deputy Head of the British Army and senior advisor to the PM on terror issues. Gentlemen, let's make ourselves comfortable.' Coffee and biscuits were on the table. Hanks availed himself to one of the pink wafers as he sat down. The Chief Constable led off.

'We have serious incidents on our hands which we cannot put on the back burner. There is a) the matter of the hostage's identity from the Brinkley's break-in. Then there is b),' the Chief Constable was counting the list off on his fingers, 'a series of intercepts from GCHQ, a possible bomb threat, which could marry in with the character who was kidnapped at Brinkley's, and c) the release of infected animals into the wild, which could, if we are unlucky, lead to a pandemic. So gentlemen, all in all we have an evil brew from a possible pandemic to bombings, which could also be big if the Lieutenant General's sources are correct.'

'Made any progress Hanks?' The Superintendent poured himself a coffee.

'Yes sir. The head of ARF should be on the way in for questioning, I'll let you know when they get here.

'That's very good news.' The Super seemed genuinely pleased to hear it. 'Get Carlton and Whittaker to do the interrogation.'

'Excuse me?' Hanks nearly dropped his biscuit. Welks was equally perplexed. 'Sorry sir, but did I just hear you correctly? I will be doing the interrogation of course, or is there something

I've missed?' Hanks was stunned. Welks looked helplessly on.

'Yes, you heard correctly, DCI Hanks. What Chief Superintendent Michaels is saying, is that we need a man of your calibre, your unique talent to run the whole show, nationally that is.' the Chief Constable explained, 'the Prime Minister personally asked for you to head the team. You will be returning with the Lieutenant General to London as soon as he has finished his business here. You're in on the think tank, in fact you're going to head the operation.' He added.

Hanks, still nonplussed about not interviewing Craig and Thompson, gradually registered the information. 'I'm a doer not a thinker,' he stated softly.

'Quite so, quite so,' the Lieutenant General agreed, 'but precisely because of that we need you at the sharp end. You 'do', and that intuitively and above all fast. You think on the run, that's what makes you such an outstanding detective. That's the kind of person we need up front where the decisions are being made. The Home Secretary has made abundantly clear what the Prime Minister wants, and I quote, 'no internecine squabbles' between either police forces,' he paused, and cast an accusing look at Michaels, 'or other government departments. I believe, Mr Hanks you have enough experience and the balls to box this through.'

'Thanks, that's putting it on a bit thick, but it's the only compliment I've had since I've been here,' Michaels pretended not to have noticed the praise of his bête noir, as well as the implied criticism, 'I've been known to be wrong though,' Hanks continued self-deprecatingly. 'How much time do we have? Does he go with me?' Hanks asked, nodding towards Welks.

'Sure, you name your own team. You will have the complete resources of HMG at your disposal. We'll leave for London on as soon as I am done here. We have the first combined think tank on this incident on Thursday. We've arranged accommodation for you, a couple of rooms in the barracks at Buck House. Not five star, but I'm sure the Officers Mess will be more than compensation for all that. Plus it's near the Yard and MoD and secure as well.'

'I presume you want in on this, Welks? The big city and all that? Doesn't scare you, does it?'

'Not in the least. I'll look back on the episode as one of life's little challenges; an exercise in cultural integration, North meets South.' he smiled at Hanks and took a little bow. 'Anyway gets me away from home for a bit.'

'Do you two ever take anything seriously?' The Chief Constable was concerned. Hanks just smiled at Welks, who winked back.

'Who'll do the leg work here?' Hanks looked in askance at the Chief Super, 'There is a lot of work to be done.'

The Chief Superintendent was struggling with the very problem that Hanks had just highlighted. Hanks might be a royal pain, but he did get results and in respect of the team he was leaving behind, the problem was worrisome.

'You'll need to pack for a week or so and remember to turn off the gas,' the Lieutenant General joked escorting Hanks to the door, outside he said in a serious tone, 'I am aware that your Department has been sitting on valuable information which should have been shared with us much sooner. I have seen the reports you have filed days ago and if your Superintendent had raised the alarm earlier, we'd all have been in London already. Him delaying to go national may have put a lot of lives at risk.' Hanks nodded, he was beginning to take a liking to this man. He wasn't a stuffed shirt, he was a 'doer' as well, not some politically correct brown-nose. They'd get on fine.

23

It had been over a week since the Brinkley's raid, and the hard-core members of Teresa Metcalf's assault group were still waiting for some sign that the government had taken any notice of them. There had been loud arguments about the wording of the letter left at Brinkley's and circulated to the press. Gavin was furious that the text had no demand for a reply except the vague deadline for the new law. Teresa was of the opinion that either the government did it, or they'd keep him until they did. In spite of the arguments, she was adamant that there would be no second letter.

They had been lucky. Jemma's desertion on the night hadn't made any difference to their operation. Clive had reported back on how easy it had been to convince the police that her absence was just a dickey tummy after a dodgy curry and a few too many beers. They'd all had a good laugh about that.

Manning's barn was ideal for them as well. Access to it was through the old canal tunnel, or over a wide expanse of open farm fields. It was impossible for anybody to observe or approach the barn without them being spotted. So far, they'd seen nobody. The hostage had regained consciousness fairly quickly and they'd given him copious quantities of codeine for the pain. Gavin performed some rudimentary first aid on the man's hand.

Khalid looked like something that had been coughed up, a

patina of sweat covering his shivering body. Gavin, who was there practically all the time, was concerned that he may have blood poisoning from the wound, although it looked relatively clean. The man had some serious bouts of coughing and flash fevers. One of the members had bought a thermometer and some pain killers, but apart from confirming his sudden extremes of temperature, their efforts did nothing to help. Khalid dipped in and out of delirium for the past day or so, semiconscious most of the time.

They'd been feeding him packet vegetable soup, which Jemma had been bringing from home for days now, and a mixture of cough syrup and paracetamol. He was looking more ghastly every day, in spite of the diet, or maybe because of it. He wasn't too bright when Clive came in to give him his soup. Khalid was semiconscious, his temperature way up again. He was sweating profusely and even Clive's attempts to spoon feed him were in vain. He went back out to Teresa in the other room.

'We ought to call a doctor. He's going to croak on us if he doesn't get help. He's been ill and getting worse since Friday when Jemma came in with that stinking cold.'

'No doctor! It's too risky! No chance! We can't back down on what we said we'd do. No negotiation!' she said emphatically, banging her hand on the table causing the others to jump. 'We'll give him another day, if he's not any better by Thursday, we will see if we can find a sympathetic doctor.'

Clive looked to Gavin for support, the thought of protesting felt like betrayal.

'Teresa, we must get him seen to earlier, he is desperately ill.' Her scowl made his heart freeze.

Gavin came to his rescue. 'Look Teresa,' he said firmly. 'We have done enough violence on this job.'

'We could just drop him outside a hospital, no one would know. But he's gonna die if we don't do something.' Clive pleaded, but knew it was a lost cause. He went back into the little room where Khalid was lying on a thin PVC covered mattress which had been rescued from an old sun lounger. The man was covered in a dirty duvet. He had put a wet towel on the man's head before he'd gone to see Teresa. Clive noticed a funny smell that wasn't there when he'd left a few minutes ago. He checked under the covers and saw that Khalid had soiled himself. A thin beige-coloured liquid, urine or faeces he couldn't tell, was flowing out of the man's underpants. He rolled him to one side, wrinkling his nose at the smell, filling the water bucket and washing the man down as best he could before dragging him to a cleaner part of the floor. Using the rest of the water to sluice away the excrement where Khalid had been lying, he then took a bottle of disinfectant and liberally doused the floor with it. At least the smell was different, no less unpleasant, just different. Khalid groaned and emitted a strange gurgling sound. Clive went off in search of more cough mixture, convinced there was another bottle around; Gavin had bought two bottles last time he went into town.

Teresa was on her way towards him. 'Seen the cough mixture?' he asked her.

'How bad is he?'

'I think it's serious. He's coughing his heart out. He's just soiled himself as well. I don't think it has anything to do with blood poisoning from the wound. The guy is seriously ill.'

'Let's go see then. The cough mixture, by the way, is all gone. Jemma was here the other day and she had a stinking cold and cough, she downed the whole bottle in a matter of a couple of hours. She seemed better afterwards though. When she left she was almost back to normal.'

'Funny, I never knew she was ill, she was right as rain this morning,' he shrugged as they walked into Khalid's room. He was quiet. He was still lying where Clive had rolled him, the back of his underpants brownish yellow from his mishap.

'See he's quiet now.' Teresa clapped him on the shoulder, 'Nothing to worry about,' she smiled. Clive wasn't convinced. He walked over to Khalid and knelt beside him, putting a finger on the man's throat feeling for a pulse. His heart missed a beat.

'Teresa,' he said quietly, 'I think he's dead.'

'You what!' she exploded. 'Dead! Are you joking?' she added incredulously.

'Stone dead, warm, but dead.' He was trying to find any sign of a pulse on the man's neck or wrist, panic rising within him. 'Nothing! There's no pulse and he's not breathing. Jesus! Now what?' He felt a lump forming in his throat.

Teresa seemed uncharacteristically at loss. 'God, we don't need that.'

'What do we do now?' Gavin asked, trying to control his voice and sound calm.

Teresa's dour expression was unreadable, her face twisted in a mixture of rage and confusion; 'We've got to get rid of him somehow.' She pondered for a moment, ignoring Clive's worries and prodded the warm corpse with her foot. Gavin looked on in horror as this handsome woman morphed into her second personality, a heartless fury, a cold witch. He shuddered at the thought that he sometimes fancied her, but there again, most blokes did, until they saw this side of her.

'Well?' he asked quietly suppressing his revulsion to please the woman. He studied the twisted face opposite, anything but attractive now in its rage.

'Put him in the woods for the wild boar to feed on,' she snarled.

Clive was about to protest that there weren't any wild boar around here, but thought better of it. 'I'll get a big plastic sheet,' he said, 'I'll move him tonight.'

Teresa just glared at him snapping, 'That's what I just told you,' as she swivelled on her heel and left him with the dead man. Clive shivered at the thought of wrapping up a body. It was the first corpse he'd ever seen.

24

Back in the foyer, Claire was in a panic, wondering how on earth 'Brown Suit' had found her. She went into the canteen and poured herself a cup of tea, her hands were shaking. Cautiously, she spied out of the window to see if he was still there. The car was gone, no, it had moved. She could see it under the trees on the far side of the road.

When she'd walked out, the first thing she had noticed had been the familiar car with the broken number plate. That's when it twigged, and then she'd seen him. What to do? She had no idea, she'd have to wait and think. She finished her tea and went back into the lab.

The virus tests from the kindergarten were in full swing and Mary would be there at eight to carry on, so Claire thought she might as well fill in time with something constructive, hoping that Mary might have an idea what she should do.

The first ferret test results were coming up. The ferrets were apathetic and inactive. There wasn't the usual kind of vigorous scuttling around. She checked the DNA spectra against the samples of common viruses. The H5N6a test sample was there, also another one. She checked the comparison chart. The match was perfect for Respiratory Syncytial Virus (RSV) and she wondered if that might explain the animals' behaviour, so she noted her suspicion on the lab report.

Her nervous hands were still shaky. She was desperately

thinking of what to do about 'Brown Suit'. With no viable solution in sight, she uneasily went back to the work in front of her.

She called up the characteristics of the virus on the company database: 'RSV,' causes infection of the lungs and breathing passages; in adults, it normally produces only light symptoms like a common cold, such as a stuffy or runny nose, sore throat, mild headache, cough, fever, and a general feeling of being ill. In infants and children, RSV infections could lead to other serious illnesses and even fatalities.' Claire continued reading the information sheet she had opened. 'RSV is highly contagious and spreads via droplets and can spread rapidly through schools and childcare centres, for example, in the food chain or via contaminated hands, surfaces or utensils. Babies are usually infected by siblings who carry the virus home from school and pass it on. Almost all children have been infected with RSV at least once by the time they're two years old. Infections often occur in epidemics that last for about six months, mostly in the cooler times of year.

Not such a big deal then, she thought. 'Kids' stuff', smiling at her play on words and keying up the online file relating to the Group 2 ferrets. She added all the text to the lab file and continued to study the DNA traces from the tests. There was one she couldn't match to anything. Mary would know, Claire thought, as she closed up the file, the memory of the old car with its broken number plate came flooding back. Risking another cautious look out of the window to the front gate, she could still see it half-hidden in the lay-by under the trees up the road and the sight of it made her shudder. She was frightened now; a hundred thousand was, after all, a lot of money.

Meanwhile

After Voss's phone call Hanks packed a few papers into his case and set for the short journey to Brinkley's. The report of the finding of a telephone hidden in the male changing rooms at Brinkley's had him excited. Hanks checked his watch, just ten past nine, he was shattered after studying the stuff from GCHQ with Welks and doing the research on the back of the Langley input, not to mention the other fronts of the investigation. He felt as if he was trying to complete a giant jigsaw puzzle only to find that there were no edge bits, no corners; nothing he could use to define the scope of it. It annoyed him as it meant they were probably researching lots of irrelevant stuff and possibly missing many relevant things.

The gate guard at Brinkley's recognised him and waved him through. Hanks parked in one of the visitors' spaces and went into the admin block. He passed the canteen and saw Mary sitting there. She was facing the door, another woman opposite her, her back towards him. She looked familiar; he felt his adrenalin flow in anticipation.

'Morning Mary,' he said brightly, 'Is Mr Voss upstairs?' The other woman turned, confirming the initial suspicion that it was the woman from the hotel bar, Mary's sister. He took a deep breath. 'Claire, well well,' he said, beaming at her, 'small world. See you managed to get your job then.' Hanks was surprised at how pleased he was to see her again and also startled at the level of attraction he felt.

'Yes, started on Friday,' Claire grinned at him, 'and kicked off last night doing the nightshift. I didn't know you worked here.'

Mary butted in, 'He doesn't. He's a detective; he's working on the break-in.'

'Blimey Mary!' Claire was shocked, 'and there was me spilling my heart out to him in a bar.' she glanced at him and then looked down embarrassed, blushing. 'You could have told me.'

'And if you'd asked?' Hanks smiled at her awkwardness and left the question hanging.

'I should have.' she said gazing directly and intently at him before turning back to her tea.

Hanks was melting inwardly. 'Doing overtime? The night shift has finished, hasn't it?' The two sisters seemed uneasy.

'Go on! You can tell him.' Mary said. Claire took a deep breath.

'You remember our talk in the bar?'

'Yes, vividly. Highlight of my week.' Hanks smiled sincerely.

'Do you want a cuppa?' Mary stood to make another tea.

'No thanks. I'm in a rush,' he said, as he pulled up a chair. 'Of course I remember our talk. I was fascinated.'

'Well, he's here.'

'Who? Your husband?'

'No, 'Brown Suit', he was outside the main gate. You know, the supposed father of the guy I married.' Claire replied with hint of panic in her voice.

'Let's take it calmly. You sure it's the same man?' Claire nodded quickly. 'Here in Sealand Road this morning?' she nodded again vigorously. 'How do you think he found you?'

'I don't know,' she appeared to be on the verge of tears. 'I'm frightened, Alan,' he was elated she'd remembered his name, 'Sorry, Mr ... er? I shouldn't call you Alan now, should I?'

'Hanks,' he said softly, 'Alan Hanks. I'm a detective, as your sister said.' He gave her what he thought was his best sympathetic smile. 'So, let's get this 'Brown Suit' sorted.'

Mary smiled and nodded to her sister saying, 'I'll let you two get on then, shall I?' as she excused herself and went off back to the lab.

'Claire, is there more to the story than you have told me? You realise that I had to start enquiries about your husband? Not that I think anything will happen to you, but he'll most likely be deported.' Claire shrugged, not caring. Hanks felt an unexpected emotional surge that brought a lump to his throat, 'This man must have been watching you to turn up here.' he continued trying for a professional tone.

Claire spilled out the whole story. She covered the lot, including the prostitution and the visits from 'Brown Suit'. Hanks thought how endearingly innocent she could appear to be.

'Did he see you as well?'

'Yes, that's why I'm still here. He was parked outside the main entrance as I was leaving. He got out of his car and was coming for me. He shouted something, but I couldn't hear what.'

'What sort of car, Claire?' Hanks asked turning automatically to the window to see.

'A white Vauxhall, with a broken number plate.' She wrung her hands. 'He's not there anymore,' Claire said glancing towards the window herself, 'he drove off up the road and parked under the trees.'

Hanks scrutinised the road up to where the trees overhung it, but there was no sign of any parked car.

'He's gone, right enough. You say he was parked opposite the main gate. When was this?'

'About six-ish, maybe ten past. My shift had just ended.'

'I'll get the surveillance camera disc from the main gate; let's investigate, shall we?'

'But you're here about the break-in, aren't you? Do you have time to do that for me?'

'Let's go see the security man,' he grinned, getting her to follow him.

The guard ejected the morning disc and replaced it with a new one. Hanks put the recording into the player and forwarded it to six am. As he hit play, there was the car Claire had described. It was a white Vauxhall Astra, about six or seven years old. The number plate was not visible on the film. At 6.12am, a non-Caucasian got out of the car and came towards the camera saying something and waving. He was wearing a brown suit and an open-necked shirt. He had a paunch, was going bald on top. He appeared to be Middle Eastern or Oriental. Hanks couldn't tell. The man was distracted by something and turned to get back into the car. Before closing the driver's door, he spat something out onto the road.

'Don't go away, I'll be right back.' Hanks upped and ran out of the gateway and across the road to where the car had been parked. He studied the tarmac closely, ignoring the car horns of irate commuters swishing past him on their way into the city. Suddenly he stiffened and knelt down, pulling a plastic bag from his pocket. With his pen, he picked up the chewing gum which was lying there and placed it carefully in the evidence bag. He ran back across the road to the gatehouse. The film was still running and the car with its driver was still there. Hanks turned to the guard.

'Did you see this man this morning?' and the guard looked over at the screen.

'Yeah, looked like he wanted to talk to her here,' he nodded in Claire's direction. 'Didn't seem too friendly either, definitely after her,' he nodded at Claire again. 'I thought he was going to try to come in, so I went out towards the gate and he just turned and got back in the car.'

'Claire, we need to talk some more. Let's go back into the canteen. This 'Brown Suit', he visited you in Chessington, right?'

'Well, only once. He came to the house because he wanted to talk to Ahmed. He played it like he'd never seen me before in his life. He'd always just phoned me if he wanted servicing, you know, to get a girl for him. I could never ring him though. The number was always different. It ...' She faltered then stopped speaking. Looking up at him with a strained expression, she said in a subdued tone, 'I hope you don't think badly of me because of the job I was doing, Mr Hanks.' It was clearly a plea for understanding.

'Claire, honestly, it's not for me to judge. History is history, you can't change it, just bury it, get a life. What you had back there, that wasn't life, sounds more like a kind of hell.' She nodded slowly in agreement, her face full of sadness and perhaps a little regret.

'Thanks. I don't know why, but I don't want you to think badly about me,' she whispered.

'You don't have to keep thanking me,' Hanks responded. 'Listen Claire, I have to go and see Mr Voss. I want you to be very careful and if you see 'Brown Suit', let me know immediately, never mind what time of day or night, here's my mobile number.' Hanks scribbled it on a bit of paper.

'Silly boy!' she took her phone back and asked him to recite the number as she deftly entered his details under her contacts. 'There see! The modern age, no bits of paper to get lost.' She smiled at him with kindly tolerance, but, all the same, he felt seriously old-fashioned, inept and rather embarrassed at his low IT rating. He took his mobile out of his pocket and stared at it. 'Would you like my number as well?' she asked, blushing faintly.

'My phone is out of batteries, and are you teasing me now?' Hanks asked brusquely to hide his feeling of discomfort that she might be just playing with him.

'No, seriously, maybe you'll need to talk to me,' she reddened more as she said it. 'You don't have to,...' Hanks was restraining the urge to reach out and touch her. Claire scribbled her number on the piece of paper and pushed it over to him, their hands met briefly. Hanks flipped his mobile open and cursed. 'Damn! Can I use your phone?'

'Sure,' she said passing it over.

'Can you please dial this number for me?' Claire dialled Carlton's number before passing the phone over.

'Carlton, anything new I should know about?'

'Well, the big wigs have gone and they've found the van, burnt out in a field behind Connah's Quay Power station. SoC are all over it right now. I tried to ring you but your mobile is switched off.'

'The battery is dead. Can you get down to Brinkley's? I need the CCTV discs from this morning taken in, get it to Welks immediately. Tell him I want face recognition; I need an ID of the face in the white Vauxhall as a matter of urgency. Tell him I'll stop his comics if he doesn't come up trumps. Got that?'

'What comics?'

'Oh, never mind!' Hanks exclaimed, despairing at the junior officers' lack of humour. 'One more thing Carlton, I'll leave an evidence bag with some gum in it at the gate house, get a DNA check done on that, will you? It should be the DNA from the face in the car. Let's keep our fingers crossed and hope we get lucky. For safety's sake, I want extra police presence in Bouverie Street; tell them to keep an eye on the Grigson house and lookout for a white Vauxhall.' He passed the phone to Claire to hang up for him, smiling at his own incompetence. He noticed her expression was one of almost adulation, as she took it from him.

'I suppose I'll have to get a new one of these,' Hanks said pointing at the old phone and grimacing.

'No chance, Mr Hanks, not a prayer.' She laughed.

Before he could decide what she meant, he saw Voss standing in the doorway. He stood to leave, saying, 'Right Claire,' as she too got up to leave, 'I hope we can identify this guy quickly, and make him to leave you alone, so you can get on with your life.'

'I don't know how to thank you...' she said, but he was already headed away. 'Mr Voss,' Hanks approached him, 'the very man I came to see.' Voss shook his hand and invited him to follow him to his office.

'Trouble with Ms Grigson?' Voss asked as they sat down.

'No, you said you found a phone?'

'Yes, the cleaners do a monthly big clean, and found a mobile phone hidden in the steel girder in the man's changing rooms. In the knowledge, that we had an al Qaida suspect working here, I thought this might be significant.' He produced a phone from his desk drawer and pushed it across to Hanks, who withdrew an evidence bag from his pocket and thanked Voss for his cooperation, whilst wondering what kind of new information they would find on the phone.

25

Mary had left her sister and the detective in the canteen, although she was burning to know what was going on between them. The way he had looked at her sister was a kind of look she knew too well. She put the thought aside and turned back to her work, remembering that Claire had mentioned the DNA traces and the mismatch. Piqued, she pulled the clipboard with the test strips down to check herself. Maybe it would give her another chance to see Voss alone she mused wistfully.

‘What’s up Mary? What’s going on in there with your sister?’ Nick nodded towards the canteen. ‘That detective is spending a lot of time with her. I mean, she wasn’t even here when the break-in happened, was she?’

‘No idea, honest, she seems to have some trouble with someone from down south, that’s all I know. I don’t think it’s got anything to do with the break-in.’

‘Oh,’ was all he could manage, ‘what’re you up to then?’ he sidled up beside her.

‘Checking anomalies that Claire mentioned.’

‘Anomalies? Let’s see.’

‘Here,’ Mary said pointing to the DNA traces from the ferrets, ‘we clearly have the H5N6A strain.’ she stopped to blow her nose, her voice croaking a little.

‘You got a cold?’ concern in his voice, ‘are you feeling okay?’

'It just started, all of a sudden. I'll be alright.'

'Don't make light of it, Mary, we're in a research establishment, and all sorts of viruses could have been set free in here since the break-in. We need to get a swab test done to find out what it is. We can't be too careful.' He fetched a swab and tube and Mary opened her mouth, submitting to the mouth swab as he deftly took a sample.

'Let's see what that brings us,' Nick said writing her name on the label and popping the sample into the lab basket. 'So what are the anomalies Claire spotted?'

'She found another strain, see? It's definitely the common RSV that's doing the rounds this time of year in schools and kindergartens.' She suppressed a sneeze. 'I don't know where this has come from. I was quite all right an hour ago.' She paused, 'Claire didn't know what it was, she suspects that it's a bit of Noro strand in it. She wanted to pass it upstairs for Mr Voss to see.'

'Good that she spotted it, her being new and all. Quite bright, just like you, isn't she?' That earned him a playful thump. 'Mind if I take those upstairs?' He took the trace. 'I'll have a look on the internet and see if we can get a positive identification of the strain. I'll give them to Mr Voss after. I'll take up the new tests on the kindergarten ferrets as well, not that I can see anything special or unusual there, but you never know. Voss might see our version of the Higgs Boson in it.' He grinned as he tucked the papers under his arm and disappeared upstairs again, leaving Mary staring at the mass of work with the kindergarten kids and their parents.

Back in his office, Nick picked up the phone and rang Voss. 'Andy, you got a minute? That new girl Claire has picked up on something; I think you should take a closer look. We have the first DNAs back from the ferrets at the kindergarten. Something has happened to the virus.' His voice broke and he coughed.

'I'll be right there. Got a cold?'

'Just a frog in my throat,' yet he felt soreness in his throat and remembered what he'd just said to Mary. 'Actually, I may have caught something. I have just done a swab on Mary; she seems to be going down with something too. I was all right an hour ago. Never had anything come on so fast,' he said, and promptly sneezed.

'Bless you,' Voss said, 'I think I'll wear a mask. It may be catching,' he added.

'Yeah, it's the season for it.' Nick hung up and called up the ferrets' file on the system and noted that Claire had been very thorough with the addition of the RSV data. He sneezed again as Voss came in with a mask.

'Bless you, again. This could be serious; I think we ought to keep the lab and you lot quarantined until we find out what this is. I'm going to call the company doctor. We can't afford to take chances. Have you had a swab test?'

'I don't want to drop dead with the dreaded lurgy,' Nick said, taking a swab pack from the shelf.

'No, certainly not on company property, you've no idea how many Health and Safety forms I'd have to fill out if you died here. If you're going to die, do it off site, that's an order. Instant dismissal if you disobey.' Voss tried to lighten the atmosphere, they both laughed as Nick took his own swab sample.

'The more human samples we have the merrier, I suppose.' he sniffed miserably.

'How are the tests coming in on the kindergarten kids and their parents?'

'I reckon they should all be done before five o'clock today. Mary's on them now.'

Voss studied the DNAs that Nick had brought up with him. 'The unidentified one looks like a mix between RSV and H5N6A. It's funny though that the middle bit has all the trappings of the Norovirus. However, it isn't Noro. '

'That's what Claire reckoned, but she wasn't sure.' He fished around the data bank and drew up the Noro virus details. 'See here, you can see the shape is all wrong and the docking points are awry. Noro, is a nasty piece of work, that little bugger,' he muttered under his breath.

Voss checked the sample number and rang the lab. 'Mary, I've put lab on lockdown because of yours and Nick's infection. I don't think any of us should go out, or for that matter no one should come in, until we find out what this is. If you are feeling well enough, do a cell biopsy on ferret A26 B II and run another DNA, will you? I want the cell walls from as many different patients as possible. Get the pictures up on the server. I've done a spread sheet; you can put the pictures in the line next to each patient's name.'

'Yes Mr Voss,' Mary answered. 'The lock-down is inconvenient, but I understand. By the way, the Health Department have just delivered a whole load of samples, new infections, people who have gone to their GPs. There are, hang on,' she paused to count, 'a hundred and fifty-six more. I'll do those as well.'

'Thanks.' He put the phone down and observed Nick, who was looking miserable, his face half-hidden behind a paper handkerchief. 'I hope this isn't getting out of control, a hundred and fifty six new cases, doesn't sound good. This is exploding. If you manage to survive the cold, can you get one of your team to test the new viruses with all our vaccines. You never know. We might get lucky.' And with that, he made for the door.

'Sure,' Nick croaked, dumping the sodden tissue in the bin, 'I'll get on to that later.'

Mary phoned Claire to tell her of the quarantine order. She asked about the girls and food.

'Where are they?' she asked.

'Off out with friends.' Claire said to the clatter of plates in the sink. 'So, how is your day going otherwise?'

'Crap, to put it mildly, this bloody quarantine thing, just what I need.'

'There's post today.' Claire put the two letters, which had arrived, on the table in front of her. 'One seems official. Shall I open it?' Mary said she should, as Claire slit the envelope open and extracted the letter. 'From the court about Derek, I suppose it's about the money. He has been ordered to pay you a hundred and forty seven pounds a week.'

'Yeah I know,' Mary said, 'but he never pays, so I am still in the shit.'

Get a court order. Have it deducted from his earnings. He has a good job, hasn't he?'

'Yeah, but he is a real bastard. He just won't pay.'

'He has to! You have proved paternity, the courts accepted that. For heaven's sake Mary, make his life difficult, not yours.' She looked at the back of the letter and saw a form to fill. Mary just had to sign it and send it off. 'There's a form for you to sign on the back.'

'I suppose you're right,' said Mary resignedly, 'but I can't sign it from here can I?'

'I reckon I can still do your signature,' Claire chuckled. 'I'll post it later. They'll probably do an attachment to earnings, so you'll get your money.' Claire said reassuringly as she sealed the envelope. 'How do you feel now?'

'About what? The quarantine or the attachment thing?'

'No, health-wise silly. You said you had a cold.' Mary stopped as if amazed by something. 'Well?' Claire persisted.

'It's gone.'

26

It was past two o'clock by the time Hanks got back to his car. The most likely reason he could think of as to why 'Brown Suit' had followed Claire up to Chester was the money, but he had more serious issues to consider. He hoped the CCTV footage would be good enough for 'face recognition' and that the man in the car was on file somewhere.

He cursed the fact that his phone was dead as he headed back to town and wondered if there was anything on the phone in the evidence bag. He turned on the music in the car, selecting at random from the changer, to be greeted with Gallagher's live version of 'Too much alcohol'. Very apt he thought as he drove, his head buzzing with snippets from the case. He went by his flat and checked his post, nothing more spectacular than a utility bill. He'd need clean clothes for his trip, grabbing a load of laundry from the basket in the bathroom and shoving it into a carrier bag. Then, checking through his wardrobe he took out two of his best suits. Viewing them critically, he realised they'd have to go to the cleaners.

He drove back into town with the stereo turned up, listening to Mayall's '82 Sydney Reunion concert. The pleasure he got from Taylor's elegant slide guitar vied with his warm thoughts of Claire. He parked illegally in Eastgate Street, put his blue light on the roof and left the hazard lights on as he disappeared into the laundry, shoving his bag at the attendant and asking for a service wash.

'Full works, Mr Hanks?' the woman asked.

'Yes, and iron and fold the shirts, please.'

'Going on holiday then?'

'Something like that. Can I collect tomorrow?'

'Sure, see you.' She was already back into her magazine offering diets, hair do's and cosmetics and all the things that would never help her regain her youth. Sad, he thought, until he saw his own reflection in the mirror on the way out. We're all past it, just glad I don't need a magazine yet he told himself.

In the dry cleaners, there was a queue, so he just stuck his card on the two suits and dropped them on the counter. The manager waved at him and nodded.

Hanks now needed a phone charger. The Phone Warehouse was over the road. He noticed with satisfaction, that his car was receiving a lot of attention parked as it was, especially with the wail of Taylor's guitar coming out of the stereo. There was a queue in the phone shop, so he didn't baulk at pulling his warrant card out and shoving to the front.

'Manager, please!' he demanded, shoving the card under the hapless assistant's nose. 'Urgent police business,' he explained, as he unceremoniously nudged the pimply youth who was being served aside.

'Over there sir,' the assistant nodded, indicating a well-dressed woman who was standing near a counter dealing with some paperwork with a customer. 'You lot always push in like this?'

Hanks was nonplussed. 'You what?'

'Pushing past everybody is not right you know. You're not any more special than anyone else.'

Hanks hesitated; instantly angry and seriously felt like saying something, but instead, just gave him a withering look. He pushed through the throng to the manageress, flashed his warrant card and apologised to the customer as he drew the woman away from him.

'Hello, sorry to do this, but I'm in a fix. My phone has packed up and I need a charger urgently. I have to go to London in an hour,' he lied, 'and I need to be contactable.' He placed his mobile on the desk, which the woman looked at in astonished disdain.

'That still works?' She made eye contact then, trying for a reaction, 'This is so old, I'm surprised it hasn't got a dial on it. Gosh, it must weigh half a pound. Have you thought about a museum?'

Hanks getting agitated, growled, 'Listen, I am on a case which could mean the difference between life and death for a lot of people. I am also in a mad rush to get to London and I don't need wise cracks about my telephone.' He had raised his voice to a level that brought the shop to a standstill, and he was entertaining a fantasy in which he lifted her off her feet by her crisp, pristine white blouse. Hanks glared around at the startled customers and staff.

'I'm sorry,' she apologised to the customer Hanks had dragged her away from. Then turning to Hanks, she stammered, 'I'm not sure we have a charger for something that old…' She paused, 'How about a new phone?' Hanks checked the time again.

'If it's charged and you can get my numbers and contacts transferred to it in ten minutes, I'll take it.'

'None of them have a charged battery when they are new. You have to charge for at least six hours. That's standard these days. What sort of mobile do you want?' she asked impatiently. Hanks did some quick thinking. Six hours was out of the question. He needed a phone and fast.

'Show me what kind of phone you have, please,' he said, putting on his polite hat for a change. The manageress, confused by this change of tactics, proudly produced her own version of the latest all singing all dancing smart phone in pink and showed it to him.

'Got it in another colour?' Hanks barked gruffly, suddenly back to his old self.

'Yes, we have a range.' She backed off again, gaining space. 'We have….'

'Got black?' before she could go on.

'Yes.'

'I'll take it, but only if you can transfer my contacts to it. Now, immediately, I mean.'

'It's three hundred and fifty-nine pounds?' She raised an

eyebrow.

'Just transfer the data and put my card in. Okay?'

'Fine,' she raised her hands in submission, taking his phone and a new, black, smart phone and turned to go through to the back of the shop. 'John will do it right away. I'll make out a receipt and the guarantee for you.'

'Make the invoice out to Cheshire Constabulary.' He thought the Super would appreciate that and smiled as he slapped his credit card on the counter. 'Hey, I apologise for being so pushy, but this actually is urgent. By the way, just one question, if I had a phone where text messages had been deleted, would I be able to recover them?'

She smiled at him for the first time, even if a little unsurely, 'theoretically, it's possible, but you'd need some kind of software to do it.' Hanks nodded taking the information in. 'The messages are stored on the card until they are over written, you can delete all you like on the phone but the SIM keeps them, only overwriting them when it's full.'

Hanks thanked her as she disappeared with his new phone and card, and went to sit on the bench in the display window, impervious to the stares and comments of the other customers. He was half-numbed listening to the gibberish being spouted by customers and staff about mega-pixels, G3, and Mbits per second and half-looking at the wonders of modern technology on display all around him. He sighed as he wondered how many people understood or for that matter needed all that stuff. It was just a phone after all.

The manageress reappeared with his card, the chit for his signature and also the new phone.

'Blimey, that was quick.' he was impressed, until she put him down with,

'Well, there wasn't much on your old phone to transfer, only the numbers which were a couple of kilobytes.' as if it was a cardinal sin to have so little data on a phone. 'Remember, you must charge it for six hours.'

'Can you put this number in?' he asked reaching into his pocket for the scrap of paper with Claire's number on it. 'Put that in the contacts would you?' Grudgingly she took the paper.

'What name?' She asked.

‘Oh, Grigson, Claire.’ Hanks was caught off balance, but caught himself quickly. ‘Can I have another look at your phone?’ he asked.

‘Sure.’ She said laying it on the counter for him as she keyed Claire’s number into his phone. Deftly, he flicked the back cover off and removed the battery pack. Ignoring her gasp and avoiding her protesting hand, he grabbed his new phone from her hand and repeated the same manoeuvre, swapping the batteries over.

‘Thanks, you’re a star.’ He stuck the phone in his pocket, tucked the phone box under his arm and was gone before she could react.

His car outside had attracted a lot more attention; people were milling around and trying to fathom out what was going on. Tough, he thought, pushing through the little group gathered around the car peering in curiously. He opened the door, grinning mischievously, as he tossed the new phone box on the passenger seat and re-stashed the blue light in the glove box. It was three ten by the clock on St Martin’s Tower, time to get back to the ranch. He started the Mayall concert from the beginning again as he drove off.

27

Parking in his space in the police garage, Hanks noticed a commotion at the other end. A police van was backed up to the doors leading to the cells and a man and woman were being escorted into the interrogation tract.

He walked into the office carrying his new phone box. Whittaker and a WPC were poring over reports on the desk. Welks saw the box in Hanks's hand.

'Finally out of the stone age then?' he quipped. Hanks ignored the comment, dropping the box on his desk.

'I've got something,' he held up the bag with the phone from Brinkley's. 'This could be Kasab's. I want everything on the phone analysed.'

'I hope you are going to give it a decent burial,' Welks joked before the impact of Hanks's words registered. 'Oh, right, that's different then. Sorry I thought it was your old one. I'll check what can be done.' He said as he took the bagged phone from Hanks. 'You know the M'Beki enquiry you asked me about? I've checked with Border Control and Immigration, there's nothing on him other than an asylum procedure, which has been dropped because he married a British citizen.' They were interrupted by a noise from downstairs.

Whittaker perked up. 'That must be Mrs Craig and partner coming in from Holyhead, wanna come and play?'

'Hanks, you're wanted upstairs,' Harris called through the

door, 'the Super.'

'Sorry Whittaker, you'll have to do Craig on your own.' He dropped his plastic cup into the bin sending a spray of unfinished coffee skywards. 'I'll be back soon. Let me know if we get anything significant out of her. Be nice to know why she disappeared. The timing was too perfect for a holiday getaway with her lover.' He tossed the phone to Welks as he left, 'see if you can find someone to get the data out of this.' He headed out towards the lifts.

The Chief Superintendent was waiting at the open door for Hanks when he arrived. His office was a scene of chaos with papers lying everywhere. 'As you can see Hanks, things are starting to move,' he waved his arm in the direction of the strewn papers. Hanks stifled a grin, trying not to show any sign of pleasure at the sight.

'Lieutenant General Richardson you already know,' then gestured to the other person in the room. 'This is Ashok Nayyar from GCHQ. He is the analyst who spotted the industrial accidents thing.' Hanks shook hands as he appraised the youngster; twenty-five to thirty at the most, a mop of black hair and bright intelligent eyes set in his brown face. He was in jeans and a button-up cardigan over a sweatshirt with a print 'The oo' in the 'V' opening at the front, which puzzled Hanks.

'What's all this paperwork then?' he asked with a sweeping gesture of his arm.

'All the requisitions and unit orders for a possible quarantine lockdown of the Northwest.' the Chief Super explained as Hanks tried to hide his satisfaction that the man was really buried in paperwork.

'Uh huh!' Hanks said noncommittally, 'What might be the purpose of this young man then?' He asked nodding at Nayyar.

'Mr Nayyar is a talented computer specialist and an astute analyst from GCHQ who will be joining us in London. As you know, Chris Hall, one of our colleagues managed to latch onto the one connection before and he thought we could get a lot more if we went over all the intercepts from the source and compared them with known email addresses.'

'Any luck yet?'

'We're still panning for gold,' the Lieutenant General said.

'Please take a seat.'

Hanks sat at the little conference table.

'What's the state of play on the hostage front? Are we any nearer to getting to him than before?' the Super asked Hanks in as polite a tone as he could muster.

'Honestly, no sir.' Hanks was a bit taken aback at the question. It wasn't often he'd heard the man asking about operational successes or failures. His last encounters with him had to do with budgets and cost savings and overtime bans. He was sceptical about whether Michaels could even connect pieces of a case together. 'As I came in, I heard Mrs Craig from the ARF and Mr Thompson are in for questioning downstairs. I believe Whittaker is questioning them now.'

'Good, any news on the other things?'

'Not worth writing home about, sir.' He studied the young man from GCHQ, 'Mr Nayyar, Ashok, isn't it?' Hanks turned to face him. 'Are you any good at getting data off a phone?'

'What do you mean sir?' Nayyar said. He undid the button on his cardigan and took it off, dropping the garment on the chair next to the desk.

'I've just picked up a phone and we'd like to take peek at the messages and call log, can you retrieve them even though they may have been deleted?'

'Doubtless!' He answered, turning towards Hanks revealing the elusive text that had piqued Hanks's interest earlier, 'The Doors'.

'You could do that?' Hanks asked, whilst thinking, boy, you weren't even in liquid form when that band was around; Hanks nevertheless grunted in personal satisfaction at having solved that little riddle at least.

'Sure, of course!' Nayyar confirmed, looking confused at the conflicting signals being sent by the detective.

'I think we'll need your skills quite a bit.'

'That's why he's here Hanks,' the Lieutenant General said. He's our rising star at GCHQ, and because of his family background; he speaks a couple of useful languages.'

'Yeah,' Hanks asked with interest, 'like what?' Hanks new phone rang before the response came. The Birdie Song trilled out electronically through the room, but it took a while for Hanks to register that it was his phone ringing. Embarrassed he answered,

'Hanks! What? You have to be joking! A recording? Bugger!' He cut off the call.

'Sorry about that. New phone.' he apologised. 'They must have set the ring tone for me as a wind up before I left the shop.'

Nayyar and the Lieutenant General smiled.

'What is it Hanks?' The Super asked impatiently.

'Craig and Thompson singing like larks, sir, it seems we've hit a dead end with them. They didn't do it. They were out of it. Even have a recording on their mobile phone to prove it. Still they've given us some leads and put some new names in the frame. Whittaker's running a check on them as we speak. Need to get back downstairs now, sir. Oh, by the way, Ashok, what languages do you speak?'

'Punjabi and Hindi.'

'Odd mix, how come?'

'My father is Pakistani and my mother is Indian.' Nayyar added for clarification.

'Bet that's caused some problems,' Hanks responded.

'I wasn't aware of them till later,' Nayyar said somewhat cagily, 'I was brought up under Islam by my father, but had the benefit of Hindu philosophy from my mother's side as well. It was a good upbringing, but yes you are right, they suffered because of the marriage, both communities rejected them.'

'Yeah, there's bigotry everywhere, isn't there.' Hanks nodded accepting the explanation sagely. 'We'll see a lot of each other I suspect,' he proffered his hand, 'I'm sure we'll get on well together, great T-shirt by the way, favourites of yours?' Nayyar looked baffled and then down at the print on his shirt.

'Err... well... yes one of,' he stammered.

'We'll get on famously then, Ashok,' Hanks confirmed, humming 'The End' as he left. Outside in the corridor his phone rang again, the Birdie Song resounding off the walls to the amusement of some passing police officers there, but at least, it stopped him humming.

'Yes?' he answered as fast he could to kill the sound.

'Welks here, I'm lonely downstairs. Where are you?'

'On my way to the interview room, I'd like to form my own opinion about Craig and Thompson, meet me there. By the way,

I may have someone to look at the phone I gave you.'

'They've got a cast iron alibi, Alan and they are being very cooperative, so Harris came out of 'Interview 1', as Hanks approached 'They've both got alibis.' he sounded disappointed.

'It's never that easy.' Hanks pushed past him into the room. The WPC sitting by the door immediately stood up, but he waved her down and turned abruptly to address the woman sitting at the table. She seemed haggard and distraught. 'Ms Craig, my name is Hanks, DCI Hanks,' he said without preamble, 'I need to know where the group that broke into Brinkley's is hiding. I need that hostage, and I need him now.'

The woman viewed him helplessly, and then looked at Thomson sitting next to her. 'I don't know.' There was an edge of hysteria in her voice.

Thomson put his hand on her knee to comfort her and added, 'We never got involved after the disaster in the scout hut. There was some talk doing the rounds a few weeks ago about a farm, but which farm it is, I'm sorry, I don't know.'

'So, what's their alibi?' Hanks asked impatiently.

'A recording of a meeting of the 'love an animal' mob,' Whittaker pointed scornfully at the digital recorder on the table, 'Ms Craig recorded a meeting of the ARF where there was talk about action against Brinkley's. She was given the pictures by one of the group,' he referred to his notes, 'Teresa Metcalf.' Heather Craig nodded in confirmation, 'In a nutshell,' he indicated the pair at the table, 'they had a big fall out with this Metcalf woman and left.'

'But the pictures came from inside Brinkley's, how did Metcalf get in there?' Hanks muttered more to himself than those present in the room.

'Kidnapping was something we didn't want to have anything to do with.' Thompson continued, eager to score favour points, now the police had seemed to accept their non-involvement in the raid. Welks just scowled at him. 'We ran out on them. When we knew they were going to do it on the 24th we arranged to be in Liverpool with our friend the Chief Veterinary Officer at a meeting about transport of livestock from Eire. His wife drove us home. We planned the ferry thing after we left the scout hut.' He sagged visibly at the end of his explanation.

'You do realise that you had a legal obligation to report this criminal act. As you didn't, we are going to have to charge you with being accessories before the fact, Whittaker, read them their rights and sort the charges.' Hanks turned and walked out angry at the time wasted. Similarly disappointed, Welks walked out to catch up with Hanks.

28

Hanks arrived home numbed by the day's events. He threw his jacket on a chair and pulled the brandy bottle from the shelf. He bent and picked up one of the CDs from the pile scattered on the floor, inserted it in the player and slumped back into the armchair with the brandy bottle in one hand and his new phone in the other. His landline rang, it was Welks. Hanks turned down the volume to hear him.

'Alan we have a preliminary result on the face recognition of the guy in the white Vauxhall outside Brinkley's. I couldn't believe it; we have opened up a wasps' nest here.'

Don't keep me waiting man,' Hanks barked.

'The Americans are pretty sure that it's a man called Masoud Baitullah. Picture quality was crap so they are being cagey about it.'

'So?' Hanks sounded irritated, 'what's the issue?'

'He's a big al Qaida man, wanted all over the place.'

Hanks was speechless. 'Oh my! This gets better by the minute. Would you believe, I had this guy within spitting distance, thinking he was just some weirdo stalking Ms Grigson. Never mind, it's spilled milk now, if there are warrants out for this guy already, that's ok, but we need to get one out for M'Beki as well, circulate nationally. He's Claire Grigson's husband. Give them all the info we've got and then wrap it up for tonight. You need to be fresh too.'

'What? Husband?'

'Baitullah appears to have set the marriage up between M'Beki and Grigson,' Hanks explained.

'Well well, there's a thing…something has just clicked into place for me now,' Welks said pensively.

'Yeah? What pearl do I get this time?'

'There was a bloke planted at Brinkley's, right?'

'Mmm.'

'So, if he's put in to do a job and can't, 'cos some bunch of vegetarians lift him and take him out of the equation, what would you do if you were running the operation?'

Hanks thought about it for a few seconds. 'Well, you'd need to get a replacement inside. Does that answer the question?'

'No, it just confirms a suspicion.'

'Heh?'

'Who's new at Brinkley's?'

'Claire Grigson?'

'Exactly!' Welks enthused. 'She could be the replacement for Khalid or Jemail. You see, he gets heisted and swoop-di-whoop Claire gets a job in the place, fits, doesn't it?' He sounded pleased with himself.

'Yeah, it's a scenario.' Hanks conceded without enthusiasm. 'Let me think about it. We'll talk more in the morning.'

After some thought, he picked up the phone and called the Yard. 'DCI Moresby, DCI Hanks here, Gillian, does the name M'Beki ring any bells? Do you have him on your radar in the Fellowship thing?'

Nonplussed by the question, Moresby thought for a bit, 'Not familiar, let me check and get back to you. What's he connected with?'

'He is connected with a certain Masoud Baitullah, who has several international warrants out after him and is a known al Qaida activist. I've just put out a warrant for him. We need to question him urgently.'

'Ok, I'll get the team on it immediately. I'll also check with special branch and MI5.'

'Do whatever it takes to get him.' He hung up. He thought back to the conversation he had had with Claire Grigson. The whole thing was somehow coming together. He was confused about his feelings towards her, especially as it was now possible that she was part of the on-going investigation. She had seemed interested in him though, or so his reading of her body language told him, even if she'd not said anything as such.

He shook his head to clear it, inwardly cursing himself for believing that a woman so good-looking and so young would even consider him. 'No fool like an old fool.' he muttered under his breath, feeling a pang of guilt as he realised Claire had replaced Kate in his thoughts.

He took out his new phone, feeling almost ashamed of his inability to use it yet. Frustrating, he thought, as he placed it on the coffee table and attempted to wipe a grubby fingerprint from the display when he heard a woman's voice apparently coming from his telephone. Surprised, he raised it to his ear and spoke into it.

'Hello, Hanks. Who's there?'

'You rang me, so you should know.' The voice was hauntingly familiar. It was her. How had that happened? He asked himself.

'Ms Grigson, what a surprise.' He said trying to cover his embarrassment. 'I was cleaning my new phone and suddenly had you on the line. But I was thinking about you anyway.'

'Mr Hanks?'

'Yes, sorry, it was a mistake, new telephone.'

'No problem, some things are meant to happen. So, what were you thinking about me? Am I a suspect?' she asked in a light amused tone.

'Not exactly, but the people you are involved with may have become suspects.'

'Brown suit? I knew there was something not right about him!'

'I am not going to comment on that,' he said meekly, taking another swig from the brandy bottle, wondering what to say next. 'Yes, well...' He stammered. 'Look, I do need to see you in relation to the case actually,' he improvised, not having considered it before.

'Well, we'll have to meet then,' she said softly into the phone. Hanks picked up on the change of tone immediately. 'I'm not busy this evening. I could come to the station if you need me to?'

'It's not that urgent. It could wait until tomorrow, I suppose, but now that I have you on the line…' his voice petered out, uncharacteristically, he was lost for words. Hanks needed a moment, rapidly planning what he was going to say, 'No need for you to go all the way into town. I'm not that far away from Bouverie Street. We could meet at the Three Bells on the corner of North Gate if that suits; it's about half way for both of us. I could ask you my questions there.' Sitting with baited breath, he expected a negative response. The pause seemed endless.

'Well, I just need to take a shower, so I could be there in about an hour,' she said coyly.

Hanks's pulse increased as he registered her acceptance. He answered, 'Okay, about 8:30 then?' as nonchalantly as he could.

'Sure, see you there.' Relieved and surprisingly elated, Hanks put his phone down and went into the bathroom to try to make himself presentable.

With a flutter in his stomach and a racing pulse, he left his flat. During the short walk to the Three Bells he began to feel more nervous than he had for many years, despite the deadening effect of the brandy he had drunk. Arriving at the pub, he stood in the entrance taking stock of the scene in front of him. The bar was relatively full, mostly with locals that he knew, but he couldn't see Claire. Just as he glanced up towards the clock behind the bar to check the time, the door behind him opened, hitting him in the back. He turned around to apologise and saw it was Claire. Simultaneously they both apologised and burst out laughing.

'Assaulting a police officer! Good start to the evening,' he joked, which raised a further giggle from her.

'Well, shall we first get a drink before you arrest me?' she asked, her eyes gleaming.

'That's a good idea,' Hanks smiled.

She looked him straight in the eye and said, 'I'll have a dry white wine, what would you like?'

'I'm supposed to be asking the questions,' he said winking as they moved over to the bar. He ordered the drinks, and then turned to pass her the wine, taking in her appearance with a long, slow, careful look. She was every bit as attractive as she had been on their previous meetings. He held his glass up in a toast then took a large swig of his drink to bolster his courage. She saw him watching her and smiled. They made their way to the back of the pub where there was only a small table with a narrow bench seat available.

'Will this do?' she asked, pointing at the bench.

Hanks was carefully concealing his delight at the chance of such close proximity, jested, 'I normally sit opposite suspects.'

'So I'm a suspect, am I?'

'We need to talk about you being here in Chester and about 'Brown suit,' he said lamely. 'We have some huge issues here. The lab assistant, who was kidnapped, turns out to be the brother of a known terrorist,' he let that sink in. Without waiting for an answer, he continued. 'What makes it awkward Claire, is that you seem right in the middle of it all, being married to the son of a known terrorist 'Brown suit', who suddenly turns up at Brinkley's and conveniently you start work replacing a terrorist suspect kidnapped from the place. I have to ask Claire, are you involved?' He stopped suddenly, appearing rueful, as he said it.

'Are you joking?' She paused allowing the accusation to sink in. 'Christ, that's a real slap in the face.' She was taken aback by his accusation. In spite of the heat in the bar, she felt a chill. 'Am I involved?' She repeated the question. 'How do you mean involved?' He coughed, unable to look her in the face. 'God no!' she said, 'Don't you realise that I arrived on the Sunday of the break-in? How could I, or anybody, have known that a break-in would happen and someone be kidnapped? And also, remember when we met, I told you my entire story not knowing who you were, would a terrorist do that? Did you ever think about that?'

'You're right,' he said, thinking back to the night they met. She had been honest and genuinely opened up to him. 'I'm sorry Claire, but I had to ask.'

Hanks paled and rubbed his face with his hands. After an uncomfortable silence she asked.

'Is Ahmed a terrorist then?'

'I don't know, but he's mixing with the wrong crowd. Can you remember anything more about 'Brown suit'? Did he have any distinguishing features or anything else that might help to find him?'

'Well, if it helps,' she paused as she sipped the wine. 'He's still calling me.'

Hanks was galvanised, 'When did he phone you last, Claire?'

'Today,' she fumbled in her handbag and placed her phone in front of him. 'I have to have a look at it, do you mind?' He picked up the phone. 'How do I find the incoming calls list on here?'

'Give it to me,' she took it back and deftly coaxed the information onto the screen. 'There.' she said, turning it round so he could see.

'Can you tell me which calls were his?'

'That's easy. I don't erase my call logs very often. Look here, see, there's one of his calls. Every Tuesday at about two in the afternoon, he'd ring and tell me to get someone to meet him at three under the bridge in St Mary's Road. So, you see, all the calls on there on Tuesdays between say one-thirty and two-thirty are from him.' Hanks heart skipped a beat.

'You mean these calls, and they go back weeks, all came from 'Brown Suit?' Claire nodded. 'I'm going to need your phone records Claire. Who is your provider?'

'I'm with Three, anything else you need?' She pushed her hair from her face in a natural and charming gesture which disarmed him again.

'Has he rung you again since this morning?'

'No, the next most recent one was last Tuesday. I was still down south then,' she turned the phone round to show him the call log again.

Hanks dialled Carlton's number. 'Carlton, can you take this down?' Hanks recited Claire's telephone number. 'I want all incoming calls to this number listed, going back to…' he paused turning to Claire, 'When did he first call you?'

'About mid-March.'

'Carlton, did you get that? Mid-March. Mail me the results as soon as you get them. You will need a court order. Miss Grigson is voluntarily agreeing to give us access to the calls. She'll sign a disclaimer, get one organised and see it that it is delivered for her signature at Brinkley's tomorrow. Have you got that?'

'Yes sir,' Carlton confirmed.

'There is one thing about Brown Suit that sticks out,' Claire said. 'He always wore a ridiculously large gold ring on his left hand ring finger. A bit like the pimps always investing in expensive watches so they could use them as money in emergencies.' Hanks made a mental note to enter the ring on the file.

'More wine?' he asked, indicating her empty glass. She passed him her glass.

Hanks stood and went to the bar for refills. They sat and chatted about her past in Chester, her sister and the scholarship to Imperial, comfortably getting through another two rounds of drinks.

'This is tough on you, isn't it?' He nodded, trying to hide his face behind his beer glass.

'Have you ever been in a position where you don't feel you can contribute anymore?' He asked out of the blue. She didn't answer. 'Or, like you know what's right and you're not allowed to do it?' She nodded. 'Well, it's like that with me. Not sure if I'm Don Quixote or a knight in shining armour. I think others see me as a kind brainless steamroller. But there are always two sides to a person, aren't there? The self-image and how others see you, yet these days I'm associating more with the image of how others see me. Am I making sense?'

'I think so,' she muttered, unsure, hating to interrupt.

'It's breaking me.' He seemed to sag, before continuing, 'I want to be a copper, a damn good copper.' She nodded encouragement. 'I didn't join to put villains on ASBOS or let them off early 'cos they had a difficult childhood. They do wrong they get punished. They…' he hesitated, his flow stopped. 'I shouldn't be... This… this is wrong.'

'It's okay, Alan.' She put her hand on his arm. 'Go on.'

'Well, the bastards get away with murder. It's not the police, it's the system.'

She tried to placate him. 'You're doing your best, I'm sure.'

'I've got two weeks 'til my early retirement and I won't have made an iota of difference.' He noted the look of confusion in her face. 'I'm getting out of the force. I'm just taking advantage of my old contract and going into the private sector.' She nodded, absorbing the information. 'No punishment to fit the crime these days. No real deterrent. The system doesn't help, the prisons are overcrowded and the courts tainted by some false sense of fairness, are letting criminals free to do it again and again.'

'What d'you wanna do then?'

'We just get the little ones. I want to get the big ones before I go.' He paused, checking his watch. 'Look, it's getting late, I don't know about you, but I have to have a clear head tomorrow. Maybe we can do this again?' he added hopefully, as they both drained their drinks. Hanks stood and held her coat for her to put on.

'I'll help you in any way I can to find 'Brown Suit', that's a promise.' she said, as they left the pub, linking her arm in his as they walked.

'You want me to walk you home?'

'My street is very safe thanks to you. We have police cars patrolling every few minutes.' she reminded him with a wink. They reached the top of Northgate Street; impulsively she leaned over and planted a soft warm kiss on his lips.

Hanks stood back, flustered. 'I didn't see that coming' He smiled awkwardly, not sure how to react.

'Right,' she smiled, seeing that he was genuinely intrigued by the kiss. 'I promised to help. You'll remember that, won't you?'

He nodded, as he stuck his hand out clumsily to shake hers before they parted. 'I won't forget, nor the kiss.'

29

Voss sifted through the data, creating a spread sheet for the results, 25 kindergarten kids entered by name, forty parents and six staff at the kindergarten, also listed by name, plus Mary and Nick, whose infections initially had caused him to panic. The nightmare scenario of a pandemic starting from his labs had ruined his sleep and he had been more than pleased the following morning to find that their infections had been short lived and the quarantine restrictions were no longer required. He had heard of 24-hour flu, but a four-hour cold? It puzzled him.

He keyed in the type of viruses identified in the mucous samples from each of them and then added symptoms. He regarded his in tray and noted the Public Health Department's list that Mary had placed there, showing another hundred and fifty-six cases. Most of the symptoms column was still empty and he wasn't sure if he was glad about that or not.

He had surveyed the results of the seven most affected patients and was shocked to see how severe some of the cases were. The only common factor between these patients that he could see was that they were all infected with the virus strain that Claire had discovered in the kindergarten ferrets, totally different to the other cases, which had been affected by the seasonal flu virus.

He added another column titled Micro RNAs as he was in the initial stages of doing some research work on these and was convinced that they played a big part in the infection cycle. He had a suspicion they were somehow connected. He added age and sex as the next columns and thought about social background, but decided against it as he didn't have any data.

He phoned the Public Health department at the Town Hall; since all the people on his list had volunteered to play guinea pigs, they were being monitored centrally. Sixteen light colds and seven cases with severe bronchial complications, which had been referred to Chester General. Good, he thought, they'll take swabs and send them to us. He'd asked if there was an increase in flu cases reported from the towns GPs, but the response had been that it was too early to tell. Voss was glad in a way that a real epidemic wasn't rearing its head, but he desperately wanted more data.

His phone rang. 'Mr Voss, Gail Marsden from Westminster Insurance. I'm sorry, but Mr Salameh won't be able to make the appointment today, he called in sick. Can we reschedule your meeting with him to next week?' Voss's antennae were up.

'I'm sorry to hear he isn't well. I hope it's nothing serious?'

'It's just the flu bug that's doing the rounds. The office has been decimated by it.' Voss thought hard for a minute, when was Salameh here, Thursday last week, time to incubate? Yes!

'I understand', Voss said frantically hunting for the man's visiting card. 'Sure, next week will be fine.' He found the card just as he hung up, keyed in the mobile number on it, hoping the man had left it switched on. Luckily, he had.

'Hi, Andy Voss here, Brinkley's.' he made out he hadn't known about the man's illness. 'Just wanted to ask if we could put our meeting back an hour this afternoon? Something's come up. Oh! Sorry to hear that. No, they haven't called. What's wrong with you?' He listened carefully to the agent's description of his symptoms, writing them down as he did so. He jotted down that Mr Salameh was also complaining of heart problems and high blood pressure. 'Well I'm sorry to have disturbed you and wish you the speediest of recoveries.' He hung up and stuck the note on the file on the computer. He was mulling over the possible ways he could get a DNA swab from Salameh and considering the possibilities of testing all the staff at Westminster insurance before discarding the idea as alarmist and impossible.

He picked up the phone and dialled the public health department at the Town Hall again. They were very helpful and being fully in the picture, only too glad to comply, assuring him that Mr Salameh would be visited and a sample taken.

His email inbox was blinking; the incoming was from Claire marked urgent and confirm. He opened it.

Hi Mr Voss, Nick asked me to look at Dr Strout's work, and the parallels between his work and ours are staggering. Now, here comes the big bit! Nobody has researched in detail about host genetic characteristics relating to the severity of the associated diseases in humans with respect to patient background, by this I mean socioeconomic background, diet, race or even previous medical history.

Like individual humans, inbred strains of mice vary in their reactions to influenza infection. Mary's type II ferrets who survived are a good example.

I suggest that we examine the genetic structure of the host animal and compare it to the severity of the illness. More succinctly, we need to compare it with that of the host that didn't get infected at all, i.e. was immune. I hope you don't mind me getting involved, but Nick's got a lot on his plate with the vaccine testing.

Regards, Claire

Voss turned away from the screen and rubbed his eyes. He could hardly believe what he had read. Claire had hit pay dirt here. On impulse he picked up the phone and dialled the lab.

'Get me Claire on the phone, please.'

'Did you read my email Mr Voss?' Claire asked eagerly.

'Yes, can you organise some sequencing tests on the swab samples that we have up to now and give me a comparison between them and the recovered ferrets from Blacon? I want to see the blocking on the binding sites data, especially in the adult human data.' He sneezed loudly and felt a hot flush run through him.

'You got a cold as well?'

'I guess so. It's crazy how this comes on so fast.'

‘Do you want me to do a swab test?’

Voss pondered a moment, ‘Okay, come up.’

‘I’ll just get Mary started on the sequencing tests and I’ll be up.’

Voss went back to his infection ‘spread sheet’, thinking how apt the term was as he flicked through the lines analysing for patterns. He struggled with the ideas that were invading his consciousness, dismissing each as implausible, unlikely, impossible or just silly as they occurred to him. Time flew. He was startled by a gentle knock on his door.

‘Yes,’ he called out, still engrossed in his data, ‘come in.’

Claire pushed the door open and stood in front of his desk. ‘Mr Voss, I think you will be also interested in this. I may have found something.’ She sat uninvited on the chair opposite him. ‘Something big, I think,’ she added, more confidently.

‘Alright,’ Voss sat upright, fully attentive now, thinking he’d struck gold in employing her. ‘Good or bad?’ he asked. ‘I’m not keen on little surprises.’

‘You ready? I think you better sit!’ she joked and laid a couple of photos from the electron microscope in front of him. ‘Here,’ she said pointing with a pen to the spot, ‘is ferret A24c second generation. This animal was infected with H5N6A on 10th October and symptoms broke out after three days. See here, the docking sites on the test cell samples are clearly visible. A24c died from the infection on Thursday, 20th October by the way.’

‘Yes.’ Voss said cautiously, ‘not much new there. Why the excitement?’

‘Now look at the pre-infection cell picture. What do you see at the docking sites in picture number one?’ Voss leaned over to see better.

‘Well, nothing, there’s nothing there.’

‘Precisely. Now the piéce de resistance, tah rah!’ She laid a third picture on top of the other two. ‘This is a group II animal B56A. This is the same infection date. When a host is infected with the flu virus, their antibodies target the hemagglutinin protein. Most viruses enter their host cells by attaching to cell-surface carbohydrates. Influenza, in particular, attaches to the termini of the oligosaccharides, specifically sialic acid residues present near the cell-surface.'

Voss interrupted with another sneeze. 'Have you come here to astound me with your knowledge of microbiology? I did study biochemistry and genetics. Does this have a point to it?'

Undeterred, Claire continued, 'Once attached to a cell, viruses inject their genetic material into the cell and take over the cell to reproduce. The cell is made into a factory and produces viruses with its own machinery and organelles, and then dies. The cell membrane breaks down releasing more viruses.'

'Common knowledge.' Voss dabbed his nose, unimpressed.

'Now, here, on the B56A ferret cells, no docked viruses. See here.' She pointed to the free-floating viruses in the plasma around the cells. 'All we had were dead viruses floating around being cleaned up by the leucocytes.'

'Where's the big bang then? I thought you were going to be spectacular?'

'Right, well, you see I thought it was a genetic thing, so I did some genome screening. I drew a blank there, so I started looking for some easier handles, and then I found it. Cholesterol!'

'Cholesterol? Are you crazy?'

'I hope not, and I think you are going to love this. The kindergarten samples reflect this perfectly and not under lab conditions. We have 25 kids and 44 adults who were exposed either directly or indirectly to infected ferrets. We have serious infections in 12 adults and 7 children. The common factor is high cholesterol. The real clincher for me was the lack of sialic acid sites in some of the marginally affected patients compared to the high number in severe cases. Sialic acid, don't you see?' Claire was frustrated at Voss's apparent incomprehension. 'Sialic acid is where the cholesterol docks on. Same place as the virus. Okay, I grant you that the cholesterol level is possibly the result of either socioeconomic background, diet or even, like my first idea, genetically ordained.' She paused and let the information sink in before continuing.

Voss sat, slack-jawed staring at the electron microscope pictures. 'No other similar studies?' he asked after a while, 'I haven't heard of anyone researching in this direction, do you know of anyone else on this trail?'

'I don't know, I'm new here remember,' she gave him a disarming smile, 'but not that I'm aware of.'

'Wow! I'm speechless. You have the backup lab reports?'

'Yes, they're also on the ferrets' file on the server if you want to add or edit anything. I mean, it would be good to know if it was diet or genes, wouldn't it?' She sat back pleased that he'd understood and yet somehow still slightly anxious in case she'd missed something. He looked at her, his mind racing through the possibilities it all suggested.

'It would be a tremendous breakthrough if we could prove that susceptibility to high cholesterol or more concisely high sialic acid levels on cell walls was the decisive factor determining how the influenza virus attacks its host.' He paused, coughing raggedly. 'If we can get there, we can literally say goodbye to flu.' He spluttered again. 'Christ, I wish I could be more active at the sharp end like you. I spend too much time in the office and not enough in the lab.' Claire was pleased with herself as Voss stood asking, 'Have you got the testing pack with you?'

30

Shener had known that Hassan was coming. Masoud had texted him. Stupid text he thought. 'Someone is bringing flowers from home. Greetings from father.' Who thought up such crap, he wondered as he flicked through the morning's post, betting that it wasn't Osama. Shener had taken on Masoud's man M'Beki last Friday. He'd been out with Murphy yesterday and was now up and running, a petrol delivery driver. He was up to dealing with four loads a day, so at least he was paying his way. He studied the man opposite him.

He was thin, even emaciated, with a hideously bony face and in the middle of it, a massively hooked nose, like the beak of some malign bird of prey, an image enhanced by the beady black eyes. The greetings over, Hassan had proceeded to discuss the plan behind operation 'Buyer'. They had studied the outline on Masoud's SD card together and Shener had made a few very pertinent adjustments to the logistics of the plan. Shener was very impressed. He hadn't a clue who had been able to do such things or how, but the calculated result was pure poetry. He smiled, thinking the world would remember this more than the world trade centre; this would hit home like, he struggled for an analogy, like ... like Pearl Harbour. This would bite to the core.

'What we need is a vehicle with 289 compliance,' Shener said brainstorming the problem, 'we have to carry a legitimate load.'

'A 289, what's that?' Hassan asked.

'A form for registering hazardous material transport with the Department of Transport, the vehicle has to be of a particular specification, safety wise, in order to get approval.'

'You need approval?'

'Ideally yes, and we also need a tanker with a special silicone lining to prevent oxidising; otherwise we could have a bomb on our hands,' he chuckled. 'Of course,' he added solemnly, 'if we don't have the right truck and the right papers, it's a no go.'

'How much is such a truck?' Hassan asked.

Shener picked up the phone. 'Soon know,' he said dialling. 'Hello, give me Norman Brewer, this is Mustafa Shener from Shener Haulage.' he waited a bit. 'Hello Norman, listen I need a tanker trailer special build. Yes, I can give you the specs. It's a UN class 3 with full static control, 30,000 litre single tank. It's just for full loads, single chemical. I'll wait.' The pause seemed endless. 'Yes, Norman, I'm still here. A what?' he exclaimed loudly and put his hand over the mouthpiece.

'Hassan, there is a four month delivery time for this type of vehicle.' He took his hand off the mouthpiece and talked back to Brewer at Fidelity. 'No quicker? My partner here is trying to get a business started up, four months will kill him. Give me a price anyway. If all else fails we'll have to bite the bullet.' He listened intently for a few moments. 'Apart from that, any ideas?' Shener listened and jotted a name on the piece of paper in front of him. 'Thanks. I'll be back to you.'

'Problems?' Hassan's expression got darker.

'Four months delivery time, that's the problem.'

'Fix the problem,' Hassan said sharply. 'We can try to hire one.'

'Paper trail!'

'Steal one?'

'Rare like virgins,' Shener replied and logged onto the ELVIS platform on the internet, which detailed shipments up for tender. No ether. He tried suppliers and came up with Allied in Leeds. 'Let's try another route.' He picked up the phone and spoke a mixture of Urdu and English to the man on the other end.

'I've sent a friend to look at Allied. See who does their

transport. I have an idea.'

'We need Allah's help. This plan is too good to die on technicalities.'

'Be patient friend, we have just started. Wait for the call from Leeds. Let's have some tea.'

They talked about getting the tanker into London and what possibilities there might be for getting ether. They had to admit the chances of them getting an order to be delivered would be small. There had to be another way. An hour passed, stretching into two. Hassan paced up and down nervously. When the phone eventually rang, it made both of them jump. Shener snatched it from the cradle.

'Yes,' he answered, 'okay, let me make some notes.' He listened and wrote. 'Talk to the man. Make him an offer. Say you must drive the Monday load,' he told the man in Leeds. 'Thanks,' he said finally and put the phone down.

Hassan was on the edge of his seat, 'What is it, what is going on?'

'Washburton's are due to collect a full load from Allied on Monday 8th November. They're using hired equipment, I T S trailers.'

'So what does that mean?'

'Don't you see? It's perfect.' Hassan's blank expression showed that he hadn't seen. 'We take over the driver's job,' Shener explained, almost shouting with excitement, 'we will make it happen on the 9th.'

'How? He will not want to lose his job. You will offer him money?'

Shener smirked, 'No, we will offer him death. 9th of November in England is 9/11, do you understand the significance of it now?' He started scribbling a calculation on a corner of his desk calendar. 'Two hundred eighty-five thousand in round numbers, let's talk finances.' He looked up at Hassan. 'That ok?' Hassan didn't need to know he had added big sum for himself onto the actual cost. Hassan nodded with a broad smile.

'9/11, magic, the plan is perfect. It matches the beauty of Buyer. By the time the driver is missed, it will be too late. You see? No paper-trails, no hassle,' Shener enthused.

Hassan nodded again, deep in thought. 'If we leave the body

of the driver in the tanker, it will disappear as well; maybe they'll even blame him for it all. There's real irony.' He sat stroking his chin. 'Yes I like it.' I will tell Qamar that he should approve.' They smiled at each other.

Shener got Hassan round to his side of the desk. 'Okay, now we do a dummy.'

'A what?' Hassan was confused as Shener called up the I T S Website.

'A copy, we make one of mine look like one of theirs.' He clicked on a screenshot of a Freuhauf tanker. 'Come my friend, I need your help. We must find an I T S tanker. Let's try the motorway services.' With that, he stood up and donned his coat. 'Coming?' The bemused Hassan, still staring vacantly at the screen for a moment, hurried after him to the car.

It took them half an hour to get to the Newport Pagnell services. The place was full and they had to search for a parking space, eventually, in frustration, settling for a disabled space, before they headed for the lorry park. Shener picked up his camera and a foldable ruler from the glove box. Huddled in their coats for protection, they wormed their way through the parked cars to the heavy goods side of the facility.

'See anything from I T S?' Shener asked squinting into the wind.

'Tankers, over there,' Hassan pointed at a line of tankers.

'Damn! Nothing.' Shener spat onto the concrete. 'Just when you need one.'

'So, now?'

'We try the other side,' they trekked across to the other side of the lorry park and were rewarded by the sight of not one but two I T S tankers in the parking area. 'Come on we have work to do.'

With Hassan holding the extending ruler and Shener photographing from every conceivable angle, they noted measurements and took photos. Returning to the car, they set off southbound again.

'Mind telling me why we need to copy a tanker? I thought we were going to take the one from Leeds.'

'Wait and see,' Shener patted the camera in his pocket as he unlocked his car for the drive back.

Thankfully, the rain had stopped as they arrived back in Buncefield and Shener was relieved when M'Beki's tanker rolled into the yard. Not that he was worried, but he didn't need anything to go wrong right now. Hassan watched the slim figure with the goatee beard as he climbed out of his cab. This was the man then, he thought, this was the instrument of Allah. He bowed slightly in respect as M'Beki passed. Shener photographed this trailer as well and then followed M'Beki into the office, where he printed off the two sets of photos and laid them out next to each other. 'We must change a few things so it looks identical, but at least it's the same manufacturer and size. We will swap it with the real one, and we have our trailer. It'll be days before they notice.'

'Okay,' Hassan said, 'you think you can pull it off? Sounds iffy to me, too much reliance on luck.'

'Inshallah, my friend, Inshallah. You will see. Allah is with us.'

The evening was dark and brooding in spite of the day-bright floodlights outside. 'I'll be in touch,' Hassan said as he hugged Shener in farewell. He bowed again to M'Beki, and said, 'My friend, we have good news for you. You will have your part to play soon. I suggest you make your arrangements with Allah.'

Shener put his arm around M'Beki's shoulder saying, 'Go home and sleep tonight. Tomorrow we have a lot to discuss and you have a great deal to learn. You'll have a new rig.'

M'Beki headed for home. Shener checked his mailbox and skimmed the incomings. Companies House with a reminder for the company year-end report and a few adverts. His mobile rang as he sorted the wheat from the chaff and binned the rubbish. He listened intently to the caller, getting tenser as the call continued.

'Good, then leave the rig at Newport Pagnall on Monday night, that's the eighth. I'll sort it from there. Leave the driver inside.' He had to tell Masoud, he checked his number matrix and sent a text from his computer. 'Buyer completes on Tuesday 7:30. Your father.' Ridiculous, stupid code, he muttered to himself.

31

The emergency services operator beckoned her supervisor over, 'Sir, I have a report of a body found on the Duke of Westminster's estate in Chester. The woman, who phoned it in, is waiting by the body. It's up the main driveway going up to the house.'

'Get a response unit out right away, and ring the number back. Tell her we're on our way.'

'Yes sir.' She put out a call for immediate uniformed assistance. TR 112, the nearest unit, took ten minutes to reach the site. It was cold and a thin layer of ground frost gave the sweep of the long drive a fairy-tale like look in the glow of the car headlights. PC Doyle used the car clock to log the time of arrival at scene as 20:38. As promised on the radio call, a woman was indeed, waiting for them; a short, stocky woman with dark curly hair. She had obviously been walking her dogs, which were sniffing around her feet distractedly.

She was visibly in shock and all she kept saying was 'Over there, over there, over there.' repeatedly, pointing vaguely in the direction of some trees just behind the ornamental shrubs which lined the drive.

Doyle got out of the car and walked over, 'It's ok ma'am,' he said, trying to reassure her. 'Can you be more precise?' The flashing light from the car roof gave the trees a surreal look; the frost crystals glittering like tiny lasers in the blue flashes. He walked into the bushes, in the general direction the woman had been pointing in, struggling through the broken rhododendron branches and undergrowth. His torch beam sliced white swathes in front of him. He was beginning to think the whole thing was a wind-up, when he stumbled over something big, black and lumpy. A bin liner, no, a plastic sheet, tough stuff like builders' damp proofing. He bent down to examine it more closely, that's when he saw the hand. It was missing two fingers. He called in the find immediately.

Within an hour, the site was swarming with SoC people and detectives. Floodlights had been set up and the area taped off, not that there were any onlookers to hold back. DC Carlton and DC Whittaker were the first detectives to arrive at the scene. Whittaker walked over to speak to the witness as Carlton approached the police doctor, who was kneeling over the body.

'Been dead for at least a day I'd say,' he'd opined, 'know more when we've done the post-mortem.' That figured thought Carlton, shivering in the cold. It didn't need a degree in medicine to suss that out.

'Got the statement of the woman?' he turned to Whittaker who was coming towards him.

'Yes, she's in shock, nothing other than how she was made aware of the body by her dogs.' Whittaker replied, 'Is it him?'

'How many IC4s do you know around here with freshly hacked off fingers? The DNA testing will have to confirm this first though. Come on, let's go for a beer before they close. Not much we can do here. It's too damn cold just standing around. Let the buttons have something to do.'

'Where?'

'How about The Cricketers? Not far is it?'

'Yeah, why not,' he checked his watch, 'only just after ten. They'll still be open.'

A short drive and then thankfully they were in the warmth of a typical, modern English pub on a Monday night, empty. A bored barkeeper sat disinterestedly passing the time in front of a darts match on one of the sports channels and music blared throughout the place. He looked up brightly as the two detectives entered. Carlton signalled for the music to be turned down, which the barman reluctantly did. 'Not a fan of Seasick Steve then?' he grinned.

'No,' answered Carlton, speech now being an option with the drop in volume. 'Two pints of best,' Carlton ordered, now that they could hear themselves think again, 'bag of crisps, Stan?' Whittaker nodded yes as he walked along the bar area admiring the cricketing trophies and souvenirs on the walls. A bat signed by John Edridge, Alan Knotts's gloves, autographed photos. He recognised Graham Gooch, Colin Cowdrey, Geoff Boycott and many others there, and several more he didn't know. Nice goodies, he thought, as he perused them.

'Nice collection.' he commented. 'See you've got cameras to stop them getting nicked then. Gotta a problem with that? Theft I mean?'

'Nah, nobody is interested in cricket any more. It's just more stuff to clean and dust. The brewery makes us keep it. If we were called 'The Coach and Horses' we'd have naffin' stuffed horses everywhere and wagon wheels as lights. Glad were not the Boars Head, dread to think what they'd do to us then. Probably put in a trough to eat from,' he laughed mirthlessly, put the beers on the bar, and then stood ready, apparently for the chance of a bit of conversation.

Carlton took the first sip of his pint before the penny dropped.

'You've got CCTV in here?' he asked quietly.

'Yeah, 'course we have. A lot of pubs have it these days.' the barman looked up at him, surprised at the question.

'You remember I came in the day after the Brinkley's break-in and asked you some questions?'

'Yeah, 'course I do.'

'Why didn't you tell me about the CCTV? I'll answer it myself. I didn't ask did I? My stupidity, so now I'm asking, do you keep the discs?'

'Yeah, I reckon so, normally six months before we chuck them.'

'You still got the disc from the 24th?'

'Sure.'

'Can I see it? Or do I have to get a warrant?' he looked at Whittaker, who appeared angry at his partner's blunder.

'You don't have to come on heavy with me fellas, I'm always willing to help the law. Who knows when I'll need 'em. I'll have a look, back in a tick.' The barman disappeared behind a curtained doorway.

'They'll string you up by the goolies if this is important.' Whittaker chided.

'Don't remind me. Christ, how stupid!'

The barman reappeared holding a CD, 'Here,' he said, laying it on the bar, 'I don't think it's been touched since the day it was taken out. Wanna watch it?'

'Silly question.' Whittaker sipped his pint.

The barman shoved the CD into the player and pressed start. The darts match disappeared from the screen replaced by scenes in the bar, which weren't particularly clear, but from what they saw, they knew they needed to talk to Jemma Phelps and the boyfriend again and also ask Craig and Thompson to identify faces.

'All right if we take this?' Carlton asked, ejecting the disc and sticking it in his pocket without waiting for consent. The barman just shrugged. Carlton paid for the beers and they headed back to Nuns Road. It was going to be a long tough night. Shame Hanks wasn't there. He'd have loved it.

Whittaker picked up the radio and called for someone to go and pick up Jemma Phelps. He barked at the officer who responded, 'No, it can't wait and yes, while you're at it, wake Thompson and Craig, get them back to 'Interview 1' and set up a CD player. We'll be there in about fifteen minutes.

'How do we get the disc into evidence? Any ideas? I've a feeling they're gonna stuff me for this.' Carlton asked dejectedly.

There was no comment from Whittaker as they walked briskly across the cold yard to the car and set off back to base.

32

The chauffeured Daimler had more than enough space for them on the way South. Hanks was taking the opportunity to fathom out his new phone with Welks's help, as well as how to get rid of the 'Birdie Song' ring tone.

Nayyar was immersed with his ultra-flat laptop, which appeared to be almost an extension of his hands as it was never out of his grasp.

'What're you up to?' Hanks asked.

'I am analysing the information we downloaded from Khalid's phone. There is not much, the messages are all the same, 'Contact father', which are all from four different numbers. There were no outgoing calls or texts made from this phone.' Hanks was silent as a germ of an idea began to formulate in his mind.

'Listen, if I give you another set of phone records, can you cross reference any commonality between the numbers?'

'Sure,' Nayyar replied. 'I would need to write a sub routine for it.'

'You can do that now?' Hanks looked amazed.

'Of course,' Nayyar looked a little hurt at the question. 'I'll start now. I can do it web-based so we can all access it from wherever we are and whatever time of day it is. I see you've got the latest smart-phone there, you could even do it from that.'

'Like hell I can,' Hanks grunted, 'hasn't got any buttons on it.'

'He can't even make a phone call on it yet,' Welks laughed.

'Here, I'll show you,' Nayyar sighed, 'we'll have you up and running in no time.'

'Great! Mobile internet for incipient senior citizens,' Welks howled with laughter at his own witticism, drawing scathing looks from both Nayyar and Hanks. 'Well, maybe we can both learn something,' he conceded.

Nayyar devoted the rest of the journey writing the sub-routine and teaching the pair how to access the internet with a mobile phone, plus how to send and receive emails. By the time they got to the end of the M1 motorway, they were getting quite good at it.

Hanks sat back eyes closed as they drove into central London, deep in thought. The Lieutenant General had been deep in conversation on the phone all the way down and had hardly spared them a word. Just as they were entering Whitehall, he turned and announced a change of plan. The accommodation for the three of them would be in Horse Guards Barracks, as it was more convenient for the Ministry, which was just over the road.

Hanks reluctantly reopened his eyes, 'Horse Guards heh?' as if he had been on the ball all the time.

The three dragged their suitcases out of the boot, where waiting soldiers picked them up and took them off towards the barracks.

'Don't worry gentlemen, you and your bags will be reunited soon. I just want you over the road for a quick run through of tomorrow's events.' he said.

They arrived at ten to nine, not bad going from Chester to Central London Hanks thought, along with Nayyar and Welks, Hanks followed Richardson across Whitehall into the Ministry of Defence. In the guardroom, three soldiers jumped to attention as they entered with the Lieutenant General.

'Easy men,' he said, 'these people are here on defence matters and I need passes for Security zone 1.'

There followed a period of furious activity with forms being filled out, photos taken and eventually, twenty minutes later each of them had a sealed laminated plastic identity card on a ribbon loop with a photo. They now had access into the bowels of the

Ministry of Defence. In addition, they were issued with a blank white card with a magnetic stripe on one side and a little golden coil on the other. RFID, one of the soldiers explained, but Welks was none the wiser as he looked quizzically at it and hung it round his neck.

'Wear them visibly at all times when you are here, or over the road in the barracks,' the Lieutenant General advised them. 'The guards here aren't all uniformed, but they are all armed and have very nervous dispositions, especially when they see civvies without IDs. We don't want to lose one of you for something silly like that, one more thing, fingerprints. Please let the officer here scan your left index fingertip. You'll need both the magnetic card and your finger to go where we're going.'

The foyer where their lift was located was deserted, apart from themselves and the officer who rapidly scanned their fingers and recorded the data; there was no one in sight.

'Lift number 2 is the one you will be using. You'll see that your ID cards have a magnetic strip on the side. Swipe the card here on the turnstile to open the door and place your finger in here for the scan.' The Lieutenant General demonstrated as he spoke.

'Once inside, the lift only goes to one floor, the one with your authorisation. It takes you down to the war room and it does it fully automatically, as soon as the door closes.'

They all dutifully swiped their passes at the turnstile, placed their fingers in the scanner and went through into the lift.

'By the way, there is no mobile reception down here. If you want calls to reach you, give the guardhouse your mobile numbers and we'll see to it that Signals gets them relayed down here for you. There's special filtering hardware that collects the signal up top and gets it down here, as if it was a straight through connection. It's the same for outgoings. Any questions so far?'

'Toilets?' Hanks asked half-jokingly, although actually, his bladder was complaining after the long drive.

'Oh yes, of course, just to the left, there,' he pointed. Hanks excused himself and Welks followed, while the Lt. General and Nayyar carried on through a massive set of double doors. On their return to the others, Hanks noted the cavernous room's modern facilities. The vast room had an atmosphere like an empty theatre and smelled musty, like ill-ventilated meeting rooms the day after an event. Lots of desks and chairs surrounded a long, central table with seating for at least twenty people. The place was eerily quiet, the hum of the ventilation system just audible and the only discernable noise.

'So,' the Lieutenant General continued once they were all together again, 'here we are in one of the country's three War Rooms. This is a remnant from the good old 'Cold War' days. It's bombproof, gas proof and has enough air and food in it to keep a hundred people sustained for months if the need ever arose. We have every mod con you can think of in here and a few you can't. Communications H band, L band, microwave and scrambled secure phone lines to every part of the world. There are also direct lines to most Heads of State. As far as presentation goes, we have overhead systems and software for doing project planning all networked with each of the workstations here, naturally. If you want, these can be released for access by outside workstations anywhere in the UK. That may be useful for you, DCI Hanks, in linking in with Cheshire and you Nayyar don't need to worry about GCHQ, we are online permanently with them.' The Lieutenant picked up on the flash of concern on Nayyar's face. 'There's a system of laser pointers and highlighters for any of the displays. In addition, the possibility exists for projecting theatre maps and real time satellite images with any overlay you could care to mention. Happy?' he finished up, rather out of breath after his lightning tour of the amenities.

'Need a big board to stick notes and photos on. A big whiteboard with coloured felt tips,' Hanks said. 'Old, tried and trusted. Don't understand all these modern media tools and scribbling is faster than programming some computer, especially in a fast moving situation, the bigger the better, Lieutenant General. About three meters long and one high should do.'

'Plus you don't have to be Bill Gates to get it up there.' Welks added.

The Lieutenant General called out and a uniformed soldier appeared out of nowhere. Richardson told him what was required and sent him off.

'Okay, gentlemen, this is where it will happen tomorrow at

nine o'clock. Don't be put off by the faces, prominent or not, nor the behaviour of some of the participants.'

'I've put up with Michaels for months now; I can cope with anyone you throw at me sir,' Hanks joked.

So, I'll get someone to show you to your billet. We'll meet again tomorrow.' The Lieutenant General turned on his heel and was gone, leaving the three in the middle of the War Room.

An Adjutant appeared and asked them to follow him. They departed via the guardroom registering their telephone numbers for continuous connectivity for when they were underground. Back across Whitehall they were shown their rooms in the barracks; as the Lieutenant General had promised it was nothing grand, but adequate.

'The mess is this way, men. You must be hungry.' The adjutant directed them to the officers' mess where a white-jacketed steward showed them to their table. It was nine-thirty, an eventful forty minutes since their arrival. Hanks ordered a brandy which he felt he'd earned. Welks settled for a pint, and Nayyar, who was sitting opposite them, ordered a tomato juice. They tossed ideas around in a hushed whisper, trying not to arouse attention from the others in the mess. The steward repeatedly came and asked if they wanted food, but Hanks kept waving him away. Eventually, he gave in and allowed the steward to bring them the menu of the day.

33

Voss sat, head in hands, trying to fathom what could happen to the virus that hadn't already happened since it was now on the loose outside the lab. The seasonal flu epidemic was in full swing as well, and the registered cases were now running into thousands.

He had just received the summary of the Salameh test results who had tested positive to the new 'kindergarten virus', which evoked the twin feelings of helplessness and dread. The telephone rang, startling him. He picked it up, knocking papers to the floor in the process.

'Yes, Voss,' he said, scrabbling to gather the papers from the floor as he listened, then froze in his stooped position half-bent under the desk before continuing in a shocked tone, 'What? Yes, thanks,' just as the door opened.

'Private call boss?' Nick joked seeing Voss half under his desk with the phone in his hand.

'No! Help me get this lot sorted.' he requested gruffly, then said into the phone, 'No, sorry, not you. I was talking to someone in the office.' Nick knelt down starting to gather and sort the papers that had fallen, Voss returned to his call. 'Testing a vaccine?' he queried. 'Well, we could try, but it is a bit early for that. Well, yes, we are working as fast as we can.' Voss clambered back into his chair and hung up. 'Public Health Department, they are worried about the insurance man. They want us to test a vaccine.'

'What's his condition?'

'He's pretty poorly by all accounts; heavy secondary infection. I have been going over the vaccine reports all morning, and I have an idea which types of antigens will be effective against this kindergarten virus, but the proof of the pudding will be in the testing. Let's go to the lab.'

'He's about the earliest case we have, so we need to know how he got the bug.' Nick replied, while they were on their way.

'Right, we all tested positive for the K virus, and strangely, none of us got as badly affected as him.' These two questions were nagging him like toothache. How did Salameh get infected and why was he so badly affected?

Downstairs in the lab, the racks of infected saliva-sample vials from the Health Department were beginning to take up serious space.

'How are we doing?' Voss asked.

'We are just adding the last of the Health Department samples to the test trays, and sending the collection tubes for incineration. That'll give us some space.'

'Good,' Voss said, eying the work they'd done already.

Mary added, 'If we get a pandemic then we can't operate from here. Just the thousand odd samples we have now are overloading us. We simply won't have the space to deal with more.'

'That's for sure.' Nick said dumping the last of the plastic collection tubes in the sack for disposal. 'We're going to need more storage if this gets any bigger.'

'I've got one big question that's been bothering me,' Voss responded, 'how did Salameh get so badly infected, so early?'

They began discussing the infection route for the poor insurance man. Nick was sitting on a stool resting his back against the workbench. 'He was here two days before the kindergarten virus was discovered and none of us had been in contact with the 'wild virus' when he was here, so he can't have got it from us.'

'Doesn't seem like it Nick,' Voss said thoughtfully. 'I can't see how it could be. It didn't exist then.'

'Does he have kids?' Claire said getting up. 'If he does and they are at the kindergarten, which would explain it.'

'Claire, I did the kindergarten list. There were no kids on it called Salameh. I mean the name is that uncommon, I would have noticed.'

'I suppose so.' Claire replied dejectedly, going back to work on the virus samples.

Voss sat down, deep in thought. The others stood around, at loss, waiting, obviously wondering what was going through his mind. Mary broke the silence, 'He seemed to be getting a cold when he was here, do you think that was it?' she asked.

'Yes Mary, I remember him sneezing, but how could that have been the K virus?' Nick was sceptical.

'The big question is where the source is? Thinking back on it, we all got our coughs and sneezes after his visit, our infections also turned out to be the K virus.'

'The incubation time is quick, we know that.' Nick added.

'Not so fast that you can get the symptoms before the virus though,' Claire joked.

'So,' Voss mused, 'when did he get ill?'

'Second question is where and how did he become infected? What is the source?' Nick added.

'Was there a secondary source, do you think?' Claire looked round at the others.

'How do we find that out?' Mary asked gloomily. Claire's face suddenly lit up and Mary studied her closely, 'What? What are you thinking?'

'Nothing,' Claire said innocently, 'it's just that I may have a way to find out. I need to make a phone call.' Voss pushed the phone across to her. 'No, in private,' she smiled, turning to leave the room picking up Salameh's sample card as she went.

Elated at the chance of speaking to him, she quickly dialled Hanks's number. 'Mr Hanks?' she asked, then more hesitantly, 'Alan?' She waited breathlessly.

'Yes, oh, hello Claire, what do I owe this to?'

'I need a favour.'

'I can't do parking or speeding tickets.'

'No,' she laughed, 'nothing like that. It's something that's maybe to do with your case, the break-in.'

'Okay,' Hanks replied, more cautiously now, 'what might the

favour involve?'

'The insurance man, who came to see Mr Voss two days after the break-in. He is sick with the virus and we need to know if he has any connection with the Rainbow Kindergarten in Blacon.'

'Why is this important?'

'We need to know how he was infected. If he has a link to someone in the kindergarten, then obviously he would have been infected there, if not, we are dealing with another source of infection.'

'Hang on, I'm writing this down.'

'Give me the man's name and where I can reach him,' Hanks paused as he noted it down, 'I'll get back to you as fast as I can.'

'Oh, right...,' she recited the information she had on Mr Salameh. 'Is that all you need?' she asked pertly, leaving the question hanging tantalisingly.

'Well, maybe you could ask that again later?' he teased back. 'Right, I'll get someone on this immediately. I'll call you back.'

'I'll look forward to that.' she answered going back into the office to be greeted by three puzzled faces.

'Well?' her sister asked, rather piqued, 'You gonna tell us what that was all about?'

34

On Friday morning when he left home, Shener was feeling tense. His wife Aysha and the kids had noticed the change in him over the last days and had been needling him about his moods. Murphy was in the Porta-Cabin when he arrived, clipping delivery notes to the clipboard on the wall.

'Morning, you doing Hendon?' he asked, as he hung his coat behind the door, 'When you come back I have a little extra job to give to you, for Tuesday. Bit of extra cash, okay?'

'Sure boss.'

'Means an early start at about 3 am. Is that a problem?'

'Nah. Where to?'

'London, taking the repair rig into the city.'

'Yeah, no prob.'

Shener saw Murphy return to his rig, and swing himself up into the cab before starting the engine, its noise partially drowned by Irish folk music blasting from the stereo. Then, as he turned away from the window to put the kettle on, he spotted that M'Beki was coming across the yard towards the office. He sat down at his desk and switched his computer on, Ahmed burst in, happiness spread all over his face. Shener supposed it was the thought of the coming operation that was buoying him up, as Shener's cousin arrived and parked his car next to the building, before also coming into the office.

'The weather will kill me,' he complained as he hung his coat behind the door.

'Welcome, Arif. Take tea with us,' he offered sliding a cup in his direction and gesturing the newcomer to take a seat. You are our rescuer in our time of need. You know what I need you to do?'

'Change the ID.' Arif said.

'Right.'

'Just swap black boxes?'

'Yes, with the one from our old trailer.'

'Okay, it doesn't take long. Where is it?'

Shener poured tea for all three of them.

'In the paint shop, you can go there and dismantle it, ready to swap. It'll save time.'

'We have to amend the valve control system on the new unit. You just want it disabled right?'

'Yeah, and don't forget the seals, they must be exactly like the original 'Customs and Revenue'. If anyone checks, we don't want them getting suspicious.' Shener sipped his tea.

Ahmed wiped his lips with the back of his hand and asked, 'You have a date now, Mr Shener?'

'All in good time my friend,' Shener nodded. 'First, you must learn what to do. We must get you trained in the delivery of our weapon. It's a very sensitive load, and very dangerous.' He stared out of the small window into the yard, pondering on just how big a bang the trailer would actually make. For a moment, scarily, he imagined that the office was getting hotter just at the thought.

'Right,' he began, 'you know you must be careful not to arouse suspicion. It must appear like a breakdown, a perfectly normal breakdown.' Ahmed nodded. 'I will send the repair truck there as well, so it all looks normal.' He dragged an old London A to Z out of his desk drawer and checked the index for the page. 'Here,' he said, pointing to a street in the City of London, 'this is Poultry. This is where you must be on the day. It is here,' he pencilled an 'X' on the spot, 'on the side nearest The Mansion House. You must break down exactly here.' He called up Hassan's photos on his computer and highlighted the ones with the newsstand. 'Here,' he pointed again, 'under this metal container there is a cover. You must lift it enough to get a six-inch pipe into it. Nobody must see it; try to hide it as best you can.' He laid the two hooks that Hassan had given him on the table in front of him. 'You'll need these to lift the cover,' he pushed them over. 'You only have the one chance. You must dispose of just over half the load into the hole under this cover and we don't know how quickly it will drain. You have to avoid any overspill into the street, at all costs. You'll need to earth the the tank, too. We don't need any sparks when you're unloading.' M'Beki nodded in apparent understanding. 'The electronic locks will be removed so you can adjust the flow manually when you unload. My cousin will go with you on Monday night and do everything necessary to the electronics. You just have to drive.

When you 'break down' you must also push down the red switch in the cab that deactivates and overrides the safety systems,' he said sternly. 'You mustn't forget!' Ahmed nodded. 'Make sure you do everything by the book. We don't need some over-zealous policeman getting inquisitive. Tell me now what you have to do. I want to be sure you have memorised it.'

'When I get to the place you showed me on the map, I pretend to break down. I disconnect the control unit for the diesel, to make the truck not work. I must stop on exactly the spot you told me. The valves must be over the news stand. Then I put the hose in through the inspection cover and earth the tank with the aluminium ladder. I drain half the tank into the hole, and press the button on the dash board that you showed me, the one that heats the ether in the tank.'

Shener nodded. 'Good, Ahmed, well done, it will be a glorious day.'

'I am proud,' Ahmed held his hand on his heart, 'I am so proud.'

Shener was distracted as a text came in on his phone with the accompanying peep-peep, and a second message followed almost immediately. Shener didn't want to read them in their presence. He forced himself to wait until Ahmed stood up, said his goodbyes and left the Porta-Cabin.

Trembling, Shener read the first message. It was simple and to the point.

'May Allah be with you and may your reward be in heaven. All is as agreed. Your father.' That was the sign, the green light.

He read the second message,'285K STG IBKK ACTIONED.' Ah, he thought, the money is there, he would have to notify the couriers. He picked up the phone to put things in motion. His first call was to the preacher and the next was to Leeds.

35

Langley had made it quite clear it was top priority. They'd been told to stop whatever other ops were going on in Swat to concentrate on this one person. Lt. Janet Cody had the man's picture and his name up in the top left corner of her screen, Qamar al Surira. This time it wasn't just a find and photo mission, this was a clear eliminate by any method job, a 'Red Flag'. She didn't feel any emotion. She didn't hate the man. Hate wasn't a factor. She was just totally concentrated on the mechanics, getting a Hellfire onto the specified target.

They had gotten the telephone number from the Brits from their special communications place in England and had photographed the user in Achar a week ago. The problem now was that there was no longer an active signal coming from Achar. Had the bird flown the nest?

First Lieutenant Cody took 'Recon 1' down another thousand feet. Maybe atmospherics were playing tricks on her sensors. 'Still nothing.' she called into her microphone. It was already light in Achar and the first villagers were out and about doing their chores. Smoke rose from the chimneys of a few of the small, flat-roofed houses and she tried to imagine what these people would be cooking for breakfast. She swept her Zephyr in an arc over the house where she'd managed to get the original photo of the target. There were only a few goats out in a paddock and a little girl with a bucket. She zoomed in on the girl, not out of suspicion, but simple curiosity. The child, in ragged clothes, had long dark hair and looked about ten years old. Suddenly Cody froze the picture. The object she'd identified as a bucket didn't look right. She zoomed in on it. 'I think I may have something,' she said softly into her mike.

'Go ahead Recon 1,' her headset answered, 'Do you have a signal?'

'That's negative. Repeat negative, control. I see a girl carrying something, not sure what it is at the moment. Am going down for closer inspection, and will put the image on your display.'

'Roger Recon 1.'

The Zephyr dropped like a stone to five hundred feet. The girl suddenly appeared startled. Cody froze, had she seen or heard the drone? No, that couldn't be. She checked she was on battery so the electric motor would be almost noiseless. No, something had happened. The girl started to move more quickly in the direction of the largest building in the village. Someone was standing in a doorway calling her, beckoning. Cody relaxed a bit trying to get a clearer focus on the object the girl was carrying.

'Any folks there who can help me?' she spoke into the mike again.

'Recon 2 here. What gives?'

'Take a look at the feed from Recon 1. Can you identify the object being carried?'

'Will try, switching now.'

Cody had the girl dead centre. The bucket seemed more like a satchel now, it had a shoulder strap.

'Recon 1? Recon 2 here. Best guess is a laptop, hope it helps.'

Her heart stopped. 'Control, we have a laptop in transit in the village.'

'Good work Recon 1. Follow it. Advise contact with target.'

The young girl slipped into the house. The door closed behind her. She circled the Zephyr over the house filming down on to as well as around it. All was quiet.

'What preds do I have on call?' she asked into the mike.

'Control here, Pred 1 and Pred 3 at your disposal.'

'Roger, understood, will call if needed.' Cody concentrated

on the signal sensors. Still nothing.

'All Recons, we have SIGINT from Langley. A text has gone out from one of the suspect satellite numbers in Pakistan. The number is currently active. Clear text will follow ASAP.'

'Good! We have him,' Cody muttered excitedly, under her breath.

'You always get this emotional Recon 1?' It was Recon 2, her backup.

'No, just a mite tense with this one, something big, maybe?'

'Ain't they all?'

The drone was coming round south again when she saw a figure approaching the house. Damn, she thought, I'm coming from behind. I can't get a facial.

'Recon 2, where are you?'

'Recon 1, seven hundred yards west of your position on auto-hold.'

'Get over to me from the north need a facial on target at GPS…' and she gave the coordinates.

'Wilco. Zephyr 2 coming in at 180° and 800 feet. Keep your distance, we don't want to play bumper cars up here.'

'Come in good and low. I want a good picture. Zephyr 1 climbing to 1000 feet course 270°. I'm taking my bird away. Site clear for Recon 2.' she said.

'Confirm.' Recon 1 added.

It was all very calm very impersonal, a tightly trained routine.

'Recon 1, I have contact. Male subject walking north towards building complex. Male, in local dress. Getting a photo,' a short pause, 'now. Photo downloading.'

'Thanks Recon 2.' Cody used her joy-stick to bring her drone back towards the building. She could see the man going in through the same door as the young girl.

'Recon 2 please clear the area.'

'Confirm clearing area, holding at point zeta one thousand feet.'

'Roger and thanks for that.' She placed her drone about a hundred meters south of the building and put it in a holding pattern, the Zephyr doing figures of eight over the building at five hundred feet. Ping! Ping! Ping! The signal indicator blinked in unison with the noise.

'We have signal traffic. I'm checking data.' Tension was building in everyone in the War Room now.

'Confirm telephone text traffic. Clear message in Urdu translation awaited.' Cody spoke into her mike.

'Control here, telephone number is confirmed. Await further instructions. Translation is on its way.'

The controller made a call to Langley, who were doubtless following the live stream anyway.

'Control, War Room, Andrews,' he announced to the agent who picked up, 'we have a confirmed contact with the target using a known number. Instructions please.'

'Your target is confirmed hostile. Awaiting message translation,' the agent answered. 'Hold until we know more. I'll get back to you.'

The translations from Urdu were coming on stream in Andrews, Langley and Cheltenham almost simultaneously.

The first was:

'May Allah be with you and may your reward be in heaven. All is as agreed. Your father,' followed by

'285K STG IBKK ACTIONED.'

The senders' number was the same; two numbers received the same messages.

The recipient numbers were unidentified. He phoned Lieutenant General Richardson with the news and mailed the messages to Nayyar and Hanks. His next call was to Langley, short and sweet. 'Take him out.'

The Controller's hotline phone beeped in Andrews Airbase.

'War Room Control.'

'Langley here, we have a go. Eliminate the target. I repeat the target is to be terminated, immediately.'

'Confirm; instruction understood.' The controller picked up the hand mike to the War Room. 'Action, Pred 1 and Pred 3.'

'Roger Pred 1.'

'Roger Pred 3,' they both responded.

'We have a go. Target Qamar al Surira. We are clear to execute. Recon 1 give coordinates.'

Cody acknowledged and sent her drone over the site. Pred 1 moved into her scanner range. Her cameras were firmly focused on the ground though.

'Pred 1, clear vision, releasing HF 2 and 4,' referring to the firing of two Hellfire missiles. The building under the drone seemed to shudder and suddenly lifted and disappeared in a cloud of dust and smoke.

'Target hit and damaged.' Cody reported calmly. She noted a little girl running from the collapsing building. She couldn't tell if it was the same one, but hoped she'd make it.

'Pred 3 coming in from the south, release HF 1 and CBs.' the third missile tore the core out of the building causing the external walls to collapse outwards. Effectively the building had been razed to the ground. The smoke was beginning to clear. There was no movement on the site, just drifting smoke. The time delay and proximity-fused cluster munitions would take care of any survivors and potential rescuers.

Cody checked her signal sensors, 'No signals or movement on site,' she confirmed. She checked to see she had filmed everything. 'Recon 1 leaving site to resume normal patrol.' she announced, feeling the let-down, the emotion she always felt after an operation. The adrenalin drained from her, she felt exhausted. Was it a success? She could never tell.

'Well done team,' the controller announced into his mike, 'back to planned flights,' he said as he confirmed the kill to Langley and texted the news to GCHQ in England. 'Any new signals let me know immediately.'

36

Welks's phone rang just as the meal arrived. 'No, his phone works now. He got a new one,' he answered, rolling his eyes. 'No, we were in a place where, let's just say, reception is limited. What's up?' He listened intently, all eyes on him. 'You what? That's... oh, shit!' he slapped the palm of his hand against his forehead. 'When? Hang on, I'll give you Hanks.' He was visibly shaken as he handed the phone over.

Several of the officers at the surrounding tables stopped talking to eavesdrop on hearing the stranger's expletive. Hanks took the phone and went outside with it.

'Bad news?' Nayyar asked nervously.

'You could say so.' Welks said thoughtfully, chewing over the information he'd just received. 'Our hostage just turned up dead in some woodland on the outskirts of Chester,' he explained.

Hanks came back in and drained his brandy in one go. He drew a deep breath and started talking. 'Whittaker and Carlton have found our hostage, dead. And now Carlton has just admitted screwing up about the CCTV footage of the break-in night. No-one thought to check if there was CCTV in the pub.'

'What a total plonker! Typical Carlton, too daft to catch a cold,' Welks sneered.

'Anyway, Carlton and Whittaker have viewed the CD. Guess who's on it, slap in the middle of the party? Jemma Phelps and her boyfriend!' Hanks looked around waving for the steward, and then turned to face Welks and Nayyar again. 'They've got people going to pick them up now. Could be an interesting night and we're not damn well there,' he fumed, 'Instead, we're poncing around in a...' the steward interrupted his tirade.

'Yes sir?'

'Bring us a brandy each. Tell you what; bring the bottle and three glasses.'

'I'd be happier being there putting my face in,' Welks said glumly. 'Carlton! What a clown! This has cost us time, lots of it.'

'What about the dead hostage? How did he die?' it was Nayyar who asked.

'Dunno!' Welks was puzzled, 'They're doing a PM tomorrow, may take a few days before we know for sure.'

'I don't drink alcohol by the way.' Nayyar said as the steward returned. 'My upbringing, you know, never got used to the stuff.'

'You will tonight,' Welks said, 'you're in the team now.'

Hanks's phone rang, this time not the 'Birdie Song' but a discreet warbling tone.

'Hanks!' he rolled his eyes up as he mouthed 'Michaels' to Welks, who reciprocated the gesture. 'Yes sir, I have heard. Yes sir, most distressing. No sir, I don't have any further information. No, I suggest you talk to Carlton or Whittaker. They are the troops on the ground now, sir.' He took a gulp of his brandy. 'Really sir, there's nothing we can do from this end. I have talked to Whittaker and he's been primed. It's up to him to squeeze the info out of them. I know, I'm as keen to find out as you, sir. Thank you.' he managed to get in before breaking the connection.

'Michaels eh?' Welks grinned.

'How do they get that far up the ladder? Can you answer me that, Welks? Pure unadulterated incompetence in uniform and it gets up to that level. It beats me.'

'Probably helped more old ladies across the road than you did, and he fills in forms better than you do, and he's also polite to people and doesn't swear so much in public. They call them soft skills these days. Oh, and I'd heard he doesn't drink either!'

'You're a solid gold arsehole,' Hanks chinked his glass with the other two. 'Cheers,' he said and downed it in one. Nayyar spluttered, his face going red as he drank his first neat brandy.

Welks looked at him, 'If you're in the team, you have to suffer like the rest of us. It's not fair otherwise. Call it equality.' That caused all three to laugh as he turned and ordered a coke from the steward. 'Here, you can mix that with the next one, it'll be easier.' Nayyar just nodded gratefully.

'I don't like the feel of this,' Hanks said refilling the glasses. 'It makes no sense to kill the hostage, no sense at all, takes all the pressure out of the threat.'

'What if he did die from natural causes though?' Nayyar queried.

'What natural causes?' Hanks scoffed. 'Bloody bad luck if your hostage dies on you of natural causes! Well, we won't know for definite until the post-mortem.'

Hanks checked his phone for any incoming emails noticing that Whittaker still had not sent the data from Claire's phone. 'I really wonder what the hell they are doing up there.' he fumed as he rang Chester Police Station to remind Whittaker to get him the phone data and then they batted information and theories around for over an hour before finally turning in for the night.

Hanks tossed and turned in his bed. Sleep just wouldn't come. There was something about Claire, the kiss and his subsequent frank, deeply personal talk with her that just wouldn't leave him alone. He was startled by a ringing noise coming from his jacket pocket. His telephone, but not his new ring tone. This was like the old metal alarm clock that he used to have as a kid, the one with two bells on the top and a hammer banging away between them. He cursed and got up to retrieve his phone, annoyed that somehow he'd managed to set the alarm function for two-thirty am. He killed the sound and put the phone by his bedside as he got back into bed, in an attempt to sleep. He had half managed, when the phone went again. He cursed, picking it up.

'Sergeant Jessop here sir, Chester Police. Thought you ought to know; the security guard from Brinkley's didn't make it. He died about ten minutes ago. PC Steadman just called in from the hospital.' Hanks thanked him and disconnected. No way of getting any sleep now, he thought. He quickly got dressed and headed for the door, fresh air was required. The corridor outside his room was empty as he walked barefoot, carrying just his phone, towards the doors at the end. His phone beeped with the incoming mail from Whittaker as he shouldered the stiff door open and practically fell out into the night, not knowing who was more surprised, Nayyar or himself as they simultaneously said, 'What the hell!'

'What are you up to out here this time of night?' Hanks finally got out.

'Damned brandy, made my stomach churn, I couldn't sleep. Had heartburn and felt sick, never again!' Nayyar looked ill.

'Never mind, you'll live. You'll have worse than that to cope with before this is sorted out,' Hanks consoled him. He saw Nayyar had his laptop with him. 'It's good I find you though, I just got the telephone data from Chester. I need you to help with the screening of the phone numbers.'

'Sure, sir, the program is still in beta version, but you can log on and have a try.'

'How do I do it?' Hanks asked.

'You could just log on to the program online with your phone, but that will probably be too slow, I reckon that we need a decent PC terminal.'

Hanks was unsure, 'What happens if I put the Grigson number in?'

'Well, we cross check our database with any of the numbers that the phone companies have sent us. What it means is, that not only can we see if, say, someone phoned Ms Grigson yesterday at 3 pm; which you could get from her provider, we can also track back whoever else they called, even if they have a different provider.'

'Okay, let's do it then?'

'We'll have to find a PC with internet access, I am using my phone's 3G out here, and there is no reception in the rooms.'

'And what gentlemen, would we be wanting reception for?' A deep voice from behind them startled both of them.

'Jesus!' Hanks managed, after his heart started beating again. 'What in God's name are you doing creeping up on folk like that in the middle of the night?'

'I might ask you, what two civvies are doing in Horse Guards

Barracks at gone 3 am, trying to get onto the internet. I'm security, on guard duty.'

'We've got passes. Lieutenant General Richardson gave them to us.' Nayyar stammered, visibly shaken and holding up his laminated MoD ID.

'And you?'

Hanks, thankfully still had his round his neck, and dutifully showed it as well.

'Better follow me then.'

'Jesus, scared the shit out of me that did,' Hanks conceded as they walked behind the man. Only then did Hanks notice the Heckler and Koch machine gun over his shoulder. Richardson hadn't been joking.

They were led into a brightly lit room where four soldiers were studying security screens covering the perimeter of the barracks. The escort introduced them to the four and told them they could use a desk in the corner, internet connectivity was given there.

They retreated to the desk. The heat in the room was oppressive and made Hanks wish he'd put a shirt on and not a pullover. Nayyar was into his programme now. 'Okay, got the data for me?'

'Sure, I'll forward the email from Whittaker to you, so you can copy and paste the numbers your new tool.' Pleased with his confidence in the jargon, Hanks was forced to put his new found knowledge to the test as he forwarded the data from Whittaker to Nayyar.

'This'll take a while; you've sent me a big xls data block. I'll have to write some code to do searches within the tables. Go have a coffee or something. It'll be at least two hours until I have something.'

Hanks, pleased to get out of the heat, went back to his room and lay down. The time was four twenty-two as he nodded off.

Breakfast was frantic. Hanks had overslept, Welks had already gone over to the MoD and come back for breakfast and Nayyar hadn't slept at all. By the time they all settled down in the mess it was half past eight.

'Nayyar, you look dreadful. Bad night?' Hanks jested.

Nayyar grunted something incomprehensible through a

mouthful of toast and beans, cleared his throat and said.

'Mr Hanks, I think we may have hit pay-dirt.'

'Uh-huh, in what way?' Hanks gulped his orange juice down.

'Your data last night.'

'Let's hear it.'

'Well, if the unanswered calls and the calls on Tuesdays between 13:30 and 14:30 are all from the same person, then we have a pattern.'

'Yeah, the bloke phones every Tuesday to get his rocks off. That's a pattern,' Welks laughed as he shoved the last piece of toast in his mouth.

'The pattern is that it's never the same provider successively, the provider changes constantly.'

'That's it,' Hanks said excitedly, 'it's the pattern!' Hanks got up, thinking franticly now. 'Look, the first call recorded is Vodafone then we go to an Orange, then Three the next one is 0_2 then we see Vodafone again. The Vodafone call numbers are five weeks later are exactly one digit apart, see,' he stabbed a finger at the display. '8769920 is the first one and the second is 8769921.'

'Bloody hell you're sharp,' Nayyar complimented, 'dammit you're right, here we have the next Orange number five weeks later ending exactly one digit from the previous time he used orange. My God, that's how they are communicating!' He said, his excitement bubbling over. 'We can now suss out the bastard's sequence.'

Welks looked at the time. 'We're late. We'd better get going.' With that, they left for the War Room.

Downstairs, after the lift drop they entered a different room to the one they were in the day before.

'Is that the Prime Minister?' Welks nudged Hanks.

'We're not in Madame sodding Tussaud's, you plonker. Of course he's Gordon-bloody-Brown,' Hanks said.

'Ah, D.C.I. Hanks, D.I. Welks, Mr Nayyar, welcome. I trust you slept well. May I introduce you to Mr Browne before we get started?' Lieutenant General Richardson stood next to them like he'd been freshly laundered.

'Gentlemen, the Defence Secretary Mr Browne. Mr Browne, D.C.I Hanks and his team.' They shook hands perfunctorily as they went to the main table.

Hanks was impressed, Welks had been busy. The whiteboard was full of the case. Pictures and felt tip lines marked various links, telephone numbers, and dates, he'd done the works. Hanks scanned it for completeness and wasn't disappointed. He saw the Metropolitan Police Commissioner, Sir Paul Stevens and nodded at him. Quite a difference to the old days. They'd both moved on.

Without much ado, the people around the table were all introduced and the division of labour agreed. There were the workers and gatherers, the deciders and the implementers.

'Good job with the whiteboard, Welks. It looks like those Rolf Harris TV shows did you some good,' he whispered jokingly.

'Thanks.' Welks gave him a scathing look back.

'Now, ladies and gentlemen,' Richardson started, 'I'd like to introduce D.C.I. Hanks to you, for those of you who don't know him. He'll give us a quick résumé of the incident so far. Mr Hanks, if you please.'

Hanks stood up and cleared his throat, 'Ladies, Gentlemen. I won't beat about the bush with long-winded introductions, backgrounds or explanations, as I assume that you have been informed. I'll give you a short synopsis of a situation which has been developing since the break-in at Brinkley's Medical in Chester on the 24thof October.' Hanks went on to outline the case to date and progress made. 'The question that needs answering is, whether this a terrorist attack on the UK using animal activists to do the dirty work for them? Speaking against this idea is the fact that our erstwhile terror suspect was kidnapped, and then subsequently found dead.

Our friends in America have identified one of our suspects; he turns out to be the man linked to the Nairobi bombings. His name is Qamar al Surira, a Saudi citizen.' He stopped to let the information sink in. 'This is him.' He went to the whiteboard and pointed at the picture.

'So, Ladies and Gentlemen, I personally feel the main event isn't the animal lab break-in. I believe that an event was probably planned, but was coincidently crossed by the animal rights front, taking a hostage they had no idea was a terrorist sleeper. Then there is Operation 'Buyer'. From Mr Nayyar's intuitive stab, we have a best guess that an accident involving ether, i.e. a big explosion with massive collateral damage is in planning. Where, when and if at all, is still a complete mystery.' He regarded a sea of stunned faces around the table. 'The hostage, if we had found him alive, could have solved a lot of questions. Unfortunately, he was discovered dead last night.'

'Do we have cause of death for the hostage yet Mr Hanks?' The question was from the tall, lanky Mr Hall, of the Think Tank.

'A post-mortem has been carried out; the results of which I'm sure will be of interest to all of us, I'm advised, will be available sometime today.'

The Home Secretary immediately picked up a phone, 'Get me the Chief Constable of Cheshire.' The remainder of the conversation was drowned by more questions.

Most of the rest of the morning was taken up with discussions about the early warning systems and activation of SitCen, the EU central committee on terror alerts. Jack Straw, the deputy PM seemed more concerned about adherence to correct protocols, than the current danger; whether SitCen should be advised and then EMIC (European Management Information Centre) or vice versa. Eventually, a compromise was reached and the decision made that the Council Secretariat should be given the information to disseminate it as they saw fit.

Hanks fumed about valuable time being wasted on this kind of mindless formality, which annoyed him intensely. Even the Lieutenant General noted his increasing frustration.

Lunch saw half the hangers-on and the ministers disappear. The two detectives availed themselves from the meagre buffet and settled in thoughtful silence at a small side table, both chewing on canapés and sandwiches. Nayyar had his laptop out again and was busily typing away between nibbling at his sandwich.

'What do you make of that load of old bollocks then?' Hanks finally asked, before biting into one of the canapés.

'Pretty boring, wasn't it?' Welks grinned.

'Specially your bit,' Nayyar chipped in. They laughed, grateful for a bit of levity.

Hanks checked his phone for emails while shoving another prawn sandwich into his mouth. 'Email from Wheeler. He sent us the coordinates from the email intercepts, forwarding it to Nayyar now.'

Hanks saw the Lieutenant General coming over. 'We've got some workrooms and staff at your disposal,' he said, 'if you'd like to follow me, I'll show you where you can get stuck into things. 'Mr Hall from the 'Think Tank' said he'd like to join your group, I hope you have no objections.'

'I think I'd like someone else here as well, if that's okay with you?' Hanks replied. 'Mr Voss from Brinkley's, we cannot afford to ignore the danger on the epidemic front, even if the cause was accidental.'

'We're not ignoring it Hanks. We're taking it very seriously indeed. However, I agree it would be good to have the man on call here in London. I'll get someone to organise it. If you've finished lunch gentlemen, follow me.'

Hanks walked past the buffet and pocketed a handful of mini pork pies as emergency rations. Who knows what the day will bring, he thought. The Lieutenant General led them off into a side room which had a whiteboard, six desks, twelve chairs and a workstation for each chair. There were telephones and printers plus a staff of four women and two men in Army uniforms. Lieutenant General Richardson introduced them. The most senior was a young first lieutenant who, the Lieutenant General said, was in charge of the team.

After Richardson had gone, Hanks briefed all of them on the incident, which proved superfluous, as they'd caught his performance in the main room on CCTV. Still, it gave everybody the chance to see who understood what and which aspects were unclear.

Nayyar was getting a little agitated, 'Mr Hanks, sir,' he interrupted, 'I think we need a big world map and a big UK map. I've got the data from Wheeler and it's practically all GPS coordinates.'

Hanks looked askingly at the lieutenant, 'Can you oblige?'

'Nothing easier, we'll project them on the wall over there.' He said indicating the clear white wall on the long side of the room. 'We'll use one of the satellite composite images.'

'Nayyar, you sort it out with him and get your data arranged into some form I can understand. I like pictures, I can understand them better than writing,' Hanks said. 'I can't handle abstracts. See what you can do.' He left them to it.

'What about the PM on Kasab?' Welks asked. 'Did I understand that correctly, that the Home Secretary phoned the Chief Constable to push that?'

'Yeah, I think he did. Get on the phone to Carlton and find out what the score is up there now.' Hanks glanced towards the door where Chris Hall had just come in.

'Hi,' he called, 'where would you like me to start?' Hall shook his hand and swept a long strand of hair out of his face.

'Join Nayyar, he's got a heap of data to sort. Best of luck.' Hanks went to the first available desk and sat down, powering up the PC in front of him. Another email from Colonel Wheeler had arrived. There was an attachment with a close-up of the face of a man, non-descript, middle eastern in appearance. A caption below stated: Masoud Baitullah also known as, Fehmi, aka, al Jamallah, aka, aka ... the list was seemingly endless. Bloody hell, one hot punter that one, he thought. He picked up the phone and dialled as he forwarded the mail to Chester. 'What's new?' as asked as he managed to reach an exhausted sounding Gunner.

'I must say, you have some powerful allies where you are. The Chief Constable's been rocking the place to get action, especially on the post-mortem of the Kasab fellow.'

'Any news on that?' Hanks asked.

'Only that the death was not caused by violence. The toxicology tests will take a while, but it doesn't feel like a poisoning either. The professor is tipping natural causes as a result of an infection. We'll know more later. Whittaker and Harris plus team have gone off chasing the ARF band. We have all the names and addresses now. I'm sure Whittaker will key you in when he gets back. The Metcalf woman got out; she's on a plane to Charles de Gaulle. Interpol will pick her up when she lands.'

'What about the Phelps woman, the Brinkley's employee?'

'She's come apart at the seams and has told us everything and more. It seems now; she's making things up, just to keep us happy.' Gunner grunted something to someone in the office which Hanks didn't pick up.

'So the ARF thing is about wrapped up then?' Hanks asked.

'Appears so.'

'Who wielded the crowbar?' Hanks asked.

'What crowbar?' Gunner asked surprised.

Hanks repeated himself, 'Yes, the crowbar from the van in Connah's Quay. You do know we're talking murder here?'

'Sorry the news hadn't reached me. I just came in.'

'From the video coverage, it has to be one of the bigger men, check the footage again, if I remember correctly, it was probably one of the two from the van.' Hanks clasped his forehead, trying to visualise the clip again.

'We have a couple in custody already; I'll push on that one. Be nice to get at least part of the mess here finalised.'

'All of it would be better. Chuck the book at them. Bloody lunatics might just have wiped out the whole population with their crass ideas of helping the world,' Hanks snorted angrily into the phone as he hung up.

He walked over to Hall and Nayyar, munching one of his pork pies. 'How's it going?'

'We've found others using the same method with one day SIM cards as well, also with the same sequencing. We've made an assumption that the cards are in blocks per provider and asked the Telecoms to tell us where they were sold. Unfortunately, we hit a blank wall as they were all bought from vending machines. GCHQ is doing a nationwide scan of the SIM card sales, checking for those that appear to be block sales. Colonel Wheeler's people are working round the clock on that. The amount of data they have to sort is massive. Sales of prepaid SIM cards run between 9,000 and 39,000 a day, depending on demand. The ones in question are vending machine sales.'

'Where?' Hanks was fully alert now. 'Where were the vending machines?'

'Heathrow Terminal 1. Why?'

'Never mind that now. When?'

Nayyar clicked from one set of data to another on his laptop. 'Between the 27th and 29th, that's the interval between machine fillings.'

'The first usage of these cards was when?' Hanks faced

Nayyar the tension inside him rising.

'27th of October.'

'That narrows it down a lot. Who has the number for the Airport police at Heathrow? I need to talk to the head honcho, now.' Hanks relaxed a bit, satisfied with himself, he stuffed the remaining chunk of pork pie in his mouth.

'What's going on?' Hall asked. 'Do we have a breakthrough?'

'Could be, could be.' Hanks smiled knowingly, chewing his pie. 'Let's just wait and see.' Nayyar was searching for the number of Heathrow police.

'I fail to see the significance of Heathrow, apart from the sale of the SIM cards.' Hall commented, still puzzled.

'Mr Hall,' Hanks explained patiently, 'Heathrow happens to be not only one of the world's busiest airports; it also happens to be one of the most densely covered with security cameras. I know, I spent half a life time studying the place on various cases.'

'Ah, I see a light,' Hall brightened; you want to study the camera footage covering the machines on that day, great lateral thinking Inspector.'

'Sod the lateral thinking; get someone to call them to send us the surveillance on all the machines in Terminal 1, between 26th and 27th of October this year. Since the machines are before passports and baggage reclaim we might try all incoming flights to Terminal 1 between those dates. We may be lucky. Welks, get onto Border Control and see what we can get on that front. Ask them to check the immigration cards. They should also check the airlines. There might be a name we can link with.'

'I'll go to Heathrow,' Hall offered. 'Since I missed the connection, I can at least do the legwork.'

'No need, just analyse the stuff we get from them. We'll lose too much time otherwise, and Nayyar, phone them and let them know what we want and where to send it to.' Hall, who was already half way out with jacket in hand turned and reluctantly went back to his work station.

'I'd feel like I was at least doing something, not just sitting here and waiting,' Hall complained.

Hanks's phone rang again. He was surprised to hear Claire's

voice and jotted the insurance man's name and address on his pad. Welks listened quizzically as Hanks voice softened during the call. Hanks dialled Whittaker in Chester and told him to find the answers to Claire's questions.

'Quite good these, want one?' Hanks extracted another porkm pie from the still bulging jacket pocket and picked a bit of fluff of it.'

'Sometimes Alan, you can be quite disgusting.'

'No?' he grinned, as Welks shook his head in disbelief before going back to his desk to get on to Border Control.

'Now,' Hanks said, getting back to the business in hand, 'what we desperately need is a handle on 'Operation 'Buyer'. Without that, we are up a bloody proverbial creek. Gentlemen, what do we have new, and any thoughts please?'

'We're talking about seriously dangerous stuff here, Mr Hanks.' One of the army staff ventured. 'This ether isn't just for kill jars for the odd butterfly for your collection. He started reading from a print- out. 'Diethyl ether, or, simply ether, is a colourless, highly volatile, flammable liquid with a characteristic odour. It is commonly used as a solvent and was once used as a general anaesthetic. It's extremely flammable, has an auto ignition temperature of 160 °C, hence it can be ignited by a hot surface without a flame or spark. The explosive air to ether ratio is between 13% and 18%. Exposure to the fumes can cause giddiness, headaches and loss of consciousness.'

'Headache is the least of our worries,' Hanks paused, putting his feet on the table, 'what else?' the man read on.

'Fire Hazard. Ether in Fire: Vapour is heavier than air with a density of 2.6 and may travel considerable distances to a source of ignition and flash back. Ether decomposes violently when heated. There's a lot of technical stuff about diffusion and such, but I reckon you'll all go to sleep if I read you that as well.'

'Bloody hell some brew that is.' Hanks stretched, clasping his hands behind his head, his chair in grave danger of toppling over as he did so. 'As our erstwhile colleague just said, we can do nothing but sit back and wait, or does anyone have any bright ideas?' There was no response, even the haggard looking Welks could only come up with a suggestion about going for a nap to keep their strength up. A suggestion which met with derision, but

Hanks did it anyway.

'Mr Hanks,' Nayyar disturbed the dozing detective nearly two hours later.

'Huh!' Hanks snapped awake, 'Information?'

'Two new intercepts. We got a clear text in Urdu, which our interpreter Aboud translated for us. Intercept time: 20:03 yesterday.' He passed the transcript to Hanks who read it out.

'May Allah be with you and may your reward be in heaven. All is as agreed. Your father.' and another strange one, '285K STG IBKK ACTIONED'.'

'Wheeler confirmed that the sender has been dealt with. We can cross the boss off the list.' the Lt. General interjected.

'So, Qamar what's-his-face is now the late Qamar what's-his-face.' Hanks stood and walked to the whiteboard and put a thick black line through al Surira's picture with a grim smile of satisfaction on his face as he added today's date. 4/11/10 and a little †. 'One down and how many to go?' He sat down again, picking up the transcript.

'He may not appreciate the cross.' Welks joked with a wry smile causing, the lieutenant to stifle a laugh.

Nayyar added, 'Second one's a money transfer, bet on it.' The others looked perplexed, '285 K STG,' that's like two hundred and eighty five thousand Sterling, to me, but I can't think what IBKK could mean though.'

'That makes sense. Don't you ever read a newspaper?' Hanks replied. 'The Daily Mail had a story on Asil Nadir and that he was coming back to Britain to stand trial and prove his innocence in the fraud case he ran from. Nadir's lawyers were providing evidence that he'd paid the money from the Polly Peck Company into a subsidiary company's account in North Cyprus and had not stolen it. The article cited that he used his mother as a witness; note that the guy himself is nearly seventy.' All faces were focused on Hanks as he spoke, wondering where the story was going. 'She stated that she deposited some 100 plus million Turkish Lira into the subsidiary's bank account in Kyrenia. And to prove it, they produced the paying-in-slip for cash, some 145 million Turkish Lira in 100 Lira bank notes.' he chuckled. 'They worked out that the old dear would have had to hump about thirteen tons of paper money into the bank.' The room burst out laughing. 'Can you picture it? A ninety-odd year old, staggering into the bank, carrying thirteen tons of banknotes?' The laughter increased, but ceased as Lt. General Richardson interrupted. 'All very interesting, Mr Hanks, but what is the relevance?'

'Yes, I remember the story,' Welks having clicked on, continued, 'it's Industri Bank Küzey Kibris. IBKK, got it! The same bank Nadir said he paid thirteen tons of cash into. A bent bank, that's for sure. One of the intercepts, sir,' he turned to the Lt. General to answer his question, 'appears to be talking about money being transferred from this bank in North Cyprus. We need to trace it.'

'I'll get Treasury on it, they're specialists.' Richardson reached for the phone.

'Won't do you much good unless you've got a cousin or two in the shambles they call the government.' Hanks contributed. 'North Cyprus is a good place for villains hiding from the law. The Met has a list a yard long of criminals living out there. We've had enough trouble with those morons they call politicians, when it comes to getting our hands on fugitives from British justice.'

A few moments later, an excited Hall arrived at Hank's elbow clutching two photographs. 'Heathrow have identified a person who fits in the frame at Heathrow Airport, Terminal 1, his name is Hassan Washiri, he travelled in from Paris.'

'Is he the one, then?' Hanks asked, thumping on the pictures on the table.

'Yes, Wheeler confirmed a clear identity match from the CIA face check. According to Border Control data, he entered the country last week. I've just checked his bio, it's a horror story; MI5 had him on a watch list three years ago, but dropped him when he left the country, and then they lost him. We should have kept him on the radar. Hassan Washiri, Age 44, born in London, England, nationality: British. I'll check 6's files and see if they have anything to add.'

'Pin him on the board.' Hanks said, handing Welks the photos. Welks walked over to the board pinning the picture next to Qamar's and Masoud's on the whiteboard. 'So the bastard's on the board now, then let's get an all points out on him.'

'The Unholy Trinity,' Richardson muttered, 'only, where are

they playing the game?'

Hanks picked up the phone and rang Scotland Yard. When he was connected to the right office, he explained why he wanted an international arrest warrant for Mr Washiri.

'We've got three names and one's dead. We've got a secret operation quite clearly being planned and funded with nearly three hundred grand and yet we haven't a clue what's going on.' Hanks hammered the table with his fist. 'We're stumped gentlemen, well and truly stumped.'

'Four.' said Welks.

'What?' Hanks face reddened, 'Four bloody what?' looking daggers at him.

'Four names.' Welks responded, 'Ahmed M'Beki,' he said softly, trying to bring Hanks back down. He was used to him, but he could see Hanks was wearing thin, this was getting to him.

'Yes, good point. We have a warrant out on him for questioning; he has disappeared from the surface of the planet. Put his face up there as well.'

'Time for food and some sleep gentlemen.' Richardson stood up. 'That's the trouble down here. No daylight, you don't realise what is going on upstairs. Horrible thought, to be stuck here in a war.'

Hanks checked his emails for the last time, an email from Whittaker about the insurance guy. He had been having a fling with one of the teachers at the kindergarten, who, according to her statement, had had contact with the infected animals two days before they were reported by the school. Good and bad, he thought. There is no secondary infection source, but who knows who else she and Mr Salameh had been in contact with. He forwarded the email to the Department of Health and to Voss.

He was just powering the computer down when Welks came over looking grim. 'Alan, you're not gonna like this. I just got this from 6. Hassan Washiri was suspected of being involved in the Mumbai massacres.'

'Why the hell didn't we know about this? We really have to get the inter-agency communications and data sharing sorted! This is a nightmare.'

37

Voss was in turmoil. Attending the post-mortem last night of Kasab, as he now knew him to be, had shaken him, with the severity of the infection the man had been carrying. He also had to deal with the uneasy thought of having had a terrorist on the premises all these months. It had left him in a state of disbelief, but now, the possibility of an epidemic had him reeling.

He'd called Mary and Claire at home, whilst fending off the mother of all headaches, getting them in early to start on the post-mortem samples. They were already at work with Nick downstairs. He was trying to concentrate on what to do next, as Claire rushed excitedly into his office.

'Oh, sorry Mr Voss, bad time?'

'No, it's alright come in,' Voss said wearily, 'take a seat.'

'I think we have something here.' She waved a USB stick in her hand. 'We spoke about cholesterol and the docking sites for the H5N6A Viruses,' Claire reminded him, and Voss nodded. 'Well, the samples you gave me this morning are almost exactly the same. The virus has docked on cholesterol sites.'

'Sorry, I'm not following you.'

'I've started a DNA on Khalid, and I'm pretty certain we'll find a similarity between his DNA, Salameh's DNA and the severe cases at the kindergarten, i.e. a tendency to high cholesterol. He has the same virus docking structure. Here, put this up on your computer. You'll see what I mean.' Voss plugged the USB stick into his PC and called up the data Claire described.

'We're up to 80 thou magnification here. Look,' Claire pointed excitedly to the screen, 'you see the small dents in the cell membranes of Khalid's lung cells and those of Salameh and the severe cases. This, if you ask me, is a genetic affinity to cholesterol. What I'm saying is that you can have high cholesterol and still not have the binding sites on the cell membranes, yet you can have low or normal cholesterol levels but genetically have the docking sites for cholesterol and thus be very susceptible to this kind of virus attack.'

'Uh huh!' Voss managed, as he studied the pictures. 'Yes, I see what you're talking about. The DNA's will give us the answer. Listen! I want the bacterium in the lung identified as soon as possible.' He stopped glancing up at Claire, who was looking slightly peeved. 'Claire, we need to speed up our work on the vaccines. I'm not being rude, but please, can you help Jemma and Mary with their work? We may need that fast now.'

'Mary's been at it for hours; you know that Jemma's in custody don't you?'

'What?' Voss almost shouted. 'Why wasn't I told?'

'Rumour has it that she was with the gang that night of the break-in.'

'Ahh! What is it with our staff? One turns out to be a suspected terrorist and the other is an animal rights activist?'

Claire just stood there, not knowing how to react. 'Anyway, at least that solves the problem of how Khalid got infected.'

'How do you mean?'

'Well, if I am stringing it together correctly, Salameh came here, infected from his liaison with the kindergarten teacher on Thursday, I remember Mary mentioning him having a cold and then you told me that Mary went to see Jemma that night. The only conclusion I can draw is that she must have been in contact with Khalid to infect him, as there was no other avenue for him to have caught the virus.'

'Now, we have no time to lose. Get on with the vaccines.' Claire set off to help the others.

Voss needed time to apply himself to the problems. He was still wrestling with these thoughts when the phone rang.

'Mr Voss? Good glad I've got you, I'm Norman Liddle from the Home Office. Detective Chief Inspector Hanks and Lieutenant General Sir Peter Richardson have asked me to contact you with regard to the break-in at your company. The government crisis unit would like to discuss the possible health hazards in relation to the infected animals that were released into the population. I believe you are already active in the Disease Control Committee at the Centre for Infectious Diseases?'

'Yes, I am. But what has that got to do with the break-in?' He thought he knew the answer, but waited for confirmation.

'DCI Hanks specifically requested that you join the team currently examining the wider aspects of the case here in London. Naturally, the expenses, within reason, will be covered by HMG.'

'What wider aspects of the case?'

'I'm sorry Mr Voss; I'm not at liberty to talk on the phone. We will be expecting you on Monday morning at the Ministry of Defence, the main building in Whitehall.'

'I understand.'

'I'll get our staff to mail you on the material you need to bring. Please report to the main security office at reception in the MoD main building. They'll be advised that you are coming and will handle everything from there.'

Voss put the phone down, stunned. What the hell was going on, he wondered as the phone rang yet again. Voss snatched it irritably from the cradle. 'Yes!' he almost barked. 'Hi Mary, what's up?' He listened to Mary on the other end, nodding and getting more and more agitated as he listened. 'You sure?' He finally added. 'Okay, I'll be down.' The email from the MoD reached just moments after the call from Liddle. He redialled without replacing the phone.

'Voss here. Good morning Inspector.' Hanks thought he sounded just as bad as he felt himself.

'You been up all night as well?' Hanks tried to sound sympathetic, but it just came out as a gruff bark.

'Unfortunately, I had the Kasab post-mortem to contend with. Nick and the team have been working flat out this morning on the tests. I will be with you on Monday, but that's not the reason for my call.'

‘Oh?’ What then?

‘I need to get a saliva sample from Jemma Phelps. I believe she’s in custody?’

‘Yes, she is. Hang on,’ he waved Welks over from the big whiteboard where he was writing something up in a blank column.

‘You need it fast? I’ll get Chester Police to motorbike it to you. What’s the angle?’

‘Our terrorist had an infection which only the kindergarten people have; the carrier in their case was the ferrets, which were recovered. Khalid or Jemail hasn’t seen a ferret since the night he was kidnapped, the K virus, as we call it, hadn’t evolved. We’re looking for the link. The only one we can think of is Jemma Phelps and I need confirmation on that, hence the sample.’

‘I see. So he died of the virus then?’

‘Yes, well, a secondary infection, because his immune system was so weakened by the virus that he died of a severe chest infection. The bacterium was an odd one, rare. It is called Pseudomonas, an unusual bug, a multi-resistant beast.’

‘Bugger, a pity we didn’t get to him in time; I would have very much liked to talk to him. Anything else you need Mr Voss?’

‘No thanks. See you on Monday.’

Voss ran his fingers through his hair as he took the stairs down to the lab two at a time. He cleared the UV sluice and made a bee line for Mary, who was standing with her back to him.

‘Okay,’ he said softly as he reached her, ‘show me.’

Mary was startled by his sudden arrival, the thrill of hearing his voice so close electrifying her as she turned to him. ‘Oh, Mr Voss, you made me jump.’ She studied the face for signs of warmth, affection, anything really. Seeing no sign of ‘interest’, she sagged inwardly, deflated and pointed to the test sheets on the workbench. ‘Here are the results. Nick has just been through them as well. The serum AS271 has knocked out the K virus in hours. This could be our vaccine. We need to test it.’

Voss studied the reports as he listened to her, obviously impervious to the proximity of her warm body. Mary fumed inwardly in frustration.

'The only way to test it is to get a volunteer,' she said. 'I think the insurance man will do it. He's right poorly.'

'It isn't legal Mary,' Voss faced her, 'but we don't have much choice. I'll take some vials of AS271 and go to the hospital now. Get on to Randell in London for me please and tell him. Then inform Nick that he's to get into full production on this immediately, if it works.' Spontaneously he hugged her and just as quickly released her. 'Well done Mary,' and with that he was gone, leaving her alternately thrilled and more frustrated than she'd been in a long time.

38

Hanks helped himself to a Telegraph in the mess. He breakfasted, spreading the paper on the table. The headline jolted him fully awake. 'NEW FLU EPIDEMIC SPREADING FROM THE NORTH WEST.' New Quarantine Regulations in Force, Northwest England and North Wales Cut Off;' despondently he laid down the paper. Through the windows he could see uniformed soldiers practicing drills and ceremonial marching. He was checking the time, seven thirty-five, just as Welks walked in, also a little the worse for wear after the previous night.

'Not my idea of a game of soldiers this,' he quipped, nodding towards the drill square as he sat down opposite. 'Seen Ashok?'

'No,' Hanks sipped the orange juice in front of him. 'Need the vitamin C this morning. God, as you get older booze doesn't half damage you more. Seen the headline?' Hanks pushed the paper over the table to him.

'Hell, that's all we need now.'

A steward appeared to take their orders and as he departed, Hanks told Welks of the developments that had reached him. They were disturbed midway through by the arrival of a soldier in khaki.

'Gentlemen,' a voice from behind reached them. 'DCI Hanks and DI Welks? Simon Philpott, Major. I am here to replace the Lt. General; he is commanding the quarantine operation up North personally. He didn't have time to inform you before he went, he got the order from the Cabinet at 2 am this morning to set up the quarantine operation. Prime Minister's orders I'm afraid. May I join you?'

He sat without waiting for the answer. Hanks regarded the figure suspiciously. An over-neat army uniform, with Medical Corps emblems on the lapels. His face was clean-shaven and shining even at this time in the morning and it made Hanks take an irrational dislike to the man. He fingered his own unshaven chin, thinking, now he knew what smart was.

'You're welcome.' he managed around a mouthful of toast and marmalade. 'You up to speed on the case as far as last night?'

'Yes sir, I spent the time studying everything since the Lt. General informed me, he's given me the access to everything. I even had access to the police files in Chester, interesting case, if I might say so.' Ashok arrived, bleary-eyed and still half-asleep. He plumped himself down next to Welks and grunted a good morning.

'You must be the miracle man from GCHQ,' Philpott continued, stretching his hand out to Ashok in greeting, 'Major Simon Philpott, your liaison officer.'

'You look ready for your own post-mortem, Ashok,' Welks commiserated. 'You okay?'

'No, I had a bad night again. Couldn't sleep, so I've been doing some work. Gimme a coffee, can't talk before.'

'First priority is to follow the money,' Hanks commented.

'We got the Treasury on that. We're waiting for them to get back to us.' Philpott pulled a tablet from his case and started typing.

'We need to track the locations of the SIMs we've got on our lists. We need as near real-time notification as we can get,' Ashok threw in. 'you guys might even be able to make an arrest.'

'Don't overestimate your 'friend and helper' Ashok, or are you being sarcastic?'

'Me?' he looked down at his plate, 'not this early in the morning.' Hanks couldn't read him so he let it ride.

'Any idea how accurate we can get the positioning?' Welks asked

'Depends on who does the tracking,' Philpott chimed in. 'We

use the telecoms and we get within maybe 10 yards. We use the military and we get to a yard plus or minus.'

Ashok snapped up sharply, 'That's the new stuff. You're not supposed to be telling people,' he chided.

'Admire your loyalty Mr Nayyar, but I wouldn't be giving the information if their status wasn't cleared.'

'The Americans have taken out Surira, we just need to locate the others now.' Hanks recapped thoughtfully.

'Yeah, that's one nil to us for now, or, if you count Mr Kasab, then maybe two nil. Problem with the analogy is, we don't know how many players are in the game, how long it's scheduled to run or what the rules are.' Welks took a mouthful of the fresh coffee. 'We don't even know what or where the game is.'

'Queensferry rules, boyo!' Hanks said in his best imitation of a Welsh accent.

'Queensbury you mean.' Philpott interjected, correcting him.

'No! No! Definitely Queensferry, kick 'em in the balls before they know it's coming. Seen it often outside the Plough on a Friday night, damned effective,' he grinned. 'In retrospect, I'm not sure the Surira thing was a good move. They'll know we're on to them now, although it's sure to put additional pressure on them.' He rubbed the stubble on his chin staring at the immaculate Philpott. 'I'm gonna get a shave. The major here makes me feel like…..' Hanks got up and left the rest of them to it. 'See you over the road in half an hour,' he called back.

Back down in the depths of the War Room Philpott proved to be an organisational wonder. The Treasury was advised of the transactional amount and given the Northern Cyprus bank details. They suspected that the sum would be sent in small amounts to avoid money laundering legislation. The Treasury boys could surely do the sums. He'd even made the suggestion that the notification procedure for UN listed dangerous chemicals be watched and he set up a round-the-clock team to keep an eye on that aspect.

Nayyar was grinding away on the phones side of things. Mr Hall drifted from one group to the next, like some malignant butterfly. Hanks confronted him on one of his transit walks.

'What's doing?' he asked perfunctorily. 'Get to me fast with anything new.' Hanks snapped.

'Yes, of course.' Hall said, miffed.

Welks looked at Hanks quizzically, 'Are you sure you're all right, Alan?'

'Bit frayed around the gills, Colin, tired.' Hanks slumped down on one of the vacant chairs. 'Are the pubs open yet? I have to get out of here. Come on.' He grabbed his jacket and pulled Welks along with him. 'We're off out for a bit of fresh air,' he informed Philpott on the way.

'The bank thing, the money trail, is coming along nicely.' he called back.

'Bravo! See you in a bit,' Hanks answered unenthusiastically. Once out in what for London passed as fresh air, Hanks felt a little better. 'Glad to be out of that Welks, I'm getting too old for all this. I haven't had a string of late nights like this since I was in my thirties.'

'You think you're the only one, Alan? Me, I'm running on the red light reserve. I hope we get a break at the weekend. I need to recharge my batteries and, no disrespect, but I'm nearly ten years younger than you and it's killing me.'

They found a pub in Parliament Street, the Red Lion, which still looked a bit Victorian on the outside. The dim, welcoming warmth was heaven for Hanks.

'Bloody Mary,' Hanks ordered on reaching the bar. 'What's yours?'

'Make it a half and a whisky to chase. My brain needs a kick start.'

Hanks ordered that too and they took their drinks to a small table at the back of the pub. It was next to the eating area where several tourists were tucking into traditional English Sunday lunch on a Friday. The smell of it made Hanks's stomach churn. He downed the Bloody Mary in one, waved at the barman for a refill and pulled the unread, breakfast-time Telegraph from his pocket.

The front page, apart from the epidemic issue, which added nothing to their knowledge, was full of Obama and his upcoming four nations' tour. In addition, there was a story with the heading, 'Police worker fired for backing psychic investigations, claims religious discrimination.'

'That figures,' Welks said, pointing to the headline, 'used to be the funny handshake brigade in charge, now it's voices from the other side. Maybe we should phone him and get his medium to talk to Kasab?' he laughed.' Probably get us further than we are now.'

'What're we doing at the weekend?' Hanks asked, breaking the mood. 'I've got no idea what we can constructively do. Suggestions?'

'I'm just a boy from the sticks, I haven't got a clue, we're so dependent on new input coming in which could lead us absolutely anywhere.' Welks said as Hanks downed his second Bloody Mary and stood up.

'Okay, I'm fit for the fight. You?'

Welks quaffed his beer back and followed. 'Ten minute lunch break, not bad Alan. Thinking of setting an example?' he grinned, but the look he got stopped the jest mid-flow.

The War Room was quiet as they entered. The Telecoms group with Ashok was busy putting pins in the map and tying little coloured tapes between them. The map was like a multi-coloured spider's web. Hanks and Welks walked over.

'Everything ok Ashok?' Hanks put a hand on the man's shoulder. 'Reckon you need to go where we were and get a top up. Make you feel better, honest.' Ashok was unconvinced.

'We're backtracking on all the available telephone conversations or texts from any of the suspect SIM cards. Assuming the first tracked call from the SIM card bunch GCHQ picked up was made by Hassan Washiri as he came out of Heathrow, then looking at the sequences, we can assume that his numbers follow in ascending order. So, now we're linking the places called with the places called from, see?' He stood back to allow the two detectives to examine the work that they'd done so far. The group over there are starting to do a matrix with the emails, but that's far more complex, since we don't have all the geographical locations for them.'

Ashok explained the colour coding for the phone calls. Brown thread was for calls made or suspected to be made by Masoud 'Brown Suit' and yellow tape showed calls by Hassan Washiri. Red was incoming from Pakistan. Green was unknown; there were two green calls, one from Hatfield and one from Hemel Hempstead. Almost simultaneously, there were 'Brown

Suit' calls from the same places.

'What's the most recent call we've got?' Welks asked

'Yesterday, open text message to Hassan and Masoud simultaneously.'

'That's the approval and the bank transfer. Nothing since?' Welks asked.

'No sir, not a peep. Pakistan has stopped sending, obviously,' Nayyar smiled.

'Wonder if the UK guys know that the Pakistani connection is mincemeat?' Welks asked pleased at his synopsis of events.

'Of course they know,' Hanks said irritably, 'we've snuffed out the head honcho. Even dinosaurs registered it when their head was lopped off.'

'There's one interesting one here, to a number in Hemel Hempstead from Southall, mobile to landline,' Ashok added.

'Who's the subscriber?' Hanks asked.

'A company called Shener Transportation.'

'Colin, we may have a lead here. Get me everything you can on Shener Transportation: Company reports, balance sheets, directors' names and addresses, anything and everything.'

The Major joined them, 'Treasury has found a series of incomings from IBKK to various banks in the UK, which have in turn been routed to a Luton account. The holder is one Nabou Fasheen.'

'Welks, that's another one for you. Check him. No, on second thoughts, let Moresby do it. Get her to do the works, the full Monty. I want to know colour of his socks and what he had for breakfast. Can we freeze the money?'

'Too late, I'm afraid. It was drawn out in cash in sixteen different transactions in five banks by sixteen different individuals. The cash was ordered by phone in advance; in other words, it's gone.' They sat and studied the transaction pathways. Hanks was amazed at how the banks involved had flouted the money laundering regulations. They spent ages sifting through the mass of data, afraid they might have overlooked something.

'We'd better send this to the Financial Services Office. Give 'em something to do on a Friday afternoon.' Hanks concluded with a grim smile, pushing the printouts from him. 'There's some big names here, kudos for someone, no doubt.' He leaned back in his chair. 'Gents, get on to the banks, they must have CCTV, and get Luton to go for the people that collected the money.' With that he grabbed a pile of the printouts of the telephone intercepts and disappeared into the back room, leaving Welks to sort the issue out with Moresby.

Three hours later, he re-appeared red eyed with the papers in his hand. He looked round the room for Welks or Philpott for an update, in case he'd missed anything, sure that if something had occurred, they would have informed him. Both had no significant news, so he decided to call it a day and go back across the road to get some rest.

He shut the door of his room behind him, leaning against it exhausted. Bed or bath? He looked at both, finally deciding on the bed, into which he sank gratefully, dozing into a troubled sleep. He dreamed a semi-erotic and half business fantasy. There was Claire, her subtle perfume and high heels. The image of her with 'Brown Suit' almost woke him before sleep reclaimed him. Her voice was echoing around him, somehow just an incomprehensible babble, with her sister constantly interrupting and confusing the message; then a police statement form, Carlton signing it, but the writing indecipherable. What was the message? Michaels looming up from the depths like a floater in the Thames.

39

All Saturday Shener was restless. He kept thinking that Monday would be busy and hoping everything would work out as planned.

The couriers had delivered the cash for 'buyer' late last night. He had cleared his safety deposit box at the bank and emptied his safe. He was busy repackaging the proceeds in the four suitcases that comprised the family's luggage. His wife had not been unduly surprised at the sudden travel plans. The four business class tickets from Heathrow were in his wife's maiden name for which he also held a passport. He checked over the cases he was packing. Each now contained three hundred and twenty thousand pounds in cash in fifty pound notes. Hopefully, any sniffer dogs on duty at Heathrow would only be trained for explosives or drugs and not banknotes.

He checked his phone was fitted with the current SIM card in the sequence. It took a while for the phone to connect to the provider, but when it did he got the familiar 'beep, beep' signal that he had a text. 'Achar is dead. Avenge.' His heart missed a beat. Achar meant the top man. Who had sent this? Masoud? He couldn't tell as the number was hidden. Shit, how far had the security people followed the trail? He locked the cases and went out to his car. 'Darling,' he called back to his wife through the open doorway, 'Just going to fill up with petrol, back in a jiffy.' She just waved.

The nearest internet café was in Harpenden. Parking as far away as time would allow and walking the rest. He sat in front of the first vacant terminal, first making and using a false account he sent a clear text to Hassan's next sequence number.

The message was simple. 'All in motion. Achar is dead. Go home.' There was nothing else he could do on that front. He logged off and erased the history in the browser just in case anybody followed him onto the computer and wanted to see what he'd done. He checked his surroundings once more for anything suspicious. Nothing. The question of where Masoud was, loomed large in his mind. Had he got out? If so how, when and where to? He was so distracted that when his mobile went off, it took him a while to realise that it was ringing.

'Yes,' he answered breathlessly. 'Oh Patsy, it's you. What's up?' He tried to sound normal to his secretary as he spoke. 'The police? When? Yes, no need to worry, thanks, bye.'

Sweat broke out on his forehead. Had a connection been made? He hit the steering wheel with the palm of his hand in frustration. Everything had been going so smoothly up to now.

He arrived home to find a police car outside. He got out of his car pulse racing, attempting to be calm; he noticed his palms were sweating, as he put the key in the door.

'Mustafa,' his wife called from the kitchen, as he closed the door behind him, 'there's a police officer to see you. He's in the living room. Would you like tea or coffee, I'm making him a coffee.'

'Okay, I'll have a coffee too darling,' as he walked into the living room.

'Mr Shener?' the uniformed officer asked.

'Yes,' Shener replied, 'to what do I owe this visit?'

'Just routine, sir. I have to ask you a couple of questions.' He said as Shener's wife came in with the coffees on a tray.

'I'll leave you two to it,' she said, backing out, casting a questioning look at her husband. 'If you need any more coffee, please shout.'

'What's it about officer?' Asked Shener nonchalantly, passing the coffee.

'Your company has received a phone call from a Mr Baitullah, who is wanted in connection with a police matter.'

Shener's heart missed a beat. He hoped his inner panic didn't show. How the hell had they picked that up? What else did they know? These thoughts flashed through his mind as he desperately thought of something convincing to tell the officer.

'I don't recall anyone of this name.'

'There was a call from his phone to your company last week. Are you sure you don't remember it?'

Shener paused, chin in hand deep in thought, as his mind raced through what he could tell, then, finally, coming up with an idea. 'The only phone call I can think of, which was out of the ordinary last week, was an inquiry to transport chemicals, but I told the caller that we only carried petrol and diesel. The stuff he wanted moving was some industrial thing.'

'Can you remember what it was he wanted transported?' The office asked draining his coffee.

'No, something about low molecular weight material, but I told him that we don't handle that. I hope that's of help to you.'

'Can you remember if you recommended any other suitable carriers to him?'

'I'm pretty sure that I didn't. If I remember correctly, he seemed quite annoyed and hung up before I could offer any further assistance.'

The officer wrote a few comments in his notebook. 'You've been most helpful, Mr Shener. If we need any more info, we will be back in touch. Thanks for the coffee.' Shener accompanied him to the front door and sighed with relief as he watched him drive away.

He told his wife he was going out, leaving her blustering and confused in the midst of lunch preparations. He drove recklessly fast to the spray shop, arriving sweating and excited. The banging and hissing coming from the shed calmed his anxiety a bit, as he swung the gate open and walked in. The air was full of car paint, a fine mist making the world hazy. A man with a face mask was at work on the logo on the rear of the tanker. Airbrush in hand, he was meticulously tracing the outline in paint. Shener had to give it to them; the painters were doing a magnificent job. The rig was looking like an original I T S tanker, the bright new logos proclaiming its provenance. His cousin was atop the tank fiddling and pulling wires.

‘What are you up to?’ he asked craning his neck.

‘Electronics, to disguise the rig, a red herring,’ he replied, dropping a spool of thin wire for Shener to catch. ‘Tuck it in the seam there,’ he pointed. ‘Make sure nobody can see it. Can you turn the ignition on?’

They spent the next two hours rewiring the rig, then went on to checking the tanker for any sign that would give it away as a bogus I T S rig; finally, satisfied that even staff from I T S wouldn’t be able to tell it apart from an original from more than ten feet away. Shener went over to Hamdi, embraced him and thanked him profusely, then pressed a wad of banknotes into his hand. He promised to see Hamdi again with the rest of the money on Monday when they would come to collect the rig. Shener felt more at ease as he drove back to the office in Buncefield to delete everything on his computers and check that there was nothing incriminating in his office, the policeman’s visit earlier had unnerved him.

40

Loud banging ripped Hanks from his sleep. He struggled dazed out of the bed, wondering how long he'd slept. He could see his watch lying near the corner of his bed, out of reach. Bang, bang, bang on the door, louder now.

'Alan, Alan!' Welks's voice, 'Wake up!'

'What's up?' he managed to croak as he lifted his watch and tried to focus on it. He staggered to the door and let Welks in.

'What's the time?'

'Seven,' Welks checked, 'we got a lot of new info, especially on the banking bits.'

'Okay, give me a minute.' Hanks backed off from the doorway to allow Welks into his room, now fully awake. 'Sit!' he commanded, searching for some clothes to put on.

He traipsed into the bathroom to change, leaving Welks sitting in the bedroom, listening to the sound of the draining wash basin.

'So,' Hanks re-entered the room dressed now, 'what's so important it can't wait?'

'Well, we hit pay dirt with several things on the bank front.'

'Did you wake me for that?'

'Not pleased?' Welks asked.

Hanks shook his head, 'Why pleased? What do we get from it?'

'So far, six potential collars, the Luton plods have leant on the banks with a little help from on high, and got the CCTV footage. They've positively identified six of the couriers.'

'It's a start, anyway.'

Welks stood to walk to the door, 'Hall traced the Baitullah call to Hatfield,' he explained smiling broadly now, 'it was to a house in Luton. Subscriber is a Mr Rahmani, 175 Moore Road. You want him brought in for questioning?'

Hanks thought about it for a bit, 'Yes, and put the fear of god into him, and send in the cavalry.'

'You don't want to just have him watched? Surely, he is heavily involved; he could lead us to Baitullah.' Welks queried.

'No, we need to pull him in now to question him as soon as possible.' Hanks insisted. 'What a start to the day,' he complained, 'come on, let's get over the road and get things organised.'

'Start, Alan?' Welks said, aghast. 'I was on my way to bed, shift change.'

'Plenty of time for that later,' Hanks joked, 'no seriously, get your head down for a couple of hours, I'll handle it.'

Back in the depths of the War Room, Hanks put Rahmani's name on the white board, aware of Philpott standing tiredly behind him.

'Right, let's get everything started to bring in Rahmani!' Hanks said firmly and picked up the phone to dial the Yard. 'DCI Moresby, please, DCI Hanks at COBRA here.' The connection took a while before the call was put through to Moresby's mobile. 'Hanks here,' he repeated, 'Gillian, need to go after a certain Mr Abdul Rahmani from Luton, do you have him on your radar in the Fellowship thing?'

'No, Alan never heard of him.' Moresby replied.

'Find out what you can, get back to me fast, it's urgent, in the meantime, send your best team to collect him, tell Luton you're coming.' Hanks doodled on the pad in front of him as he spoke.

'Got that. How's your operation progressing?'

'One can of worms after the other. We haven't a clue what the main event is yet. A bomb as it seems, but no clue about where and when. We're working round the clock here. Lots of leads, lots of suspects and no idea what's happening.'

Moresby returned the call a few minutes later, 'Rahmani's a

lecturer at Hatfield Uni,' she announced without preamble as Hanks picked up, 'you're not going to like this I think.'

'Come on woman spare me the bloody drama, out with it.'

'He's a civil engineer, a tunnels expert. He's working on ventilation systems for the London Underground.'

Hanks uttered a stifled, 'Shit!' before he reined his thoughts, 'hold on a second Gill,' he covered the mouthpiece with his hand, 'Philpott!' he shouted; his sense of urgency causing heads to turn as the Major ran over to him. 'We have the possible target; the London Underground. Inform Transport police and get them on the highest alert status and tell the Home Secretary as well.' Philpott looked shocked as he departed. 'Okay Gill,' Hanks returned to the call, 'get the man's university office, or whatever he has there, and his house turned over, everything and anything. I want it all back to base for analysis. We need to move fast on this.'

'Alan, do you realise it's Saturday morning, the University will be closed. We have to get a warrant to get in there as well.'

'Gill, don't give me excuses, give me results.' Hanks growled into the phone. 'Understood?'

Yes sir, my team is already on its way to Luton and Bedfordshire Constabulary is instructed. I'll get back to you with news immediately we get some.' she answered formally.

'Shit, I'd forgotten it was Saturday.' Hanks muttered, slamming the phone down hard, as he considered his options.

Philpott was looking frayed, gesticulating wildly as he spoke to someone on the phone as Hanks walked over to him. 'So?' he asked as the Major hung up.

'Transport police and the Met are on highest alert. All tube stations are getting extra surveillance.'

'We just have to wait for the buttons to pick up Rahmani now.' Hanks massaged the back of his neck. 'Where is Nayyar?' he asked.

'Probably still asleep.'

'Haul him out of bed and get him on to transport police. I've got a feeling that this is beginning to break. I want the tube station CCTV's fully monitored and recorded from now on. Get GCHQ on it to put their resources behind it. Talk to Wheeler.' Hanks was in full flow. 'If they are going for the London

Underground, and this Rahmani chap is a tunnel expert, where the hell are they going to hit?'

An adjutant came over, saying that he'd organised breakfast to be sent over today, as things were a bit hectic. Hall appeared from the lift, excited, announcing that he had an idea. 'Under UN regulations, any movement of certain chemicals is a notifiable transport. If our 'chummy' is going to try the Ludwigshafen thing, then there has to be an unplanned movement of a large quantity of ether. The manufacturers must notify the DfT (Department for Transport) on a 289. Then via GPS, they monitor the position of each dangerous cargo. The DfT Centre in Swindon is responsible for coordinating and tracking registered loads.'

'So, what are you waiting for? Get going on it and keep me up to speed on what you find.' He turned to Nayyar, who appeared next to Hanks rubbing the sleep out of his eyes, 'What in hells name is a 289?' Hanks asked quietly.

'Should I google it, or ask Hall?'

'Just find out for me.' Hanks smiled for the first time this morning, pulling out a map of the London Underground. 'I wish I knew where to start. It's worse than finding a needle in a haystack.'

'Maybe, breakfast and coffee will help. Let's get some nourishment in.' Philpott suggested.

They sat in silence confronted with the full fat boy breakfast, their steaming cups of tea untouched in front of them, as each was lost in his own thoughts. Hanks saw the clock tick over to 9:30. 'Why haven't Luton got back to us yet?' he asked apropos nothing. Philpott just shrugged tiredly.

Hanks got up and made his way back to his desk and dialled Luton to see what progress had been made on the arrest front. The duty officer was very apologetic and referred Hanks to the Chief Constable's Office. Hanks slammed the phone down, fuming. Saturday, Hanks thought, Chief Constable's Office, they have to be bloody joking. He looked over at Philpott, and said 'Fed up with the bullshit I am getting from Bedfordshire Constabulary, instead of doing something, they refer me to the Chief Constable's Office, on a Saturday! There's no one there.'

'Got the same problem,' Philpott sympathised, 'we need men

up in the quarantine line, but as you so succinctly put it; no one there.'

The day dragged on. The number crunching Telecoms teams were pinning more and more suspected 'related' calls on the board, as Hanks wandered through the room waiting for the crucial piece of evidence he needed for the breakthrough.

The only new thing on the white board was a burst of five calls from a non-sequenced pre-paid mobile phone to a known SIM card on that morning between 8:46 and 8:52 emanating from St Albans. The calls had all gone unanswered as the recipient's SIM card was no longer active. Nayyar had the suspicion that, whoever called the number was panicking; the calls had all gone to the number that had called Rahmani's landline in Hatfield, and he reminded the group that these numbers were only used once, hence the call didn't get through. Hanks wrote St Albans on the white board next to the numbers and stood back, wondering what the old Roman town had to do with things.

After lunch, Hanks was disturbed by a call from the Met Commissioner, during which he expressed his frustration of the lack of arrests in Luton, and that he was being referred to the Chief Constable's office for excuses. Sir John promised he'd find out what was going on for him, as he thanked Hanks for his efforts. Hanks had hardly put the phone down, when it rang again. This time, the strident voice of Gill Moresby greeted him. 'Alan, not sure how to tell you this, but Rahmani is nowhere to be found. His wife says, he came in very flustered, picked up his laptop and left the house again without saying where he was going.'

'Have you tried tracing him with his phone?'

'It's apparently switched off. He is underway in the family car; we have an all points out on him at the moment. Will let you know as soon as we got something.'

'Thanks Gill,' he broke the connection, and ran his hands through his hair in frustration.

It was in the evening, back in the mess at Horse Guards when Sir John got back to Hanks, the call interrupting his dinner with Welks. Hanks listened, his face got redder and redder the longer the call went on. Finally, he thanked the commissioner for calling and exploded. ‘What the hell is going on!’ He stood up, shouting, causing alarm all around him. Welks pulled him back down again, trying to calm him.

‘What happened, Alan?’

‘I don’t believe it!’ Hanks continued unabated. Nayyar and Philpott both stopped eating, shaken by the outburst.

‘Rules of engagement? Rules of fucking engagement?’ Hanks was livid. ‘Ashok, get on that laptop and get me the Bedfordshire rules of engagement.’

‘Calm down Alan.’ Welks attempted to get his friend back on track.

‘You wouldn’t believe it,’ Hanks said calming down somewhat, ‘they have new guidelines relating to suspected Muslim terrorists. Restrictions on police actions! We are tracking extremists involved in suspected acts of terrorism and there are restrictions during a national emergency?’

‘Here sir,’ Nayyar passed him the laptop, the screen filled with the Bedfordshire Constabulary ‘Rules of Engagement – For dealing with suspected terrorists’.

‘Have you seen this?’ Hanks stammered in utter disbelief as he read, ‘What half-crazed morons dreamed this up? Am I imagining this?’ He slammed his hand down on the table ignoring the spillage caused to the drinks. ‘Here,’ he ranted, ‘listen to this,’ by now causing everybody in the mess to stop eating and listen. ‘Quote… ‘Community leaders must be consulted before raids into Muslim houses.’ Quote…‘Officers should take their shoes off before raiding a Muslim house.’ Quote…‘Use of police dogs in searching Muslim premises will be considered serious desecration of the premises.’ Simple idiocy, sheer lunacy!’ he raged. ‘No wonder Rahmani got away. I bet the so called community leader has tipped him off. Find out who he is and haul him in. Let’s get back over the road, I need the Home Secretary, we have to get these restrictions lifted immediately.’

‘We are not allowed to contact Cabinet members directly,’ Welks reminded him.

‘Then get me Richardson, now!’

‘But he’s up North doing the quarantine thing.’

‘I don’t care if he’s in a meeting with the Pope,’ Hanks’s was boiling, 'if they don't lift these restrictions, we can't do our job. This is madness!' he fumed.

Welks finally got through to the Lt. General and he, in turn to the Home Secretary. Within the hour there was an emergency order rescinding any restrictions on police raids in the Home Counties for an interim period of 30 days under the Prevention of Terrorism Act. One for the good guys, thought Welks, as he announced the news to Hanks.

'Too bloody late, Rahmani got away!'

41

His inner rage from the day before had caused Hanks indigestion. Welks and Philpott were already in discussion over the Sunday papers and coffee as he arrived in the mess to announce that he was going to Luton to sort things. Philpott said he'd get a car organised for him and went off. Hanks sat opposite his partner, ignoring the offer of coffee, staring glumly out of the window.

'You look pissed off Alan.' Welks commented.

'The fact that I'm a little more than mildly aggravated must be plain to a blind man in a dark room,' Hanks muttered darkly, 'not belittling your observational skills Colin, but upset does not get near it at the moment. Between you and me, I have never been as frustrated as I am right now.'

'I feel for you Alan, but it's the system, not the people.'

'How the hell can you separate the two? They are one and the same thing, the people make the system. You know the old saying about the horse and the camel; a camel is a racehorse designed by a committee, our system is perfect governance, engineered by well minded cretins,' he breathed in deeply, 'sometimes I wonder about the well minded bit.'

'Wow, that's probably the most politically incorrect description for 'Nanny State' I've ever heard you say, but since the Bedfordshire rules issue, I have to agree with you one hundred per cent. We've just been in the lunatic asylum for so long we don't hear the screams anymore.' Philpott arrived back and told Hanks that there was a car waiting for him outside.

'You two keep an eye on things over the road. I've got to see that they come up with the goods on the Rahmani guy, this desk bound detective stuff, and the politicking, is pissing me off. I'll be back this evening.' Without breakfasting, he turned and walked out, calling over his shoulder, 'Colin, do me a favour, ring Luton and tell them I'm coming.'

The car out front of the building came with a uniformed driver, a smart young guardsman.

'Where to sir?'

'Luton nick, Buxton Road.' Hanks sank into the passenger seat as London started to flash past. The army driver was adept at slipping through the traffic knots that threatened to bar their way. They made swift progress. Hanks sat back and shut his eyes, wondering what the day would bring. The horrors of what was being planned, with the money already disbursed must mean the deadline was looming. He had to get Rahmani, this man was the only connection they had; his only chance.

Luton, on first impression did more than live up to its dreary reputation. Decaying sixties architecture and litter strewn streets gave the place an aura of disillusionment, almost despair.

'We're here, sir.' The driver's call came, as the car pulled up at the Buxton Road police station, breaking Hanks's none too complimentary thought train about the place. Hanks told the driver to wait, before barging through the front doors into the reception area.

'Where's the officer leading the Rahmani hunt?' He slammed his warrant card down in front of the flustered desk sergeant, without further ado.

'Welcome, sir, we were expecting you. Markham DS, sir.' he read from his list.

'Where is he?'

'It's Sunday, sir.'

'I don't think you understood me. I didn't ask what bloody day it is, I asked where he was.' Hanks felt his blood rising, his face heatıng.

'I think he's off today, sir.'

'Get him on the phone. No, don't get him on the phone. Get

him here.'

The desk sergeant proceeded to search for the errant DS's number while Hanks stood at the counter unable to comprehend how an officer in charge could have a day off in such an important investigation.

The desk sergeant took Hanks to a small office where two women were poring over a computer screen. He introduced them to Hanks, a DC and a civilian support worker.

'These are the two working with DS Markham sir. They will fill you in with the progress. Markham is on his way now,' the sergeant backed out shutting the door.

'So?' Hanks ignored the pleasantries 'what the situation up to now?'

The DC responded, 'We have an all points out on Rahmani's vehicle sir. We know he left home in it.'

'What've you checked?' Hanks asked. 'Petrol stations? Traffic cameras? The two women regarded one another, unsure of what to say. 'Before you tell me how many traffic cameras there are and what a lot of work that is, answer the question.' Hanks pre-empted.

Somewhat piqued, the DC replied as politely as she could, 'We're checking those sir.'

Unfazed by her reaction, Hanks changed tack. 'What did the search of his house bring?'

'Nothing of any significance, sir.'

'Bank statements? Credit card statements? Address books? There must be something.'

'Yes, we have his bank and credit card statements, but there is nothing out of the ordinary to see on those. There's been no movements on any of his accounts.'

With that the door opened and a breathless Markham burst in. 'Sorry,' he panted, 'just went home to shower and change, we've been at it since Friday solid.'

'You and me both,' Hanks responded unsympathetically. 'Your plan?'

Markham hung his coat on the back of the door. 'We've got his wife in for questioning; she's been cooperative, but of no help.' He pulled a chair out and sat. 'I'd say she knows zip. I tried her for two hours yesterday and nothing.' Traffic picked up on Rahmani's car though, through the cameras in St Albans, yesterday around noon; coming off the M25 at the Noke roundabout.'

'Okay,' Hanks answered, getting more comfortable with the operation as he listened. 'Do we know when he actually ran for it?'

'The wife says, round 8:00 am, why?'

Hanks nodded sagely at the information. 'It confirms a suspicion. You operated by these stupid rules, I suppose?'

'Glad you think they are barmy as well,' Markham smiled, 'yes, we had to contact the imam at the Moore Road Centre before we went for him.'

'Same street as Rahmani,' hanks muttered, 'When did you talk to him?'

'We got to him just after prayers around quarter to eight.'

'The bastard tipped him off then. Go and get him, charge him with aiding and abetting, and hampering police enquiries, wasting police time, littering and anything else you think you can make stick. I don't want any excuses that he has a flock to preach to today. Arrest him.' Markham reached for the phone and instructed someone to go and pull the Imam.

'We can only hope that he knows where Rahmani may hide. Can I see the address book you have recovered? I suppose we have to go banging on doors.'

One of the women passed him an evidence bag with a neatly bound address book. Hanks opened the first page to see the names and addresses listed in what he assumed was Rahmani's meticulously neat hand writing, noting, as he leafed through the book that most of the addresses were overseas. Something MI6 could follow up on, he thought, mentally filing the idea for later. Only as he flicked to the last page, did he notice a horribly scribbled telephone number in pencil, in a different hand writing.

'01727, where is that?'

'St. Albans sir.'

Hanks blood froze. He grabbed the phone, dialled the number, and got the engaged tone. He passed the book back to the woman and told her to get the number traced as he turned to Markham saying 'Get some discreet surveillance round to this house now, look for any indication that Rahmani may be there. It may even be worthwhile to knock on the door pretending to be a door to door salesman. They should be careful and not scare him off.'

'The address is 12 Melbourne Close, St Albans.' One of the women clarified.

'Thanks. Contact Herts Constabulary and tell them that we need an ARU (armed response unit) on immediate call for a possible raid in St Albans. Have you got a map?'

'I can do better than that,' she zoomed in on a program on her screen that looked like Google Earth; the address was a small terraced house in a cul-de-sac between the railway lines and the main road. They examined possible exit routes and Hanks concluded, 'there's no road access to the front of the house, the main London Railway line is just across the field and the old ancient earth works to the North. If he goes out on foot, there's two ways out. If he goes out by car, there's only one.'

Markham said, 'There's not much point in plotting a raid on this place without confirmation that our guy is there.' he turned around to one of the women, 'I suggest we take a break and organise some coffee until we hear back from surveillance.'

'Coffee, music to my ears,' Hanks exclaimed, 'I haven't had a coffee all day.' After the bustle and hum of the War Room, Luton CID offices seemed tranquil, the lack of 'happenings' lulling Hanks almost to sleep. His semi doze was interrupted by Markham.

'Sir, we have had a call back from Melbourne Close, Rahmani's car is outside next to the garage. There are two men in the house as far as we can tell.'

Hanks leaped out of his chair at the news; instantly wide awake, 'Okay, let's see how good the Herts boys are then. Who is in charge there?'

'DI Rossington,' Markham answered, 'I spoke with him earlier. I took the liberty of calling him before I disturbed you. With respect sir, you look like you could do with some sleep.'

'Even without the respect, I need it.' Hanks laughed humourlessly. 'Okay, let's go where do we meet up with them? How long will it take us to get to St Albans.'

'About thirty minutes.'

'Ask this guy, Rossington, where to meet him.'

Forty minutes later they arrived at the Britannia Inn St Albans, to find the pub car park seething with police vans spilling more and more police by the minute. Hanks walked over to a man in a suite who was directing things and introduced himself.

'How far away is the house?'

Rossington pointed with his thumb over his shoulder, 'Over there, two hundred yards. We have the other side covered as well.'

'What are we waiting for? Let's go!'

The small house in the middle of the terrace offered no resistance as the armed response unit team battered the door down. Two men ran out the back, straight into the arms of the waiting officers. Hanks turned round to Rossington and put his hand on his shoulder, 'Nice one, thanks. Let's take them to Luton. Get forensics down here and SoC, we need this place thoroughly turned over.'

The armoured van, with the two suspects, followed Hanks and Markham back to Luton, where the two men were put under guard in separate interview rooms.

'I'll take Rahmani, you take the other one.'

Hanks opened the door to interview room one, and found a balding olive skinned man sitting at the desk.

'Mr Rahmani?' The man's eyes flickered but he didn't answer.

'What did Masoud Baitullah want from you?' He noted the fleeting look of fear in the man's eyes. Hanks tried again, 'We know you've had contact. What did he want?'

'I don't have to tell you anything. I want a lawyer.'

'Yes, that's your choice. I was trying to do this the easy way,' Hanks turned to the officer in the corner, 'Lock him up, charge him under Section 28, the terrorism act, aiding and abetting, he's going nowhere for the next month.'

Hanks got up to leave, Rahmani pleadingly said, 'I can't tell you anything, they'll kill me and my family.' The man's fear was causing sweat to run down his face.

'Baitullah?' Rahmani nodded slightly. Hanks stood up walking to the door, saying, 'Look, if you help us, we can bring your family in for protection.' Rahmani remained silent. 'Take him down, and call me if he changes his mind.' He said to the officer, before going back to Markham's office.

'Get me Rossington on the phone.' he told the DC. She connected him almost immediately, 'Hanks here, head of the COBRA team, we met earlier. 'Any news on the house search?'

'They're finishing up now, sir. They found nothing of significance. A few bits of broken plastic in the garden, we're assuming they may have been part of a PC or laptop, we've collected the pieces, but no other computers, no mobile phones, nothing else.'

'We have the mobile phones here. Thanks a lot for your help. We'll be in touch.'

Markham returned, excited, 'Rahmani's friend was quite talkative; seems to have no idea what's going on. He said that Rahmani turned up on his doorstep and was in a real flap, he borrowed a hammer and smashed his laptop to smithereens in the garden, before he came back in to announce that he was in trouble.'

Hanks called out to the DC to get Rossington back on the line. 'Rossington, your guess about the bits of plastic is right. Rahmani smashed a laptop with a hammer in the garden. Get back there and put the garden under the microscope,' he paused, 'check the bins and the neighbours' gardens as well.'

'We'll have to get special equipment like flood lights, as it is going to be dark soon.'

'I don't care if it takes all night, but I want that laptop found. Here's my mobile number, phone me instantly the moment you find something.' Seeing it was almost four o'clock, he remembered that he hadn't had neither breakfast nor lunch.

'Markham, Ladies, you've done a great job. Let me know if you get anything else out of Rahmani, I have to get back to London now. Thanks for your help.' Markham walked him through the building to his car.

It was gone seven o'clock when Hanks's car drew up in Whitehall outside Horse Guards, where a wary sentry inspected his pass. He went straight to the mess, his premise that the 'workers' would be at their evening meal proving correct.

'Good day?' Hanks asked plonking himself down next to Welks.

'Depends, you look smug, yours must've been better than ours then.' Welks continued eating. Philpott was on the verge of saying something when Hall butted in.

'We got the message about half past six, but it's from yesterday'

'What was yesterday?' Hanks was too tired to pick it up.

'It's happening Tuesday, this Tuesday, in two days.' Philpott added attempting to contain his excitement.

'Woah! Slow down,' Hanks put his hands up. 'What intercept and what is happening on Tuesday?'

'Buyer is on Tuesday.' Welks answered as Hanks stole a chip from his plate.

'Why didn't you phone me?'

'Just had it translated, Alan. Eh, get your own chips.' Hanks waved for the steward, he was starving he realised.

'Sorry, it's a text out of literally a billion, it simply slipped the net.' Nayyar said guiltily, 'That's what Wheeler told me anyway.' he added quietly.

A softly exhaled 'Jeeesus!' escaped Hanks lips. 'All we needed, another foul up.'

'Come on, Alan,' give a little slack, these guys are doing what they can. To filter a threat text from billions of messages is a fantastic feat.' Welks said defensively.

'Yeah, sorry you're right, I'm just tired. Show me the text.' Nayyar flipped his laptop round and showed him. Hanks read out loud, 'Buyer' finalising contract 7:30 Tuesday. Greetings from Father.' Could be any Tuesday,' he commented as the steward took his order.

'We've been discussing that,' Hall said, 'but using semantics; it must be this coming Tuesday,' he stopped as if that was self-explanatory.

'The logic being?' Hanks asked, as his beer arrived.

'If it was another Tuesday there would be a date, or Tuesday next week, or a week on Tuesday.' Hall finished the line of reasoning. Hanks just nodded.

'I phoned Lt General Richardson to see what we can offer on the manpower front. Searching the London Tube system for explosives is going to take a huge amount of manpower.' Philpott added.

Hanks sipped his beer, deep in thought as his food arrived. Pulling his plate towards him, he suddenly brightened. 'You don't need men to search all the stations; just the underground ones. Nothing else makes sense. Now, gentlemen give me a minute; I haven't seen food all day. By the way we got Rahmani.' With that he started, with gusto, to attack the steak on his plate, leaving the questions, for the moment, unanswered.

42

Masoud was nervous, the Buyer operation was underway, but he'd heard nothing since Hassan's last visit. The Chester operation appeared to be a total loss. The whole of the North West was cordoned off by the army, and he was worried about the disease up there as well. He was sure the papers weren't telling all. The rumours circulating, spoke of hundreds of deaths and panicking in some towns. What a shame they couldn't take credit for this disaster, he thought.

Frustration wasn't enough to describe his agitated state, as he drove his car into the Luton Community Centre car park. He performed his ritual wash before taking off his shoes and going to prayer. He entered the mosque, its tranquillity soothing him, reaffirming his sense of belonging and righteousness. He stood there in the throng of the Al-Wusta midday worshippers, before his God, leaving all his other worries and concerns aside for the moment. The drone of the sermon and praying relaxed him, he felt at ease for the first time in days. The Imam was reciting the ritual first verse of the Koran, Masoud let the words drift through his head, like music, he heard the words without listening,

"In the name of Allah, Most Gracious, Most Merciful. Praise ...." without thinking, or comprehending. This was how it should be, he thought, prostrating himself with the rest of the congregation, uttering the automatic response "Glory be...." He spoke the words feeling comfort and inner warmth from them.

The session ended, leaving Masoud in the scrimmage of men trying to collect their shoes in the outer area. People were gathering round the Imam, showering compliments on him for the wonderful sermon. Masoud had just finished tying his laces, as he heard the police sirens approaching. The relaxation he'd just felt instantly disappeared, he sensed an adrenalin rush. Three police vans arrived seconds later followed by a police car. Masoud sidled down the back of the atrium and out through the side door. Police were all over the forecourt of the Mosque, as he got out, they were barging through the worshippers towards the front entrance.

Masoud made his way to his car, attempting to appear unconcerned at the events. Inwardly he was raging at the desecration of this holy place. He struggled with the car door lock and managed to get in behind the wheel all the time watching as the Imam was unceremoniously bundled into a police van and driven away to loud protests of many of the worshippers, who were held back by heavily equipped police.

Driving out towards the football stadium, he decided it was time to change vehicles. Traffic on Dunstable road was light as he pulled out, both angry and afraid now. The Imam had been taken by the police, why? What had happened? Still puzzling this, he pulled into the side road leading to the lock-up garages.

Within minutes, he'd swopped cars and was driving his red Nissan back into town. In the light of what had just happened at the mosque, he needed to get information, and check his mails. The Internet Café he often used was just up the road, the next turn off left. Net-Europa café had just the one benefit, that of being the only one open on a Sunday. He ordered coffee, which from past experience had proven undrinkable, but it seemed expected of the clientele. Sitting at the furthest unoccupied terminal, he keyed up his account. One message, sender unknown, some Mickey Mouse name, he opened it. The text from Shener was short and jumped off the screen at him, '*Buyer finishes contract 7:30 Tuesday. Greetings from father.*' Masoud's coffee tasted better after he'd read that. He checked the date, feeling a frisson of pleasure as he realised it was the 9th of November, 9/11, but in England this time.

Next day

On Monday Shener followed Ahmed up the Motorway to the Newport Pagnell services. As arranged, the trailer with its load from Allied was waiting as Ahmed reversed his truck next to the rig from Washburton's. Shener was pleased, the trucks were practically identical. They sent Ahmed off to have tea while Shener checked the tanker's Hazchem and number plates before swapping them with the ones on M'Beki's rig. The Washburton tanker's signage was now proclaiming, non-dangerous vegetable oil with a label 'Foodstuffs only', his cousin climbed on the top of the tank to change the GPS unit over.

'You have the heater?' he called down to Shener.

'Here.' grunting with the effort, Shener passed it up to him.

'Where do you want it?'

'Up there.' Shener pointed, getting his breath back.

'And the timer?'

'We will need to screw it to the inspection cover.'

'What does it do?' Arif asked, spitting a bit of insulation tape out onto the ground.

'When he closes the valves on the tanks and presses the button that you are installing in the cab, the timer starts, and after exactly fifteen minutes it allows power through to the hot plate, which, if the manufacturer's data are correct, will reach 190°C in approximately four minutes. So exactly nineteen minutes after he has 'unloaded'...' He left the rest unsaid. His cousin's smile was evil as he started drilling.

'We'll do all the rest at Hamdi's. We've been here too long already. Anybody could be watching the surveillance cameras at the moment.' Shener was indicating to Ahmed to get into the cab. He did as he was told calling, 'Where to?' as he started the engine then edged the rig forward.

'Follow us back to Hamdi's. We'll rejig your unit there. It's safer.'

'Agh! What the hell is that!' M'Beki screamed panic stricken, as the dead Washburton driver's arm flopped out from the curtained sleeping bunk behind him, touching his shoulder. He jumped down. 'In the name of Allah who...?'Ahmed was shaking.

'Calm down Ahmed, it's only the driver, he is at peace now. Allah will welcome him, don't worry.' Shener climbed up into the cab and stuffed the arm back behind the curtain. 'See? He's gone now.'

'Okay,' Ahmed said tremulously, his eyes riveted on the curtain. 'Follow us,' Shener shouted up at him as he got back in his cab. He smiled broadly all the way down the motorway and his smile grew each time he looked in the mirror and saw the Washburton's tanker, with Ahmed at the wheel behind him. His cousin sat tinkering with the GPS box in his lap, oblivious to the motorway and its traffic. At Hamdi's paint shop they were greeted by the man himself, standing alone in the middle of the yard.

'I sent everyone else home.'

'Good.'

Ahmed got down from his unit pale and shaken.

'Ahmed, you okay?' Shener thought that he looked nervous, even frightened.

'I'll be fine, it's just the body, a dead man in the bunk behind you is…' Ahmed stuttered to a stop. Shener dismissed the whole issue of the body with a wave of the hand. Yet, Ahmed seemed no easier, even though he was no longer in the cab beside the body.

Shener's cousin set about installing the fake GPS unit in the Washburton's trailer. As far as the rest of the world or anyone else was concerned the Washburton's trailer with its full load of ether was still parked in Newport Pagnell services. Only a physical inspection of the tanker would reveal that it was empty, which was something Shener believed wouldn't happen for at least twenty-four hours, but by then, it would be far too late. He sighed happily at the thought.

43

The War Room was tense as the team sat round the meeting table discussing the weekend's developments. 'So the crux lies in this bloody laptop,' Hanks stated, 'Herts are searching the garden for Rahmani's hard disc. We have to wait and see what they get. I think is going to be crucial, since our friend Rahmani hasn't uttered 'dickey' since we arrested him.' He pulled himself upright, 'Tuesday, tomorrow 7:30.' He turned on Hall, 'am or pm?'

'Er, guess is am.'

'Why?' Hanks fired back, his voice hoarse.

'7:30 as opposed to 19:30.'

'Ok, Philpott, can you talk to the DfT and the Home Sec about locking down the London Underground tomorrow morning?' Philpott nodded picking up the phone. Hanks walked over to Hall, 'Progress on the transport front?'

'Sort of, sifting the 289's has been a nightmare; we got there in the end. We are down to four that appear relevant. We have a load registered from Leeds to Bermondsey, thirty-five tons diethyl ether to Taymar Pharmaceuticals. That's a regular monthly drop. It goes through on the last Monday of the month, every month. Picked up on schedule this morning and currently at Newport Pagnell services. Driver has probably done his time, and having a forced break. The second is from Southampton, a container full of diethyl ether that's going to S.P.& N. Chemicals in Havant. The container is stuck in customs at the mo. Some papers aren't correct or something. I think we can rule that one out. The third is a twenty-five ton load of diethyl ether from Liverpool to Tunbridge Wells, also a regular drop to a chemical reagent purifying company called Crystallex. The truck is currently stuck in traffic on the Dartford crossing, in the middle of the QEII Bridge. Here, you can see it on the screen.' Welks leaned over and saw the red blinking dot hovering over the River Thames at Dartford. 'The last we have currently in transit is a thirty-five ton load from Liverpool, for a new customer in Margate. This could be a possibility.' He pulled a note pad from beside the keyboard. 'The company is a Dutch pharmaceutical company, they have just set up a manufacturing and drug refining operation here in the UK and are going on stream this week. I spoke to the operations manager there, a Mr Van Walraven, and he seems genuine. I say it could be the one, not only because it's a new customer but, because of the manager's name, sorry the MD's name.'

'Go on man! Don't let me die of suspense.' Hanks suppressed a sneeze.

'He's a German, Dr Manfred Bayer.'

Hanks' heart missed a couple of beats. 'How long have you had this info?' his face drained even more colour as he asked.

'Just got the email from Van Walraven.'

'Where's the load?' Hanks shivered involuntarily.

'Here.' Hall pointed proudly to the screen. The truck was at Keele Services on the M6. 'He's been there for about an hour now.'

'Follow it! This could be the one.' He was absorbing the information when his concentration was broken by the arrival of Voss.

'Hello. I'm after DCI Hanks or Lieutenant General Richardson. Voss is the name, Andy Voss. Do we shake hands or do I salute you?' Voss said, stretching his hand out, smiling.

'Oh, Major Simon Philpott, I'm the liaison officer standing in for the General. He's off on business up north, the quarantine exercise. He should be back here any moment. How can I help?'

'I was told to be here at the disposal of Mr Hanks and his team.' Voss said, craning his neck to see where Hanks was.

'Hang on just a minute I'll get Hanks for you.' Philpott left Voss to follow, as he went over to Hanks. Voss took in his surroundings. Then he saw the familiar face of Hanks coming towards him, haggard and pasty, in a word, unwell.

'You okay Mr Hanks?' he asked with concern in his voice. 'You look like death warmed up.'

'Thanks for the compliment Mr Voss. I may have caught a bug. Came out of nowhere.'

'Really!' Voss's antennae were up. 'When did it start exactly?'

'Started out of the blue, one minute fine, hunky dory, next minute flu. Started about an hour ago.'

Philpott interrupted, 'I must agree with Mr Voss, you look grim, Mr Hanks'.

'I'd like to take some saliva samples,' Voss turned to Philpott, 'just as a precaution. Can we do some swab tests here?'

'I'll check, let me make a call,' he reached out, 'I'll get your coat put away.'

'If this proves to be the K virus, we better get a few dozen swab sample sets down here, the virus is highly contagious. Can we have the samples sent express to my team in Chester? I'll ask them to send some of the vaccine here; about 200 doses should do it.' He said the last bit more to himself. 'The last thing you need here is an epidemic knocking out your team.'

'I'll get back to you.' With that, Philpott was gone. He returned with the information that a medical team was being checked in upstairs at the moment and asked Hanks and Voss to follow him.

'Where to?' Hanks asked.

'Medical centre.' Philpott called back over his shoulder.

They arrived outside a double door with red crosses on it, Philpott ushered them in. 'I think you'll find everything you need here, gentlemen, I must rush to attend to Mr Hall.' He left hurriedly.

Voss and Hanks were in the anteroom of a small, but well-equipped mini hospital containing four beds with all the trimmings of an intensive care station. Hanks plonked himself down on one of the beds causing the metals springs to creak ominously.

'The serum Mr Hanks is a possible antidote. We've tested it,' Voss's was tone confident, '100% success rate so far. I bought a sample with me.'

'Sounds good,' Hanks croaked, 'how many have you tried it on?'

'One,' Voss grinned grimly, 'but it worked out fine. I'll get a nurse administer it to you, just in case it is the K virus.'

Hanks sighed, laying back. 'If it works, do it. That's always been my mantra.' The Horse Guards medical officer arrived, followed by a nurse.

'We need a throat swab to be sure.' Voss turned to the nurse. 'Can you please give him this?' A small glass vial changed hands.

Hanks eyed the nurse suspiciously as she opened a case and pulled out the sample tubes. 'Open wide,' she said, as she expertly swabbed the inside of his cheek. 'There, that didn't hurt did it?'

'If you're going to treat me like a kid, I should at least get a sweetie!' Hanks grumbled at her. She ignored him as she prepared the syringe and jabbed it in his arm, Hanks groaned in mock agony.

Voss stood next to his bed. 'According to your symptoms, I'm almost sure that you have the K virus, so if it's any consolation, you should be out of your misery soon.'

'What? Am I gonna die?' Hanks looked up. 'Man flu is always the worst,' he tried to joke weakly.

'No, Mary, Nick and I have all had it. It comes suddenly and goes suddenly. Only lasts about four to six hours, seems to have hit you hard though.'

'He won't get better by us staring at him and it's not exactly a spectator sport.' Welks chuckled mirthlessly, turning for the door. 'Just stay there Alan. We'll come and get you if the world ends.'

'Up yours too.' Hanks whispered weakly as they left, bumping into Lt. General Richardson on their way back to the main War Room.

'What's up? Why the sick bay?' Richardson asked.

'Hanks seems to have caught the K virus,' Welks replied, 'by the way, this is the famous Dr Voss from Brinkley's. Do you know each other? Mr Voss gave Hanks the antidote, he should be fine within an hour.' They sat down at the conference table and were interrupted by Hanks' phone ringing. Welks snatched it up, 'No, Welks here. Who? Sure. It's for you Dr Voss, a Mr Kitson.'

'Ah, right,' Voss said, puzzled that Nick had phoned Hanks taking the receiver, Richardson and Welks looking on as Voss started an animated cross-examination of things he was being told on the phone. Finally, apparently satisfied, he put the phone down. 'My phone isn't working,' he said checking the display, 'I have no network.'

Richardson ignored the comment as he was still mulling the antidote issue. 'You say you have an antidote that works?'

'Yes,' Voss answered, 'but we haven't tested it properly, yet! Just mice and one volunteer, well two,' he said nodding in the direction of the sick bay, but we are so confident, that we are in production now.'

'We have to get the Cabinet advised, there have been a spate of flu-related deaths already.'

'Usually I would put it down on this time of year. It takes out the weak, but it seems that all age groups are affected.' Voss replied. 'I agree we have to get the top layer involved.'

'At least we have a vaccine. That's a start.'

'Not tested.' Voss underlined again.

'Yeah, but it bloody well works so it's fine in my book.' Sir David persisted.

'Wish you were head of NICE,' Voss smiled, 'getting drugs approved would be a heap easier.'

'So, how many doses can Brinkley's produce, if this epidemic takes off?' Richardson asked.

'We started yesterday, so by the end of next week about a half a million units a week.'

'I'll get back to you, let me make some calls. I don't think that's enough.' Voss could hear the cash register already. With that Richardson was gone.

Hanks's phone buzzed again, Welks picked it up. 'DI Welks, Hanks's phone.' He answered. 'DI Rossington? No sorry DCI Hanks is unavailable, I'm his deputy. What's up on the Laptop front?'

'We've found bits of laptop over a wide area, the surrounding gardens and the field on the other side of the roadway outside. But the hard disc is still eluding us.'

'It must be there, we need to find it desperately. Put everyone on the task and let me know immediately when you find it.' Welks hung up.

Hall was still hovering over the dangerous transport screen. The Dartford Crossing load was moving again and seemed innocuous. Southampton was still in Customs, and the Newport Pagnell shipment hadn't moved. The suspicious load had left Keele and was heading south on the M6 followed discretely by two unmarked ARU cars.

Philpott stood beside him staring at the board. 'How's the patient?'

'He'll live,' Welks said, 'he'll be up again in an hour tearing the walls down.' He put more confidence into the sentence than he felt. 'Anyway, Major, I'm dying of starvation here.'

It took a while for the army catering corps to get the food over the road into the bunker. The plates were lined up and the sweet smell of curry wafted into the room from the big open pot.

'Fine, let's get stuck in then. Give me an update Welks.' A pallid Alan Hanks stepped back into the arena.

'You okay?' Welks asked surprised to see him. 'I was just checking central ops on any progress about Baitullah and M'Beki.'

'Do you mean that they still haven't found them? Tell you what, it's time to get Joe Public involved.' Hanks was standing beside him looking like a dog's dinner, wiping his running nose, while he picked up the phone. 'Who am I talking to? DCI Hanks here.'

'Nicholson sir, DC Nicholson.'

'Listen up, I want a photo of M'Beki and Baitullah sent to all the papers and TV stations with the headline; Britain's most wanted terrorists, no, make that terror suspects, just to keep the legal guys happy. Get someone to authorise some sort of reward, say a hundred grand for information leading to…, the usual legal footnote, etc. Got that?'

'Yes sir.'

'Good! Try and get the TV stations and the evening papers to go with it tonight, the sooner the better.' He started coughing heartily, then continued, 'Oh, and make sure every copper in the country gets a picture of this man. I mean everyone, even the Special Constables and Community Watch people. We need as many eyes out there as we can get.'

'I'll get on to it right away ...,' was all he heard as he hung up. Hanks sat staring vacantly at the whiteboard.

'Good to see you up, Mr Hanks. How are you feeling?' Philpott asked 'You still don't look too good.'

'Should see me in the mornings,' Hanks joked.

'I have done sir,' he came back dryly. They sat and ate, not talking. Hanks poking around at his plate and scarcely eating as they stared at the whiteboard and checking the additions.

The Lt. General, in contrast, ate with appetite. 'Good!' he said while he was grabbing another plateful then adding, 'I think we have everything covered that we usefully can. The PM has asked if we can convene earlier tomorrow morning, for 7:00 am. He has to deal with a visit from that EU chap Barosso; some economic stuff. Bet he wants us to join the Euro,' he grinned impishly.

'Seen the news on TV?' Sir David asked.

'No, unfortunately, we had other things to do.'

'Someone has leaked that the hostage from Brinkley's was a Muslim and that he had connections with suspected terrorist groups.'

'Oh my God,' Hanks put his hand over his face, 'that'll put the cat amongst the pigeons, won't it? How did the virus containment exercise go?' Hanks asked Sir David.

'Nightmare, simply a nightmare, no-one takes it seriously. They're more worried about the tailbacks on the M62 than stopping the world dying. This country is going crazy.' He rummaged in his attaché case for a moment. 'If you want a light hearted interlude, I have something for you.' He placed a folder of reports from the 'front line' the CR units, the complaints relations section of the operation. 'Here, read this, a Mrs Wilson of Salford was threatening to sue for missing a hair appointment. A school outing with kids on the way to a footie match wasn't prepared to stop, because the little darlings would have been disappointed. The Territorials had to remove the driver and the teachers physically from the coach. No-one wants to believe this can be real.' Sir David continued, 'We're putting out a National emergency in all the media starting tonight to inform the public about the containment measures. We've got every hospital in the country on standby and all GPs are advised.'

'Are we competing now for front page headline space, Sir David?' Their laughs were interrupted as the collator called out urgently, 'Call from St Albans.'

'I'll take it here,' Hanks snatched Philpott's phone up. 'You have the hard drive?' The group were galvanised. 'How badly damaged is it?' He listened for a few seconds, 'Get it sent to specialists for recovering the information on it. Nothing has greater priority!' Hanks put the phone down and announced that they had the disc, but it was found in a gutter and was badly damaged and wet. It would be hours if not days before they could get any information recovered.

He walked over to the white board with Welks, studying the state of play. Minutes later, Philpott interrupted the two detectives, as he arrived breathlessly to announce the Cabinet were not prepared to shut down the complete London Underground system for Tuesday morning. The reasoning, so he reported, was that there was insufficient evidence for such a drastic move; to quote the Home Secretary, 'no reason to overreact'. Philpott also stated that the Deputy Prime Minister said that the financial loss for something that might not happen would be astronomical and with elections coming, politically impractical.

Hanks exploded, a barrage of expletives stopping all activity in the War Room.

'I know,' Philpott said recoiling from the violent outburst, 'the Lieutenant General is still trying to convince the Home Secretary.'

Hanks calmed down fast, outwardly at least, realising he had to focus, he was now confronted with the possibility of thousands, if not tens of thousands of casualties. 'In Hell's name what more do we have to give them to convince them that there's an imminent attack planned?' He dragged Welks from his chair 'Come on, we need to talk, you realise that any one of the Central London Stations could be a target.' He pulled him off towards the back room.

'What makes you think it'll be Central London?'

'The out of town stations would not have sufficient propaganda impact for terrorism. We know the operation 'Buyer' is happening at 7:30 tomorrow morning. I have an idea to minimise casualties. Let me talk to the Commissioner of Transport for London. I also need the TfL Press Officer. Get them on the phone in here.'

44

Whilst waiting for the Commissioner of Transport for London to get back to him, Hanks joined the discussion with Voss and the team from the Department of Health about the epidemic. The discussion dragged on into the night, filling time rather than progressing. Hanks listened with half an ear, fretting about the call to TfL and when they were going to get information about Rahmani's hard drive.

When Richardson finally arrived back from Downing Street, he looked ten years older. Hanks looked up in the hope he was bringing good news, but the Lieutenant General shook his head imperceptibly; just enough for Hanks to get the message before he advised that the government were keen to keep up the Muslim terrorist angle on the release of the virus, and not the Animal Rights Front. The Home Secretary has issued a D notice, there was to be no information to the contrary.

Hanks was too sick of all their manoeuvring now to be upset by it, his inner sense of justice jaded by so many days with little or no sleep. Normally he would have raged, now he was just focussed on one thing, 7:30 tomorrow morning.

Hopefully his plan would work. Welks nudged him awake at one point with a comment about how the government spin doctors were already hard at work in the media. As far as Hanks was concerned it was business as usual, manipulation of the media for effect. Plus they had Voss's new vaccine; surely they should concentrate on that. The vaccine would probably save more people than anything. Large scale tests had begun in the North West now, but the quarantine was staying. No-one could move in or out of the zone. It gave the soldiers something to do, Hanks thought wryly as the talking went on into the night.

Welks had managed to get him the Commissioner of TfL on the phone around midnight and the press officer had turned up an hour later, giving Hanks the excuse to leave the meeting amid puzzled looks.

It was a matter of only hours now, and he still had no idea where the action would be. They had tried analysing likely targets with the TfL people. A number of possibilities being examined, Victoria with some 12,000 passengers and 500 plus staff was being considered as the most likely, with St Pancras and Euston coming in as joint co-favourites.

'We're looking at the best part of 15,000 casualties if we choose wrongly.' Hanks said as the orderlies brought fresh coffee at just after four in the morning. 'We can only hope and pray we've limited that,' he added.

The TfL press officer had drafted his press release with Welks's help and had left to go to Lots Road with a police escort to get things sorted there. There wasn't much more they could achieve Hanks thought gloomily, conscious of the clock ticking round.

They had decided to skip breakfast to prepare for the politicians. The Prime Minister's request to move the meeting forward didn't make things easier. Hanks had set out his list of suspects and assembled a 'PowerPoint' presentation. Welks started working at the whiteboard; whilst Voss who'd appeared shortly after them busied himself with a visual presentation on the virus front.

'The army is missing,' Hanks joked as he worked.

'Do we panic?' Welks asked over his shoulder.

With the words hardly out of his mouth, Richardson marched in accompanied by Philpott, Nayyar and another army type. Hanks wasn't sure, but thought, as he had more scrambled egg on his hat than Philpott, that he must be higher-up the totem pole. He continued punching furiously at the keys on his laptop, cursing the lack of time or more specifically, his lack of typing skills. Orderlies were placing thermos canisters of coffee and tea on the central table along with the usual selection of juices and mineral waters. The polished glasses were being put in place as the first grumbling participants began to take their places. It was 6:50 am. There were still a number of empty seats, not just ministers, but junior members as well. Hanks could hear the mumble of complaints about the chaos on the Tube this morning; he smiled grimly as he heard them.

At 7:00 am on the dot the Prime Minister and Home Secretary entered and sat down, nodding curt greetings around the still half empty table. After a little small talk about the absentees, the Prime Minister tapped a glass for silence.

'So, shall we get on?' The Prime Minister said looking at the clock which was now showing 7:05.

Hanks liked that, no messing around, no inane small talk, and straight to business. Sir David introduced the new faces to the group and briefed the politicians. There were apologies from some, who'd phoned in due to the Tube crisis. Hanks noted that the new military man was a colonel. It turned out to be Wheeler from GCHQ, Nayyar's boss, which explained the lad's earlier absence. He was hardly concentrating when Welks nudged him, whispering. 'You're on.'

'So now I'll hand over to DCI Hanks who is leading the enquiry and let him give you a progress update.'

Hanks stood as Richardson sat down. 'Thank you Lieutenant General, Ladies and Gentlemen,' he began, 'I'm pleased to advise that in spite of some 'restrictive' procedures we've made some arrests, albeit at the lower end of the spectrum, but at least progress.' He had the first screen of his presentation beamed up on the projection wall, a simplified sketch showing the various lines of enquiry and who was leading each of them.' Hanks mobile rang. Irritated, he examined the display and seeing Rossington's number, he cursed under his breath. He apologised to the meeting saying, 'This is urgent, Mr Welks, please take over.' He pressed the accept icon and was galvanised by the news Rossington had for him. 'It's Bank, you're sure of that?' he confirmed. Hanks cut the call and interrupted Welks in mid discourse. 'Ladies and Gentlemen, the specialists have just recovered sufficient data from a terrorist's laptop to confirm that the target is Bank Station in the City of London. The attack is due to happen in,' he paused to look at the clock in sheer shock, 'exactly eight minutes.' Without further ado, he began to shout instructions.

'Nayyar, get me all CCTV coverage of Bank Station and put it on the big screen, 'Welks, Transport Police and Bank Station, evacuate everyone! NOW! Then get Central Traffic Control to put all traffic lights on red. A gridlock will stop at least some getting into the area.'

'On my way,' Welks grabbed a phone, and started issuing instructions.

'Get the emergency services on the way,' he nodded at Voss in the absence of the Health Minister, 'get the Health ministry to alert all the London Hospitals.' Hanks checked the time, 7:28. He was sweating, thinking what else he could do to minimize casualties.

The first traffic cam pictures were appearing on the big screen amidst looks of incomprehension at the speed of things from the politicians.

'That's the Mansion House camera,' Sir John the Met Commissioner said, 'and that's the Bank of England,' he announced the information in running commentary as the screens showed the coverage of dozens of bewildered people being ushered out of the Bank Station entrances into the road.

The first Transport police cameras started coming in showing the platform 1 on the Docklands line. It was strewn with apparently lifeless forms lying on the ground. 'Shit, it's the ether, they're unconscious.'

'7:29,' the Commissioner announced as the camera in Poultry came up on the screen.

'There it is,' Hanks pointed shouting. There was a tanker with three people next to it. Suddenly a sheet of flame erupted from the underground Station entrance opposite, then all the screens went blank. The room was silent.

A second later, glasses rattled on the tables, the surfaces of drinks showing concentric ripples in them as the overwhelming reality of what had happened sunk in. Shocked faces, some with tears streaming down them, some helpless, some uncomprehending turned towards Hanks. Somewhere in the background an alarm bell was ringing.

'I thought this place was bombproof.' The Prime Minister managed to break the silence. 'What was that?'

'Operation buyer sir,' Hanks said quietly, to no one in particular, as bedlam broke out in the room; people reacting hysterically, questions upon screamed questions. Hanks put his hands over his ears. …'How many dead?'…'Why wasn't it stopped?'…'Who was going to carry the can? He felt like jabbing the Home Secretary in the chest and asking her how much more evidence she would have needed to shut the Underground down, but it was pointless, there were more important issues now. He tried to imagine what that truck load of ether would have done to the station. The unconscious ones underground were lucky, if that was the right word to use, he thought despairingly, as the magnitude of what had just happened sank in on him.

Welks spoke white faced next to him, 'Jesus fucking Christ, the bastards, we'll make them pay for this!'

'This meeting is over,' the Prime Minister announced, 'I want an emergency Cabinet session in 20 minutes at number 10. All Cabinet members come with me to Downing Street. In the meantime, follow emergency plan 'Alpha'. Sir David, I want immediate notification on all pertinent issues.' the Lt. General nodded. 'The rest of you gentlemen, sort out this mess as best you can. Shut London's traffic down.' The Prime Minister ordered, not heeding the Lt. General's attempt to interrupt. 'Everything except for the supply of food, water and medicines, stop it. I want every vehicle leaving London searched. I want these people found and fast!' The Prime Minister walked towards the lift, the Cabinet members drifting after him one by one.

Hanks sat still in shock, watching the departing Cabinet members heading for the lift. The Prime Minister's last word, 'fast', echoing in his head.

Hanks slumped back into his chair, drained of all energy; numbed by it all. Welks was also in shock, operating like a robot, as he tried to get information from the emergency services.

Hanks face contorted with anger. 'He wants 'em fast, bloody

comedian!' he spat out in a harsh whisper, venom in his tone. 'They are the ones who put the hurdles in our way, now they want fast action.'

'We both know that the ones who did this are probably with their virgins now.' Welks added. 'We couldn't have stopped it in the time we had.'

'I wonder if Joe Public will see it like that.' Hanks was getting less pleased by the minute. 'Who is doing the PR on this?'

'The PM's press office with Scotland Yard I imagine.' Richardson answered.

'We have to be careful of how the press is going to handle this,' Hanks responded, 'racial tensions and all that. Let's get City of London on the line and find out what's happening. Get Nayyar to put the TV news on the big screen. Maybe we can see the damage there, any reports on casualty counts?'

A uniformed soldier po-faced dropped the late editions of the morning papers on the desk in front of them. The headline on the top one read,

'Huge Power cut cripples London Tubes. Commuter Chaos, Millions stranded.'

'You sly one you,' Philpott said admiringly, 'that's what the TfL Press Officer was doing here in the middle of the night. You couldn't get them to shut it down, so you did it for them. I bet it's not often the media gets prior notice of a major power cut. I should think you've probably reduced the casualties by 70%.' He patted him on the back, shoving the newspaper across to the Lt. General Richardson, who glanced at it and gave Hanks a wry smile and a thumbs up.

'Well done Mr Hanks. You've just confirmed that we picked the right man for the job, quick thinking that one.' The Lt. General whispered across the table. 'Any idea about casualties yet?' he asked in a louder voice.

'Initials coming in, but still only the tip of the iceberg,' Hall told them. 'The Fire service and TfL have four trains destroyed in the tunnels, max capacity would mean over 1200 people in each.' He appeared strangely pleased.

'What's to be happy about?' Welks looked daggers at him.

'I did a calculation based on the TfL statistics. On a normal day at this time there would have been eleven trains in the system round Bank Station at that time, some 4,500 passengers exiting the Stations at Bank and Monument.'

'Well?' The Lt. General asked gruffly, 'Nothing to be smiling about.'

'No,' Hall answered winking slyly, 'but the fortuitous power cut saved thousands, at least seven trainloads.' Richardson just grunted in response.

'Lucky power failure then,' Welks said, surreptitiously patting Hanks on the back.

45

Hanks wasn't sure what he felt, the shock had been put on the back shelf, he was raging at the injustice and wanted to take this rage out on anyone and everyone. He tried to be as calm as possible. An outburst now, however understandable, would not be constructive. How could he get the group all focused again? He was pondering this as Nayyar came over with Hall. They sat either side of him.

'We have had an idea!'

'An idea, great! Do I need this idea now?' Hanks answered annoyed.

'We think it might just flush out our suspects.' Hall said very seriously, 'We have the telephone card numbers and sequences. If this 'Brown Suit' and 'Hook Nose' are still using this method to communicate, we could simulate a message from one of the numbers.' he sat back as if all was clear.

'You've lost me. What message? What do we tell him, or them?'

'How about, 'Congratulations. I have a safe way out of the country join me, or something along those lines.'

'Too obvious,' was Hanks's first reaction, 'but then, maybe the psycho boys at MI5 could get some text worked out, maybe if we do it in Urdu then it will seem more authentic. Yes, it has a certain appeal to it. Let's do it. Any suggestions for the meeting point?'

'Philpott has been talking to Hereford. They say a Motorway rest area would be ideal, not services, that would be too dangerous, too many people around, but just a car park and rest place,' Hanks nodded, 'where a crack group could hide and surprise our two suspects.'

'Where and when?'

'Colonel Wheeler has an SAS team in Marston in Kent. He suggested the old disused petrol station on the Whitfield roundabout in Dover directly on the A2. There's plenty of cover for our people and it's enough out of the way, not to be a danger to the public.'

'You prepare everything. Let's see if I can get the rest of our team back on track now.' Hanks said as he slowly stood up and addressed the room, all eyes turned to him.

'Ladies, Gentlemen,' Hanks raised his voice to make himself heard over the general babble. The room went quiet, 'attention, please. This morning, we have had probably the heaviest peacetime loss of life ever in the UK. I want you all to know that we know who did it. We are on the trail of the masterminds behind it. The man who gave the command in Pakistan has already been eliminated by our American friends.' A low rumble of approval greeted this information. 'Furthermore, we made several arrests in the Luton area yesterday and expect more today. We are not stabbing in the dark anymore; we have clear and definite leads. Please, I know this has been a shock, but the only thing I can say is keep focused and don't let emotion blind you. With discipline and a systematic approach, we will catch these bastards and bring them to justice. I need the fullest cooperation and maximum effort from all of you now, it's not over yet.' Hanks voice rose in power and intensity. 'We are a top team, and together we will crack this terror cell.'

He sat down again in silence. There were grim smiles of determination visible around the room as one by one people got back to work.

'We should visit the site.' Sir David commented.

'No thanks. I've seen the aftermath of enough bombings. There's nothing we can do there, we'd only be in the way of the professionals who have an enormous job.' Hanks responded. 'Let's hear what the lads have wrung from our canaries at

Paddington Green. Maybe we can charge them with being accessories before the fact.' He looked at Welks with a mixed expression of sadness and determination. 'Could we have stopped it? I can't help but think that if we had found Rahmani just before he destroyed his laptop..., but the stupidity of political correctness...' his voice tailed off.

'I know Alan, I know,' Welks comforted him. 'the Bedfordshire rules and all the namby-pambying have cost thousands of lives today, but your stunt with TfL and the power cut was brilliant. That power cut probably saved about 20,000 people.'

Hanks smiled at him wearily. 'Keep it to yourself, Colin. No one can know this.'

'Mr Hanks, you may want to see this,' someone from Nayyar's team on the telecoms side called out. 'a clear text email from a 'Brown Suit' number in English and Urdu.' Hanks walked through to him.

'Who was it sent to?'

'All the national papers and TV Stations, it's a claim from the bombers.'

'Print it off and give it to the specialists in MI5; the use of language from it may help them make our text more authentic.'

Nayyar came in, 'Seen it then?' He seemed disappointed at not being the messenger.

'Yes, just confirms what we know about who was behind it. Wheeler has pinpointed it as coming from Luton, an address in Moore Street, outside number 54. Want to send the locals in?' Welks said. Hanks raised an eyebrow.

'You've been watching too much TV. By the time plod gets there, he'll be long gone. Pity we don't have those UAV things here. I'd like to fly one up Bury Park Road and take a look.' He turned to Philpott. 'If only we could intercept some of the texts or mails from these numbers and doctor the answers. The problem is we have to deal with four providers.'

Philpott shrugged helplessly, 'Ask the experts.' he pointed with his chin at Wheeler and Nayyar.

'Well? Can we?' Hanks asked again.

'Difficult to get all four to play ball in such a short time. We would need court orders and that would take all day.' Wheeler looked glum.

'We don't,' Nayyar chipped in brightly, 'we transfer all the numbers to one central server. A server under our control and we transmit what we want text wise. GCHQ has the capacity for that; I mean it isn't millions of calls is it? Conversations we can let go through, we just monitor and record those. It may need some pressure to get cooperation from the telecoms though. It's not exactly legal.'

'Blowing half of London off the face of the planet ain't legal either.' Hanks fumed. 'Who do we need to talk to? Philpott? Where the hell are you?' Philpott reappeared from the other room.

'Sorry.'

'Whose patch is Telecommunications in the Cabinet?'

'Business Innovation and Skills,' Philpott recited.

'Right, Nayyar tell him or her exactly what you need so we can do it from here. Let's get the Right Honourable Member for Wapping North or wherever, to be a bit 'innovative' with our Telecom buddies. I want results before lunchtime.' Philpott and Nayyar left.

'Paddington Green on the phone sir,' an aid from the backroom called out.

'Can I take it here?'

'Sure push line 4.There, where it's blinking.'

'Right, Hanks here. Ah, Coleman! I haven't heard from you for a time. How's it going? You pulling fingernails yet?'

'This is the 21st century, Alan.'

'I know, not allowed.' Hanks smiled ruefully.

'Going soft Hanks?' Coleman jested, 'Actually, we don't need much pressure here; they are all so shaken by what's happened, they're telling us everything; they'd cough up when their daughters lost their virginity, if we asked. Will take us a year to sort out all the information we're getting. Beds Station have pulled in two more of the money collectors and two social workers from the Moore Street Muslim Centre.'

'Most important for us is the information about Masoud Baitullah. We need to know everything about him, especially possible hiding places. What about Shener?'

'Mustafa Shener; he's cleared his accounts, the signs are that he's gone. The Redbourne guys are at his home address right now and everything's locked up. Neighbours say the family left by taxi with lots of suitcases around nine o'clock last night, seems like he's skipped. The Hemel police are at Shener's company in Buncefield, they've found out that M'Beki worked there and he and another driver, an Irishman, never turned up this morning. Oh, and the computer hard discs have been wiped clean.'

'Sod it; we've missed him.' Hanks was getting edgier by the minute, thinking what if 'Brown Suit' and Washiri had bunked as well. He could hardly bear to think about it. 'Have you checked flights out last night?'

'In progress, we're checking tickets in the wife's name as well.'

'Thanks Coleman, see you around.' Hanks broke the connection and found there was a queue of people awaiting his attention.

'Fancett, MI5 sir, I realise you're tied up, but we have the message ready for texting.'

Hanks read the English version and then asked, 'Is the Urdu okay? Checked?'

'Double checked sir.'

'Good, take it to Nayyar next door and tell him it's ok with me, and to send it to both of them, he'll know what I mean.' the man disappeared.

The Lt. General plonked himself down heavily beside him. 'I've a briefing with the PM in twenty minutes. Anything we can give him?' he toyed with a pencil that was lying there, 'anything to put out to the public?'

'You can tell him we're wrapping the Luton and Hemel ends up. We have about a dozen in custody in Luton and a lecturer from Hatfield whose laptop had the plans for the atrocity on it. The two head honchos are still at large. One is definitely still in the country and his last known position was Luton. I don't think he needs to know about the Dover thing yet. You never know, it might not happen. Did Wheeler pass that by you, sir?'

'Yes he did. It's a long shot, but we don't have much else in the arsenal, do we?' The pencil snapped in his hands. He put the pieces down embarrassedly on the desk. 'Sorry, a bit up tight with all this.'

'Who isn't?' Hanks sympathised. 'Let's get on with it.'

'You lot get some lunch. Then we'll see what else we can get up and running.'

Hanks didn't feel like eating in the circumstances. He glanced at the lunchtime edition of the Standard with its pictures of the remains of the Bank of England and the tanker. The headline read. '**Thousands Die as Tanker Causes Huge Terror Blast**.' The back page, showed photos of Washiri and Baitullah. Hanks tossed the copy on the table, and walked over to Dr Voss, not having the stomach to read the report.

46

Since leaving the MoD the Cabinet had been in emergency session in Downing Street. The Prime Minister was vacillating between bouts of outright rage and indecision, all in all giving the impression of someone not in control of himself. The Minister of Defence was trying, more or less in vain, to console and advise him on the one hand and get some semblance of sense out of him on the other. The Secretary of State for the Health Department was one of the last to arrive.

'Home Sec. here yet?' he asked, irritably.

At that, the Home Secretary arrived out of breath from the run across Whitehall, slamming the door behind her as she came in.

'So, what's the latest, Home Secretary?' Straw demanded.

'DCI Hanks is trying to set a trap for the two main suspects.'

'Hmph! I detest the word trying. I'll try to get it done on time, is a self-fulfilling prophecy,' he fumed. He turned on the Defence Secretary. 'So what's your plan eh?' he managed to say it without prodding the man in the chest, but the aggression was all there in his stance and facial expression.

Browne was a little taken aback, he was still reeling, like the others, from the news of the disaster and the horrors shown on the TV. 'Well,' he stammered at last, 'we should declare a state of national emergency, in my mind. We need the troops in to sort the mess out and a lock down on all travel for the next two days.'

'Brilliant.' Straw said derisively. 'Shutting the sodding door after the horse has bolted, terrific. Any idea what that would cost the country?'

'Now, now, Jack there's no need to let personal antipathy get in the way of getting this thing sorted,' the Minster for Food and Fisheries interjected, 'we won't be getting anywhere scoring points off each other.'

'Quite so,' Gordon Brown slipped into the conversation again, 'call in the UN perhaps?'

'Bloody imaginative, isn't he?' Straw jibed cruelly. 'Let's get sat down and see what we can make out of this mess.'

'What is the situation at Bank?' the Prime Minister asked.

The Home Secretary stood and shuffled her papers, 'I have to inform the Cabinet that as of 10:30 this morning we have an estimated body count of 4,307 dead, a known 413 hospitalised injured, and as many as 8,200 missing. The last figure is, however, only a best guess at the moment. The tube tunnels are still being searched, but we expect no more survivors down there. Thanks to the power cut only about 25% of the normal traffic was caught in the blast, and there would have been many more people in the stations at that time, had the power cut not happened. Last I heard, only three trains, about 3,000 casualties have been reported, under normal circumstances we estimate that it would have been about 16,000.'

'Happy coincidence, I dare say, we don't have to make heads role for the outage?' the Transport Minister asked rhetorically.

'The injured toll is relatively low. The head of the London Fire Brigade tells us that many of the victims were, mercifully, unconscious because of the fumes when the explosion happened. Whatever consolation that gives us. What we do need however is mortuaries.' the Home secretary continued.

'My staff are going to commandeer some of the cold storage houses in Smithfield's. I don't care if they have to give the meat away, but we need somewhere to store the bodies until we can identify them. We need that space desperately. The lockdown on travel at the ports and airports is causing huge problems, the atmosphere at Gatwick and Manchester is, putting it mildly, explosive. The police and border control are trying to screen everybody, but honestly, it's no better than absolute chaos.

We're doing our miserable best with the resources at our disposal, but if any of the bombers are there, it's unlikely we'll find them, unless chance plays a big part.' She paused and took a sip of water.

'Good, right Des,' he said turning back to the Defence Secretary, 'how are we going to rid the country of terrorists? What's the plan?'

The Defence Secretary was nonplussed, 'Prime Minister,' he flustered, 'We have never made any plans for this sort of thing in any of our 'Think Tank' scenarios. We have the 'Nettles' plan, which involves rounding up every person in the country suspected of radicalism, espionage or terrorism and putting them in camps to interrogate them. We have the old Army bases in Yorkshire and Somerset available, plus two secure facilities in Scotland.'

'What are we talking about here?' Jack Straw asked.

'Well, we would need to provide accommodation for about thirty thousand people who have been denounced since the blast and that's in the last few hours alone. Surely, it's a civil issue, not one for the armed forces, although we could argue, 'State of Emergency', a special case. However, I think it's a parliamentary issue. Not that the armed forces won't help of course.' His eyes sought help from Jackie Smith, 'Am I correct, Home Secretary?'

She looked daggers at him for passing the buck. 'Thank you Des.' She said sarcastically, aware that the road she was about to tread, was not going to be popular, but there was no way to dress up the truth here, not now, not today, not after what had happened. 'Gentlemen, as you are all aware, all the cuts in public spending have put a great strain on the domestic security services. Policing and intelligence gathering services have been on a shoestring for years now, which is why we are in our current predicament. Sure, we have lists of suspected terrorists and their affiliates, and sure we know of certain organisations which support these people and fund them.

We have,' she continued, 'been inundated with phone calls and emails denunciating thousands of people, who according to the callers are everything from al Qaida to members of secret cabalistic societies. There's doubtless valuable intelligence to be gained, but we don't have the resources. As far as 'Operation

Nettles' is concerned, this was conceived back when there was no internet and we had twelve pence to the shilling. It was made to deal with suspected Warsaw Pact spies and KGB moles, not a significant slice of the population, who we know already, will be denounced for one reason or another by neighbours with an axe to grind, people settling old scores and grudges. It'll take years just to sort the wheat from the chaff on that front. We don't have the capacity to manage anything on that scale. Just the interrogations, with the manpower we have, would take decades.' She looked glum the room was eerily silent.

'So enough of this maudlin self-pity,' Jack Straw took a lead, 'what options do we actually have? I don't think listing the things we can't do is being helpful here.'

'You're right Jack,' The Prime Minister said, 'what measures can I announce to the public in the TV spot?' His words were met with silence.

47

Voss was glad to be outside the claustrophobic atmosphere of the War Room. After the events of the morning, he was also glad to be out of underground tunnel systems. The very thought of what had happened at Bank made his skin crawl. The bunker was not for him, he wanted to see the sky, wanted the fresh air unfiltered in his face. He'd never considered himself a claustrophobe before now. The news coverage on the car radio was now just background noise since the initial shock about the magnitude of the atrocity had surfaced, with commentators' voices, and a babble of so-called expert opinions, he was submerged in a sea of numbness. The Commissioner for Police was on air sounding very stern and serious, pleading for calm and public participation.

When he arrived at the DoH (Department of Health), there were three people in the small office to greet him, all studying a map of the Midlands and the North West of the country. There were red markings around the north west of Chester, a red circle just north of the centre of Manchester and another in Leicester. These were the flu outbreak centres. Not really epidemics, but certainly the start of one, large outbreaks with a high enough incidence level to rate careful observation. Nearly ten per cent of the population of Chester had come down with the bug, and so far thirty two fatalities, sixty in hospital with complications. Manchester had over ten thousand cases, with two hundred and eighty-one dead, and over three hundred in hospital. In Leicester so far, there were two thousand registered cases and seventy-eight dead.

All had one thing in common; the Chester kindergarten virus. Admittedly there were the seasonal fatalities connected with the current flu that was also doing the rounds, but nothing to compare with the K virus figures. Voss and his team were telephoning as many people as they could to try and find transmission routes and interfaces, so far with only marginal or no success. Voss's hand ached from holding the phone and the only thing he'd managed to get out of the morning's graft was to transfer his data from his Excel chart to the DoH database, which was now fuller by some thousands of new entries and the samples from these patients were winging their way to Brinkley's for testing and cataloguing.

The clock over the door showed eleven twenty-seven, the big digital display advised as the minutes clicked over loudly. The thing was a monster, reminding him of the old departure boards at stations and airports, clattering as they changed to reflect the latest updates in the timetable. He painstakingly dealt with the drudgery of collating patient details. The work required his full concentration, but, if nothing else, it kept his feelings at bay for the meantime.

He immersed himself in his spread sheets, searching for links, for common factors. The only one that he'd managed to find so far was that the three towns with major outbreaks had all been Roman at some point in their history. As a connection, he discarded the idea as ludicrous. No, there was something else that he wasn't seeing. Frustrated, he plodded on, continuing to try to analyse the ever-growing list.

He flicked through to the notes he'd made to discuss with Randell and read through them again. AS271 was the first antibody which could fight all types of the influenza 'A', to be discovered, he mused, and smiled as he opened the file with the test results. Hanks and the insurance man were an added bonus, something positive, and something to help lessen this horror-filled morning. Randell had phoned him worried about his brother who'd been up to Bank that morning, Voss tried to reassure him that he was probably alright. Randell also informed him that the COBRA team had been in touch. They were to start supplying vaccines as fast as they could. He'd taken the order for a preliminary ten million doses. Voss's eyes lit up at the numbers. The not so good news was that, because of a possible pandemic, the company was to release the manufacturing methods to the European majors, so they could swing into production immediately.

He listened patiently to his boss's lamentations about the profit situation and how he wished he could go it alone. Given the situation, Voss thought it was out of place. It should be people before profit if this epidemic was going to be that big a problem. It was the fatalities which continued to bug him. No apparent correlation in the number of reported outbreaks to the number of fatalities. Normally, he would have expected a common ratio.

Randell was particularly proud of his research into the costs of an epidemic. Here, he was sure that they could put pressure on governments to pay virtually any price for a vaccine like that. The latest flu epidemic in Britain was placing a significant burden on the emergency services and was costing the country billions in lost work, medications, and hospital capacity, all for a comparatively mild strain of influenza. Having a universal treatment, which could be given in emergency circumstances, would be economically invaluable, not to mention the added benefit of guaranteed alleviation of human suffering. Yet, this was a scenario unlikely to be played out, kicked into touch by the clear order to cooperate with the pharmaceutical biggies.

Whoever bid the most got the biscuit. Voss was uncomfortable with the callousness of his boss's stance on the issue. The benefits to mankind were considered quite secondary, it would seem. Voss reflected on this dejectedly as he put the phone down, deferring the question of the ethics of the issue.

48

'Sir,' the collator called out, 'I have Inspector Moresby on the line.'

'Yes, put her through.' Hanks pulled his chair up to the desk and took out a pen. 'Hi, bit rough down on ground zero then?' he asked grimly.

'Talk about it! This just defies description. I've showered, I've changed my clothes and have been spraying the office with pink floral mist, but I just can't get the smell out of my nose. It's awful. Your reward idea has put a lot of public-spirited folk out on the streets rooting out terrorists. There are vigilante groups lynching anyone that remotely looks like either one of the two culprits.' She paused and mumbled something to someone else in her office. 'Sorry about that,' she came back. 'We've had nearly four hundred calls from the public saying they've seen them. Sightings spread from Dagenham to Scunthorpe. And before you say it, no sir, we don't believe the C's in Scunthorpe even if Typhoo did put the T in Britain.'

'So, where does it leave us?' Hanks grinned at the jest.

'Thin on the ground, we just can't check all the calls quickly enough. Things are crystallising though, around two areas. Southall and Luton. We got a call from Patel's Superstore in Park Road Southall saying someone resembling Washiri bought a telephone card. Took the daft woman an hour to realise it was the bloke on the front pages of the papers.' she stopped, 'you still there?'

'Certain it was him?' Hanks grunted.

'They got him on the security camera. Rubbish picture quality, but it's him all right. No turban and long dark straggly hair. There's no doubt that he's our man. Want me to forward it to you?'

'Of course,' Hanks said curtly, 'what manpower do we have in Southall?'

'The local bill, say twenty uniforms and maybe half a dozen plainclothes, plus a fast response group of another twenty-five in Hounslow, which we can get in at short notice. I suppose we could call one of the Heathrow teams, but I bet they're stretched to the limit with the airport closed. Oh, I've got three 'Operation Fellowship' people under cover there as well.'

'What about communications between them? They all got radios?'

'Apart from the Fellowship people, yes, why? You think we'll need them?'

'No idea. It's nice to have options though. We have a text from our suspect, Masoud. He's claiming responsibility for the explosion. No real details, just a 'we did it' thing. There's a video attached to a mail which was sent to the BBC, we presume M'Beki doing his martyrdom bit, haven't seen it yet. His location at the time was Moore Street in Luton. You get any joy from showing the picture?' Hanks asked.

'Yes, we got five positive ID's. One guy even lent a room to the man to use. We're having it searched now. I'll let you know what we find.'

'Keep the Southall crew on standby. You never know your luck. Where are you now?'

'Back at the Yard, Paddington Green depresses me.'

'You and me both,' Hanks conceded, 'I'll ring if Southall develops. Hanks hung up just as Nayyar rushed over.

'Just got a text from one of Washiri's batch, here.' he put the slip in front of them. It read '*Pleased to hear father is well. Please phone him 0208 3525552 on one hour.*'

'So what's the telephone number?'

'They are changing the pattern; maybe he's sniffed a rat.' Nayyar scratched his head, 'The number's a phone box on the corner outside Southall railway station and Washiri's call came from the park down the road. We've got him down to a couple of yards. Looks like a bench by the play area if you check the 'Google Earth' site.

Hanks thought for a minute. 'How long have we had this?'

'Minutes, five max.'

'We have about fifty-five minutes until he goes back to the phone and waits for 'Brown Suit's' call.' He called over to the dispatcher, 'Get me Southall nick fast. I need someone with local knowledge, someone who knows the geography. Thanks Ashok, that's amazing work again. I never cease to be impressed.'

'Chief Inspector Hanks! Sergeant Shah from Southall, sir, line two.'

Hanks picked the phone up. 'Hello, DCI Hanks here,' he barged in without waiting for an introduction from the other side. 'We need a bit of local knowledge. Hope you can oblige.'

Hanks put the phone on loudspeaker calling to his partner, 'Welks get on the phone to Moresby. We'll need her people in Southall. Tell them to get them ready to move. Washiri is there.'

'Sergeant Shah here,' a crisp almost Oxford accent came on the speaker phone interrupting him, 'what may I be of assistance with.'

'We have a suspect on your patch, possibly one of the minds behind the Bank thing this morning. Our latest info is that he's in the park by a children's play area, about a hundred yards from the station. Can you tell me if there's a way we can approach this site without being seen?'

'Oh, that is very difficult, this time of year especially. You see the hedges and trees have no leaves.'

'If he leaves the park, how many exits are there?'

'I will be looking now, one moment please.' There was a pause, 'Ah there are, let's see one, two, three ... seven exits.'

'Excuse me! Where are you counting from?' Hanks asked, perplexed.

'The surveillance cameras, we have the park under observation because of drugs and petty crime.'

'I want a live feed from your cameras into the MOD immediately, if not sooner; hang on,' Hanks turned and shouted, 'Nayyar, how the hell do I transfer this call to you? What extension?'

'323, sir.' Nayyar shouted back.

'Okay Sergeant Shah, I'll put you through to our technical wizard. Thanks, you've been more help than you'll ever know,' with that, he transferred the call to Nayyar.

'Welks I think we may have our boyo on TV in a minute. We'll need feet on the ground fast. How's Moresby's crew coming on?'

'She can get us seventeen uniformed offices and five plain-clothes to Southall Station within the next twenty minutes.'

'Tell to put her men in the side streets covering every exit from the park. Better still get this Shah chap at Southall nick to tell her where to put them.'

'Right, I'm on it.' Welks picked up the phone again.

Hanks googled a street map of Southall onto his screen and saw the park and station; lots of side roads, the aerial photo also showed lots of alleys. Twenty-two men weren't going to be enough. He punched Philpott's number and asked him if he had any ideas where they could get extra men in from. A couple of minutes later Philpott got back with a suggestion that they send a sixteen man trained anti-terror group by train from Paddington. The suggestion was at first ridiculed until Philpott explained that it was easier to sneak them in that way without raising suspicion. They could be on the next train, and be there in twenty-eight minutes.

'Okay, get them there in civvies; I don't want a squad of heavily armed uniformed officers storming out of the station frightening our boy off. Move it! Go! Go! Go!' He slammed the receiver down. Hanks was getting excited, the people around him became affected by his surge of adrenaline and they were all watching him partly in anticipation, partly apprehensively.

Nayyar shouted through, 'I've got the park pictures.'

Hanks jumped up and almost ran into the next room, causing a stir and questioning looks all round as he did. Nayyar mumbled something incoherent as he and Hall hunched over the screen peering at the shadowy picture of a children's play area in a park. The cold weather meant that even the hardiest of kids were not out playing on the swings, so that, at least was something they needn't worry about.

'There he is!' Nayyar pointed with his pen to a lone figure hunched on a bench.

'Looks like more a wino to me. Right scruffy sod,' Hanks commented, 'you sure it's him?'

'Here is the GPS of the last call and here are the GPS coordinates of the bench.' Hall said, as if Hanks were an imbecile for even asking the question. Hanks ignored his tone and continued to study the picture.

'Can we get this on the big screen up there?' he pointed to the projector screen still running 'Breaking News' on the attack.

'Sure! The quality will be rubbish, though. Not enough pixels,' Nayyar explained.

'Try it. If it doesn't work, we still have this.' Hanks nodded at the screen.

Seconds later the TV commentary was replaced by a snowy grey picture of the man on the bench in the play area. At least they could see the basics.

'Split the screen and put the map of the place next to it. We can mark the positioning of the men on the ground then,' Hanks ordered searching for his colleague. 'Welks, you got men in motion yet? Come have a look at this.'

Philpott came and stood at Hanks's elbow, 'The Paddington boys are on their way. Your chum suggested getting Sergeant Shah to meet them at the station and tell them where to go.'

'Magic, get Shah out of uniform and down to that station fast.' He was beginning to get a good feeling about this.

'The AT team are equipped with small arms and Tasers. We need a Home Office 'Okay' to use them, though. Your territory I think, Mr Hanks.'

'Quite.' Hanks walked over to the group from the Home Office. 'Home Secretary?'

'Here,' a woman's voice emerged from a scrum of people round a desk, 'what's up?'

Hanks explained briefly what was going on in Southall and what resources he'd put into play, and he requested authority to use all means at his disposal to arrest the suspect Washiri. The Home Secretary wasn't happy to give Hanks 'carte blanche' so she sanctioned provisional approval, with force only to be used if the suspect threatened the safety of officers. Hanks thanked her.

'Bloody politicians,' he grumbled as he walked away, his face like thunder, 'sodding weak-kneed politicians.' he kicked a wastepaper basket in frustration.

'What's up Alan?' Welks asked, as he returned to the group.

'We have clearance for the use of extreme force to capture Washiri.' He announced, shortening the version of the Home Secretary's 'permission'.

'Great!' Welks looked surprised.

'Just make sure that if they use it, every report must say that Washiri was threatening an officer.'

'Check the screen; he's nervous, see, jigging his leg fast then holding it, then almost uncontrolled jigging again. He gets up, walks to the hedge, looks up and down the road and sits down again. He's very alert. We mustn't do anything to frighten him,' Welks said. 'I'll get the psycho blokes to analyse his body language. Maybe that'll give us more of an insight.'

Traffic on Park Road was very light, relatively few people were out on the streets considering it was the tail end of the normal rush hour. Of course, the country was still in a state of shock at the enormity of what had happened and they were at home in front of their TVs, waiting for matters to unfold, dreading the terrible news that one of their own could be amongst the victims and hoping to see the culprits apprehended. Absenteeism was going to peak, today, Hanks thought as he watched a train pull in at Southall station. About thirty or so people got out, spilling quickly into the street. Washiri seemed to pay little or no attention to them. Good, Hanks reflected, he wasn't expecting anything from the station side then; he was concentrating on roads and cars, checking for threats.

'I've put a timer on the screen,' Nayyar said. Tapping away rapidly at his keyboard, a backwards running digital timer showed on the bottom of the screen. It displayed a mere 27 minutes until 'Brown Suit's' call was expected.

'Where are our people now?' Hanks asked, 'Have the Paddington boys left?'

'Sergeant Shah has just called in. He's on the platform waiting to meet them.' Philpott was still holding the phone as he relayed the information.

'Right, is there any chance of getting into a house

overlooking the park? Maybe get a sniper in there?'Welks asked.

'Now there's a thought,' Hanks smiled. 'Check please, but I've no idea how we'd get him there, as the tube service is at a complete standstill. A helicopter would be our only chance.'

Welks eyes lit up. 'How about Capital Radio's 'Eye in the sky', they have a heli over London to monitor the traffic. Can't we commandeer it?'

'Have to put the bugger off the air then. Don't want this in every living room in the country. Try it! Speak to Mrs Smith.'

'Major Philpott, a word if I may.' Hanks pulled him down to whispering level. 'You got any snipers over the road in Horse Guards?'

'I'm not sure Mr Hanks. I'll check.'

'If we have one, I want to get him by heli into Southall in half an hour.' Hanks let the man stand up again. 'As soon as you know if one is available let me know. I'll organise the transport. But it's between us,' he winked.

The timer was ticking steadily backwards, only eleven minutes to go now. Washiri hadn't moved, apart from standing to stretch his legs and presumably keep warm.

'You notice something?' Hall said, fast forwarding a recording of the surveillance camera in the park, 'He hasn't looked at his watch once in all the time he's been there. Doesn't that strike you as funny?'

'You sure?' Hanks asked, perturbed.

'Just re-running the film, but I'm pretty certain of it.'

'That doesn't make sense. Someone who's set a time for the return call surely always checks how much time he's got.' Welks commented.

'You're right.' Hanks replied, 'There's something not right here.'

'We've got the Southall men positioned all around the park and there's now a new camera team in one of the houses overlooking the park. If you switch to the Southall link you should get the feed.' The collator gave the link to Nayyar. 'I'm marking the position of the police on the road map aerial photo composite.' A series of red dots appeared on the big screen at junctions leading away from the park. By now, everyone was gathering round to follow the events.

'No sniper, sir.' Philpott came back, breathless. 'Sorry.'

'No time now anyway,' it was nearest Hanks got to thanking the man.

The timer was down under two minutes now and Washiri had still made no sign of moving. 'The team leader in Southall wants to know what to do, sir.'

Hanks tore himself away from the image of Washiri sat in the park. 'Wait!' he said, 'no-one moves until I say so. Have you got contact with Shah?'

'Yes sir,' the collator answered, 'Shah is putting one of the ATU team as a busker by the phone booths, guitar and mouth organ holder and all; 'borrowed' from some unsuspecting street musician. He's got a camera and mike on the mouth organ so we should be getting live streaming from him as well. Two of the men are going into the park as winos complete with brown paper bags. There're going in at the far end of the park away from Washiri.'

'Let everything appear totally normal. How are they kitted up?' Hanks stamped his foot in disappointment as the timer went into the minus zone. 'Shit!' he said, pointing at the timer. 'What now?'

'Hang on, I'll get an update.' Nayyar uttered, burying himself in his computer again.

Welks brought some coffee over. 'Steady the nerves, Alan.' he sat down next to him, 'What if the original message was a code?'

'Why is he waiting then?'

'What if one hour means another time? The number plus something?'

'It obviously wasn't a bloody hour was it?' Frustrated, he turned to Nayyar, 'We do have the right bloke, don't we?'

'Affirmative sir,' Nayyar quipped back, 'I'm running a word check through all the old mails we have, there's a poor use of preposition in '**on** one hour' instead of **in**. We're checking if it may be deliberate, then again it could always be a typo.'

'Let me know if you find anything. Any movement?' he asked anxiously.

'No, the situation is still the same.' Welks clutched his coffee mug like it was precious. 'Washiri walked around the park past our guys just now. Presumably it was a check-up. He seemed unperturbed and he's back on his bench now. The winos look great! One's apparently out for the count.'

Hanks looked at the screen to be rewarded with the picture of a man holding a bottle to his chest, lying flat on his back on the grass. 'I'd like a pint of what he had,' he joked. 'When this is over, I'll need it.' A few smiles greeted the remark.

'Why don't we just go in and get him?' Nayyar asked. By this time the Home Secretary was hovering behind Hanks as well.

'If we go in now, we will lose 'Brown Suit'. That's why,' Hanks grunted. 'I want both of these creatures. I want to stamp on their livers.'

'I'm quite sure that's not allowed Inspector,' the Home Secretary added from behind him, ostensibly shocked by the very thought of it.

'Oh, come on, Ma'am!' Hanks chided. 'You're not gonna give me the, 'He probably had a tough childhood. He's not really an evil man, just a product of his environment crap, are you?' He pushed his chair back. 'These bastards are responsible for killing a vast number of people this morning. An enormous figure that I can't and don't want to get my head around at the moment. And you are bleating about how they get treated. We're not at Magistrate's court now Ma'am, with all due respect.' His tone left no doubt where the respect was. Welks put his hand on Hanks's arm to calm him.

'Mr Hanks,' Nayyar broke the uncomfortable hiatus, 'We have the 'on' preposition wrongly used in three emails that I've found up to now. Each time, if I'm is correct; they denoted a time period's difference i.e. one week equals two; an hour, two and so on, you know? My bet is that Washiri meant two hours not one.'

'Let's hope you are right, minus nine minutes now. Fifty- one minutes to go, if you're prediction is correct.

'We have to incapacitate him even if he only appears to be getting away. Shoot him down if need to be!'

'Under no circumstances, Mr Hanks, no way!' the outraged Home Secretary jumped in again. 'We definitely don't do that sort of thing here. We do things by the rules here. That's what makes us better than the terrorists.'

‘Okay, Ma’am, we don’t do that sort of thing here.’ Hanks gave in, rolling his eyeballs skywards with bad grace, thinking to himself that’s what makes us deader than the terrorists. ‘I want to speak to your sergeant Shah when he reports in.’ Hanks added as Philpott walked over to him. ‘A word, my friend,’ he whispered quietly into his ear, pulling him away from the group. ‘How do we ‘legally’ take this nasty piece of work down if he does a runner?’

‘Only possible if, a) he poses a direct lethal threat to either an officer of the law, a member of the armed forces or a member of the public or b) if the Prime Minister declares the region under a state of emergency. In which case, if we tell the suspect there is a state of emergency and he fails to stop, we can inform him we may use force, then a warning shot and then we can ‘disable’ him.’

‘I prefer the Queensferry rules.’ Hanks said, ‘Shoot the monster and tell everyone we did ask him nicely to stop running away. I’m sure we could find enough witnesses.’

‘Sure, just hope there is no passer-by videoing it and stuffing it on Youtube. You never can tell these days.’

‘I want the bugger alive though.’ Hanks added.

‘Of course,’ Major Philpott put his hand on Hanks’s shoulder. ‘You’re doing a grand job,’ he said. ‘I know it’s tough. If it backfires, the shit lands in your lap.’

‘Don’t I know it,’ Hanks replied.

‘Washiri is moving again,’ Welks called to Hanks, ‘still in the park, seems to be scanning the perimeter.’

‘He’s just looked at his watch for the first time since we’ve been on to him,’ Hall managed through a mouthful of sandwich. ‘Only twenty-two minutes to go.’

‘Any signs of ‘Brown Suit’? Any contact?’

‘No, sorry.’ Nayyar said, ‘Anyone else got any info from the Luton end?’

‘Seen the Home Secretary?’ he asked. Welks nodded in the direction of the group round the conference table. ‘She’s wanted at Number 10, urgently,’ he explained. Hanks was relieved that she was going. Having her gone meant she wouldn’t be able to see what he was doing.

‘Right, Nayyar, can you make the phone in the kiosk ring

without actually putting Baitullah's call through?' Hanks restarted the proceedings.

Nayyar conferred with one of the telecoms guys. 'Yes, we can.'

'Can you also make the incoming caller believe the number is engaged? Or even better out of order?' Again, after a short discussion this was confirmed as doable. 'Right, then here's how we do it.' He looked at the timer. There were still some eight minutes to go as all the teams gathered around him to hear the plan.

'Mr Hanks? I have Bedfordshire Constabulary on line 3 for you,' the collator called over. Hanks reached to pick up the phone, 'Yes,' he said as he put it to his ear, 'Hanks here.' Welks watched his colleague closely as the remaining colour drained from his face. 'I understand.' Hanks finished the call and sat down again, heavily.

'Not good news Alan?' Welks asked.

'No Colin, they've found Baitullah's Vauxhall outside some lock up garages in Luton. 'Now we have no idea.' Hanks was despondent.

'We'll keep tabs on all the SIM cards; you never know, someone might still be active. It always seems to end differently to how you plan it.' Welks put his hand on Hanks's arm consolingly.

Hanks smiled at his partner, 'Never lose your optimism, do you?'

Southall

There had been non-stop coverage since just after eight in the morning. New bulletins coming thick and fast, Hassan could hardly tear himself away from the pictures. They'd all done their jobs, all of them. Shener had done well. They had all done well. The end result was more than they'd dared dream of, now he had to get away. He'd jumped the country before and he'd do it again, but with his picture and that of Masoud's being all over the media, it would be immensely more difficult this time. How the hell they'd got pictures of them both he didn't know. What had they missed? What had they overlooked?

Hassan's phone beeped, a text had arrived. He stood motionless spellbound by the images in the TV showroom window, as yet still oblivious to the risk he was taking standing openly in the street. He was sad Qamar was not there to see this. He opened his phone and read the message. It was from Masoud.

'Have a safe way out. A2 Dover. Father has it organised.' It was in Urdu. Funny, they'd never discussed escape plans. It never occurred to them that they might need them. Now, with hindsight, it seemed like a grievous omission. He had to get back to Masoud, but how?

He considered his options, somehow the security services had been on to them. His mind was in turmoil as he tried to figure out how they had managed this. Had he and Masoud been careless? Had they stuck to a particular pattern too long? He didn't know, but decided to change his method of communication after one last mobile contact. A Public phone, yes that was the answer, he searched around for one cursing the fact that the few that were around were practically all card phones; he had to risk buying a telephone card.

He also had to change his appearance. Looking around to check if anyone was paying attention, he dipped into a disused shop doorway and removed his Pashtu hat, discarding it in the accumulation of rubbish lying there. Hassan shook his hair loose and combed it with his fingers, checking his reflection in the dirty window. Once satisfied with the result, that his image was different enough from the newspaper photo, he went on.

A few doors along was a 24-hour supermarket. The sign over the door announced it as Patel's Superstore; the place was crammed with every conceivable thing. The gangways between the shelves to the cashier's desk were so narrow; he had to go sideways to get down them. The young dark-skinned girl on the till was plugged into her not so personal stereo, jigging to the loud swishing sounds emanating from the headphones. She was perched on a stool, her chubby legs bulging inelegantly in her over-tight hot pants. Hassan had to tap her on the head before she even noticed he was there. The girl lifted one earpiece off her head, obviously annoyed at the interruption.

'Telephone card,' Hassan said, 'twenty pounds.' Wordlessly, she opened the till and took one off a stack bound with an elastic band. He put the twenty pound note on the counter and left her with her music. The likelihood that she'd recognised him was minimal, he'd bet she didn't even know what day it was. However, as he left the shop, doubts wracked him, shocked by seeing the store TV on with his and Masoud's pictures. 'Reward! Wanted terror suspects!' 'Killers at large. Reward for information.' How by Allah, had the dogs got on to them so fast?

Equipped with his card, he set off in search of a telephone box. The corner of Park Avenue and South Lane by the station offered him a choice of three. He picked the middle one, noted the number and walked away round the corner to the park where he found a bench and texted Masoud. 'Pleased to hear father is well. Please phone him 0208 3525552 on one hour.' He pressed send, hoping that Masoud would get the message. Hassan retreated to a bench in the park opposite. Although it was miserably damp and cold, from where he sat he could observe the phone boxes without being conspicuous. Although not enamoured by the prospect of a two hour wait in the cold, there was no alternative; Kahn's was out of the question. Hassan checked around him, reassured that there were ample exits from the park. He'd still be in a position the make a break for it if the need arose; Southall was home territory for him, after all. Apart from the passing traffic, which was very light; there was nothing unusual, nothing to arouse suspicions. Hassan began to inwardly relax; no-one knew his whereabouts. How could they? He could only wait now. Wait for Masoud's call.

49

The officers were all in their positions surrounding the park and the station. The phone box was the centre of attention as Washiri made his way towards it. Hanks was glued to the screen as the camera in the house zoomed in on their target. The excitement in the room was tangible. What if the terrorist was carrying a bomb? What if he was armed and a threat to the forces on the ground? The two drunks who had begun to wander in the general direction of the station, now followed behind the man. A busker was strumming 'My ol' man's a dustman', the only tune he knew, for the umpteenth time.

Washiri checked round for anything suspicious. Convinced everything was clear he proceeded to the phone box and waited outside. He looked at his watch nervously, and Hanks and his team automatically did the same. The counter which Nayyar had installed showed less than a minute to go. There was an audible intake of breath, and relief, as the phone started to ring. As Washiri put his hand on the door grip, Hanks shouted into the radio to take him, now. The busker dropped his guitar and the two drunks materialised at Washiri's side before he knew what was happening. Yet, Washiri reacted incredibly fast and bolted into the station entrance where he was confronted by three waiting members of the anti-terror team. He saw the levelled weapons and tried to flee in the other direction. He put his hand into his jacket, pulling out a knife, but then began to lower it, realising the gesture was futile. The oncoming officers didn't give him even a moment's time to make a threat with it as the Taser darts penetrated his shirt front. Washiri went down like a felled tree, hitting the pavement with a loud smack. The busker quickly knelt on him and put the cuffs on. A cheer went round the room as they saw the struggling figure being safely bundled off to a waiting van and heard the confirmation that he had been taken, was unharmed and safely in custody.

'I want that one personally, Welks. Get him to Paddington Green. I want to do him myself,' Hanks growled ignoring the backslapping and congratulations. 'Settle down people, we still have the other one to deal with. Nayyar, has he got the unavailable tone?'

'Yes, he has just tried redialling, he must be panicking.'

'Glad someone else is showing signs of nerves,' Philpott quipped. 'Is he still in Luton?'

'You wish, Hall said, 'He's in Hemel Hempstead.'

'What the bloody hell is he doing there?' Welks exclaimed.

'Do we know any closer than that?' Hanks asked.

'Not sure,' Hall conferred with Nayyar, 'there's some kind of interference, Radio signals confusing the triangulation.' Hanks was worried.

'What is causing it; he hasn't got some jamming technology I hope?' Hanks looked over at them.

'Checking the local stations now,' Nayyar contributed, 'we have such a mass of signals there. A GPS black-spot; there's traffic radio, the radar sensors on the bridge, the Police frequencies and the oil companies stuff, pipeline monitoring and communications.'

'So how close can we pin that last call?' Hanks persisted.

'Plus minus 50 metres,' Nayyar said.

'So where does that put us in Hemel?

'Buncefield Terminal, more or less,' Nayyar answered. There was a sharp intake of breath all round as Nayyar broke the news.

'What about the Dover meet?' Hanks said seemingly ignoring the information.

'He's southbound, in Hemel now and he could take the M25 round to the Dartford Crossing and on down, so the three pm slot is still theoretically possible.' Nayyar advised.

'Are all the troops in position?' Hanks checked with Philpott for reassurance who nodded in confirmation.

'What's plan B?' Welks asked.

'Bloody pessimist, aren't you.' Hanks grunted. 'Plan B? What plan 'B'? Firstly, we get plan A off the ground, and then we do a plan B,' Hanks stated, then leaned back in his chair and cracked his finger joints loudly. 'Plan B,' he mumbled to himself, wondering what the hell that was going to be, and hoping that he wouldn't need it.

'The PM's going live on TV in two minutes direct from Downing Street.' Someone from the Home Office group called over.

'Mr Nayyar, can you put it up on the main screen please?'

The big picture of the park in Southall disappeared, replaced by the dour face of a reporter outside Number 10 repeating for the umpteenth time what had happened at Bank that morning and how shocked everybody was.

'Does the PM know we've got Washiri?' Welks asked. 'He may need some good news.'

'There's absolutely no way, we'll tell him,' Hanks said, 'We don't want to scare Baitullah any more than we have to, you never know, he still may turn up at Dover.'

The clock said 2:30 pm. With all the ferment, everyone had missed lunch. The trolleys with food for the teams still stood where the army catering corps had left them outside the lifts. Hanks got up and took the lid off one of the trays, uncovering neat little triangles of white bread filled with salmon paste. He lifted one and bit into it as Philpott appeared at his elbow.

'What, no pork pies? DCI Hanks you disappoint me,' he jibed.

'I've disappointed the nation letting someone blow the City of London off the map,' he cursed.

'The telephone was last active in Buncefield. Could he be there? Shener Transport is in Buncefield.'

'Doubt it,' Hanks munched on dejectedly, 'Buncefield has probably got more police in it than petrol at the moment, any news on Luton?'

Philpott helped himself to a stack of sandwiches and saw Hanks look at him, 'I'm taking some for the team back there,' he nodded over his shoulder. 'They're not all for me,' he muttered guiltily. 'Luton, no, the local police are doing house to house enquires, but it's a huge task'

'Waste of time,' Hanks poured a coffee for himself, 'he's long gone. We got his signals southbound on the M1 and in Hemel. We can only sit and wait until he shows face again. If you ask me the airports are better open than closed, he has to go past a scanner if he's leaving the country. At the moment, he can't leave, so he doesn't have to walk past any cameras and can't pick out his face. My advice is to open the ports and airports again, that gives us a much better chance. A car ferry is my bet, there's nothing easier for smuggling someone out of Britain than on one of those. It's dead easy, minimal checks. Covered with a blanket on the back seat or in the boot, and whoosh you're away. 'La belle France' and invisibility.'

Nayyar came over, 'You want to see the PM on the box?'

Hanks looked over at Nayyar, 'You do it for me, I didn't vote for him anyway.' I'm going for a break, a little lie down, just to collect my thoughts. This is all a bit much for a Tuesday.' Hanks headed off back to the rest rooms at the rear of the underground complex, a few perplexed stares following his progress.

Hanks reached the sick bay and sat down on the first bed. He needed breathing space, away from the expectant eyes of everyone in the crisis centre. He sank head in hands and rocked backwards and forwards trying to get some kind of realistic plan together. Nothing survived even superficial examination. He lay back on the bed wrestling with memories of old cases of fugitives on the run, and ruses to lure them out. Nothing, nada, zilch. He dozed fitfully for a while, everything passing by in slow motion as he dreamed of the flames envisioning the panic in the tunnels at Bank. He pictured the families waiting for the dreaded news that their loved ones were amongst the confirmed body count.

He woke feeling helplessness, rage, impotence. With the word impotence still in the forefront of his mind, he was disturbed by a tap on the door. On impulse, he took out his notebook and wrote the word down. He didn't know why, he had no clue as to what the significance was, if any. He just had a gut feel that it was important.

He stood and opened the door to be confronted by a worried Welks.

'You okay Alan?' It was nearly four o'clock.

'Thanks, I knew you'd be good for a motivating pep talk.' He backed off, allowing Welks into the room. 'I've been racking the old brain about how to get out of this mess. How do we lure 'Brown Suit' into the open?' He splashed water on his face as he spoke. 'What's new out there?'

'It hasn't got any better; the public backlash has started. First, a couple of stabbings, terror suspects in Durham nick, then one in Long Martin, now we have several more, the death toll keeps climbing.' He paused. 'Christ, it's a bloody shambles. As if the body count from the Underground isn't enough. The press are going ape shit at us, there are asking why we haven't stopped the disaster from happening, if we knew who was behind it.'

'Clever buggers, all of them, but, of course, with a degree in hindsight they can afford to be. They can throw stones without any responsibility for their actions, but we have to be seen to function. What's with Washiri? Is he at Paddington Green yet?'

'Yes, but there's worse news.'

'My cat's dead! Come on, Colin, it can't get any worse, don't wind me up.'

'Well. You want the bad news or the really bad news?'

'Great! I get a choice, do I? Come, sit and tell all.' He sat back on the edge of the bed. Welks joined him.

'The Prime Minister is threatening to resign. The Queen has been on TV practically ever since sending messages of peace and national reconciliation. The Cabinet is debating whether there is a legal precedent for calling a coalition government.'

'Not sure which is worse, a PM giving up in the face of the opposition, or an afternoon listening to Her Imperial Maj. chuntering on for hours, 'Mai husband and Ai,'' he imitated scathingly, 'gimme the really bad news.'

'There was unrest in a couple of high immigration areas earlier; it's turned very nasty now. Vigilantes are touring neighbourhoods of Bradford and literally lynching anyone they find on the streets who looks remotely Muslim. There are gangs of Muslims out there as well, trying, with violence and threats, to counter this. It's a war going on out there, a bloody civil war.

Mosques have been burnt down as well as churches in retaliation. We have the Fourth Crusade going on in our back yard, Brown has declared a national state of emergency and troops are being deployed to the hotspots. We both know it's not going to put the cork back in the bottle, though. Richardson is at the end of his tether.'

'Hell,' Hanks expounded as he exhaled and jumped up, 'what a mess. What's our prissy Home Secretary doing, apart from covering her arse, that is? Any news on the Dover end of things? Not that I expect him to go there now. He must surely have twigged that we are onto his mobile phones trick.' he punched his fist into his palm. 'Damn!' he swore causing Welks to flinch.

'You can't blame yourself Alan. It's not your fault.' Welks tried to console him.

'It really is my fault! Analyse it! Since when do we know about Baitullah?'

'No good crying over spilled milk, Alan. What's done is done. Can't put the genie back in the bottle.'

'Alright, let's get back to it then. I don't see what we can achieve, but we can busy ourselves with damage control at least.'

They walked back out into the main room; some nods of acknowledgement greeted them. Nayyar and Hall were like Siamese twins at the computer console and a woman in army uniform sat a discreet distance behind them taking shorthand notes of the main bits of their actions. They're documenting everything, Hanks raged inwardly. Still there wasn't much she could constructively do otherwise, he supposed.

He reached his desk and looked around for the Lieutenant General. Missing him, he saw that Philpott seemed to have aged a decade during the course of a day.

'You alright sir?' he asked Hanks with some concern. 'Don't want any more casualties, do we?'

'Not if one of them is me,' Hanks agreed, 'how are the riots?'

'Horrendous if you want the truth. The Media are fuelling it by keeping a damn tally. It's like a gruesome football match: Christians 14 - Muslims 19, Mosques 7 - Churches 5. Every time the score changes more go out onto the streets to even things out. It's complete bedlam in about six or seven major cities now. Latest we heard was that half of Leicester was a war zone, we have reports that there are small arms and even explosives being used in the fighting. There are army units entering Leicester city centre now with orders to enforce a curfew, but the truth is that we even have problems in the units going in, whites refusing to go in with Coloureds and Asians. Asians are refusing to go against their own people. In a word, chaos! The Lieutenant General has gone off to a senior officers' conference in Rugby and has authority from the Cabinet to ask the UN for help if he thinks we need it.'

'Jesus wept! Bad as that? I never dreamed it could happen, not here, not in good old Britain.' Hanks said outraged.

'Nor did any of our 'Think Tank' worst case scenarios.' Philpott admitted ruefully. 'Not in our worst nightmares did we consider a situation like this.'

'Well, who's doing something about it?' asked Hanks. 'Who's stopping the media keeping score and egging the great unwashed on? What the hell is happening in Downing Street? Are they all blind and paralysed?'

'Not our job, not our problem,' Philpott countered.

'You're not serious are you? If we're in the midst of a civil war, it is our problem. It's everyone's problem.' Welks countered. 'If it was your house they were burning down, whose problem would that be?'

'We're here to bring the perps to justice, whatever that happens to be,' Hanks stated baldly. 'If our 'Bleeding Heart' Home Secretary had her way they'd all be back on the streets next day with a pocket full of cash and new clothes to help them get over the trauma of being arrested. Just so that her government can slap itself on the back and say how much they've reduced the prison population,' he hissed. 'The country can let all the others cock up, but the police can't be seen to fail. If I didn't know I was retiring on Friday, I'd get depressed. It's all a load of bollocks!' he ended emphatically.

'You surrendering?' he asked astounded. 'I don't believe it. They won't let you retire, not until this is sorted, you know that.'

Philpott said nothing as he followed them over to Nayyar and Hall. Nayyar saw them coming and turned to stand up, but Hanks waved him down. 'Long hard day,' he commiserated, 'stay where you are. Anything new?'

'No, Mr Hanks, the telephone is as dead as a dodo. Nothing since he went off the air in Hemel earlier. Chris here has been talking to Mr Voss at the Health Ministry; the flu thing is spreading faster now. They have three people just entering statistics now. He says he'll see us later in the mess. They are releasing the antidote tomorrow. The news of the vaccine availability is going on TV tonight.'

'At least the Queen has stopped blathering on the telly,' Hall countered, 'some small mercy. The talk about dissolving parliament and putting an all-party coalition in to deal with the crisis has taken the lead now. Would you believe there are laws stopping a National Unity Government except in a case of war?'

Hanks nodded, in what he considered to be his most profound manner, 'Sounds about right.' he grunted. 'So where's the problem, eh?'

Hall looked at him almost compassionately. 'The debate is whether such a government can be formed since the Declaration of War can only be made against a country not an individual or a diffuse group. You see?'

'I see more than you give me credit for.' Hanks smiled at him knowingly.

'They'll be more worried about who carries the can than sorting the problem.' Philpott said bitterly in a short, uncharacteristic outburst. Hanks raised an eyebrow.

'Yes? Tell more.'

'I sat in with the COBRA team and they want the coalition, so that if it goes pear-shaped, they can say it was the others who cocked it up. It's all about saving their own skins. Totally sick!'

'Nothing's changed on that front then.' Hanks thanked the pair and moved on. The Home Office team was huddled together, incredibly busy coordinating forces to combat or at least contain the violence in different parts of the country. The onset of darkness had emboldened a lot of people to come out onto the streets. A map on the wall showed the hot spots. West London, Cardiff, Luton and Bradford were the biggest red spots followed by Leeds, Leicester and Bristol which were marked as amber, as were Brixton and Manchester, Maidstone and Slough. Watford and Dagenham were in yellow. The head of the group came over to them.

'A mess, isn't it?' he pointed to the map. 'We have nearly 190 dead as of half an hour ago and the night hasn't begun yet.'

'I thought Leicester was the worst hit?' Hanks queried.

'That was the first flare up with any venom. The real hate fights are going on in the West London Boroughs, in Southall and Hounslow. Whole streets are burning and the Sikhs and the Hindus are out with the British vigilantes tearing into Muslim dominated areas and destroying everything that they can. It's like I imagine the pogroms in Nazi Germany to have been like. There's no planning behind it, yet. It's purely spontaneous.' He added, 'If they get organised there's going to be real trouble. There are reports; however, that some factions are using the social media 'Facebook and Co.' to get groups together to coordinate things, but it's all very disjointed at the moment. The All British Nationalist Party is fuelling it up on their website as well,' he went on, 'and it's got a half a million likes on the media.' He pointed to the green arrows at the bottom of the map, 'Those are army units which are on the move to the red bits. We anticipate them being in position sometime in the next few hours. We're even sending light tanks into West London, for what good it will do.'

Hanks was mesmerised by the big TV screen on the wall. Sights he'd only seen in news clips of race riots in America were being broadcast live from Bradford. Shop-fronts were smashed in, cars ablaze, a burning mosque and gangs of mostly white youths running amok through the town torching anything that would burn. There were two limp bodies hanging from a makeshift gantry next to the burning mosque, both had crudely written signs around their broken necks. The camera panned round to take in the signs, the commentator describing the smell of the burning building and the fact that the fire brigades were completely overstretched, but not without mentioning that the report contained flash photography.

Hanks shrugged his shoulders helplessly. 'Not much we can do here, let's focus on getting a sniff of 'Brown Suit'. As you had the foresight to mention, we need a plan B. Let's go over to the mess and put our thinking caps on. Ashok, Mr Hall, would you care to join us? I think the sun is over the yardarm. The telecoms blokes can let us know if there's any movement on that front. You lot go ahead, I'll catch you up. Major Philpott, care to join us?'

There were minor complaints about work to do and people to contact, but all in all, they knew that there was little they could achieve before Baitullah showed himself and then they would have to be ready. Hanks picked up the phone as they all left and rang Paddington Green. He asked to be put through to Moresby.

'Hello, Gillian,' he said as she answered. 'What's our evil little turd doing? Done anything nasty to him yet? Given him a bacon sandwich or nice pork sausage roll?' he quipped.

'No, just a bit of friendly water boarding, thumbscrews and electro-shocks.' she joked back.

'Great! Nothing like tried and trusted police methods. So what have you got from him?' Hanks asked feeling more tired that he had in weeks.

'Nothing at all,' Moresby continued, 'he's not said a word since we bagged him. He wrote down that he wanted a lawyer, that's all.'

'Charge him under the act, that'll give us 28 days to squeeze him,' Hanks grunted, 'I'll come down tomorrow, if you've no objections. I'd personally like to meet this creature, alone, no cameras, no tapes and above all, no witnesses. Do you get my gist?' His anger came over loud and clear.

'Sure, Alan, but we, or better said you can't work like that. Good grief, it's gotten you into enough hassle in the past, even with minor villains.' She pleaded with him. 'This one here is premier league; the world's media are camped out front here. You rough him up; it'll be the end of you and your pension. We've got the psycho guys from MI5 coming down; they're very good, let them handle it.' Moresby was practically begging him to stay away.

Hanks thought hard about it for a few seconds and decided that Moresby was probably right. 'I was joking,' he said half-heartedly, 'but if he doesn't cooperate by Thursday, I want in on the interrogation. Can we do it like that?'

'Still not sure it's a good idea Alan. Let's wait and see,' she tried to placate him.

Hanks put the phone down, feeling totally drained. The clock showed just after 5 pm as he walked to the collator and told him where he could be found. He got into the lift alone and went up to ground level, hardly noticing the newly placed armed soldiers standing in the entrance as he left. Whitehall was wet, grey, and above all cold. He pulled his jacket collar up and dodged through the traffic and the drizzle.

50

Something wasn't right. Masoud was sweating profusely, his hands clammy. Not sure if it was nerves or adrenalin from the euphoria of the morning's success. He'd seen the early editions of the news and was elated to see the devastation they had caused, the casualty figures were in the upper thousands and still climbing. Allah would be pleased with him.

His phone started to vibrate, a text message. Taking his eyes off the road to look at it, he nearly side-swiped a car in the next lane whilst doing so. It was a long message, and unable to read it and drive at the same time, Masoud decided to stop somewhere. The radio was reporting the news about 'Buyer'. He nearly crashed the car again as the announcer said the police were searching for a Hassan Washiri and Masoud Baitullah in connection with the atrocity.

Masoud had to get off the motorway to read his message. The next exit was signed 'A4140 Hemel Hempstead ½ mile'. Trembling now and desperately needing the toilet, he took the turning too fast, the tyres of the unfamiliar car screeched alarmingly as it left the road completely in the curve, slashing and destroying half a dozen of the white reflective way markers. He managed to keep the car upright through the scarily tight curve and get it back onto the road. Then as the road straightened out, the discovery that he had reached the Buncefield Terminal shook him further, the place was swarming with police. He tried not to look in that direction, but his panic level increased as he slowed down enough to take the roundabout, sedately.

The Breakspear Hotel loomed up on his left, he instantly opted to hole up there and consider his options; he had to read the text and make some decisions. Masoud calmed down a bit at the thought as he manoeuvred his way into the car park.

He parked as far back as he could, even though he knew this car couldn't be on anybody's watch list. It had been bought and registered in Luton to a man down on his luck, who had been prepared to lend his name and his licence for the insurance and other formalities in exchange for a wad of cash. Since then it had been garaged. Masoud's emergency suitcase was on the back seat; it held extra money, new passports and credit cards. With his picture all over the media now, he needed to change his appearance fast.

Angling the rear view mirror round so he could see himself he started on his disguise. He leaned back and pulled his case from the back seat and placed it next to him, taking out the envelope with the passports in it. A French passport with a photo of a man with glasses and greased back hair was about the easiest to achieve in the car. He grabbed his toiletry bag and smeared some hair cream into his hair, combing it vigorously back. He also had a pair of spectacles with plain glass in the case along with a credit card in his new name Mansour Afridi from Calais. He put a few visiting cards into his wallet identifying him as a salesman from a company in Calais selling kitchen equipment, which completed this quick identity change.

Masoud walked into the hotel, it was eerily quiet, its clientele of reps long gone; on their way to their next customers. Two receptionists were watching the TV coverage on a screen beside them as Masoud walked passed straight into the Gents. He finished his ablutions, touched up his hair, then came out into the reception area again, where the cleaning crew were in full swing vacuuming the carpets, dusting and emptying the bins.

Masoud stopped one of them, 'Excuse me; do you have an internet terminal here?' the man glanced up at him and pointed in the direction of the restaurant door.

'You 'ave to pay mate, it's coins or credit card, y'know.' Masoud thanked him and went over to the bank of pay internet machines next to the restaurant entrance. He put five pounds in the coin slot and considered using an online booking service to reserve a room in the hotel, as he felt he would need internet access, which was not available in any of their safe houses. As he was sitting there, he noticed a constant flow of TV crews and the occasional policeman checking in at reception. The safe house would be better he concluded, staying here was too risky. He turned to check his mails. Nothing from Pakistan, but the most important mail, a response to his earlier request for assistance, had arrived as he was scanning his inbox; it was a coded message from his London contact, '*Organisation is in process, c u @ prime-point Wednesday 2:00 pm.*'

Tomorrow, good he thought, he felt his tension abating. He then turned to check the phone message from Hassan, who had sent him a number in London to contact, that was the message he'd received in the car on the way down, it wasn't part of any plan. Masoud checked how long he had; Hassan was expecting his call in just over an hour. The second one was older, a plan about escape via Dover, he assumed that the contact number was to do with the Dover plan. The more options he had, the better it would be. Now he was ahead of the game, but for how long, he wondered. He needed to hide until his 'friend' got his escape organised. The organisation had a safe house in Hemel Hempstead, 'kasan e noor', the steps to freedom, how apt he thought, I'll go there.

It was nearly two o'clock, a mere six hours after the blast. Up to now he'd been elated, now he was just exhausted and hungry. The hotel restaurant, offered somewhere to while away the waiting time and eat. The meal, mediocre as it was, occupied him until he could phone the number Hassan had sent to find out about the plan from him. The staff left him to himself, more interested in watching the events on the big flat screen over the bar than serving, which suited him fine. He tried not to show indifference to the events being screened on the TV and to hide his joy as the body count rose.

The odd occasion that the waiter did bother him, Masoud obliged with small talk about how terrible it was and how sorry he was that so many had perished. The first reports of a civil backlash were coming in on TV, small incidents in Luton were the first mentioned.

Their success this morning was now beginning to give him his usual excitement. The clock ticked round to two thirty. Normally he'd have phoned Claire for Hollie or one of the girls at this time. He hardened under the table and fantasised about Claire. Distracted from his lust by the need to phone the number Hassan had sent. Masoud checked the SIM card in his phone was the right one for the day, so Hassan would recognise it and waited for the exact time before dialling. The call failed, the unobtainable tone; panicking, he redialled immediately, with the same result, his thoughts far from erotic now, something wasn't right. In desperation, he dialled Hassan's mobile, using the next number in the sequence, the number was unobtainable. Now he was sure that something had gone wrong and decided he had to rely on his own skills to get away. He left the money for the meal on the table and walked through the bar, noticing the emphasis of the TV news had changed.

The new announcements, that riots were starting up in parts of London and the Home Counties, stopped him in his tracks to watch. The commentator was careful to avoid the term race riots. None the less it was plain that there were vigilante gangs roaming the streets hunting for suspects, or just victims.

The BBC News interrupted the program to show an announcement live from 10 Downing Street, a ragged looking Prime Minister giving an address to the nation. He was about to leave when the PM announced that the police expected to make imminent arrests.

Masoud made an instant decision; stepping out into the empty smoking area, he pulled out his mobile, took out the battery and the SIM card, stamped on the phone in an effort to destroy it, but achieving little more than twisting it out of shape. He ditched the remains plus all his remaining cards in the waste bin.

In his car again, the presence of police vehicles and satellite trucks from TV stations unnerved him more, his decision not to check in to the hotel reaffirmed, it would have been suicidal. Solitude was required to analyse events and evaluate. Drained now, after his earlier euphoria and fretting about what to do next, the thoughts about the woman coming to the forefront of his consciousness as he turned on the ignition and drove off towards the town centre.

The house ‘kasan e noor’ was a known fall-back point, one of the many safe havens the organisation had dotted around the country. He drove to Cotterells and parked the car in the garden of the small terraced house. The lights were burning as he got out of the car taking his suitcase from the back seat. He unlocked front door with his key code, happy that the time switches made the house look occupied. He called out cautiously, just in case, shutting the door behind him. There was no answer; he checked the small ground floor, nobody there. The narrow stairs reminded him of Claire and Hollie as he climbed them. The house was empty, nervous exhaustion took its toll of him, he lay on the bed and slept, dreaming. He started to fantasise about her again, deeply erotic visions coupled with his image of the explosion in the City, explosion, orgasm, explosion, orgasm, the sequence repeating itself as he lay there finally ejaculating at the thought of her. He checked the time 5:00 am still dark outside, sweaty and still exhausted; he got up and went off in search of a telephone box to phone her.

He was dejected as he left the telephone box; it was hard to describe his emotion. It wasn’t panic, it wasn’t fear. Why had he done it? He couldn’t answer that, he didn’t want to face the truth. She hadn’t answered him, she just hung up. What had he expected? She knew who he was and she’d be petrified of him. There were few people in the market at this time in the morning, the empty stands offering a skeletal silhouette of dark sparks against the pre-dawn sky. He’d chosen to use the bus stations’ phones, as they were far enough away from the house and would be difficult to keep under observation without the watchers being obvious. He’d gone back into the house, his mind in turmoil with images of the Claire woman filling his thoughts.

Switching on the TV in an attempt to get her out of his mind, he flicked through the channels to be confronted with pictures of Hassan being bundled out of a police van at a police station somewhere in London. He couldn’t help wondering if he would crack under, what would doubtless be, intense questioning. The rest of the news about the formation of a government of national solidarity consisting of a coalition was of little interest to him, even less than the ‘expert’ opinions about terrorism and Islamic extremism.

He decided that a change of clothes and a bath wouldn't go amiss before he set off on his trip to meet his contact in London later. He went off in search of fresh clothes and toiletries and possibly scissors to optimise his disguise.

The prime point mentioned in the mail was Harrods café; Masoud had deliberated how to travel, considering public transport to be too risky, he'd decided on his car.

Harrods loomed in front of him as he manoeuvred his way into the car park in Lancelot Place. He was a little early for the 2:00 pm meeting, but that was fine by him. He tried to behave as normally as possible and yet attempted to see if he was under observation as he walked the short distance from the car park to the shop. He nervously entered the building through the Hans Road entrance, conscious of the CCTV coverage he was walking into and holding his head down. He dodged through the pharmacy and headed for the lifts. The attack yesterday had destroyed trade; Harrods was almost empty, the staff standing in groups waiting for the occasional customer to pass. The Attaché was not waiting in the café when he arrived. Masoud took a corner table with a good view of the sales floor and waited, his mind still racing, considering everything that had happened. He was suddenly startled by a hand on his shoulder.

A dark-skinned man loomed over him, 'Masoud?' he looked up at him and nodded his acknowledgement.

There were no pleasantries, just a matching nod from the man as he sat next to him. Masoud sat expectantly waiting for the dour faced man to speak.

'I come at great risk to see you,' the man said.

'Sure, me too, what do you have for me?' Masoud was anxious now.

'We have organised an escape route for you. We have sent for a diplomatic passport, we are waiting for a courier to bring it. Our interior minister is advised, it will be issued quickly.'

'How quick?'

'We can get you out by next week, but not before Wednesday.'

'You can't want me to wait a week!' Masoud said loudly.

'My friend,' a brief flicker of a smile crossed the man's face, as if dealing with a child, 'you've seen the press and TV. You are the star at the moment. In a week, your face will be replaced by the next big thing, a shipwreck, a plane crash or a sporting event. We have to wait for things to cool down and the public to be distracted by something else.'

'A week, what will I do?' Masoud asked.

The embassy man shrugged, 'You will wait. You want us to help you out, you do it our way. I will be here the same time next week with the documents, in the meantime stay low.' With that, he stood up and left Masoud open mouthed.

51

Voss was numbed by the effort of trying to make patterns from lists of new flu outbreaks, especially as the crew in Chester were now totally overwhelmed by the sheer mass of testing. He had to get more resources into play. If they needed to react quickly to the changing situation then the information feed had to be drastically improved. It was taking too long to collate each patient with the type of flu virus they had. Mary, Nick and Claire were being run ragged in the labs at Brinkley's. It was still taking about four hours to determine the type and email the results. He'd talked to Chester earlier and heard the sample backlog was now over ten thousand and the disease was spreading faster now. The weather conditions were perfect, cool, moist and with little wind.

Aerosol weather he thought, as he boarded the taxi for the ride back to Horse Guards. The taxi driver, a West Indian, was very verbose about the terror attack, angry about the way people were allowed to destroy the country. Voss tried to put his own reaction into some kind of perspective. He'd been pushing it to the back of his mind all day, the terrible injustice of killing all those people for what? He couldn't come to terms with it. No selectivity, no differentiation, just madness, a slaughter of thousands of people, whatever their race or religion, just boom, and gone. Overall, he felt immeasurably sad. Yes, he thought, that was his overriding feeling, sadness.

The taxi had stopped in the middle of Whitehall. It took Voss a while to register it. Only when the driver turned and spoke to him did he look out to see that the road was blocked by two armoured vehicles and soldiers checking traffic.

'Think this is the end of the ride sir,' the taxi driver said, as he wound the window down to talk to the young soldier standing next to the cab.

'Where to?'

'MoD', the taxi driver said, 'he's got business there.' indicating Voss in the back with his thumb.

'New rules I'm afraid, no cars, you'll have to walk sir.'

Voss wasn't going to argue. He opened the door, paid the driver and walked through the roadblock, but not without being searched and having his laptop examined. Even the Lieutenant General's MoD pass didn't spare him that.

Walking through the drizzle, he noted a lot of cars parked in Downing Street. Unusual, he thought, and wondered what was going on there. What would happen to the government after today? Britain had never had anything like this before.

He reached the doors of the MoD and was immediately aware of the increased security, with armed soldiers inside and out. His pass was scrutinised very carefully as he asked about Hanks and Lieutenant General Richardson, to be told they'd both left for the day. Voss had an idea where to find Hanks and his team. He crossed the road to Horse Guards; the guards there had been replaced by khaki-clad soldiers instead of the men in ceremonial uniforms. Again, he was thoroughly checked over before being allowed in. The inseparables were in the mess as he'd expected, both looking shattered. He sat down next to them, dumping his damp raincoat over a chair behind him.

'What's the progress?' he asked, breaking the silence between the two men.

'Got one, the other one got away. Well, if you count the bomber we got two.' Welks answered dejectedly. 'The other bastard must have somehow realised that we were on to him and just disappeared.'

'How's the flu front?' Hanks asked resignedly, relieved to have a change of topic at last. He was totally on edge with his seemingly insolvable problem of Baitullah.

'We have an overwhelming number of new cases and an interesting spread pattern.' he flipped his laptop open. 'The problem is we can't keep up with the testing. My people in Chester are inundated with thousands of samples from all round the country now. We actually could do with some technical help on that front.' His computer had booted up as he spoke.

Hall and Nayyar arrived and sat with them at the table, both showered and freshened up. Hanks thought about it, sniffed himself as unobtrusively as he could and almost decided against the idea. Welks watching him, smiled.

'I know it's not Christmas yet, but it would do you good. Not just to clear the air. Maybe the hot water will get the brain going again. I'm going to have one.' he stood up. 'See you guys in a bit.'

'Maybe he's right. I need to switch off for a bit as well. I'll have a quick freshen up and see you back here in a bit. Mr Voss, no disrespect, but I hope your data can wait. I haven't slept much in two days. I'll see you in about an hour, maybe we can eat together and discuss.'

'Of course,' Voss agreed, rather surprised by the sudden disappearance of the two detectives.

It was nearly 10:00 pm when Hanks made it back to the mess, Nayyar, Hall and Voss cramped around the laptop, its power cable strung dangerously across the aisle to the wall socket.

The atmosphere in the mess was tense, the officers naturally unsure of what the next day or days would bring. Iraq, Afghanistan, Northern Ireland, they'd done all that and it had been bad enough, but this was their own back yard, an invisible enemy on home ground. There was muted conversation all around. The TV was on, with the sound turned off, showing riots in Leicester, Birmingham and Manchester, with pictures of burning barricades, houses and angry mobs throwing anything they could get their hands on.

Pictures came up of frightened women and children being bundled away by police and emergency services to any place of safety. They were ugly, terrifying scenes. The news ticker was still giving tallies of victims killed in the blast that morning. As Hanks sat down with the group, he noted the score at which mosques versus churches was running at. It was 9:6 for churches at the moment. He asked for Welks, but he was nowhere to be seen.

'What have I missed?' Hanks asked, as the steward took his order for a beer.

'We're trying to fathom how the Chester virus is spreading. It's not a contagion thing. You don't get it from touching. It's passed solely through aerosol particles. Someone sneezes near you and whoops you've got the 'kindergarten virus,' Hall replied.

'Uh huh. So do we have any patterns?' Hanks probed.

'Many, not that any of them are making much sense at the moment, though,' Voss answered. 'We have the outbreaks that are all in towns next to a motorway, which makes sense, but doesn't help much.'

'The problem is made more complicated by the fact that we have the seasonal flu epidemic starting here as well and the spread pattern is also along the motorways,' Voss added, 'we have a major challenge coping with the number of samples flooding back to Brinkley's, we can't cope anymore.'

'How many registered cases do we have now?' Hanks asked.

'148,300 and rising,' Voss said, turning the laptop for Hanks to see. 'Here, take a peek at the spread sheet for yourself.'

'What's the system here?'

'Oh, it's organised quite simply. The front end of the table is the type of infection and there we have K and S for Kindergarten and Seasonal flu, then we go to name, sex and then town. After that, the main sort keys are virus type, severity and location, that's done by post code for want of a better handle. If you click there, you can also get a graphic of the distribution superimposed on a map of the British Isles,' he pointed to the tool, 'You'll see the counter of total reports keeps changing; that's because the database is online and each new case is uploaded immediately.'

Hanks nodded, as he scrolled through the entries, not sure how to start. He was about to give up, when on impulse he skipped across to the names. Draper, Hafeez, Fellows, Holmes, Milner, Skelton, Zia, Patterson, just a few in the list that confronted him. Checking the different types, he saw they were all S types. A feeling in his bones rather than a concrete deliberation caused him to go back and click 'sort by virus K' and then he flicked over to the names. Aboud, El Saugani, Al Ibrahim, Bin Afranu, Saleh, Shah, Zinaba..., he couldn't believe it. He flicked over to the S list again, running the cursor down the names, the list was mixed.

'What is this?' he exploded leaning back from the display. 'What on earth have we been sitting on?'

'Why?' Voss asked, concerned that something was wrong.

'Have you analysed names?' he asked, with bated breath, not sure if he could believe his find.

'How do you mean, names?' Voss asked.

'Here, all the K type severe infections seem to be solely foreign names. That's just on first glance, mind you, but the K types all seem to be foreigners, with very few exceptions.'

'You what?' Hall stammered, 'You have to be joking. Let me see.'

Hanks pushed the laptop over towards him. 'Bit of a quirk if that turns out to be true, a flu that only foreigners get,' Hanks thought out aloud, 'no...,' he paused, getting his words together, 'actually, the S list is mixed. The seasonal flu hits both groups equally hard, but the K virus gives only a fleeting cold to the majority of people. The reason why they don't appear on this list that they wouldn't go to the doctor for a cold that lasts just a couple of hours, would they?'

'That, gentlemen, is the crux of the matter; we seem to have a racially specific bug here.' There was initial silence, as Voss digested the magnitude of Hanks's discovery, 'It's not a quirk, Mr Hanks,' Voss continued after a while, his excitement mounting, 'but a magnificent breakthrough, if it's true.' Voss was beside himself with excitement. 'I had a discussion with Claire the other day about selective infection and the reasons for it. We had a preliminary inkling about this, yet how the hell could we have missed that? Something so blatant, it appears to be a genetic thing. Claire spotted the indications in the electron microscope pictures. The viral docking sites for the K virus were where cholesterol normally gets to grips with the body's cells. We were going to do some detailed work on it, thinking it could be the clue to a universal flu vaccine. That was our initial interest.'

'Sorry to seem thick, but what's that got to do with foreigners or race?' Philpott asked.

'Not all foreigners, Major, just some. There have been parallels in the past. Take the 1918 Spanish Flu pandemic as an example. There were complete racial groupings which were unaffected; Eskimos and American Indians were for all intents and purposes immune. It would appear that on this occasion, we have an influenza strain that Caucasians are practically spared from. The genetic trait towards cholesterol sensitivity is definitely far more predominant in the Mongol, or Arab stems of our great family tree. We'll have to do a heap more testing, but it certainly looks that way at the moment.'

'Wait!' Hanks had to raise his voice to get heard in the excited babble that had broken out around the table. 'Can we put the spread of the K type down solely to people who have been in contact with people from Chester, who either had the cold or the flu from there?'

'Sure, I'd say it looks like it.' Voss answered.

'How does it spread?' Philpott asked.

'Aerosol, it's an airborne disease. It needs moisture and warmth. It gets taken up by the lungs. However, it dies quickly if it dries out or the ambient temperature drops too low.'

'Before we do anything, I want Nayyar and any other non Caucasians in our team to be given the vaccine, because if our theory is right, they are high risk candidates, and I can't afford to have any of them out of action at this stage in the proceedings, especially Nayyar. By the way, how long does it take, the incubation for the infection to take hold?' Hanks asked.

'This is a fast one, but it varies from individual from individual. Some cases have been quicker; the first symptoms appeared within 24 hours.' Voss said.

Welks walked into the mess as the people stood, the meeting breaking up for the night.

'What's up Alan?'

Hanks took a while to react. 'Just an idea I'm mulling over,' he said, a heavy frown on his brow, turning into a curious mixture of a grimace and a happy grin, which Welks couldn't fathom.

'I need to talk to Voss, confidentially.'

'Okay,' Welks said stepping back as Hanks pushed his chair

back to stand, 'I'm none the wiser, though. By the way sorry I was late, I wasn't feeling too bright.'

'You may be getting what I had, better get the medics to take a swab, but if you don't have foreign ancestry, you won't die of it.'

Welks's puzzled look evoked a sympathetic pat on the shoulder from Hanks with a promise that all would be explained. 'Who do I need to see about sample testing assistance then? Any ideas?'

Philpott turned back to them, 'Ideas about what?' he asked.

'I thought you'd left already.'

'I came back to get my case.' Philpott explained.

'We need virus testing help. Voss's team is going under with the work load.' Welks replied, Voss, nodded agreement.

Philpott opened his attaché case and pulled out a file. On the outside, it carried five letters in bold type, COBRA. He leafed through the contents, 'How about the Port of London Authority chap, Dr Rogers? He offered his help on the first meeting.'

'Yes, I know him,' Voss said, 'they have superb labs, two big electron microscopes, top equipment. Yes, they'd be a great help. If I can get my team in there with them, we'd have everything we need on our doorstep. We'd have to bring a heap of stuff with us, though, and there's the quarantine to get through,' he added as an afterthought.

'It shouldn't be a problem, apart from the quarantine aspect. Shall I start getting it organised?' Philpott was in the starting blocks, Hanks nodded as he jumped up and left, keen to do something constructive.

'I'll phone Nick Kitson to organise getting the team from Chester ready to move.' Voss was also galvanised now.

'Well then,' Hanks said a little more upbeat now there was something actually being done.

As the night passed, the TV bulletins were running in the background, news of the riots, or more accurately, the attacks on immigrant communities was getting more serious as time progressed. Lieutenant General Richardson had phoned around one o'clock. He had called up the Territorial Army, since the last available reserves of the mainstay army had just left their barracks in Coventry. Although earmarked for UN duties in

Kosovo, the 101 Force Support Battalion had been put in to quell massive unrest in Luton. The area had been declared a disaster zone and a dusk to dawn curfew was supposed to be in place, only no-one was adhering to it. Fire-fighting teams were unable to function. Many buildings and vehicles were in flames, burning uncontrolledly in the Moore Road area around the Cultural Centre. Infrared shots had shown lifeless bodies lying in the streets, the ticker tape at the bottom of the screen showing the grim balance of deaths.

'Someone should get that stopped. Now!' Hanks shouted, as he turned the set off and tried to get the sickening images out of his mind. Nayyar looked at him uncomprehendingly. 'Get the tally off the screen; it's like pouring petrol onto a fire to put it out.' Hanks clarified.

'We would need a D notice for that.' Welks added.

'Sod the D notice just get in touch with the TV stations and get them to take it off. Tell them to act responsibly, people are worked up enough. Nayyar, have you had your antidote jab yet?' Hanks slumped back in his chair. 'We need to get the media to stop putting the score up on the telly and internet. Mr Hall can you sort that? Suggest that they put on the subject of the vaccination being available and advise everyone to stay calm and get inoculated.' Hall set to the task. Hanks and Welks spent time picking over the case, arguing about ways of trapping Baitullah, before Welks fell asleep and Hanks had to wake him to finally go to bed to a restless sleep of his own.

The noise of departing troops woke Hanks around half past five. The Horse Guards were being thrown into the breach. Hanks showered quickly and made his way to the mess. The smell of crisping bacon wafted tantalisingly in the air. Picking up the newspaper, he sat in the window, seeing the Lorries depart into the dark morning. As the last one left he turned to the headlines, not really interested in the reports, he was somehow empty. There were messages of sympathy and support from leaders all around the world. All grateful, no doubt that it hadn't happened to them. Also reports from Holland about attacks on Malaccan communities and in Germany some Turkish quarters were under siege from fanatical skinheads and right wingers; thankfully, as yet, there were no dead on those fronts. Hanks patted his pocket for his phone wanting to reach the Lieutenant General, but realised he'd left it in his room. Annoyed, he got up and went back for it, passing the steward just coming on duty.

'Six o'clock start, sir.' he said, 'be with you in a minute,' as he disappeared into the kitchen area.

As Hanks arrived in his room, his mobile started ringing and he just managed to catch it before the vibrations sent it off the edge of the bedside table. The display showed Claire Grigson. What on earth could she want from him at this time of day? He felt more than curious; normally he only got catastrophe calls this early.

'Hanks,' he announced, 'this is a nice surprise at this hour. What's up?'

'God I'm glad you finally picked up! I'm frightened, Alan.' she managed to get out. Before Hanks could respond, she exclaimed, 'he just rang. The bastard phoned me again.' Hanks was galvanised, feeling the goose bumps rise on his arms.

'When?'

'Just now, round 5:30 this morning. Why would he call me at this time? I'm scared. It's him who did this horrible attack!'

'Yes Claire, I'm afraid so. Did you answer?' he said, as he wondered to himself, if this was a catastrophe call after all.

'I picked up, but when I heard his voice I cut him off. I never said anything.' she paused, 'I didn't know what to do. Did I do right?'

Hanks didn't think so, but left it unsaid and instead soothed her, 'You don't have to worry; he's miles away from you.' he sensed her doubt, 'Last we knew he was in Hertfordshire, well away from you. You want us to send someone for protection?'

'No, no, I just thought you ought to know,' she sounded nervous, but relieved, 'I feel safer for telling you already. Funny isn't it.'

'That's good; we want to keep you safe. You haven't got the number that he phoned from by any chance, have you? Can you check for me?' he walked to the bedside table and put his notebook down while Claire fumbled with her phone.

'Yes, its 0441 539892.' she read it off her display.

Hanks scribbled it down next to the entry from the night before, one word 'impotence', a connection or just a coincidence? He put the thought aside to carry on the conversation. 'Listen, I have a feeling he may call you again. This time you have to talk to him, and you have to keep him talking, just keep him on the line. Can you do that if he calls again?'

'Sure,' she seemed more confident now.

'Tell him you want money. Tell him you'll go to the police, the media, anyone if he doesn't pay up. Say you want two hundred thousand.'

'Wow!' she took an audible gulp of air, 'that much?'

'He is calling you for a reason, Claire. He will want to meet up with you, and the money would make him believe that you also want to meet him.'

She was silent for a moment, and then said with a pleading voice, 'You're going to get him, aren't you?'

'Yes, Claire, we'll get him.' he said as encouragingly as he could, 'We are going to have to monitor your mobile phone calls from now on. At the moment you are our only connection to this animal. I'll still have to get a court order but if you can sign a chit to say you agree, it'll save a hell of a lot of time.'

'Of course, I'll help in any way I can. The only calls I get are from Mary's girls and Mary, apart from 'Him' that is.'

'If it's any consolation, I think he definitely fancies you,' Hanks added sarcastically.

'Leave off! He makes me wanna puke.'

'Was meant as a joke, sorry. Are we going to see you in London, by the way? Has Mr Kitson spoken to you and your sister?'

'No, why? What's happening?' he could sense a little panic in voice now.

'Nothing to get upset about, we're moving the testing from Chester to the Port of London Authority labs in Bermondsey. Mr Voss thinks the facilities there are better and we can liaise more quickly with a lab on the doorstep.' Hanks paused; maybe he shouldn't be telling her this. 'I'll get DC Whittaker to come to see you at Brinkley's. The telephone forms are a formality, but we have rules,' he grimaced as he said it, 'I'll send him as soon as I can reach him.'

'Okay,' she said, 'I just hope you get him.'

'We'll get him!' Hanks emphasised the '*we'*. His next call was to Nayyar. Who responded with a groggy,

'Yeah!'

'Hanks here,' he shouted into the phone. 'Wake up! Are our telecom guys active this early?'

'How early is this?' Nayyar groaned.

'Not quite six. Good morning.'

'Six! Shit!' he cursed. 'D'you know when we finished last night?'

'No. So what's the answer?'

'To what?'

'Don't piss me around, Ashok. I need to know if the telecoms guys are active. Now!'

'Sorry,' Nayyar pulled himself together. 'What do you need?'

'I've got a number and I need to know where the phone is. It's a landline from the number. Who do I have to talk to?'

'Let me have the number. I'll sort it.'

Hanks recited the number and asked him to be quick, explaining that it was a 'Brown Suit' call. That woke Nayyar up completely.

'See you at breakfast in a few minutes. I should have something by then.

'Oh, and I need this number tapped.' Hanks recited Claire's number and told him the paperwork wasn't ready yet, but on the way; the subscriber has agreed.

'Got that,' and Nayyar said and was gone.

Walking back to the mess Hanks kicked spitefully against Welks's door, calling out, 'Good morning campers. Rise and shine!' and had the satisfaction of an angry grunt from the other side of the door. Back in the mess, the TV was on again. The floodlit pictures of the area around the still cordoned off Bank Station showed nothing more than a few fire engines and a police incident van. Hanks could see no sign of the tanker they'd seen before the explosion.

Philpott was the first of the 'Team' to arrive, spick and span as ever, his face drained and grey. He sat next to Hanks without comment and poured himself a coffee, not even venturing a grunted greeting before the first mouthful.

'Busy night?' Hanks asked.

'You could call it that.' he smiled wryly, 'The logistics for moving the Brinkley equipment and staff down through the quarantine cordon is all organised and Voss is talking to his people now. The move is underway. They'll be up and running some time tomorrow.'

'That's good. At least we'll have the lab on our doorstep from now on.' Hanks poured more orange juice into his glass, then as Welks shambled in; he reached over and poured one for him.

'Thanks,' Welks grunted and sat down, downing the liquid in one. 'my swab test was negative you'll be pleased to know.'

'That was quick!'

'Yeah, they are just testing for the antigens now, much quicker than DNA.'

52

Hanks noted the muted atmosphere as the six of them entered the war room. The teams were at their places and alert, but he was immediately aware that they were looking for guidance and more to the point, were expecting it from him. His mind kept going back to the aside about 'Plan B'. The fact that he didn't have one made it a tough move to motivate the shell-shocked staff. Sure, he had some lines of enquiry unfinished: Masoud's call to Claire for instance, and Shener; then there was the cash trail, as well as that evil man Washiri. He could also include the lecturer from Hatfield and his computer.

I need a crystal ball he thought, a gipsy Rose or some such. Putting these depressing thoughts aside, he called for the overnight team leaders to give their update reports. Telecoms were quiet, with nothing to report from the SIM cards. One exception was a call, which had gone out from a London number, to one of 'Brown Suit's numbers, but the number was inactive. All it said was, 'Message understood. Will advise on Wednesday'.

'Where does it come from?' Hanks asked.

'You'll like this,' the team leader answered. 'The Embassy of the Republic of Yemen.'

'Have we got the place under observation? Hanks asked. 'I know we're stretched, but if 'Brown Suit' goes there...,' he left the rest unsaid.

'Mr Hanks.' Wheeler interrupted. 'Cheltenham has very close tabs on all communications to and from that particular embassy. They won't get an electron in or out without us knowing about it.'

'So, what about the physical side?' Hanks persisted. 'People going in and out. Can we keep tabs on that?'

'I don't think they'd risk having such a high profile person come to their doorstep. If they meet, they'll do it outside, somewhere prearranged,' Wheeler concluded.

'I know MI5 are working round the clock on a lot of these embassies,' Philpott chipped in.

By 10 am, most of the Cabinet and shadow Cabinet members had taken their places in the War Room; a heated discussion was underway. The PM was the only one absent,

'I'm not that stupid,' Jack Straw snapped at Jacqui Smith, 'it was a cop out.'

'The coalition thing?' she stared at him astounded.

'No, the Prime Minister going sick. Just expedient, if it goes pear shaped it was the others. He's out of it, not involved.'

Hanks listened in to the conversation half-heartedly, his mind more on Claire than on the ministerial tattle around him. Who cared about Gordon Brown he thought. They should be talking justice and retribution; anything rather than passing the buck. He got up and moved away, leaving the 'experts' to it. He poured himself a coffee and leaned against the wall slurping it gratefully, the warm liquid doing his system good.

'What's going on?' Welks joined him out of nowhere.

'Sweet F A,' Hanks said disparagingly, 'the PM's sick!'

'Usual then?' Welks also poured himself a cup. 'Anybody said owt?'

'Heh? What, for example?' Hanks grunted in annoyance at his partner.

'Bout you slurping your coffee like that. Surprised they can concentrate.' He chuckled as Hanks started to protest then just glared at him. They stood, leaning on the wall, in silent contemplation as the Home Secretary put the overnight reports in front of the Cabinet members. 'First task is to get this civil unrest problem under control,' she said to general agreement.

'Give us an update. We've all seen the TV coverage, but what is the real situation?' Straw asked.

The Defence Secretary stood up. 'With your permission, Jacqui?' turning to her for the go-ahead, she nodded.

'The situation is dire, worse than we are seeing on TV. We've put a briefing together, showing the hotspots and where we believe we could have problems in the near future. The 'backlash' is against all foreigners. Strange that even Caribbean groups are being targeted. We have a fatalities list which runs around two hundred and fifty at last count, with many, many more injured. We need to put a brake on that, by whatever means. Just putting troops between the parties doesn't hack it. What we have put together is a package of measures to de-escalate the situation.' A few murmurs of agreement greeted this. 'In a nutshell, the vigilantes, if I can call them that, are getting more and more organised. There are cohesive and coordinated attacks taking place, which are being directed via social networks. The social network companies are aware of this and are cooperating fully with us by removing offensive groups, but as fast as these companies take a group offline, another springs up.'

'Nothing new there. The method has been used often, the Tottenham riots, the Brixton riots, Toxteth, Bradford, I could go on.' Straw said, sounding almost bored.

'We propose some radical methods to combat this.' Browne continued. 'Our first thought was to shut the internet down completely. Initially, we could have passed it off as an incident caused by the destruction of a nerve centre due to the rioting. We decided against it for two reasons. One, it's not plausible, we can't take the internet down by destroying one switching centre, and two, we must be seen to be actively doing something. Not relying on accident or fortune to stop the troubles.'

'We're closing down all the social networks as of,' the Home Secretary looked at her watch, 'ten minutes ago.' There were astonished gasps around the table, but no complaints.

'Secondly,' the Secretary for Defence went on, 'we are imposing a dusk to dawn curfew from 6pm tonight. The news is going out through all the media outlets from 11 o'clock this morning and is being plastered on billboards, as well as being broadcast from police loudspeaker vans.'

'Our third measure involves unblocking the ports and airports.' The Defence Secretary continued. 'I know it sounds counter-productive, but we really need the manpower elsewhere. I've talked at depth with the investigation team as well and they favour the idea. DCI Hanks is hopeful that known suspects will try and make a run for it. By so doing they will pass our face recognition scanners.' There was another murmur from around the table.

'We do have a little more ammunition in the locker,' Jacqui Smith added.

'Tell us,' said David Forester as he walked in with Gordon Brown, fresh from Buckingham Palace.

'Sorry,' the Prime Minister added, 'we didn't mean to interrupt, please continue.'

'Good morning, I thought you were ill?' she greeted the Prime Minister and the newly appointed Deputy Prime Minister, 'Welcome.' She carried on, 'We have the options of selective power cuts and complete media censorship, but I don't think we want to go down that route, do we? We haven't been taken over by the Chinese, at least not completely yet.'

'Quite, Home Secretary,' Forrester agreed, Brown nodding consent, 'Good that we have the threat of being overrun by the yellow peril still up on our radar, but that's not today's problem is it? We implement the first three measures, now. Let's get down to damage control and casualties. Just two more questions, Home Secretary.' He paused as the room went quiet.

'The press will be over us like a rash looking for solutions as soon as the reaction to the attack begins to pall. What are we doing on that front?'

'Prime Minister,' the Home Secretary stood, 'we have an effective vaccine being deployed as we speak. The Brinkley's incident, I think we can consider is fully under control now and we have quarantine measures are in place. Our greatest challenge at present is the civil unrest going on out there. Our security services are stretched to the limit. If we don't get it under control it could destabilise the whole country. We'll be back in the dark ages if we don't get assistance. I have spoken to the Secretary for Defence and he has agreed to withdraw our troops from Germany to be deployed here in Britain and also the contingent in Northern Ireland will be reduced to reinforce the homeland. The problem here is anarchy, not terrorism.'

'Why don't we tell everyone the Influenza outbreak is spreading like bushfire, and as such they should all stay indoors?' The Health Secretary said quietly. There was a stunned silence around the room.

'What?' Forrester asked, 'What are you suggesting?'

'Well, how about we spread the word that all the deaths are flu related and people going out onto the streets are endangering themselves and their families by going into severely affected areas, like Leicester for example.'

'Mmmmm!' Forrester mused, 'that might just work. Get the PR people on it right away. What with that and the vaccine programme, we might just get to put the lid back on this.'

53

In the depths of the ministry an agitated Lieutenant General Richardson was loudly ordering the redeployment of troops from Germany back to the UK. He was quite red in the face as he greeted the detectives with a wave of the hand.

They moved over to the group dealing with the phones. Telecoms had had a bit of an 'event' it seemed. There was an email message from the Yemeni embassy to an unknown addressee. Just one simple text in plain English, '*Organisation is in process, c u @ prime-point Wednesday 2:00 pm.*'.

The Health Ministry crowd weren't so upbeat. The flu counts were skyrocketing. Hanks sat there, incommunicative, deliberating.

Philpott advised that the overnight testing at the Port of London labs seemed to be confirming Hanks's hypothesis about the racially specific aspect of the virus. The Health minister seeing logic now in the inconsistency of the infections to death ratios; where the immigration levels were lowest was matched with the lowest fatalities. Hence there were hardly any rural deaths. He'd pushed this information to the spin doctors for their media campaign about the vaccination programme. Maybe if people believed certain sectors of the community were more infectious, others may keep away from them.

'You know, I still feel rough; sore throat.' Welks said.

'I thought you tested negative?'

'I did,' Welks answered defensively, 'maybe a mistake, what with thousands of samples and the lab moving.' He sneezed hard, earning him a 'Bless you!' from somewhere behind him.

'Get tested again then, I can't afford to lose you at this juncture either,' suddenly, as if stung Hanks snapped out of his cocoon, 'Welks, do me a favour. Hold the fort here, will you? I need to talk to Voss.' He said before disappearing into the back office to call Voss on his mobile. He was gone for quite a while.

'You look upbeat.' A snivelling Welks said from behind his handkerchief as Hanks re-joined the group. 'What's cooking?'

'Major Philpott?' He ignored Welks for the moment. 'I'm expecting a delivery shortly from Mr Voss upstairs. Can you see to it that it is accepted and that I'm informed please? I know there is top security here, but don't let anyone open the package. Did you get retested yet?'

'Yes of course, they took the sample off straight away.'

'Good, Colin. What day is it today by the way?'

'Thursday, Alan. Why? Are you losing touch?'

'Not at all, I'm just getting into form; you know I retire tomorrow?'

That stopped everyone in their tracks.

'You are doing what? Retiring? Not in the middle of things!' Philpott admonished.

'No I'll be on overtime from then on,' Hanks chuckled, and then a slow smile came over his face.

'Are you ever serious?' Richardson asked, good-naturedly this time. 'That's been asked before, hasn't it?'

'Never more so, sir. Can someone get me Moresby on the phone? I think it's time we paid Washiri a little visit. How's your cold?' He observed Welks critically, 'What do you think? Reckon we'll get any more out of him than Moresby?'

The collator called over, 'Moresby for you, sir.'

Hanks realised all ears were tuned on him as he took the call. 'Gillian, Hanks here. How is our little friend doing? Choked on his bacon yet?' Hanks laughed cruelly as he listened, nodding a couple of times at what he was hearing. 'Okay, Welks and I will be over later. I promise we'll behave just me and Welks in there alone with him. I don't suppose he's made any formal statement, has he?' Hanks played with the telephone cord twiddling it round his fingers as he talked. 'Quite. Who's his brief? Kerim Zamana? That toad!' Hanks rolled his eyes theatrically, 'No, I don't mind if he's present. Let's have it all above board and honest. Right, see you later.' He hung up, ignoring the expectant faces gawping at him.

It rang again as soon as it settled.

'Hanks it's for you,' Welks said handing the phone across to him, as he burst into a coughing fit, 'Ms Grigson,' he whispered. Hanks's ears pricked up at the name.

'Hanks here' he said as warmly as he could manage.

'He called again. Wants to meet me,' she sputtered out. 'I'm really scared now.'

Hanks beckoned at Nayyar and scribbled a note. 'It's alright, calm down and tell me everything, you'll be quite safe,' he reassured her. 'What did he say?'

'He wants a meeting, next Tuesday. He wanted to know why I was in Chester at Brinkley's.'

'Interesting,' Hanks commented. 'and?'

'I told him my sister works there and I went for a visit. I don't think he believed me. He was obviously mad at me. I asked him about Ahmed and the bomb, he didn't answer.'

'Did you make a date?'

'You told me to keep him talking so I did. I told him I wanted money, like you said.' She stopped for a moment, as if thinking of something, 'We arranged to meet him in the usual place, you know, where he used to pick up the girls, 3 o'clock, Tuesday. I'm scared rigid, Mr Hanks.'

'That's Surbiton, right?' She grunted affirmatively, 'Where are you staying? I'll come and see you as soon as I can get out of here.'

'Nick and I are in the Travel Lodge, in what used to be County Hall.' Hanks made a note of the room number as he finished the call. The thought of seeing her again so soon was a needed fillip.

'Jesus!' he roared, 'I thought we had her phone tapped. Why didn't we get all this. Who screwed up. Nayyar?'

'Just checking, but it looks like 'Three' haven't received the court order yet, sir. We're trying to find out where it is.'

'Get on the phone to Whittaker; find out what is going on!

Good job this woman trusts us, or we'd be stuffed. The meeting is in Surbiton on Tuesday.'

'We'll have to get to Surrey to do a recce of the place.' Welks stated.

'Yes, suss out the meeting place so we can make a plan.' He turned to Welks, 'You wanted a plan 'B', and I think we're getting one.' Welks just looked miserable and ignored the comment as an aide appeared at his elbow.

'Sir, there's a package upstairs waiting for you.'

Welks, get your coat. Let's go visit our friend.

54

The drive over to Paddington Green was punctuated with roadblocks and rioting damage.

The armoured doors and razor wire gave the detention centre a depressing atmosphere. They were screened in through the main entrance. In the foyer, Gillian Moresby was waiting for them.

'What's the deal Hanks?' she asked gruffly. 'You expect to get more out of him than we have?' she added aggressively.

'Not sure, just need to get a sniff of the man,' Hanks replied. 'Got his brief with him, has he?'

'Yes, he got here about forty minutes ago.'

'Found out who's paying him, then?' Hanks asked, seeing the woman reddening as she quickly make a note.

'We'll check into it. I'll get someone onto it now.'

'Oh, hell!' Hanks smacked the palm of his hand against his forehead. 'I forgot the package. Hanks turned to one of the officers standing there, 'Be a chum, will you go and get it for me, please. It's just a taped-up paper bag on the back seat of the car. Where are we talking to Washiri?' The officer who wasn't pleased to be playing errand boy, went off to get the package.

'Room five.' Moresby told them.

'Bring it to me in room five.' Hanks called after him. 'Come on Colin, let's have some fun.'

'I wish I wasn't feeling so rough, I may have been more use

to you then. How are we doing this?' Welks sneezed dramatically.

'You still got your cold?'

'Very observant,' Welks's voice dripped sarcasm.

'Good.' Welks was baffled.

Moresby bustled past them and led the way down a corridor past numerous cells. The smell of detention centres was always the same Hanks thought, piss and stale socks. He shuddered as he thought of the evil he was about to confront.

An armed officer stood guard outside a door with the number five on it and he checked all their IDs before opening the door. The smell of stale cigarette smoke hit them as they walked in. Hanks took in the familiar room, its two-way mirror facing the prisoner whose skinny ankle was cuffed to the leg of the steel chair, which was in turn bolted to the floor. Washiri was every bit as deathly looking as his picture. Hawk featured; with deep-set dark ringed eyes he was grossly underweight for his height and positively cadaverous. His brief, Zamana, was the opposite, dressed in a voluminous black suit and white shirt, more like Jabba the Hut from Star Wars.

Hanks ostentatiously wafted the smell of stale cigarette smoke emanating from the lawyer's corner away from his face.

'What's it smell like to you, Welks? What do you get when you mix shit with the contents of an ashtray?'

Welks could think of all sorts of things, but unsure of the tactic, just shrugged, 'Got a cold Alan, can't smell a thing.'

'A fat slug lawyer straight out of the sewers,' Hanks finished and laughed as Zamana tried to rise from his chair in protest. Hanks pushed him back down as he started to remonstrate. 'Just shut up and listen,' Moresby looked like she was going to say something as the door opened and the uniformed officer Hanks had sent to get his package came in. He pushed it into the DCI's hands, and looked relieved as he made a quick escape out of the hostile atmosphere. 'Thanks!' Hanks called after him as the door slammed shut, 'I'd advise you to get your client to cooperate fully. Otherwise, he's looking at multiple consecutive life sentences, in fact, we may be able to charge him with high treason, which is, as you well know, one of the only two crimes left on the statute book that carries the death penalty.' He unwrapped the package, revealing a black plastic box ignoring the blustering of the lawyer.

'Gillian, outside please. I need a word.' Bemused Welks gaped after the pair as they went out, then turned to glare fiercely at Washiri. The officer inside the room sat apprehensively watching Welks.

'Said anything yet?' Welks looked at the officer.

'Not a word, sir.'

'He won't either,' Zamana's deep voice came from the corner of the room. Welks turned to glance at the lawyer and suddenly sneezed again. He apologised and turned back to the prisoner, sneezing once more before he could get a tissue from his pocket to stifle the next one.

'Bloody cold,' he complained.

The door opened again and Hanks, accompanied by a smiling Gillian Moresby, came back in. Welks noticed the black box had disappeared.

'You alright? Don't want a doctor, do you?' Hanks asked, anxiously, consoling Welks whose nose was buried in a tissue.

'Don't namby-pamby him, Alan. Are you finished with the prisoner?'

'Yes, I just wanted to see what real evil looked like actually, never thought I'd be able to get any more out of him than you.'

'You lost the thread, Alan?' Welks asked confused.

'No, sunshine, I don't think so,' he grabbed Welks's arm and said, 'Okay, let's go home.'

Welks just followed him to the car where the driver was waiting for them.

'County Hall Travel Lodge. What's the time?' Hanks ordered as they got in.

'Five to five, Alan,' Welks said. 'Mind telling me what the hell's going on, Alan? You've lost me completely.'

'All in good time, Colin,' was all Welks could get out of his partner, who appeared sublimely pleased with himself. 'You need another hanky? Your nose is running. Here!'

'Thanks,' he dabbed his nose with it. Shaking his head in disbelief, he added, 'I think you need a psychiatrist, more than I need a bloody hanky. Seriously, you're off your trolley.'

Hanks laughed. 'Welks, that's what I like about you, the

undying devotion and the complete confidence in me.' Hanks leaned over. 'How would you feel about arresting me?'

'What on earth for?' Welks asked, amazed.

'Not sure, hasn't panned out yet. Could be GBH, could be manslaughter, could be premeditated murder, because I knew what I was doing, you see.' Hanks studied Welks hard. 'You know what I'm talking about?'

'In a word, no, none the wiser. Enlighten me.'

'You know we think we found a link between the K type and the ICs?' Welks nodded. 'Good, you were listening. Well, Voss just gave the of vaccines for our colleagues? Ring any bells?'

'The black box?' Welks looked at him as if he was not quite all there.

'Uh huh, well done, Sherlock. Gillian is having all the staff there inoculated as we speak.' Hanks smiled and leaned back. 'Voss reckons the first symptoms will occur within twenty-four hours, we'll have to wait and see how Washiri is feeling. If he's ill and we have to medicate him, maybe we'll even have to drip feed some sort of narcotherapy to help him remember things. The Lieutenant General tells me there's a very secure medical facility at Waterloo Barracks and our friend the Major is not just Medical Corps, he's also been on tour in Northern Ireland quizzing Paddies. Now you know what it's about, are you going to arrest me or what?'

'Bloody hell, Narcotherapy? 'What...?' Welks was practically speechless, 'what the hell are you talking about?' Then the penny dropped. How do you even know that he's infected Alan?'

'Well?' Hanks noted the change in his partner's demeanour.

Welks slowly began to smile as the significance of the afternoon visit sank in. Hanks noticed both the slight smile, and the slow nod of satisfaction as his partner twigged what had happened.

'What if I don't have the K virus?'

'Mr Voss confirmed your retest before we came here.' Hanks added.

'Oh, thanks for telling me, what would you have done, if I hadn't have had the K virus, but just a normal cold?'

'You don't want to know.'

55

The police car dropped the pair of them off outside the main entrance to the hotel. The army had closed the road to through traffic, an impressive roadblock in the middle of Waterloo road, backed up by an armoured car to make sure nobody misunderstood the message. Hanks told the grateful driver he could finish as they got out in front of the hotel, to watch the man drive off home to his wife and kids.

'We need room 426, she knows we're coming.'

'Sure you want me here?' Welks asked mockingly. 'Don't want her on your own do you, given your predilections?'

'Get away!' Hanks punched him on the shoulder.

'Just a thought.' he laughed

The lift took an age to get them up to the fourth floor, room 426 was opposite as they stepped out, Hanks knocked.

'It's open,' a female voice answered. 'Oh, it's you Mr Hanks.'

She was wearing a thin kimono robe and drying her hair in front of the window looking out over the Thames and the lights of the city.

'Are we disturbing anything?' Hanks asked, with what for him was consideration.

'No, not at all, come in.' She flicked her still wet hair over her face and bent forward to blow-dry it, exposing her long legs and tight figure to the two of them. Welks blew on his fingers and shook his hand.

'Hot stuff,' he mouthed. Hanks felt the same way, but he was sure his feelings were far more intense.

'Nick and I were going to try and find a pub for quiet drink.' She stood up and threw her hair back, 'Just to unwind and chill out. Please sit,' she offered, 'I'll put something on,' as she pulled on a pair of jeans.

'What did 'Brown Suit' say to you exactly?' Hanks said, plonking himself unceremoniously on the bed in the small room, trying hard not stare at her body.

'Try and give us it verbatim, Ms. Grigson,' Welks coaxed dabbing his nose.

'Well, I'll do my best,' she paused for thought, continuing to rub the ends of her hair dry. 'Well, he said,' she thought for a moment, then started falteringly, 'Claire, I saw you in Chester in that medical place… What were you doing there?' He was angry. It wasn't just a casual question. He was steamed up about something; I don't know what, though. Maybe it was just me he was uptight about.' Hanks felt the surge of frustration when he had realised they hadn't had the tap in place in time. Whoever cocked that up might as well have been working for the other side. Claire went on, 'So then he said that he had to go away soon and wouldn't be back for a while. I told him I wasn't stupid and that I already knew the score. I had seen his face all over the news. Then he got all Mr Nice Guy. So, I hit him with the money thing.'

'And? How did he react to that? Angry?'

'No, not really,' she said, 'it was like he was chewing over the question; thinking about something,' she explained, pausing to pull her sweater on. 'Anyway,' she continued, 'then he says, 'Well, you're sort of a widow now and you know we look after the families of our martyrs. I'd like to reward you. He's in paradise soon, and I want to give you your bit of paradise as well.'

'Stop!' Hanks burst out. 'He said that?' he stood abruptly, 'Those words exactly?'

She was taken aback. 'Yes, well more or less. That's what he said; I'll give you your bit.'

'Of paradise. He's not talking steaming orgasms here.' Hanks frowned, 'How did it go on?'

'He asked where I was. I told him it was none of his business. Then I asked him if he was going to give me the money. He said it depended on how good I was to him when we met. I sort of insinuated that we'd get it off together.' she blushed. 'Then he told me to be at the bridge in Surbiton where he used to pick up Hollie and then we'd go to the apartment to 'talk'. He said Tuesday at three o'clock. That's about it.' She tossed the towel on the bed next to Hanks. 'You think I should meet him?'

Hanks turned to Welks frowning, deep in thought. 'We'll have to decide whether it's safe for Claire to meet him. Personally, I'm not in favour of her going unless it's one hundred per cent safe.'

Welks took the lead, bridging the void left by Hanks's inertia. 'We'll organise everything at the bridge and bag him. It can't be that difficult surely?'

'I think we need a bit more thought on the matter. We can do that over a drink.' Hanks finally interjected. 'Good company always stimulates my brain, three heads are better than two,' he joked. It was not so much the need of a drink, more that he just didn't want to leave her. They were interrupted by a knock on the doorframe as Nick popped his head in. Hanks finished his sentence, 'that is, if you can stand our company.' He joined Welks and looked out of the window embarrassed and afraid she might say no. Gazing out at the lights on the Thames from the opposite bank sparkling in the wavelets flowing past, waiting for her answer and wishing the others would just disappear and leave him alone with her.

'Of course we can.' she stepped swiftly over to him and grasped his arm. 'I'm sure Nick won't mind, and I'll feel safer with a police escort.'

'Where do you reckon on going? D'you know the area?'

'No idea, somewhere with a bit of character, a London pub.'

'I'm sure we'll find at least one out there.' They walked over to the lifts. Hanks was silent, lost in thought as Claire's arm linked through his as they left the hotel.

The detectives had stayed in the pub with the two from Brinkley's for about an hour before deciding to take time out for some deep thinking. They excused themselves and left, with

Hanks promising to phone. They went back to the MoD, calling Philpott to join them and then spent the night there ensconced in discussions and phoning Richardson frequently throughout. Sleep was a luxury they didn't get much of, and their breakfast was minimal, coffee and a biscuit.

The War Room was as quiet as a graveyard, yet seemed to throb with apprehension. After the chaotic events of the week, an almost physical aura of anti-climax hung around in the room. Faces were drawn and grey from the long hours they'd all put in. The room was no longer prim and tidy. A discarded jacket here, a paper cup there, even the remains of dinners on disposable plates lying around, were witness to the unrelenting pressure all the staff were suffering.

'Mess in here today,' he commented to Welks. 'No cleaners by the look of it.'

'Not seen the news or read the papers then?' Nayyar asked, surprised.

'Nah, we normally make the news, not watch it,' Welks quipped, sarcastically.

'A national day of mourning has been announced, for the riot and virus victims,' Nayyar explained. 'It's to be considered like a public holiday.' Nayyar turned his laptop screen around so they could see it. 'Everything is shut, apart from emergency services and utilities.' The screen showed a convoy of hearses driving past Buckingham Palace where the Queen and the rest of the Royal Family stood on the balcony, heads bowed under the Royal Standard flying at half-mast.

'She'll earn her money today if they drive all of them past her. At least she's learned something,' Hanks mumbled to no-one in particular.

'Heh? 'What?' Welks said quizzically.

'Flags, at half-mast,' Hanks grunted.

'It's been all over the news and newspapers since yesterday evening, that and the vaccination programme.' Nayyar commented, 'You should see the queues at doctors' surgeries. At least the news about the epidemic has put a kind of lid on the rioting. People are more worried about not dying than going out and killing someone.' He shook his head in disbelief. 'Oh, and we have Claire Grigson's phone tapped now. Sorry about the cock up.'

'Has he been in touch again?' Welks asked, to be answered by a negative shake of the head.

'Is there anywhere decent to stay in Surbiton? I think we have to see the lay of the land down there this weekend. Not a mob, just me and Welks here with a few of the locals. No more than that. We need a nice quiet look-see.'

'I'll get someone to check. Not my neck of the woods.' Wheeler admitted.

'Moresby is on the line and wants to talk to you. Sounds like she's got the humdinger of all colds,' the collator called over, 'You want her?' Hanks smiled

'Yeah, go on then. Surprised she's talking to me, especially if she's gone down with a cold. I did warn her.' Welks appraised him with a complicit grin, 'Glad I clued her in though.' Nayyar looked as if he was hearing Hanks speaking a foreign language.

'Hanks here,' he answered, listening for a moment. 'Don't sound too bright, Gill, didn't the stuff work?' He winked at Philpott, 'Oh, you probably took it too late then.' Hanks commiserated as he sat on the corner of the desk his leg dangling, expression strangely happy. 'Has one hump short of a camel started talking yet? What? You want to send him to hospital? His temperature is over 40? Yes, he needs medical attention.' Hanks had to suppress his joy at the news, and twiddled the phone cord happily. 'I'll check with Philpott, I'm sure they have a secure facility at Waterloo Barracks.' Philpott was listening in and nodded with a broad smile. 'I have a yes on that. Get him over there fast,' Hanks grinned gleefully. 'and Gillian, your cold will be over in a few hours, it'll be like I said, don't worry.' Hanks hung up and fisted the air and emitted a loud whoop of joy. 'That's a real bit of luck. Just when we needed it' He gave Philpott a high five.

Better let Washiri's brief know where we're moving him to, hadn't we?' Welks asked with a complicit grin. 'Think he'll be up for it? Might need the next bed, if you ask me.'

'If it blows up, it was an emergency, so we didn't have time to let him know,' Hanks replied, an edge of malice back in his voice. 'Monday will be fine. After all, we don't have a private number for Mr Lard tub, and it is Friday.' Hanks pulled Philpott off to one side.

'You know what to do now?' Philpott nodded. 'Okay, you'll maybe want the MI5 team there as well. I know they have some tongue-loosening tricks in their repertoire.'

Philpott shook his head. 'Later maybe if we don't have any success.'

'It's your ball game, so you decide. He's army property now.' Hanks patted him on the shoulder. 'We're off to the PLA labs. We want to talk to Voss and Rogers. If you need me I'm there.'

Welks and Hanks walked over to the lift. 'What we need is more time,' Hanks said, as the lift doors opened.

'I know, if we want to infect the terror cells, the lapse between infection and outbreak is too short.' Welks pondered as the two of them stepped in.

'If the bastard is too sick to travel, we defeat the object; I'll have to talk to the experts. You know this is illegal?' Hanks asked his partner, 'after calling me crazy at Paddington Green yesterday, you still sure this is where you want to be?'

'Nowhere else!' Welks confirmed with grim determination as the doors closed. 'We just need to be sure there is no way to trace it back. Will Gill stay quiet?'

'She didn't sign a contract, but yeah, she's ok. I'm cool with her on that front.'

'Good, let's do it then, shall we?'

56

The investigating team had spent hours over the weekend looking around the area near the St Mary's Road Bridge. There were a couple of small shops and a lay-by, two bus stops and a zebra crossing. The road past the shops was built up with solid, between-the-wars semis flagged here and there with the occasional for sale or sold signs. The other direction took the road past the park with its kiddies' playground and the cricket pitch. Hanks couldn't help but think about parallels with Washiri in Southall and the park there, but this time, there wasn't a hope of getting the same kind of all-round video coverage.

The railway bridge itself was an unspectacular iron girder construction that had enjoyed the company of years with hundreds of pigeons. Their droppings were simply everywhere. What Hanks had now come to regard as 'Claire's corner' was just out of range of the excreta from the birds. In spite of the efforts of Elmbridge Council, the pavements under the bridge were a disgrace and a real test of pedestrians' nerve.

Hanks made sketches and occupied his time with a stopwatch and talking with the local mini market owner. Welks measured the widths of the roads and radii of the corners, to check what kind of backup vehicles could be accommodated. The local officers from Kingston and Surbiton were only too glad to assist. The thought of being in on the arrest of the number one terrorist in the UK was something they didn't want to let slip.

'Used to be your stomping ground here, didn't it?' Welks asked, reeling his tape in.

'A lifetime ago,' Hanks concurred, 'back in the days when a pint of mild cost ten pence.'

'Jeez, you really that old?' Welks stepped back in mock amazement, 'So what's the night life like?'

'This is it chum, we're here.' Hanks joked and then continued more seriously, 'Now, listen, this has to be watched discretely to make sure our friend isn't doing the dirty. I didn't like that quote, 'giving you a bit of paradise.' If you say it to your girlfriend it's different to what I'm sure this mad dog has in mind.'

'You're worried about her, Alan, I have been watching you, it's obvious that she means a lot to you.'

'You don't think I'm too old?' Hanks asked with concern in his voice.

'Doesn't matter what I think.' Welks studied his partner closely, envying the fact that he looked younger and fitter than he did. 'I told you it was about time you to let go of the past, go for it! She's great.' he paused, 'I think we've got enough info to make do. Let's get back to the nick and get some ink on paper.'

Hanks called the local liaison officer and said they were ready, and soon a car arrived to whisk them back to the station in Kingston. The national emergency meant that the place was buzzing for a Sunday and not just functioning with the normal weekend skeleton staff. They went up the stairs to the CID offices, where a planning room had been put at their disposal. Hanks and Welks laid out a large-scale street plan on the table and, together with the local officers they decided where they needed to place people and vehicles, plus what kind of extra observation techniques could be unobtrusively installed.

Hanks was adamant that he wanted to be part of the team on the ground. He was fed up with being stuck in the bunker. He was, after all, his own man now. Officially, he'd gone into retirement the day before. He was determined that the operation would remain ultra-low profile: it needed to be as low-key as possible to avoid being noticed. He was also quite sure that he was going to be in the forefront of the action.

'Where are we staying?' Welks asked the liaison officer, 'I could do with a shower and a bit of a wind down. It's been a cow of a week.'

Hanks nodded agreement. 'Yeah, we've had a bitch.' He started to fold up the maps and put the notes in his case. 'We'll be in first thing in the morning to fine tune the details,' he said. 'I think three cars and a back-up on the edge of the park should be sufficient. We should put another back-up at the beginning of St Mary's as well. That's just in case he doubles back. I don't think he'll be expecting anything, so we can be relatively relaxed about any escape plans. I just wish we knew what car he was using. It would make the initial identification easier.'

'A sniper on the bridge would be nice,' one of the local DCs commented, 'and another in the park would be even better.'

'Don't let the Home Secretary hear you talking like that. I nearly lost my job from saying it when we were going for Washiri,' Hanks chided, 'We have a nanny as Home Sec.,' he laughed softly, amidst a consensus of nods. 'Let's go team, thanks and we'll meet here Monday at 9 am.

They reached their hotel in the early evening darkness. It was a big Victorian building on the edge of Richmond Park. Instead of nightlife, their day was just beginning. They went to Hanks's room. The first call was to Philpott.

'What's the news on chummy?' Hanks asked without preamble. 'Has he started to talk?'

'Could put it like that,' Philpott sounded smug.

'Come on man, out with it, what's happened?'

'We had to give him antibiotics by infusion. He was very sick indeed. That virus is a very nasty animal for some.'

'Can't exactly say I'm sorry to hear that,' Hanks interrupted.

'Unfortunately, there was a mix-up with infusion bottles and we gave him Pentothal by mistake. No doubt the medic in charge will get his leg smacked,' he paused.

'Get on with it, Philpott! Save the fairy tales for the enquiry, if there is one. What has he given us?'

'MI5 have been talking to him all afternoon. The one thing he's adamant about is that he won't talk about Abbotobad. We never even asked him about Abbotobad, which is a town in Pakistan by the way, although we have no idea what its significance is.'

'Hmm. Anything else worth hearing?'

'Got a list of names and addresses that'll fill your notebook, Chief Inspector, a good harvest, I'd say. Question is, do we cure the rat or do we let the virus exact justice?'

'I don't care, but I suppose you'd better at least try to save him. Give him some of that antidote stuff, another statistic for Voss,' Hanks smiled, 'do your best anyway. Pass the Abbotobad thing on to the Americans. Maybe they can do something with it. They might have a better idea of what it could mean. Major, thanks. You've done a great job!'

'Have you talked to Voss?'

'Not yet. I'm ringing him in a minute. Want me to pass anything on?'

'No, but I don't think you should talk about the plan on the phone to him.'

'What?' Hanks exclaimed. 'Why?'

'They could be tapped. At least the MoD phones are safe.'

Hanks put the phone down and took a deep breath. 'Nearly there Colin, nearly damn well there,' he exhaled slowly and dialled the Port of London lab number. After a few rings Voss picked up personally. 'Listen, Philpott just gave me some advice about the phones. You understand?' the answering grunt confirmed that Voss did. 'So, making progress?'

'Yes, I think so.'

'When are you likely to know?' Hanks asked.

'The team at PLA are running the final tests now. We'll know in an hour, two at the latest.' Hanks checked the time. It was six-fifteen.

'You've got my mobile number, so ring me as soon as you know. Oh, and can you ask Claire if she'd come and see us here in...' he turned to Welks, 'What's this place called?'

'The Warren.'

'The Warren in Kingston. Tell her to bring her stuff and give her the vial and the vaccine as well. Let her know we appreciate everything she's doing. Great woman that. You're lucky to have her.'

'I'll tell her. I'll get her a taxi. You'll sort out a room?' he finished.

'Sure, hear from you later.' Hanks put the phone down.

'The vial, you cannot be serious,' Welks stated aghast.

'Voss reckons they can retard the virus by several days, so the incubation and infectious period are prolonged. All Baitullah's contacts thereafter will get the disease, we'll target the terrorists specifically this way; a bit like the magic bullet cancer drugs.'

'You know that's illegal,' Welks said.

'The plan is to infect the bastard when we get him. Then deport him back to wherever he wants to go. He then infects all his buddies and if he doesn't want to go, we let Philpott 'cure' him.' Hanks made the little inverted commas sign as he said cure.

'Another Washiri? They'll goose you if they find out.'

'Yeah, it will be worth it though.' Hanks smiled, leaving Welks shaking his head in disbelief.

'We'd better go down and book her a room or do you want her in yours?' Welks said grabbing the chance of needling Hanks again.

'Get off! Let's book a room.' They walked together down to reception, each immersed in their own thoughts.

57

Claire was centre stage in the restaurant that evening. She'd been out shopping with a couple of WPCs during the day and shown Hanks and Welks the skimpy top and skirt she was intending to wear for the next day's meeting and wore the revealing glittery outfit at dinner, not that there was much of it to put on. The policemen thought it was great though, hardly taking their eyes off her. Claire lapped up the attention.

'Seen the news?' Welks nudged him. The evening news on the hotel bar TV had shown racc riots spreading across Europe in a backlash to the events at Bank; the death toll was climbing hourly.

'Which bit?' Hanks asked between mouthfuls.

'The riots here are supposedly abating.'

'Propaganda! The politicos think they can manipulate folk into believing what's on the news. Let's tell them, 'the riots have stopped', so no-one turns out for them anymore. Same crap every time,' he added despondently, attempting to catch Claire's eye again.

'Seriously, Richardson says the same. You must read the same books.'

'Sure. It's like a sodding bush fire in Europe, completely out of control. How many are going to die because of these maniacs.' he thumped the empty glass down, causing a reaction around the table, with heads turning expectantly in his direction.

Hanks held his palm up in apology for the disturbance. 'You know Colin, there's no such thing as fairness.'

'I'm beginning to think you're right, but the maniacs and zealots are everywhere, not just in religions.' Welks added, his voice serious, as he refilled their glasses. They clinked glasses.

Welks toasted, 'At least the riots have slowed down. They've caught onto the fact that the disease is deadly and everything is at a stop. They are all trying to get the vaccine. There's an exodus of Asian families rushing out of the infection zones and the medical centres are full of people waiting for the vaccine. There are a lot of people fleeing the country.'

'What about the indigenous rioters?'

'God, you're so bloody PC these days Alan,' Welks took another sip of his wine, 'they don't want to go anywhere near areas that may be 'infected' so it is working both ways.'

'Humph!' Hanks grunted, 'Working you call it? Manipulating public opinion I'd call it.' He cast a look at Claire who was fending off compliments from one of the local DCs. 'Anyway here's to Justice!' He toasted Welks; they drank together leaning towards each other, an almost intimate pair. Claire was watching them closely now, curiosity clear on her face.

'You drinking to something special?'

'You and justice,' Hanks smiled at her.

'Justice, you believe in it?' she said quizzically. 'You said that there's no such thing, that the punishment never fits the crime.'

'You're right, but we're going to change that tomorrow, aren't we?' he winked at her conspiratorially.

'We hope,' she smiled back warmly, 'if it all goes to plan.'

Hanks nodded, taking another sip of his wine. 'If you don't mind, I think I'll turn in; all a bit hectic for an old soul like me.' He smiled in self-deprecation. 'Gentlemen,' he said standing and raising his glass, 'I leave you with a toast.' Conversation stopped and all eyes were on him, 'A toast to our success tomorrow.' The group all stood ceremoniously.

'To success!' they uttered in solemn unison. As they placed their glasses back on the table, Hanks pushed his chair back out of the way.

'Good night, and happy hunting tomorrow.' He placed his

hand on Welks's shoulder and squeezed it. 'See you at breakfast.'

Back in his room Hanks had never felt more tired, more drained. He threw his jacket into the armchair and slipped his shoes off as he flicked the remote to turn the TV on, zapping through the channels trying to find some distraction, some soporific to send him to sleep, the endless selection of seemingly identical chat and reality rubbish, offering him nothing of the sort. He tossed the remote onto the bed in frustration. Going into the bathroom, he undressed and got into the shower, all the while thinking about Claire and their eye contact throughout the evening. Was there something there? Was it only him who thought there was something special between them? The hot water soothed and relaxed him as thoughts about tomorrow and about the past cascaded through his mind. He let the water stream over him, enjoying the harshness of the spray and the steam it created. He felt alive again, buzzing. This was what he was here for. In his reverie, he almost didn't hear the knock on the door outside. The persistency could only mean Welks. Hanks cursed under his breath and turned the shower off.

'Coming Colin, coming, just a minute.' he wrapped a towel round his waist and went to the door as the knock was repeated. 'I'm here. Where's the fire?' He drew back the door lock, to be almost bowled over as the solid wooden door flew inwards.

'Jesus!' He was totally taken by surprise as arms went round his neck and he was pushed back into the room. He heard the door slam as his mouth was covered by her soft lips, the kiss slowly expanding from initial contact to something deeply passionate. He was so off-balance he stumbled back and fell helplessly onto the bed taking Claire down with him. 'I thought it was...!' he managed to gasp as she pulled away his bath towel.

'You didn't expect me to wait forever, did you?' she chided, pulling fiercely at her top. He sat up and kissed her neck, reaching behind her to release her bra.

'You really don't need this you know,' he murmured, dropping it on the floor as he nuzzled her breast with his mouth. 'They are just perfect.' She pushed him back onto the bed and sat astride him. His hand went under her short skirt to discover the thin line of her thong which he pulled aside. 'You are so beautiful,' he began, but she put a finger on his mouth silencing him as she drew him into her.

Next morning, Hanks woke with Claire's head, her blond hair in disarray, on his chest,. He moved causing her to awaken and hug him, kissing his chest.

'Mmmm,' she murmured sleepily, 'that was nice.' She snuggled up and stroked him. In spite of his arousal, he disentangled himself from her long legs, reluctantly but with determination gently pushing her off him.

'We have a lot on, Claire,' he admonished. She lay back and stretched, showing the full length of her beauty. Hanks eyed her appreciatively and for a moment, he was severely tempted, but shook his head. He kissed her softly, and then unwillingly pushed himself away. 'It's late and they'll all be waiting for us, plus I need all my faculties to protect you today. There'll be other times, better times.' She nodded. 'Just to keep things clean, you'd better go down first and I'll come down a few minutes after.' Claire looked at him, the sadness in her face obvious. 'Listen, I'm crazy about you. Welks suspects it, but we don't need the whole team to know just yet. It may be a distraction and we need total concentration today.' Hanks took her in his arms and hugged her, the scent of their night together strong in his nose.

58

By noon they were all in position in Surbiton, Claire, nervously nibbling at her nails, was sitting next to Hanks. They had a couple of folding chairs set up to the side of the window in the little corner mini market.

'You all right?' Hanks asked concerned.

'I feel a bit shaky, but probably just the nerves.' she dabbed her nose with a tissue.

'You still want to go on?' He was watching her carefully now.

'Yes, of course. You'll be in the car keeping an eye on me anyway, won't you?'

Hanks had an unmarked car parked outside in a lay-by and Welks was around the corner in St Marys Road, just the other side of the bridge. From where he was, he had an unobstructed view of Claire's corner, as did the police on the park side. The foot officers and back up crews on the far side of the park, stationed there in case Baitullah made a run for it on foot, were invisible.

'Yes, and it'll be okay,' he reached out and stroked her hair. 'you just make sure that you run. You're gonna do fine, you'll see,' he said. The previous night had changed things in him and he felt uneasy about Claire's role, his mind was in turmoil.

She looked up at him like a helpless doe, her eyes moist as she began nervously to repeat some of the concerns she had already aired, 'What if he gets out of the car? What if he has a gun? I mean, I can't wear a bulletproof vest under this outfit, can I?' She sneezed loudly.

Hanks concealed his worry by hugging her, 'Hey, you know that you don't have to do this. I can get a policewoman to dress up, but he may just not stop for her, it's you he wants.' with an appreciative smile, he continued, 'I can see why. You're a stunner.'

'Are you trying to hit on me, Mr Hanks?' she smiled teasingly, her smile fading to a nervous frown.

'If I wasn't, would you be disappointed?' for a long moment they held eye contact until she finally nodded and he relaxed. Hanks looked out of the window as a passing bus caught his attention.

'Any action out there?' he called over the open channel on his radio.

'Negative, nothing untoward, one car has been past twice in opposite directions, a woman with a kid going one way and returning with no kid the other. That's the only double.'

'Thanks.' He turned to Claire, 'Want some fresh air? We've got nearly half an hour.'

'Want a wee desperately. I'm so nervous, I'm frightened that I'll have an accident,' she shivered.

He looked over at the proprietor, who was sitting at the cash desk, still in mild shock at having the police nesting in his shop. 'You got a loo?'

It seemed like an age before she returned, pallid, wiping her nose with a bunched up tissue, with her make-up retouched. There were endless minutes to go. Hanks put his jacket around her shoulders, 'We'd better get you on station soon, just in case he's around. Wait for the bus to stop outside and then pretend that you've just got off it. Walk naturally to the corner. We're here, we're watching.' He squeezed her arm. 'You know exactly what to do Claire, don't you?' he prompted her yet again.

'Of course,' she sneezed softly stifling it by pinching her nose.

'Don't take any chances, Claire, and good luck.' he hugged her briefly, rubbing her back, getting a nose full of her perfume. 'I want you back whole, ok?' He gave her a deep intimate kiss and took off towards the door.

'Detective Chief Inspector!' she called after him breathlessly, 'Ever heard of the police complaints board?'

'Not enough or too much, what's the complaint?' they both laughed. 'Alright, we're off everyone.' Hanks said pulling the door open. 'All stations, Claire's coming out when the bus stops. There's one due in two minutes. Listen Claire, I'm going to swap places with Welks.' He called back into the shop. 'I don't want to risk anything going wrong.'

Claire had caught up with him in the doorway and nodded apprehensively catching his glance before he turned away again. He wasn't sure now who was the more nervous, him or Claire. He could feel his own hands trembling. He knew if this went wrong, it would be not only a political and professional disaster, but also a deeply personal one, but strangely, Hanks felt optimistic.

'Welks?' Hanks keyed the radio on Welks's channel, 'Change of plan, take over here and I'll watch Claire from the car.'

'Okay, I'll wait till you get here.'

Hanks gave Claire another hug, before closing the shop door behind him. Welks's BMW was just the other side of the bridge, Welks opened the door puzzled at the change of plan as Hanks approached.

'What's up?' Hanks just raised a hand to silence him as they exchanged places in the car.

'Just get to the shop and use the backup car if we can't stop him.' Hanks said pressing the keys for the other car into his partner's hand.

'You are worried about her, aren't you?' Welks looked concerned. Hanks just nodded, 'Ok,' he patted Hanks shoulder as they changed places.

Welks saw Claire huddled in Hank's jacket in the doorway. He heard the hiss of airbrakes outside as the single-decker bus stopped, disgorging its passengers. The driver waited for a moment for the two people at the stop to board, then shrugged surprised, when they didn't, and moved off again. He wasn't to know they were policemen.

'It's time. Welks said, 'If you are in danger, just leg it, we'll do the rest afterwards. Run under the bridge. Hanks is there.'

Claire left the mini market without a backward glance, and walked slowly to her corner. She was alone, and this was now her pitch. She shivered in the cold and sneezed again, rubbing her arms for warmth.

'Three o'clock, no sign of him,' Hanks's voice crackled on the radio.

Welks left the mini market and got into the other car. He wound his window down and breathed in deeply as he nervously checked the time again.

'Car coming from the park side,' a call came in on his radio, a white Renault drove past, the driver almost missing the corner, as he stared over at Claire. It wasn't Baitullah. A different voice came over the radio, 'Another one coming,' a transit van with some plumbing company's insignia on the side slowed to a stop and the driver offered her a lift. Hanks's stomach knotted in tension as he saw Claire tell the van to drive on. The driver gave her two fingers as he pulled away.

Hanks started the engine nodding at the two plainclothes at the bus stop as he did so. He hit the steering wheel with the palm of his hand impatiently. 'Come on, come on, let's get this done,' he muttered to himself. Claire stood stiffly at the corner. He could see her dabbing her nose. Wrong time to get a cold he thought. The radio crackled into life again.

It was one of the Kingston DC's, 'Car coming down the hill. A non-white, wearing glasses in a red Nissan, 06 plate, male, looks very tense. Wasn't there something about a big ring?'

'Yes, big and gold.' Hanks answered nervously, 'Where is he now?'

'Coming down past the Ditton Inn pub, it's him.'

Hanks was sweating profusely now and his hands were sticky as he released the handbrake and put the car into gear, craning his neck to get a good view of the corner.

The Nissan pulled to a stop next to Claire. Baitullah wound the window down and spoke to her.

Hanks watched the scene unfold through the windscreen of his car. Claire was nodding her head, he couldn't see her mouth as the window lowered and cursed inwardly for not playing safe and putting a wire on her. She backed away from the car. Hanks could hear the man shouting at her, but not the words. Claire was almost at the brick bridge support as Baitullah sprang out of the car ran round and pinned her to the brickwork, his hand around her throat.

'He's got a knife!' Welks shouted into the radio.

Hanks, turned on the siren, and put the flashing blue strobe on the dashboard as he drove the car forward. The shock and surprise on the face of Baitullah was plainly visible as he spun round, releasing his grip on Claire's throat. Hanks' sole focus was Claire as she ran towards him. Baitullah raced to his car and jumped in, revving fiercely in panic, pulling away, tyres spitting gravel.

Reaching the car, Claire ripped the passenger door open and threw herself in beside him, sobbing, 'God, he is evil that man,' she gasped slamming the door shut behind her. Hanks put the car into gear and floored the accelerator to give chase. Suddenly a cloud of grey pigeons descending from the underside of the bridge in panic at all the noise distracted him.

'Fucking pigeons,' he screamed as he wrenched the wheel causing the car to swerve abruptly across the road, clipping the side of the bridge with a screech of metal on stone and scattering dozens more pigeons. A car sped past him hooting angrily at his abrupt manoeuvre. The other police car coming from Parkside didn't have a chance. The police driver, momentarily blinded by a huge cloud of pigeons flapping across his line of sight, didn't even see the other car until the collision. Hanks's car narrowly avoided them both as they slithered across the road into the park fence. The pigeons cleared, the Nissan had no option but to turned left towards where Welks was waiting. There was a moment's eerie silence.

Hanks saw Welks's car swerve abruptly out of the lay by. The huge flock of pigeons that emerged from under the bridge, a distraction he hadn't anticipated, had gone. He held his breath as the Nissan gathered speed and hurtled towards Welks, a smash unavoidable. He could hear Welks on the radio, his channel somehow still open.

'Shit!' Welks screamed, 'how can everything go wrong?' Hanks saw the blue strobe on the dash come on, a futile gesture under the circumstances. 'Shit!' Welks screamed again as Hanks saw Welks's hands leave the wheel, pushed away by the exploding airbag, holding his breath as his colleagues face disappeared into the cushion. The car ricocheted off the speeding Nissan and veered wildly over the road into the iron railings of the park. The two officers at the bus stop who had initially started to run to the first accident froze at the sound of the second crash behind them, unable to decide which one to attend first. Hanks car stopped beside the wreckage.

Stunned seconds passed, before the radio filled full of garbled messages and requests for information and instructions, officers were streaming across the park towards the accidents. Hanks was shouted into the radio 'He's got away, the bastard is moving in the direction of Hampton Court, all units between here and the A3 concentrate on a red Nissan with severe front end damage.' Claire stared horrified at the sight of Welks's car.

'My God! What ...?' Claire's tears were flowing freely now.

Hanks jumped out of the car and rushed over to Welks. He tried to pull the door open to get to him, it was jammed. He picked up a stone from the ground and smashed the door window. Welks was motionless his face in the airbag.

'Colin,' Hanks shouted, 'Colin, can you hear me?' Welks's face turned slightly towards him.

'Get this damned airbag out of my face,' Welks managed to mumble.

'You're alive, thank god, it was your round in the pub, you had me worried for a second.' Hanks said, obviously relieved as he pulled on the car door. Hanks checked the road for signs of the departing Nissan. 'Where did the son of a bitch go? He stood, staring down the road in the direction Baitullah's car had gone. 'This bastard is not going far and he's not getting away.' Hanks struggled through the crowd of police officers and bystanders gathering to gawp at the wrecked car back to his BMW.

'I'm coming with you,' Claire shouted running after him.

Hanks was in no mood to argue, 'We'll follow the oil slick,' Hanks growled, as he floored the accelerator, 'I reckon a mile at the most from the size of the oil loss.'

59

It had always been a risk. The combination of killing the woman who'd demeaned him so badly, with the reward of blissful gratification at the same time was too much for him to let go. All the same, he was glad to be out of the prison of the safe house at last. He was happy that this was going to be his final act before he collected his escape documents tomorrow. How fitting, he thought, to crown this incredible success with her blood.

He'd cruised the area in the late morning, checking for any tell-tales signs of police activity and had seen nothing. His date was for three o'clock and he'd made sure he was punctual; the decision to kill her was an easy one, because he had to. She was special, beautiful, but he had to teach her a final lesson. The disrespectful bitch, thwarting his desires and humiliating him, now he would show the slut what respect was, before he dispatched her to whatever hell was waiting for her.

Masoud toyed about how he could play it out, after he'd done his thing with her. When he was finished he would cut her throat like a goat at the Eid and let her bleed out at his feet and then leave her in some dirty alleyway by the Thames. Another nameless corpse, no-one would care. He was aroused and jittery at the same time, hormones and adrenalin creating a confusing mix. These sluts were all the same, just stupid women to be used and disposed of, even if this one was different in some way that he couldn't quite fathom, she had to go.

He drove down the hill noticing a car parked on the left, almost at the same time as he saw her. She was breath-taking and she filled his vision. Forgetting the parked car, he drew alongside her and wound down the window, conscious of the knife in his pocket. His eyes were almost level with the hem of her skirt. He felt weakened, intoxicated and wondered fleetingly what this feeling was. Was this what everyone called love, a helplessness that lamed? He told her to get into the car and she nodded, but instead of getting in, she backed away. Annoyed he jumped out of the car and pinned her against the wall of the bridge, the feel of her body delicious against his, as he squeezed her throat. She tried to knee him in the groin, but he'd anticipated that. In anger he slapped her with enormous force and still gripping her throat, he went for his knife. The sex would have to be sacrificed, he was enraged now. Suddenly she spat straight into his face, the warm saliva unexpected and shocking, as was the loud noise of a police siren which sounded almost on top of him. He snapped his head round seeking the source of the sound and saw that the parked BMW was rolling towards him with a blue light on the dash. Terrified, he thrust the woman away, ran back to his car and frantically jumped in.

He panicked completely as he saw her running towards the police car. Cursing loudly, he floored the accelerator and sped away from the kerb. None of it made any sense. Claire! The police! With his heart pounding and no time to deliberate, he desperately wiped his face, clearing the spittle from his lips. It tasted of mint. A blur entered his field of vision from the left, big and grey and swerving into the middle of the road. A car came racing out of the lay-by opposite and careered across the road at him. Instinctively, he wrenched the wheel away from the vehicle, but too late. He hit the other car, sending the driver slamming into his airbag and forcing the car to slither across the road towards the park fence. Baitullah's windscreen crazed instantly robbing him of forward vision, almost simultaneously his head hit the door frame and his side window shattered. Another siren started behind him, nearer this time. He was frantic now. He stuck his head out through the broken window, the cool air helping clear his muzzy head for a moment as he tried to see where he was going. The engine was still just about running and he was not going to stop. He drove towards Hampton Court, struggling with pain, a loud rushing noise in his ears, limited vision and a faltering engine. His speed dropped to practically walking pace after just a few hundred yards. He cursed loudly slamming his fist into the dashboard, as the engine failed and the car rolled to a complete halt. Masoud listened for any signs of pursuit, but the rushing noise blotted the world out. He was quivering with a mix of overpowering rage and fear. The bitch had gone to the police; he'd underestimated her nearly fatally. The car was a mess, with the bonnet crumpled and steam hissing out from under it. He was still rubbing at his face where she'd spat at him. No woman had ever done that. Not to him! Unsteadily, and panting for air he got out of the car. He kicked the front tyre in frustration as a BMW cruised to a halt to halt beside him. He turned and ran, in panic, from the grey suited man, who'd jumped from the car. His attention focussed on his pursuer, he failed to notice the other figure in front of him. Claire's face contorted in a mixture of hatred and pleasure as her foot connected with his groin and he collapsed in agony in the gutter. Rough hands grabbed him and jerked his wrists behind him. Masoud felt the cold steel on his skin as the cuffs closed.

'You're nicked,' the policeman said smugly to the back of Masoud's head as he yanked him upright, 'you don't have to say anything, but whatever you say may be used against you. Someone will give you the official version back at the station.'

'Kalet!' Masoud hissed. 'I made history!'

'You didn't make history scumbag, you are fucking history. He turned to the woman saying, 'Well done Claire. Good that you are not a police officer, that kick could have been deemed as excessive force.' He smiled 'accidentally' banging Masoud's head hard against the car door frame as he rudely shoved the man inside.

'I could do more to this evil turd.' she spat at him again.

'It's okay Claire.' Hanks tried to calm her as he put his hand in his pocket for the vial from Voss. Panicking when he found it wasn't there.

WEAPONS OF MASS DESTRUCTION

By Robin Melhuish

A war on terrorism based on what? An illegality? Hanks is drawn into a web of conspiracy that not only jeopardises his professional career, but also throws his deepest beliefs to the wind as he attempts to fathom the real reasons for terror and who is behind it..

Isolated incidents, things that on their own make no sense and yet coupled together become simply preposterous. Is the unbelievable true? A plot with more layers than the skins of an onion. Hanks's beloved Claire, faced with the twin threats of British Justice and prison, on the one hand and radical right wing extremists who are set on destroying her on the other. Endeavours, in a race against an invisible enemy, where there can only be too many losers.

AUTHOR'S FOOTNOTE

It wasn't until I'd finished writing this book that I discovered the following which almost makes a mockery of the fiction.

Bush, Cheney, & Rumsfeld are involved in the Project for a New American Century which published its 'Rebuilding America's Defences' in Sept 2000. In that paper it states:

'...the art of warfare will be vastly different. Advanced forms of biological warfare that can target specific genotypes may transform biological warfare from the realm of terror to a politically useful tool'.

Seen the news? SARS (Severe Asian Respiratory Syndrome and more recently MERS in Mecca and Korea? (Middle East Respiratory Syndrome)?

No cause for alarm. Is there?

Robin Melhuish
2015

ABOUT THE AUTHOR

Born in Hertfordshire in 1950. His other works include 'April Fools' Day' and the sequel to this work, 'Weapons of Mass Deception'.

He is keenly interested in technology and science, especially its impact on society.

12082890R00223

Printed in Great Britain
by Amazon.co.uk, Ltd.,
Marston Gate.